Breeder

By
K.B. Hoyle

TWCS
PUBLISHING HOUSE

First published by The Writer's Coffee Shop, 2014

The Writer's Coffee Shop
(Australia) PO Box 447 Cherrybrook NSW 2126
(USA) PO Box 2116 Waxahachie TX 75168

Paperback ISBN- 978-1-61213-291-4
E-book ISBN- 978-1-61213-292-1

A CIP catalogue record for this book is available from the US Congress Library.

Cover image: © Dmitrij Skorobogatov / Shutterstock.com,
© RYGER / Shutterstock.com
Design by: Jennifer McGuire

www.thewriterscoffeeshop.com/khoyle

Sanctuary

Chapter 1

I awake in a sea of darkness that changes quickly to hazy yellow light. I'm in pain, but I can't remember why. I blink, and the light changes from yellow to pale blue. I blink again, and it sharpens, as does the pain.

Pain is a sensation almost foreign to me, one nearly forgotten. I groan and press my hands to my abdomen, the nucleus of my pain. My stomach feels flat and smooth to my touch, but inside I feel swollen, ballooned, ready to burst apart.

I blink again, but the light does not change this time, and all I can see is the pale blue of the ceiling. There is a soft beeping beside me. I try to turn my head toward it, but I can't move.

Then there are voices.

"She's awake."

"She should still be sedated. What went wrong?"

"Nothing went wrong. The procedure went just as planned."

"Then why is she awake? Is she in pain?"

There is a tugging on my arm, gentle. I don't think they mean to hurt me, but they do. I gasp, and a tear slides from my eye to my ear.

"She *is* in pain." A cold hand on my forehead. "The poor dear. Her bag ran out."

"Rectify it. Immediately."

"Another thing that should not have happened. You don't think—"

A hiss. A sharp intake of breath. "Not now. She can hear us."

The hand is removed from my forehead. I hear movement around me, and the tugging on my arm increases before it ceases altogether.

A door opens and closes, eliciting a quick rush of air against my skin. I'm left alone. Coolness descends on me, first into my arm, then traveling through my veins. I sigh and another tear slips out as the pain diminishes. I don't know why I'm crying, and I don't remember why I'm here.

Someone new enters the room. I can tell by the cadence of the footsteps, which are almost silent, and the shadow that enters my periphery. I'm not afraid. I have nothing to fear in Sanctuary. I blink again, and this time when I open my eyes, my vision is filled with the pale green shirt of a person standing over me. A Protector. Only Protectors wear that color in Sanctuary.

But there is something wrong with this Protector, or maybe it's just the fuzziness in my brain making me think there is. I scrunch up my eyes, fighting to stay lucid. The Protector's form is tall and broad in the shoulders, flat across the chest. The Protector is a man.

But Protectors are never men, and a man should never be here alone, with me.

He bends over me, and my view changes. His visor—opaque, reflective bronze—hovers inches above my face, and I catch my breath. Not because I'm afraid, and not even because I'm startled, but because I see myself reflected in it. Myself. Large brown eyes above narrow cheeks, nose, and full lips, features that are optimal for survival, since I am nearly genetically perfect. Features I haven't seen since I came here five years ago. In Sanctuary, we only see others, never ourselves.

My vision blurs as the coolness in my veins swims into my chest. The pain is gone.

The Protector is still here. His bronze visor turns to gold as the light spangles on the edges of my vision and then blends with green.

"Who are you?" I ask. My lips are heavy and want to stick together as I speak. "What's your name?"

I don't know why I ask this. It's a foolish question. Nobody goes by names in Sanctuary, and for good reason. I must be losing my head with the cold wave that is carrying me away.

But he answers. I haven't heard a man's voice in five years. It's deep and pleasant and warm, even as it sounds canned behind his helmet and visor. Maybe he *is* supposed to be here. Maybe he's supposed to calm me back to sleep.

"My name is Pax," he says. Then he leans lower, his helmeted face just inches from my ear. "What's yours?"

My name? I don't have a name. "Seventeen," I say. My speech is slurring now, and I lick my lips. "B-Seventeen."

"No," he says. "Not your designation. What's your *name*?"

I close my eyes as memories from a life almost forgotten swim through my mind. My name. My name. I had one once, didn't I? The other girls gave me one. We named each other, before we knew better.

It comes to me like a fish rising in circles from the bottom of a pond.

Pria.

I part my lips to speak it, but I'm carried under instead, and all I release is a breath of air. But it's best. Names create dangerous divisions. It's why we don't have them here. Who does he think he is to ask this of me, anyway? Who did I think I was to ask it of him?

It's best he doesn't know it.

Chapter 2

I am an approved Breeder for the Controlled Repopulation Program. Years ago, Gaia Earth was dangerously overpopulated, resulting in three Great Devastations: the Great Famine, the Great Pandemic, and the Great Incursion. Entire nations were wiped out as humans fought, unsuccessfully, for survival, and Gaia Earth's population plummeted to fewer than 100,000 people, threatening the extinction of the human race.

Then the Unified World Order stepped in to take control, to create peace out of the chaos, and to ensure the controlled repopulation of Gaia Earth would take place under optimal conditions. I am privileged to be a part of that effort, to be approved as a carrier of genes that will make humanity better, stronger, smarter, and more versatile. And here, in Sanctuary, I want for nothing. My life is perfect.

I will remember this. I will repeat it until I remember it is true, and I will cease these foolish doldrums.

I'm sitting with my feet curled up beneath me on the settee facing the Looking Glass in the gathering room. With one finger, I curl the hair around my right ear. It's just long enough to almost wrap around the tip of my finger, which means I will be called in for a shave soon. My hair grows faster than most of the other Breeders', overhanging my ears in just two weeks. Any longer than it is right now and it could incite feelings of vanity on my part and jealousy on the part of my sisters. We all submit to the regular shaving of our heads to avoid these feelings, to make us equal. It is wise and good, but I can't help acknowledging I like my hair when it gets longer. It is thick and smooth and loosely curled, and I can almost remember what it looked like before I came here. But that is why it must be shaved. I close my eyes and mouth my admonition. *My life is perfect.*

"What's wrong, Seventeen?" The cushion depresses next to me as a familiar voice asks, "Why were you gone all last week?"

I open my eyes and smile at her—at Breeder Eight. She's younger than I am by three years. She replaced the previous Breeder Eight, who was reassigned just last year.

"Nothing is wrong," I say. "I had a procedure done. That's why I was away." I hadn't realized it had been a full week, though, and the revelation makes me feel disoriented for a moment. I put my fingertips to my forehead.

Eight's brow creases and she touches my arm. I flinch away. Unlike many of my sisters, I am wary of touch. I don't know why.

"A procedure? Is everything okay? Would you like to talk about it?"

"Everything is fine."

No. It isn't. I avert my eyes so she can't read my lie.

"I'm just tired from it, that's all," I say.

She gives me a sympathetic smile and reaches to touch me again. "You should rest in our dormitory, where it's quieter. Would you like me to walk you?"

"Eight, I . . ." I sigh and pat her hand. For a fifteen-year-old girl, she has maturity beyond her years. "Thank you, but I would rather stay here."

"May I stay and talk with you?" Her expression is open, hopeful. Like all the Breeders, she is lithe and strong, with brown eyes, flawless olive skin, and even, white teeth. It is fitting we call each other "sister," for we look so much alike.

All of humanity looks like us now, although we've been told it has not always been that way. Once, there was a wide variety of recessive traits saturating the human gene pool, but that was before the Great Devastations almost wiped out humanity. Most of those with genes on the fringe—with too much melanin, or not enough, or an eye color with a tendency for weak sight, among other things—died out in the Devastations. And because of their weaknesses, and their inferiorities, it is now our job to make sure those sorts of genetic flaws never infiltrate the human race again. It is our great honor as Breeders, as Carriers, to ensure the survival of a more perfect human race.

"Seventeen?" Eight asks again.

"Of course you may stay. I enjoy your company." Best to not seem too disturbed by my procedure. It was, after all, not the first time it's happened to a Breeder since my time here at Sanctuary.

She gives me a brilliant smile, revealing a dimple in one cheek, and settles in more comfortably. "So," she says with the air of one beginning a long conversation, "why are you tired? Is it just because of your procedure, or is there another reason? Are you sleeping enough? Are you eating enough?"

"I believe so, yes," I say with an indulgent smile and tip of the head, twisting my finger back into my hair.

"Oh, *oh*! You're Carrying, aren't you?" She pushes herself up onto her knees and grasps my shoulder. "Of course, why didn't I see it immediately? What an honor, Seventeen! What contribution number is this for you?"

I shift so her hands fall away and say, "Actually, I'm not Carrying. I . . . *was*, but something must have gone wrong, because I'm not anymore." I press my hands to my abdomen. I have been so unsettled since the procedure it's difficult to remember exactly what happened.

Her expression turns crestfallen. "What do you mean, something went wrong? Isn't that why they choose us? Because our genetics prevent things from going wrong?" She leans away, wrapping her arms about her ribs as though to shield herself from my imperfection.

Heat rushes to my face. "It can happen to anyone, perfected genes or not," I say. "Sometimes Mother Nature just says *no*." Without meaning to, I've drawn myself up and folded my hands in my lap like an older sister. I have no right to claim that title, as I've contributed only one healthy Carry to the Program so far, but I feel the need to put Eight in her place.

To her credit, she lowers her lashes and bows her head. "You're right, of course. I'm sorry for judging. But . . . it frightens me."

I deflate and tap her chin, encouraging her to look up. "What frightens you?"

"The possibility of carrying—of passing on—flawed genes," she says in a low whisper. "They would kick me out of the Program, wouldn't they?" Tears cling to her lashes, threatening to spill over, and I mentally chide myself for revealing what happened to me.

"They didn't kick me out," I say. "Even with a problem here or there, they have chosen us because we are their best opportunity of restoring humanity. There is no need to be afraid."

She nods and wipes at her eyes, her gaze going to the long, curving window we call the Looking Glass. Outside, beyond the foot-thick glass, is a stunning vista of pine-swept mountains. We do not have a view of the

Commune here, from this side of Sanctuary. Over here, we watch the world through the privacy of the one-way Looking Glass.

"Have they scheduled your first Carry yet?" I ask Eight. "You have been here a year already, haven't you?"

She nods and continues staring out the Looking Glass as she says, "Yes. I have one more month of preparatory vitamins and exercise, but Mother says I should be ready after that. She evaluated me herself."

There is such a proud note in her voice I don't tell her Mother evaluates all the Breeders before their first Carries. I just nod and say, "That's wonderful."

A medical technician comes around with a tray of little cups, each numbered and containing pills. I hold out my hand for mine, as Eight does for hers, and we are quiet for several moments as we swallow them dry, one at a time. We have never been told what each pill does, other than being given vague references to their being necessary for our "health and wellbeing as Breeders of the Unified World Order," but I have always trusted that they are for our good. The UWO has every reason to keep us healthy, and one look around the room at the strong bodies and shining complexions confirms they are doing their job.

Each Breeder has her own drug regimen, so I don't pay attention to the quantity or size of Eight's pills, but I'm missing one—a small pink one I've taken every day since I first arrived. I frown and stir my finger around the bottom of the cup just to make sure it isn't hiding beneath a bigger pill, but it's definitely not there.

"Excuse me," I say to the med tech who is waiting for us to return our cups. "I'm missing one. The . . . well, I don't know what it does, but it's the one that is about this big"—I hold up my fingers a quarter-inch apart—"and light pink."

"Yes," the med tech says with a smile. She wears a wrap around her head because, beneath it, she has a full head of hair. Only Breeders are required to have shaved heads, but Mother doesn't want us to feel jealous of the medical technicians who serve us, so she requires the wraps. "Mother has determined you no longer need that one after your recent procedure," the med tech says. "She made the change in your prescription herself."

"Oh. So . . . it wasn't anything necessary for my nutrition, then?"

The med tech's smile widens. "I'm not at liberty to say, B-Seventeen. But you can trust Mother's judgment. She would never prescribe anything that would not be to your benefit."

"I still have mine," Eight says, holding it up between her thumb and forefinger with a slight frown. She gives me a narrow-eyed look that says she's jealous I've reached a milestone she hasn't yet, and then puts it on the back of her tongue.

I finish my pills and hand the cup back to the med tech. I swallow several more times, trying to clear the feeling of the dry pills traveling down my esophagus, a feeling I can never quite get used to. But another technician will be around with glasses of water soon, as it's almost time for our midmorning meal.

After the med tech walks away, Eight settles back against the cushions of the settee with a deep sigh and says, "Do you ever feel anything, Seventeen? When you're Carrying, I mean." Her gaze flits around the room, and I know she's taking in the several sisters who are in various stages of Carrying—some of them with hardly a bulge beneath their cotton gowns, others so distended they look about ready to deliver, and all of them with languorous expressions on their faces. Many sit with half-closed eyes, rubbing vacant circles on their bellies.

"I mean, I know they give us drugs to calm us through the process, and other sisters have told me I'll barely know I'm Carrying until it's over, but . . ." She bites her lip and looks out the Looking Glass again.

I shouldn't push, but I'm curious where her thoughts are taking her. No other sister has ever approached me like this before—with fears before their first Carry. I wish I'd felt comfortable enough to talk with someone before mine. "But what?" I ask gently.

"Why do they touch their stomachs if they're not fully conscious of the procedure?" She asks the question in a rush, as though afraid I'll find it stupid.

"Well, I suppose a part of the brain always knows," I say.

"But you never felt anything?" she asks again.

It's my turn to look away. I study the giant tree that grows through the floor in the center of the gathering room. The Tree of Life, we call it, and it's our emblem here at Sanctuary, signifying our contributions to the human race. Its branches don't yet reach the greenhouse skylight far above, but they will someday. I wonder what they'll do when it gets too high. It would be immoral to cut it down. They'll probably have to raise the ceiling.

My gaze travels from the tree to the Carrying women sitting in its shade. Eight wants to know if we *feel* anything when we Carry. I think about my experiences.

The first time I Carried, I didn't feel anything—that is true. The drugs I was on made the forty weeks seem like mere days. I have very few recollections beyond vague remembrances of yoga exercises and time spent lounging here, in the gathering room. But the second time, before my procedure, and after, it was . . . different.

My fingers flex and I realize I'm pressing on my abdomen again, and Eight is watching me do it.

I look into her earnest expression. She does not need more anxiety than she's already feeling. The first Carry is always the scariest.

"No," I say, relaxing my hands. "I never felt anything."

Chapter 3

Another week goes by, but my memory of what happened before my procedure does not return. It shouldn't bother me, but I can't get it out of my mind.

When I Carried my first contribution to full term and delivered it for the Program, I experienced similar memory loss—all to be expected, of course, due to the drugs. The med techs keep us sedated for the deliveries to spare us what I've been told is extreme discomfort, and we are given calming drugs for the recovery time before we are sent back to live with our sisters. Although I've delivered. only once, I remember the experience as being rewarding, to know I'd contributed to the betterment of humanity, but otherwise unremarkable. I don't know why this last experience, when I didn't even Carry the contribution to full term, should be any different, and it's worrying me. I have difficulty sleeping, and when I do sleep, in my dreams I remember an encounter that feels like it's from a dream. I'm speaking with a man who asks my name and gives me his in return.

"Pax."

"What's that?" Eleven asks, not even breaking her gait on the jogging machine beside mine.

I am jogging as well, my arms pumping in time to my quick, even steps, sweat trickling from my newly shaven scalp.

I break into laughter and close my eyes, tilting my face to the ceiling. "It's . . . nothing," I say, composing myself. I don't know where the laughter came from. I must be internalizing more anxiety than I thought. "I

K.B. Hoyle

didn't mean to say that out loud."

"You only said the one word. What was that—a *name*?"

"No!" I say, too quickly. "It was nonsense. Something from a dream I had." I hit the slow button on the machine, suddenly wanting to be far away from Eleven and her questions.

"Done already?" she asks.

I look at my time. I've only completed thirty minutes—half my usual run. We are on such a schedule here at Sanctuary that any change is notable. I've always loved the routine, knowing what every second of my day will look like, but now the thought of staying on this machine a minute longer makes me want to scream. "I'm not feeling well," I say, slowing my walk until the machine is stopped.

"Are you Carrying?" Eleven asks, her eyebrows raised. She excels at physical activity. She hasn't even broken a sweat yet, and she's been on the machine as long as I have.

"No," I say through gritted teeth. I step down and grab my towel to mop at my head.

"Oh, I suppose not. You'd be over there with them." She jerks her head toward the crowd of ten or so women who are doing yoga stretches on the other side of the room, led by one of the exercise techs. They all look half-asleep. The sight of it puts me on edge, and I grimace.

"Seventeen," Eleven says, and her voice is full of concern. "You should go to Medical. You really don't look well."

My hands are shaking, and I can't hide it. I cover my face with my towel and take a couple of bracing breaths behind the terrycloth. How can I be sick? Illness is so rare here that the medical wing exists mostly to monitor our nutrition and help us through our Carries. If I'm sick, it means there is something wrong with me—something beyond whatever it was that made my last Carry fail.

My breath hitches in my chest as I feel a stab of the fear Eight expressed to me the week before. What if they kick me out of the Program? How would I survive in the Commune outside Sanctuary? It's been five years since I've lived outside, and I barely remember what it's like. I would be expected to make myself useful to the UWO in some viable way, but I don't know how to do anything other than what I am doing now. And I would be around *men* . . . like Pax.

"What's your name?"

"Pria."

I didn't tell him that, did I? I shudder and lower the towel. I can't go on like this. Eight noticed last week, and now Eleven. I have to get a grip on my anxiety. *My life is perfect*, I remind myself.

"You know," I say, pasting on a smile, "I believe I'm actually just dehydrated. I'm going to get some water, and I'm sure I'll feel better."

I fold the towel with deliberate calm and wait just long enough to see Eleven relax and focus once again on her own workout, then I deposit the towel in the laundry basket and go to the water cooler. I drain two cups in quick succession before slipping out of the gymnasium. There are still thirty more minutes before afternoon meditation, and I can probably blend in with the rotation of sisters in the gathering room until then.

I have to walk past the broad double doors to Medical on my way there, and through the glass I see a flash of light green. I stop and backstep, curious. Of course we have lots of Protectors here at Sanctuary, Protectors who are just like the Enforcers in the Commune except they work exclusively at Sanctuary. But Protectors are always female. I'm sure what I'll see through the glass is a female Protector, same as always, but I can't shake my dream remembrance. I want to prove to myself Pax was just a figment of my imagination.

I position myself so only half my face shows through the glass and peer down the sterile hall with the white walls and blue ceiling. At first I see no one, but a swinging door far down the hall indicates someone just exited from my sight.

I sigh and bite my lip in frustration. I can't investigate because I can't get through these doors without pushing a buzzer to be let in, and I don't exactly want to have to explain myself. Curiosity is frowned upon in the Unified World Order—that was part of my education at the Agoge. Children who are overly curious tend to put their own interests over others' and are not good candidates for usefulness to society. I saw what happened to those types of children, and I was smart enough that I learned to suppress my curiosity at a young age. If I hadn't, I never would have been chosen for this most perfect of positions in the UWO. I never would have been chosen to live in Sanctuary as a Breeder.

And here I am, risking my perfect life on a curious whim.

I shake my head and step back from the door, breathing hard. I'm feeling an almost desperate desire to know who just exited the Medical corridor, a desire that prevents me from walking away. Why now, of all times, does my curiosity have to rear its ugly head?

"My life is perfect," I murmur, taking another step back and pressing my hands to my abdomen. I turn my back on the glass just as a chime sounds, signaling the unlocking of the door, and I look over my shoulder in alarm. With the locking mechanism disengaged, the door slips open with a soft click and quivers on its hinge.

I look up and down the corridor, but all the other Breeders are engaged in activities of some kind, and there are no technicians in sight. I step back to the now-open door and peer through the glass again, my heart slamming in my chest.

Standing at the far end of the hall is a Protector, and it is most definitely a man. And if it is a man, then it is not a Protector at all but an Enforcer, and Enforcers only belong outside this compound.

His back is to me, but he turns his face to the side so I can see the reflective bronze surface of his visor. He stands very still, and I sense him studying me out of the corner of his eye, even though his face and head are completely obscured. Then he opens the door to his right and walks through.

It's more than I can take. I have to know what this man is doing in Sanctuary, for my safety and that of all my sisters—at least, that's what I tell myself as I pull open the door of the Med wing and spring through. I run with light steps down the hall, so nervous my palms are sweating. A med tech could appear out of one of the side doors or hallways at any moment and challenge my presence here, and what would I tell them? That I saw a *man* in Sanctuary?

Well, why not? Wouldn't they want to know so they could report it, so they could rectify it? *I'm doing the right thing.*

I reach the end of the hall and wipe my palms on my pants. There is a sign on the wall beside the door he disappeared through, and I know the symbols on it are letters, but I can't read them. Only those whose professions will require reading are taught to read after their Agoge education, and Breeders do not qualify.

The door is heavy and cold to the touch, probably made of some strong metal, and it has a large, old-fashioned knob. Blinking lights on a panel indicate that it is usually locked, but right now it, like the door to the Med wing itself, is unlatched and hanging slightly ajar.

I pull it open and I am at the top of a staircase. There is a landing just ten steps down before the staircase turns a corner into darkness, and I let the door rest on the jamb behind me, careful not to let it latch. I don't see the man—the Enforcer—anywhere, and my nervousness is beginning to outweigh my curiosity.

I should leave.

But I came all this way. I have to go just a little farther before I turn back.

I descend to the landing and crane my neck to look around the bend and down into the darkness. There is no telling how far down the staircase goes. I hear a soft click somewhere far below, and then a green form materializes out of the darkness and ascends the steps just in front of me.

With a sharp exhalation of breath, I back up until I trip over the stairs behind me. I sit down hard, wincing as my tailbone strikes the concrete, and then he is standing over me, his head tilted down and his gloved hand extended as though to help me up.

I gasp. "Don't touch me! I'll scream!" I scramble to my feet and onto a step up so my head is even with his, my face close enough to his visor to see my reflection.

He lowers his hand, and I study him, my breath coming in scared hitches. His form is so foreign after five years among women that it captures my interest despite my fear. Although he is not much taller than me, his shoulders are much broader and his hips more narrow. He is clothed head-to-toe in the green uniform of an Enforcer, which extends even to heavy boots and gloves. Not even his neck shows below the helmet that covers his face, and the only other color is the bronze visor that stretches from his forehead to his nose. I wish he would lift his visor so I could see his face, and for more reason than wanting to read his expression. I haven't seen a man's face in five years, and I'm curious. I hate myself for my curiosity. I wouldn't be standing here if it weren't for that.

I should run away. Why am I not I running away?

"You're different than the others," he says, his voice just as low and even as I remember it from my dream. Or rather, my dream was just as accurate as the reality.

"No, I'm not," I say. "I'm exactly the same as my sisters."

"That's not true," he says, but there isn't any malice in his tone. He holds himself so still I can almost imagine his voice is coming from the walls instead, if it weren't for the air of energy I feel in his poise, as though he could spring into action at any moment.

He has a holstered weapon at his side—the same light celery green of his uniform. My eyes flick to it. I may be strong and quick, but he could kill me right now if he wanted to.

"Why do you say I'm different?" I ask.

"Because you're here." No malice. Hope. He sounds hopeful.

I fight the urge to look around the stairwell. I must keep my eyes on him if I'm going to survive this encounter.

I lick my lips. "Why did you come to me?" I ask. "That *was* you, wasn't it?"

"Yes."

"You're . . . Pax."

He inclines his head, acknowledging my statement.

"Do you all have names? All the Enforcers, I mean?"

"Everyone has a name, whether they choose to acknowledge it or not. Even you."

I don't want to acknowledge my name, that's true. I never should have had it in the first place. "What's your designation?" I ask, clinging to what I know, trying to take control of the conversation.

He opens his mouth, then hesitates for a moment. "E-Fifteen."

"And what, exactly, are you doing here, E-Fifteen?" I try to put authority into my voice, like I did when chiding Eight, and fold my arms over my chest. "You're aware, I'm sure, that no men are allowed inside this compound."

He leans closer, eliminating my illusion of control. "I'm here for you, Seventeen. I'm here to let you know I can get you out, should you ever desire it."

"Why would I want to leave Sanctuary?" My voice drops to an incredulous whisper. "I am a Breeder. I am one of the most valuable components of the Unified World Order. I have an obligation to help humanity. My life here is perfect, I—"

"Your world is a lie," he says. "And when you're ready, I'll be here, waiting for you."

I laugh. "A lie? How can you—"

"Shhh!" He puts a finger to his visor and tilts his head toward the dark stairs below. "Listen," he says.

I do. Of course I do. I can't get my curiosity to obey my better judgment. I lean forward and tilt my head also, and a moment later I hear a sound I haven't heard in years and years, even though I am a Breeder. I must be pulling it up from the semiconscious recesses of my memory of when I delivered my healthy Carry, even though I can't remember the delivery itself, and I never held nor saw my contribution. It's a sound of shared humanity, and maybe, for that reason alone, I recognize it.

It is an infant crying.

The sound is faint and pitiful, and it rises in pitch until it reaches a scream before it abruptly cuts off.

Pax turns his face back to me, and my mouth falls open.

The cry and the way it cut off fills me with dread, and I clutch my abdomen as shooting pains course through me. Shaking my head, I turn and flee.

I'm out the door and back in the sterile hallway of the Med wing before I have time to register anything other than my desire to get out of there. I sprint down the hall and slam through the double doors into the main corridor beyond. My momentum carries me to the far wall where I crash up against it, my sweaty palms stopping me from banging my forehead on the cold white tiles.

I'm hyperventilating, and I can't control the heaving of my stomach. With a retch, I vomit on the wall and then slide to my knees.

I stay like that, curled in the fetal position on the floor near the puddle of my own sick, until a gasp lets me know I've been discovered, and then cold hands carry me away.

Chapter 4

"How are you feeling, Seventeen?" The voice is soothing and familiar, and I blink my eyes open and turn toward it.

Mother. Director Mother has come to see me.

"You had quite a turn there." She caresses my forehead, and it is warm and dry and comforting.

"Oh, Mother, I'm so sorry!" I screw up my face and tears slide from the corners of my eyes. "I don't know what came over me. I—"

"Shh," she says. "It's okay. You were very dehydrated. Eleven told us you left exercise early."

"Are you going to kick me out?" I ask, my eyes wide and my lips trembling.

Mother laughs lightly, making fine lines appear around her dark eyes and her mouth. "Kick you out? Now why would I do something like that?"

"I'm sick! I—I lost a Carry. I think there must be something wrong with me. I'm unfit to be a Breeder."

"Nonsense," she says. "The only thing wrong with you is that you must take better care of yourself." She draws her silvery brows down in a stern expression. "Your body is not your own. You belong to the Program, and to the Unified World Order. You are superior, Seventeen, and you are very valuable."

"Yes, Mother. I know."

"Too valuable to let go over a couple of bad days," she adds with a twinkle in her eyes.

"Yes, Mother."

"We're getting you hydrated," she says, patting my arm where an IV drip is attached, "and then we'll get you back on your vitamins."

"Why did you take away my pink pill?" I ask.

"Because you've outgrown it. You don't need it anymore."

"What did it do?"

"It was just a supplement. Don't worry. Remember, curiosity is just skepticism and doubt masquerading in innocent clothing."

It's one of the maxims from the Agoge, and I finish it for her. "And it leads to individualism, which causes divisions in society."

She smiles and taps her finger on the tip of my nose. "That's my girl," she says.

Curiosity. And guilt. I look up at the pale blue ceiling. "Mother, there's more."

"Oh?"

I swallow hard. "I saw a man in Sanctuary. Right here, in Medical."

There is a long pause as Mother goes still and gives me a long stare. "A *man*?" she says, almost breathing the words. "That's impossible."

"He was here, dressed as an Enforcer."

To my surprise, Mother laughs. "Oh, Seventeen. You know Enforcers wear the same uniforms as our Protectors. You did not see a man. You saw a tall woman."

"I *did* see a man. He—"

"Think about it." She spreads her arms wide. "How could a man walk around here undetected? It doesn't make sense."

"I know, but—"

"That's enough," she says, and her voice is firm. "Dehydration can cause all sorts of symptoms, disorientation and hallucinations among them. If you thought you saw a man, even if you thought this man spoke to you, it was surely a figment of your imagination."

I chew my lip. I want to believe her, desperately I do. I want to believe everything I heard in that stairwell wasn't real. I want to believe *Pax* wasn't real.

"Do you really think so?" I whisper.

"I know so," she says.

I breathe a sigh of relief and press my hands to my face. Of course Mother is right. How could a man walk the halls of the Med wing undetected? It's absurd of me even to consider that what I experienced was real.

"Now, get some rest. I've given them orders to keep you here through tomorrow," Mother says, rising from my bedside. "We have to get you healthy again so you can begin your next Carry."

"When will that be?" I ask, eager to get back to being useful.

She gives me a thoughtful look. "In a couple of months, I think. But don't worry, it will be here before you know it."

I nod and smile, and then she's gone, and I'm letting myself drift off to sleep.

But sometime in the night, I hear an infant screaming, and I dream of a faceless man leaning over my bed.

Chapter 5

"What's through that door at the end of the hall?" I ask the med tech as she escorts me from my room the next day. I nod toward the door, and she follows my gaze.

"Medical supplies," she says without hesitation. "It's a storage closet."

"With a mechanized lock?" I ask, raising an eyebrow.

"*Valuable* medical supplies," she says with a smile.

"So there's not a staircase through there?"

"A staircase? Goodness no. We're on the ground floor, and there's nothing above or below us in this part of compound. Where do you imagine a staircase would lead?" She gives me a quizzical look.

I shrug, feeling relieved. It *had* all been in my head, and Mother is not going to kick me out. I will get back to my normal routine and put this whole episode behind me.

The chime sounds when we stop before the double doors, and the med tech holds them open so I can exit. "We'll see you in a couple of weeks for your next assessment," she says. It's a generalized "we," for she probably won't. They rotate the medical staff with such frequency it's unusual to see the same technician twice in a year.

"Thank you." I duck my head and leave. They gave me a new tunic and pants in the Med wing, so I feel clean and fresh and ready for my day. Even so, I put my hands on my hips and consider where to go.

It's exercise time, but Mother doesn't want me exercising for a few days. I could join the earlier rotation of meditation, but focusing on being still does not appeal to me right now. If I go back to the dormitory, I will most likely be alone, but I'd like to avoid the thoughts that could arise.

It would be best for me to go to my favorite place in Sanctuary—to the gathering room and the Looking Glass. Sisters who are on their usual leisure hour will be there, and I will surely be welcomed into a game or activity.

I hum to myself as I walk, trying to stay distracted. I've never craved a good friend before, but I crave one now. I wish I had someone in whom I could confide, someone who understands that my curiosity is not an expression of desire to leave Sanctuary, someone who could assure me I'm not going crazy.

I descend the three steps into the broad gathering room. It is lit with pale yellow sunlight that suffuses the white furniture and walls with warmth. The trees beyond the looking glass are bending and swaying in a wind I can't hear, and I go straight to the glass and lay my palm against it. We aren't allowed outside, but whatever nutrients we need to get from the sun, we can get right here. It's why so many of my sisters are stretched out on the settees facing the glass.

A mule deer ambles past, not ten feet away, and I watch, captivated by its beauty. It is young, its spots still visible, and it stops to graze in the tall grasses that are poking through the snow cover. Several of my sisters give shouts of delight and step up beside me, watching it as I do. It is not spooked by us, for it can neither see nor hear us. The glass is tinted on the outside so no one can see in.

I smile, and then I feel a nudge of cold wetness on my hand, followed by silky fur, and I look down. Flora, our resident pet dog at Sanctuary, has joined us at the window, drawn by the sight of the deer. She presses her nose against the glass and wags her tail, whining.

"No, Flora," I say. "You can't go say hello."

Flora looks up at me and barks.

"No, no!" I say with a laugh.

Flora sits but keeps wagging her tail. I kneel beside her and stroke her fur. It's a strange thing that we name our pet but we aren't allowed names ourselves. And Flora, technically, isn't even a legitimate dog. The Unified World Order is always working toward perfecting the cloning process, and Flora looks like a normal dog—a golden retriever, the breed used to be called—but in fact she's nothing more than an experiment. Cloned animals die quickly without the computer implant that's inserted at birth at the base of their skulls. I run my fingers over the slightly raised bump on Flora's neck. If I'd never been told about it, I probably wouldn't have recognized the bump for what it is, but everybody in Sanctuary knows Flora is a clone. The computer implant gives Flora's brain added instructions that the cloning process hasn't been able to replicate. I've never been told exactly how it works, other than that Flora would die without her implant because her brain would cease working properly.

Cloned animals, also, are bred to be sterile. Until the UWO can perfect the process and create genetically perfect clones that don't need the computer implant to survive, they won't release any of the animals into the wild. Since the goal of the cloning program is to help rejuvenate some of the animal populations that have been devastated by humans over the years, it's probably wise that they're waiting until they have the process just right.

Flora whines and stands, and my hand drops from her head. "What is it, girl?" I ask. But then I see what she sees—a glint of gold in the trees beyond the grass. I draw my breath in sharply. Several of my sisters do the same as they also see the mountain lion approaching.

"Oh . . . run away!" cries a sister to my left.

"Run, run!" The chorus is taken up by those of us paying attention.

The young deer lifts its head and twitches its broad ears, poised and quivering for flight. The mountain lion inches closer, its head low and its shoulders hunched. Some of the sisters have begun to cry, and Flora barks and barks.

Then a Protector runs into view, waving her arms and shouting words we can't hear. She shakes her head back and forth, and the deer springs away. The mountain lion gives a swipe of its paw and bares its teeth at the green-clad Protector, but the woman unholsters her weapon and fires a shot into the air. With a flick of its tawny tail, the lion turns and bounds away.

My sisters cheer, and I feel a great surge of relief and rest my forehead against the glass. If the lion had eaten the deer, it would have been the right and good circle of life, and we all know that. But nobody wants to see *how* the fittest survive. There are some things best left to the imagination.

Chapter 6

Two weeks have gone by since my imagined encounter with Pax, who doesn't exist. But instead of feeling better, I feel worse. I'm still having disturbing dreams, and every morning I wake up with phantom pains in my stomach and a feeling of lethargy that weighs me down like anchors on my wrists and ankles. Getting out of bed is an act of will, but act I must if I want to stay here.

I smile and talk with my sisters, exercise when I'm supposed to, take my vitamins and medications, meditate, eat my prescribed six small meals a day, and partake in leisure activities. But in my free time, I sit and stare out the Looking Glass at the woods and the grass and the sun and the breeze that stirs it all. It's not as though I want to go out there, but I long for an answer to my sadness, to my . . . I'm not sure there is a word for my indescribable sense of discomfiture and grief. And there's no one to whom I can really talk. If only I could know why I feel this way, I could remedy it, I think. But I don't.

I mark off the days until I will be declared fit for my third Carry. I crave the drugs they will give me.

Eight has joined the ranks of the pre-Carries. She's across the room from me now, laughing and chatting with a group of girls around her same age, all of whom are scheduled for their first Carry within the week. They will leave as girls for their implantation and come back as women. I wonder if I should go tell them how it will change them, but I don't. That's not the sort of information we share in Sanctuary.

"Seventeen, come with me, please."

I look around and drop my finger from where it was twirling in the hair at my ear. A med tech smiles down at me from the stairs by the entrance to the gathering room. She is flanked by a hygiene tech—a severe-looking older woman with knobby knuckles. One look at her and I know she was not a Breeder in her younger life. She never would have qualified.

It's time for my medical exam and my haircut already. How did I lose track of time? They must have told me to come to the Med wing at this time today, and I must have forgotten.

I rise, dislodging Flora, who has been snuggling up to me, and go quickly to them, my tunic swishing around my thighs. It hangs away from my body too much, and my pants beneath it are sagging on my hips. I haven't thought about my weight in weeks, but now that I'm going in for an exam it occurs to me I've gotten too thin. But I've eaten everything they've prescribed for me, and I've made every effort to stay physically healthy. Still, they won't be pleased. I circle my fingers around my bony wrist. Chances are my next Carry will be postponed again. I bite my lip and discreetly adjust my pants higher on my hips.

They direct me to one of the first rooms off the main hall in the Med wing, and I sit obediently on the examination table as the med tech attaches the plastic and metal cuff to my wrist that will measure my vital signs. It buzzes and hums, growing warm against my skin until it tingles, but that's normal. The hygiene tech takes up her position behind me and adds the buzz of the clippers to the buzz of the cuff. My soft, dark brown locks fall around me on the bed, and I twist my fingers into my tunic, resisting the urge to pick up a lock of my hair just to feel its silkiness. It, like the rest of me, belongs to the UWO.

"Hmm," says the med tech, checking the display on my cuff. "Muscle mass is good, but body fat is low. Are you eating your full rations?" She taps on her screen and doesn't look up.

"Yes, Sister Tech." I address her formally. "I am." I don't know why she bothers to ask. All our consumption is recorded by the technicians at Sanctuary, and dereliction of duty is never tolerated.

"Then your activity levels must have climbed. Are you spending more time in exercise?"

"No, Sister Tech. No more than usual."

"Hmm," she says again. Her fingers fly over her screen. "Your pulse is increased, and I'm detecting lowered levels of serotonin. Usually serotonin increases with increased activity levels, but not if that activity is a result of anxiety or depression."

Depression. That's the word for what I've been feeling.

"How are you feeling lately, Seventeen?" There is genuine concern in her voice.

I smile. "Great," I say.

She narrows her eyes and studies me, her hand hovering over her screen. I school my features into the most relaxed expression I can manage and keep my lips upturned in a pleasant smile. I expect her to ask me next if I've experienced any more hallucinations of men roaming the Med wing, but she doesn't. Mother must not have reported what I told her. I am at once relieved and puzzled. Wouldn't that be relevant medical information to have on file if I'm supposed to be producing perfect offspring for the UWO?

My cuff tingles sharply in a spot on the inside of my wrist, and a whole new string of colored letters and numbers fly across the med tech's screen. She splays her fingers over a few of the lines, magnifying them, and gives them her attention. Her screen is transparent, so I can see the lines of colored text. If only I could read them.

"I feel ready," I say after several moments of silence.

Buzz, buzz, buzz. The hygiene tech drags the electric razor over the spot above my forehead, and the soft locks fall across my vision, some of the hairs settling on my moist lips. I pull them off with trembling fingers.

"I'm sorry, ready for what?" the med tech asks.

"Ready for"—I pull another hair out of my mouth—"my next Carry."

A crease appears between her eyebrows and she consults her screen again. "Oh, I'm sorry, Seventeen," she says, "but your weight is nowhere near where it needs to be. You need another six weeks of recovery from your procedure, and I think we will have to push your next Carry off another four to six weeks beyond that."

I add up the weeks and flinch as the hygiene tech pokes my ear with the sharp prongs of the clippers. "Ten or twelve weeks? What am I going to do with myself all that time?"

She smiles, showing perfect white teeth. "Rest, get healthy, enjoy some leisure time. Really, most girls appreciate the time off between Carries."

"I—I do." I let the hygiene tech push my head to the side to finish the shave. "I'm just eager to be useful to the Program. It's what I live for."

"Well, now, *that* I can appreciate." The med tech smiles again, but it doesn't quite reach her eyes. She lifts my hand and removes the cuff, then pulls her bottom lip between her teeth and considers me. "I tell you what,

I'll reevaluate you in six weeks, and if you're up to optimum health, I'll send you straight off for implantation that very day."

"Really?" My voice is suddenly too loud as the hygiene tech turns off her clippers. "You would do that?" I ask, lowering my voice.

"Certainly. I see no reason not to."

The hygiene tech packs her clippers away in her bag and exits without a word or a backward glance.

I quirk my mouth to the side. "Of course, it won't really be you. It will be someone else."

"What's that? Oh . . . yes, of course. Someone else." She taps something on her screen, and then it goes opaque and milky white. "I've put it in your notes."

"Thank you," I say. "That means a lot to me."

She pats my hand and tucks her screen beneath her arm.

I stand and tilt my head. "I don't think I've ever been seen by the same med tech twice," I say. "Why is that?"

Her expression tightens ever so slightly so that lines appear around her mouth, and I notice a funny little whorl of skin above her lip. But she doesn't break her gaze with me. "You *are* an inquisitive one, aren't you?"

Is that in my records? I blush and look down. "Sorry, Sister Tech."

"No need to be sorry," she says. Then she takes a deep breath. "Working in a Breeding compound, like this one, presents many challenges to those of us in this profession, and it's one reason the Unified World Order keeps medical technicians on a rotation. We travel constantly." She gives me a forced smile. "I love it. I get to see all the many ways the Unified World Order is healing Gaia Earth." She sounds as though she's reading from a script.

I bite back all the questions her brief explanation raises in me and nod instead. How many Breeding compounds are there? How many Communes? Has she ever been in the medical rotation that cares for the contributions we make? Is there a nursery in the basement here—is that why I heard a baby cry? Has she ever seen an Unfamiliar, and are they as terrifying as their pictures suggest? Does she ever wish she could stay in one place, like us?

But I can't ask all these questions. I've already put her off with my idle curiosity, despite her claim to the contrary. I can see it in her rigid posture and the slight pursing of her lips. So instead I just say, "That sounds lovely. Thank you for telling me."

"Certainly."

"Six weeks, then?"

"Six weeks." She leads me out of the room, and we head back to the double doors.

But I can't help myself. I have to ask one more question. "What's through the heavy door at the end of the hall?"

"Medical supplies. It's a storage closet," she says without even looking toward where I'm pointing. Her response is so similar to the previous med tech's it's almost eerie. She fingers the button to let me out, and the chime sounds. "Why do you ask?"

"No reason," I say. "Just curious. Thank you for everything." I turn to leave, but she places a hand on my arm.

"I wish you all the best, Seventeen," she says, and there is a strange earnestness in her gaze, as though she's holding back from saying more.

"Thank you," I say again.

After the door closes between us, I watch her through the glass as she turns and walks down the hall. She's tapping on her screen again, and I know it's probably information about her next patient, but I wonder if she's adding more to *my* chart. Something along the lines of "Too inquisitive." I bite the inside of my cheek and curl my toes inside my shoes. Why can't I just keep my mouth shut?

When she reaches the end of the corridor, she looks over her shoulder and sees me still standing at the glass. She smiles and raises her eyebrows, and I smile back and duck away.

I stand beside the door, out of sight for a few seconds, and then peer back through the glass. The med tech is gone, and the light on the security panel beside the door to the "storage closet" is green. Green for unlocked. It was red a moment before.

I suck my teeth and widen my eyes even as I mentally chide myself. It doesn't mean anything. She probably just needs some supplies.

But I can't help wondering if she means for me to see.

Chapter 7

"You're crazy, and paranoid," I whisper to myself. It's early morning and my dormitory mates have all left for breakfast. "Stop trying to ruin your life." I cover my face with both hands and take a couple of deep, meditative breaths. Talking to myself has become an unhealthy habit as of late—something else I need to work on.

It's getting harder and harder to get out of bed every morning, and I'm feeling an irrational desire to cry . . . all the time. I'm usually a loner, but now I've pushed all my sisters even further away. I go through the motions of my days without even bothering to smile anymore. My sisters whisper about me, and I can tell many of them are offended by my seclusion, but I can't even bring myself to care.

They are not the only ones watching me. I feel eyes on me all the time. Med techs seem to be everywhere, always showing up when I enter a room. They tap away on their clear screens, and I think constantly that they are studying me. Protectors come and go, too, and every time I see the celery green of their uniforms, I do a double take, certain one of them will turn out to be a male Enforcer instead. I even see Mother a couple of times, but when I try to catch her eye, she looks away. I can't help feeling it is deliberate.

In my dormitory at night, I listen to the soft breathing of my sisters, but I can't sleep. I do everything I've always done, and still I get thinner and thinner. My six weeks will soon be up, but there is no way they'll let me Carry again in this condition. I'm ruining my perfect life, and I can't make sense of why.

I decide to spend more of my leisure time in dance. The flowing, synchronized choreography used to give me a sense of euphoria and restfulness, but now it just makes my chest ache with a longing I can't define. But I keep trying, keep grasping after a solution to my depression—a solution that seems ever out of reach.

I cannot live like this.

But I must. My life is perfect.

"Perfect, perfect, perfect," I whisper with my eyes closed.

A chime sounds and the voice of a nutrition tech comes over the intercom into my room. "B-Seventeen, are you coming to first meal? You don't want to miss out on your nutrients."

"Yes, I'm coming. I'll be there soon," I say. I notice she didn't add that she would have to log that I missed a meal, an offense for which I would be reprimanded. I swing my legs over the edge of my bed and stare at a spot on the wall. I'd better get moving.

After breakfast, exercise, and meditation, I'm back in my favorite spot before the Looking Glass. I sit with my eyes closed, soaking up the warmth coming in off the glass and down through the skylight above the Tree of Life. A shifting of the settee beside me lets me know I'm not alone, but nobody speaks, and I stay absorbed in my own thoughts. I'm fine with that.

"Ooh, look!" an older sister says. "Is that what I think it is?"

"It is! Oh, it's a *child*."

My eyes shoot open. The other Breeders in the room, all except for those who are Carrying, are crowded in front of the Looking Glass, obscuring my vision.

"She's precious," another sister says. "How old do you think she is?"

"She must be older than seven to be out of the nursery," someone replies.

"Her Agoge instructor will *not* be pleased," says an older sister—Three, I think—to a titter of laughter.

I press my way forward through the bodies to reach the glass. A few of the sisters make way while others give me scowls, but I manage to get to the front to look through at the scene.

There is a small girl out in the grass. She has a branch in her hand that she's brandishing back and forth, as though pretending to cut the grass with it. She's wearing the simple, one-piece tunic of the Agoge, although it's hanging askew, and her hair is dark and cut in a chin-length bob. Her mouth is moving like she's talking to herself, but obviously we can't hear what she's saying.

"But how did she get back here?" a very young sister asks. She's only been with us for about six months. "Isn't there a fence?"

"No," Three says. "No fence. Just dense forest and the Protectors. We wouldn't want to inhibit the wildlife from roaming freely."

"She's lost, then," another sister says. "Poor thing."

"She doesn't look too upset about it," Three says. "Look at her!"

The little girl drops her stick and stares at the Looking Glass, as though seeing it for the first time. Parting the tall grass with her hands, she wades through it until she's standing just before us. She raps the glass with her knuckles, a puzzled frown on her face. Several of the sisters crouch down to be closer to her, smiling and waving even though they know she can't see them.

I stumble back a pace as the sister beside me crouches and bumps my knees.

The little girl shades her eyes to try to see through the glass, and then she presses her nose flat against it and puffs out her cheeks. The sisters around me laugh, but I just frown. Why hasn't a Protector come around the building yet to usher this girl away? We've never seen a human wander by here before. The Commune Agoge is a couple of miles away—has she really walked so far on her own without getting caught?

I search the trees for green uniforms but see instead a glint of tawny gold.

"No . . . oh no." I press closer to the glass, kneeing the sister who made me stumble, but I don't care. Animals, especially predatory animals, are territorial. This must be the same mountain lion we saw a few weeks back.

"Somebody has to help her," I say. My heart is pounding in my chest as though the lion is bearing down on me instead of the girl. Somewhere in the room, Flora starts to bark.

By now, some of the other sisters have also noticed that the lion is approaching the girl just as it had approached the deer. Lowered stance, flicking tail, wide eyes. Several sisters are making similar exclamations to mine, and the ones crouching in front of the girl are now pointlessly shooing her.

I slam my palm against the glass. "Run!" I shout. "Run away!"

The other sisters' voices rise with me, as though I gave them permission to shout. I use my fists now, pounding on the glass and screaming, "Run, girl, run! Someone has to help her!"

The lion is so close to the girl, and she still doesn't see it. She tilts her ear toward the glass instead, as though she can almost hear us.

"*Please!*" My voice comes out in a shriek. "Someone get a Protector!"

"No."

The word, spoken loud and authoritatively, comes from Mother, and everyone in the room falls silent.

I spin around and push through the crowd to get to her. "Mother, please, please, do something!"

"What would you have me do?" she asks. "It's already too late."

A scream pierces the room, and then several sisters are crying and wailing. My knees weaken as I turn back to the Looking Glass, but all I can see is a spray of blood across it. The girl and the lion are gone, the only traces that they'd been there a swaying swath through the grass marked with a smear of blood.

I stumble back to the glass, tears obscuring my vision, and fall on my knees where the blood is turning to droplets that run down the surface. I press my hands, then my forehead, to the glass as a wrenching sob escapes me. I can't remember the last time I cried like this, but now that it's coming, I'm afraid it won't stop.

"That's enough," Mother says, her voice carrying over the noise in the room. "Girls, enough."

Quiet falls faster than it should, considering what just happened, and I'm the only sister left crying. At least, I'm the only one left crying out loud. I dig my forehead into the glass as though I can push through it. I try to listen to what Mother's saying, but I can't seem to focus like the others can. Did they not all just see what I saw?

"There is no need to carry on," Mother says. "It is sometimes sad, but it is the circle of life. Repeat it after me, *the circle of life.*"

"The circle of life," the other sisters say in monotone.

I don't join in; I'm still crying too hard. I don't *want* to join in.

"Seventeen," Mother says.

I raise my watery eyes to her.

"Come with me, please."

As if moving in a dream, I rise and walk toward her. She smiles as I approach but doesn't offer a hand or arm for comfort. Instead she folds her hands in front of her and walks away. I follow her down a side corridor to the elevator. She presses the button that opens the elevator doors and raises her hand to stay the Protectors who have followed us. Once she and I are inside the elevator, she presses her thumb to the access pad that will take us to her personal floor, and the elevator begins to rise.

On the outskirts of Sanctuary, there is only the ground floor, but in the middle, there are more floors that rise above, getting consecutively smaller as they get higher. Mother's office and living quarters are at the top on a floor of their own. The elevator shaft is glass on the side that borders the gathering room, to give the impression of climbing the Tree of Life as the elevator rises. Here, the upper floors press against the empty space of the high-ceilinged gathering room, and it is only when we get to the top floor, to Mother's living quarters, that the elevator is enclosed in walls and we lose sight of the tree.

Mother doesn't speak to me until we have exited the elevator and are sitting at her broad, empty desk in her office. Everything in this space is white, from the desk to the chairs to the walls to the carpet. My beige tunic and pants look dingy next to the white of the chair I sit in, and Mother's steel-gray hair, short as it is, looks almost black in comparison.

As soon as she is settled, she folds her hands on the desk and says, "Now, Seventeen, I'm concerned about you. Tell me what you're feeling."

By this time I've gotten a hold of myself, but the tears are still dangerously close to the surface. I clear my throat before answering. "I'm feeling sad, Mother. Is that wrong? All the other sisters are sad, too," I say. I know my voice sounds petulant, but I feel as though I have to defend myself.

"Yes, but your sadness is different." Mother leans forward. "Yours betrays an unhealthy emotional attachment to the girl, whom you didn't even know."

I raise a hand in a feeble gesture. "Is it an unhealthy attachment to feel sorrow over the death of a defenseless human child? Do we not love our own kind?"

"What is our own kind?"

I don't answer because I remember what I was taught, and I don't want to say it aloud. All living things—humans, animals, insects, and even trees—are one kind. Except that feels wrong now, the logic flawed. I don't dare speak that thought, though. To even think it is treasonous.

Mother sighs at my silence. "It is unhealthy because you think the girl has more merit than the lion, when, in fact, they are equal. Think about your education. We are all just animals. Would you cry as much for a lion cub killed by a human? For a tree lost in a fire?"

I bite my lip.

She sits back, an indulgent smile on her lips. "Oh, Seventeen. It is antiquated thinking like yours that led to the Great Devastations, don't you see?"

"But . . . we're supposed to be *re*populating Gaia Earth because of those Devastations," I say. "Wasn't that child a contribution of the Program?

Wasn't she one of ours?"

Her smile drops, and the lines in her face disappear. "You must never think of them as *yours* or *ours*. They belong to the Unified World Order, as do you. The loss is shared by all of society, not by any individual or organization, which is why I cannot allow your uncontrolled display of emotion to go unchecked."

"I'm sorry, Mother," I whisper.

There is a long pause during which I study my hands.

When Mother speaks again, her voice is kinder. "Survival of the fittest can be difficult to witness, but remember, it is right and necessary for the furthering of the very best in the animal kingdom."

I close my eyes, seeing the splash of blood on the Looking Glass behind my eyelids. *Right and necessary?* If that is true, then we all indeed are just animals. "We could have stopped it," I whisper.

"What's that?"

I look at her, trying to gauge her reaction, but her expression is tight and forcefully pleasant. I can see it, though, in the slight flaring of her nostrils and the lines around her mouth. "I said we could have stopped it. A Protector stopped that lion from killing a deer only a few weeks back. Why not the child?"

"The mule deer is part of our protected ecosystem. An ecosystem, I might add, that humans once nearly destroyed." She raises a finger when I part my lips to speak. "If the science techs ever discover the glitch in the cloning process, we'll be able to add yearly to animal populations worldwide. But until that time, or such time as the Oligarch determines they have reached self-sustainability, the deer are under our protection, as are the lions and a number of other native species."

The Oligarch. The three rulers who make up the highest authority in the Unified World Order. Their decisions are law, although it seems strange to me that they should concern themselves with the mule deer population in Colorado Province.

"But is it not survival of the fittest to allow the mountain lion to eat the deer?" I ask in a rush.

"Not when the deer is under state protection, and certainly not when there is something we can do to prevent it," she says. "I'm sorry, but it is simply not the same scenario."

"But the girl—"

"Has now effectively failed out of the Agoge. For wandering off as she did, she would not have been allowed to continue her education anyway."

Failed. Mother is saying being eaten by a lion is *failing*. My eyes dart around the room as I imagine the fear the girl must have felt, and the pain. I hope it was over quickly, that she didn't suffer too long.

Why am I the only one who is sympathizing like this? The white walls feel suddenly as though they're closing in on me. My pulse increases, and I grip the arms of the chair.

"You have a tender heart," Mother says, and I jump because she's kneeling next to me and I didn't even notice her approach. She touches my chest. "Just remember to direct that love to the state. We live in a world of big pictures. Do you know what I mean by that?"

I nod, but she goes on as though I didn't.

"Small sacrifices must be made to ensure the propagation of the ideal human race. That girl was not suited for life in this world, in this vision we bear for a better future. We would have figured it out eventually, but nature, Gaia Earth, figured it out first. Her sacrifice ensures that one stronger and better can take her place in our society. Do you still desire to help us build this future?"

I feel as though the whole room is spinning and I'm in the center, at the vortex of a white whirlwind. Her words are both horrifying and encouraging. They validate my beliefs and challenge them all at the same time.

I don't know what I believe.

I put my hands over my face and nod because there's nothing else for me to do.

"Good," she says, her voice soothing. "In order to make that happen, though, we must get you healthy. I've been watching you lately."

I look up sharply. So it *wasn't* in my mind.

"And I've decided you need some time of focused meditation. I'm prescribing three days in the solitary meditation chamber. This is both as a discipline for your outbursts in the gathering room and for your own benefit. Do use the time wisely."

"I will," I say in a croaking whisper. She's not kicking me out, not even now. Although I'm beginning to wonder if that's not what I desire after all.

"Come along now." She rises and presses a button on her desk. It glows green, and she leans toward it. "B-Seventeen is in need of her escort to the meditation chamber in Medical."

"Yes, ma'am." The light goes red, and then it's back to white.

The elevator door opens, and Mother waves a hand in its direction. "Please get on and ride it down, Seventeen."

"Yes, Mother."

"I'll see you soon," she says, putting her hand on my cheek and smiling at me in such a way that I know she loves me. Though I wonder why she summoned the Protectors to escort me. Was she expecting me to fight my sentence?

I step into the elevator, and the door closes between us. When it arrives on the ground floor, there are two Protectors waiting for me.

I go with them willingly, back down the corridor into the Med wing. The solitary meditation chamber is in a far corner, down two separate branchings off the main corridor. It is the farthest removed one can get from anyone else in Sanctuary.

When we reach it, a med tech keys the pad to open the door, and then she walks away without a word. I step into the dark chamber and look around at the sleeping mat, incense jars, and toilet. There is also an audio player with headphones beside the sleeping mat—the most recent dispatches from the Oligarch for me to listen to, most likely.

I turn back to the Protectors and start to say "thank you," but then one of them lurches into the other. Their helmets crack, the sound alarmingly loud in the confined space.

A third green-clad figure is behind them—the one who cracked their heads together—and I know despite the obscured features it must be my imaginary man. E-Fifteen—Pax. I gasp and stumble back as he kicks one of the Protectors in the chest, sending her flying against the far wall of the meditation chamber. The other Protector gives a cry and grabs her weapon, but he twists her arm until it cracks, and she screams and drops the weapon to the floor.

"Pick it up!" he shouts at me, but I'm too aghast to do as he says.

"What did you—*why* did you—" I start toward the Protector who is slumped against the wall, but Pax grabs my arm and spins me around. I wrench away from him. How dare he touch me?

"Run. Now."

I'm shaking all over. "*Why?*" I cry.

He snatches up the gun the Protector dropped. She's on the floor, whimpering and cradling her arm. He aims it at the intercom on the wall and shoots, the ball of green energy frying the button and leaving a charred hole.

Then he shoves me out the door and into the hall before slamming the chamber closed behind us and engaging the lock.

"Because they were going to kill you," he says. "Now *run*."

Chapter 8

I careen around the corner of the first branching, Pax's words echoing in my brain. Why would they kill me? They wouldn't kill me. I'm a Breeder!

Pax is running behind me, his slapping footsteps urging me forward. I can't think like this. I have to stop.

I plant my feet and skid to a halt. Pax lets out an exhalation of surprise as he slams into me. I stumble forward, but years of dance and exercise pay off as I nimbly stay on my feet and swing around to face him. "Tell me what's going on," I say. "Why did you say they were going to kill me?"

"Because they were. I've been tailing them all day, and I heard their orders come through clear as day. 'Terminate B-Seventeen. She's asking too many questions.' I followed them when they came back with you. I just saved your life."

I ask too many questions? I know curiosity is frowned upon, but would they really kill me for it? This doesn't make sense. "Who gave the order?" I ask in a whisper, narrowing my eyes.

"Who do you think?"

Mother. I close my eyes. "No. She wouldn't. I don't believe you."

"She did."

I think of the conversation I just had with her. Of her cool assessment of the death of the girl. Of her assurances of our place in the animal kingdom. But Mother loves me! Doesn't she? I clench my jaw and hold back tears, giving Pax a blazing look. Why must he plant these doubts?

"If she wants me dead," I say, "why hasn't she given the order before now?"

"Because they hoped they could get you under control. Breeders are valuable commodities, after all—difficult to replace. But now . . ." He shakes his head, and I could almost scream with the frustration of not being able to read his expression.

"Now?"

"Now you know what they are capable of." He lowers his head and his voice. "Your response was exactly what they were looking for, exactly what they can't allow."

"What . . . with the girl?" I swallow hard, trying to push the images away. I close my eyes. "They didn't have anything to do with that. As Mother said, it was already too late."

Pax steps closer, his visor hovering just in front of my face. "But *would* she have done anything about it, even if she could have?" he whispers.

I study his visor, my stomach sinking because I know the answer. "No," I say.

He steps back and holds out his hand to me. "Then why are you still here? You know in your heart it's wrong, and that's what separates you from the others."

"But I don't get it. This is a place of *life*."

"It is a place of death, and you'll never know the truth if you don't come with me now."

I ball my fists and look away, becoming slowly aware of a muffled pounding that can be coming only from the Protectors locked in the meditation chamber down the hall.

Pax gives an exasperated sigh and asks, "Do you need proof?" He reaches toward my head and I flinch, thinking he's going to strike me, but instead he grabs a tablet from a slot beside the door I'm leaning against. He keys it on and taps in something that makes it come to life. I don't have time to wonder how he knows the access codes before he turns the screen toward me and points to a line of glowing green script. "There. Read it for yourself."

I look at it for only a moment. "I can't read," I say.

For the first time, Pax falters. He tilts his head in a jerky motion, clearly surprised, and says, "What?"

The pounding at the end of the hall grows louder, and I can now hear muffled voices. Pax looks over his shoulder. "Fine, here . . ." He taps rapidly, and then says, "Computer, play back last transmission, volume low."

As clear as day, Mother's automated voice comes through the tablet. "Terminate B-Seventeen. She's asking too many questions."

My breath leaves me in a rush, and I slump against the door at my back. "It . . . can't . . ." I press my hands to my mouth and take deep, bracing breaths. I will not cry. I will not cry.

Pax replaces the tablet in its holder and says in a low voice, "Do you believe me now?"

I nod. How could I not? "But I don't want to leave Sanctuary," I whisper, my voice hitching. "It's my home."

"You must leave," he says.

I shake my head, terror like I've never known coursing through me, seizing me and making me clench my chattering teeth.

Pax's tone drops another notch as he asks, "Don't you want to be free? Let me save you. Please, Pria."

My eyes fly wide and I look at him, my heart slamming in my chest. "How do you know that name? Did I tell it to you?"

"I know a lot more than that, but you'll never know how if you don't come with me." He holds out his hand again. "The Program got one thing right—you *are* very special. Too special to die. Please."

Slowly, as though my arm weighs fifty pounds, I reach for his outstretched hand. When our fingers touch, he envelops my hand and squeezes it. This touch, this single touch, even though he's wearing a glove and I cannot feel his skin, is treason to the Unified World Order because I did it on purpose. I am a Breeder, physically set apart for the propagation of a more perfect human race. Touching a man is forbidden to me by law. But until now, I'd never had the opportunity.

Holding his hand marks the end of my life, but somehow, it feels like the beginning.

Chapter 9

I don't have time to dwell on my treason, for at the moment of my consent, Pax pulls me after him. We don't run this time but walk briskly, and when we come to the main corridor, he puts his finger to his visor and releases my hand. A door opens with a *snick*, and we hear voices.

"It was false labor, probably brought on by all the excitement today," a med tech says. "I've given her a higher dose and instructed her to rest. Her genetic map is particularly promising, and all scans of the fetus have revealed optimum results. See here . . ."

There is a quiet tapping for a moment. Pax holds his weapon near his ear and waits, while I hold my breath behind him, every beat of my pulse screaming, *What are you doing? What are you doing? What are you doing? What are you doing?*

"Ah, yes, I see," another med tech says. "And the fetus *is* male, yes? No mistakes this time?"

The first tech must nod, because the second tech says, "Good. I don't think I could stomach another one this week."

"Shhh," the first voice says. "Not here."

Then there are footsteps walking toward us. I press to the wall, shielded by Pax's taller frame. They walk past the entrance to the hallway in which we are standing, but they don't even look our way, absorbed as they are by the information on the first woman's tablet.

Once they are past, the first med tech says, "When is your rotation up?"

"Next week, thankfully. I can't take much more of this. *We're* the ones who could use the drugs."

The first tech sighs. "I don't disagree. Where are they sending you next?"

I don't hear the second technician's response because they pass through another set of doors and the corridor falls silent.

"Let's go," Pax says.

I let out the breath I've been holding and follow him. He doesn't reach for my hand again but keeps both his hands on his weapon. He turns us toward the end of the hall and the door that marks the entrance to the storage closet or, as I must now admit it is, the staircase.

Just as we near the end of the hall, another door opens and a med tech steps out.

"The code is 1859," Pax says to me, training his weapon on the tech.

"How do you know that?" I ask.

"Not now. Just get it open."

I stiffen and stare at the startled tech. "Don't kill her," I say.

"I wasn't going to! Now get it open, Pria."

The use of my name jars me again, and I back toward the security panel while Pax says to the startled technician, "Don't move, and don't say a word. Put your hands up where I can see them."

Shaking, the med tech raises her hands, her blinking tablet quivering in her grip. "Who are you?" she asks.

"I said don't speak! Pria, I don't hear that door opening."

I tear my eyes from them and fumble with the keypad, entering the code incorrectly the first time. I take a deep breath and try again. 1-8-5-9. This time the door gives a chime and clicks open with a puff of air.

"Do you need help, sister?" the tech asks me.

"Quiet," Pax says. "I'm warning you."

The med tech gives me one more frightened look, then turns and starts to run.

Without hesitation, Pax shoots. I hear the *zip* of the energy burst leaving the gun, and then the woman topples over with a cry, blood blossoming on the back of her thigh.

Blood. Blood splashed across the Looking Glass. A little girl dying.

I gag and double over, but Pax grabs me around the middle and hauls me through the door. He pulls it closed behind us, and we are engulfed in blackness.

I'm gasping and heaving, and stars dance across my vision. I expect him to order me to pull myself together, but now that we're through the door, he stands perfectly still, one arm around my waist. He's not embracing or comforting me; he's only keeping me from falling on the floor. And he's letting me get it out of my system.

Mother had ordered me to stop.

I push away from him as soon as I'm able to stand without support and wipe my mouth and my eyes, which are adjusting to the darkness. Our light clothing seems to glow in the dark, so I can see his form when he extends his hand to me again.

"I can't ever go back, can I?" I ask in a hoarse whisper.

"No," he says. "Would you want to?"

I huff out what is almost a laugh but without humor. Then I shake my head and grip the railing instead of his hand. Without waiting for him to lead, I start down the stairs into the darkness.

They go down and down. I stop at the first landing where there's a door and look over my shoulder, but Pax shakes his head and passes me by. "All the way to the bottom," he says.

We pass three more landings with doors before we come to the bottom. A heavy-looking door with a security panel beside it reminds me of the one above, and I tilt my head, listening. There is no sound of pursuit.

"Why isn't anyone coming after us?" I ask, my voice sounding dead. I'm resolved to this fate, but it doesn't yet feel real. "They will have found the injured med tech by now."

"I changed the passcode on the door," he says, deftly keying in another passcode where he stands. He puts his hand on the handle as the lock disengages.

"You . . . how do you know how to do that?"

"I have a diverse skill set," he says. "It will hold them, but not for long. Come on." He makes as though to open the door, but then he hesitates and looks my way. "Prepare yourself."

I frown.

He opens the door and the stench hits me like a wave. I cough and cover my mouth, my eyes watering. I've never smelled anything like it before.

"Come on," he says again and nudges me through ahead of him.

Still holding my hand over my mouth and nose, I step forward into a vast chamber lit by strange, pale, oblong lights. The walls are bare concrete, and there are three other closed doors leading to who knows where. I never knew there was a basement in Sanctuary, let alone a vast underground network, and I look around with wide eyes. A rushing sound I can't immediately identify fills my ears, and as I look for its source, I see an enormous contraption in the center of the room.

It's made of dull burnished metal, and there is what looks like a vent of some sort sticking out of the top and covered in a black substance. Tubes and pipes run out of its top and up to the ceiling where they disappear into the concrete. A door large enough for me to crawl through stands ajar on one side of it, and although I can't see anything in its dark interior, it seems to be the source of the stench. There is a shovel leaning up against it and several buckets stacked nearby. Dust covers everything.

Pax comes up beside me and holsters his weapon.

"What is that?" I ask.

"Incinerator," he says.

"Incinerator for what?"

He turns his face to me so that I see my pale reflection in the bronze. "Later," he says. "Can you swim?"

I blink and recoil. "What?"

He jerks his head to follow him, and we walk to the shadowy recesses of the underground chamber. About five feet down and running between the floor and the wall is a channel of frothing water—the source of the rushing noise.

"It's the only way out." He points to where it runs through a culvert in the wall, into darkness. "It's a natural underground stream that eventually empties out into the river, south of the Commune. It will be cold with winter runoff, but it's our only hope."

"Are you crazy?" I shake my head. "We'll drown! How do you know there will be air for us in there?" I jab my hand toward the culvert.

"Because I've done this before." He steps closer and looks down at me. "Now, can you *swim*?"

I raise my arms. "Of course I can't! What reason would there have been for me to learn?" The Unified World Order doesn't waste resources on nonessential skills.

"Then you'll have to hold on to me." He holds out his arm, but I hesitate. Touching him is almost more frightening than the churning, rushing water.

"I don't think I can," I whisper. I've already touched him so much today. I've already committed treason ten times over. This is simply too much. I've made a mistake. I should go back

Pounding sounds on the door through which we came, and Pax and I both look toward it. Without waiting for my permission, without even removing his helmet, he grabs me around the shoulders and throws us both sideways into the water.

A short drop, then a slap of icy water all over my body. I gasp and choke, and water floods my lungs. I cough and gag, floating on my back with Pax's arm an iron bar beneath my chin to hold my face above the water, and then I'm swept through the culvert and into blackness.

Pax

Chapter 10

What follows next is a series of terrifying minutes during which I'm battered in total darkness against rocky walls and shot through curves and twists, carried ever downward, sometimes able to breathe, sometimes drawn under, always within the circle of Pax's arm. I feel him kicking his legs and stroking with his free hand, but I'm not sure what the use is. We are hapless twigs borne on this current, and I'm half-certain we won't survive the journey.

I have no idea how long it goes on before we are shot out a cave mouth and over the lip of a drop. Suspended in water and air, my scream catches in my throat. Then we plunge into a deeper current and spin around, still drifting downward but at a much slower pace, and I swallow my scream entirely as my head breaks the surface. Pax holds me yet, although the water has grown tamer, and he strikes off toward one of the shores. The sun is high in the sky, and I gasp in fresh outside air as I try to catch my bearings. It's been five years—five *years*—since I've felt a breeze on my face.

Pax drags me onto rocky shoals caked with ice, but I'm so battered and numb, I can't feel the cold through my sodden clothes. He deposits me onto the shore, laying my head gently down, and then he pulls his arm away and I'm free. I'm so dizzy, though, that when I try to rise, I only flop over onto my hands and knees.

With my limbs shaking, I raise my head and look into the forest. Staring right back at me are the amber eyes of a coyote. I go rigid. I recognize this creature, and I know what it can do. A girl in the Agoge with me was attacked by one once. I can't remember what happened to her.

The rocks next to me shift, and Pax is there, on his feet, pointing his gun at the coyote. He doesn't shoot, just stands at the ready, and after several tense moments, the coyote turns tail and runs away.

With a sigh and a mutter, Pax holsters his weapon and offers a hand to me. "You'll want to get out of those clothes," he says. "It may be warm out, but the water is frigid. You'll catch hypothermia."

When I don't respond, he takes my shoulders, but I shrink away and say, "Don't *touch* me!" I sit back on my heels and wrap my arms protectively around myself. The dizziness is passing, being replaced with a sense of horror at what I've done.

Pax keeps his hand outstretched for a moment more, and then says, "Will you at least let me help you up? There's a place not far from here"—he looks over his shoulder—"where I have supplies. I have clean clothes," he adds. "But we should go . . . quickly."

I nod, shivering violently. I'm holding in tears, and the back of my throat feels about ready to tear apart with the effort. Scorning his hand, I get unsteadily to my feet and lift my chin.

Pax raises his hand to his helmet as though to remove it, and I catch my breath in spite of myself. How I can still feel curiosity over the sight of a man's face at a time like this, I don't know. But I'm disappointed again because Pax seems to think better of it and lowers his hand. He turns to the woods and says, "Keep close."

I follow him into the dense tree cover, taking care not to twist my ankles on the bulbous rocks that stick out of the groundcover at unexpected twists and turns. My shoes, which are lightweight and made for life inside, are no match for the rough ground, and I wince repeatedly as sharp sticks and rocks prod at my numb feet. I know I'd be in a lot more pain if the feeling had fully returned to my extremities. But I don't utter a single word of complaint, and I blink back any remaining tears. I can't have Pax thinking I'm weak. This is a hostile world, and whether or not I agree with Mother's practical enactment of the philosophy, it is a world where only the fittest survive. I am the fittest. I am a Breeder. I will survive.

After several minutes, we come to a shelf of rock that overhangs a shallow cave. I can see all the way to the back of the cave, as it's only about eight feet deep, but I probably wouldn't have seen the cave mouth at all if Pax hadn't been leading me. Several strewn boulders and a thick growth of gorse bush camouflage it, and a trickle of a mountain stream dribbles over the lip of the shelf above.

"Here," Pax says. He ducks inside the cave and reemerges a moment later with a bundle. "Clothes." He hands them to me.

I snatch them as quickly as I can. I'm alone in the woods with a man I don't know, and he's asking me—no, *telling* me—to undress.

I'm so cold I can barely think straight, and I don't know what to do.

Pax puts both hands on the sides of his helmet and lifts. It comes off the back of his head first, so that he has to tilt it forward to extract his face. And then he's holding it before his chest and lifting his eyes to meet mine, and I forget about my cold, wet chill.

His dark hair is sticking up from the helmet, but it's somehow dry even after the dunking we've been through. His complexion is much paler than mine—in fact, it's much paler than any complexion I've ever seen before, and I take a step closer to see him more clearly. There seem to be some sort of darker spots all over his face, but they, too, are pale, and with the sun mottling in through the trees above, it could be just a trick of the light.

His face . . . it's so different from all the feminine faces I've grown used to. Where I have soft curves, he has sharper angles. His eyebrows are thick and straight, and his brown eyes are level and serious over high cheekbones and cheeks that are slightly concave. His lips are full and larger than mine, and his jaw and chin are square. A slight crease runs down the center of his chin, something I've never seen before on any female face.

He stands in silence and stillness, letting me study him. Perhaps—probably—knowing this is the first time I've seen a man since I was a child in the Agoge.

His features are curiously attractive to me. I've appreciated the beauty of my fellow Breeders before, as I think it's in human nature to acknowledge beauty, and it would be impossible not to acknowledge the beauty of a bunch of genetically superior women, but my appreciation for his face feels different somehow. I'm having a physiological response as well. My pulse is increasing and my face flushes with warmth. I feel embarrassed, shy, and drawn to him all at the same time. Why merely looking at him should cause this response is beyond my understanding.

Pax shifts and begins to unzip the high neck of the collar of his suit, and my breath catches in my throat. I spin so my back is to him and say, "What are you doing?"

"I'm soaked through," he says. His voice sounds different outside his helmet, quieter and clearer. "We can't stand around staring at each other all day." The underbrush crackles as he walks toward me, but I don't turn to look at him. "You change clothes inside the cave. I'll be out of sight, a few paces away. Call out when you're finished."

He walks away into the trees, a bundle of clothing grasped in his hands, and I make sure he's completely out of sight before I tuck myself away in the cave.

I'm exposed only for a few moments, and as soon as I've donned the new tunic and pants, I feel warmer. The clothes are of the style I'm used to but made out of coarse material that itches my skin. The pants are a little too large, and I roll them down at the waist and look around for new footwear. There are a couple of pairs of brown boots in the very back of the cave, and I hold up both pairs, choosing the one that looks closest to my foot size. As I slide my feet into them, I remember I'm supposed to let him know when I'm done.

I stick my head out of the cave. "Pax," I say. My voice sounds too loud in the stillness of the forest.

I'm ready for some answers.

Chapter 11

Pax returns wearing pants and a tunic similar to mine with the sleeves half-rolled up. He's barefoot and carrying his green Enforcer uniform in a bundle wrapped around his helmet and boots. He sets the bundle carefully on top of a boulder outside the cave before extracting the holster for the gun and strapping it around his waist. The sterile light green against the coarse brown of his tunic is an odd combination. He hands me the second gun—the one he took from the fallen Protector in the meditation chamber. I never saw where he'd tucked it away, but clearly he got it out with us.

This time I take the gun without hesitation. If this is survival of the fittest, I need a way to defend myself. But I don't have a holster for it, and I don't know how to use it. It's made of polycarbonate, a material I learned about in the Agoge. Lightweight, durable, and cool to the touch, it doesn't feel like something that could kill someone.

"Do you know how to shoot one of those?" Pax asks.

I shake my head.

"I'll have to teach you, and soon. Hand me those boots, will you?"

My hands are still shaking, although I'm much warmer, and I hate the betrayal of my weakness. I retrieve the other pair of boots from the back of the cave and toss them at his feet. He bends to retrieve them without a word.

"You . . . you had clothes my size," I say. Even the boots are almost perfect.

"I've been planning getting you out for a long time," Pax says without looking up from lacing his boots. "It wasn't difficult to figure out your measurements once I'd accessed the med computers. There was surprisingly little security to get through."

"Why would they need security?" I ask. "Our lives belong to them, and we couldn't read the files even if we got a hold of them."

Pax nods. Once he's finished lacing his boots, he stands again and walks toward me.

I shrink back against the cave wall near the entrance, but he doesn't seem to notice. Instead he tilts his head below the trickle of water coming over the lip of the rock shelf and drinks deeply. I study him again while he's not looking and find him . . . captivating. The bulge in his throat moves up and down as he swallows—I touch my smooth throat—and there are definitely some sort of speckles on his skin. It's not just a trick of the light.

He finishes beneath the stream and steps back, wiping his mouth. There is something odd about his pale complexion next to his dark hair and eyes, eyes that are troubling to me the closer I look because I can see that his eyelashes are pale. They don't match the color of the rest of his hair. I feel like I'm looking at two people put together.

"Drink," he says, gesturing toward the trickle of water. He backs away toward the scattered boulders outside the cave to make space for me.

I keep the gun clutched in one hand as I approach the water with as much caution as the deer in the grass beyond the Looking Glass. But I don't really think Pax will hurt me. If he wanted to, then why would he have saved me? So I tilt my head and drink, not realizing how thirsty I am until the cold water touches my tongue.

Pax is still watching me when I finish, and another moment of silence passes. Now that we are free of Sanctuary, it's as though he doesn't know what to do with me. I don't know if I *want* him to know what to do with me. I have a million questions, but I don't know where to begin, and the discomfort of being alone with a man is making me tongue-tied. So we stand and stare at each other in the mouth of the cave, the afternoon light slanting through the trees warming our shoulders and heads.

Finally Pax parts his mouth to speak, and from this close, I immediately notice his teeth. They are white but not perfectly straight. On the upper right, one tooth slightly overhangs the one beside it, making it stick out.

He must notice the direction of my gaze and my surprised expression, for he gives a humorless laugh and says, "Not used to seeing anything less than perfection, are you?"

I shift my gaze up to his eyes, but I don't respond. It was a rhetorical question anyway.

"There's more you should see," he says. "And you should see it before anything else, before you ask any questions, because you won't believe my answers if you don't."

I raise my eyebrows.

With a sigh, Pax brings his thumb and forefinger up to his right eye. I cringe as he touches the surface of his eye and pinches, pulling away what looks like the first layer of membrane. I cover my mouth to keep from crying out, wondering what sort of pain he must be in, but he doesn't utter even a whimper. He takes a small case from his pocket and tucks the membrane inside it, then does the same with his left eye before putting the case away. He rubs his eyes for a moment, and then, blinking, he looks back at me.

"Do you see?" he asks in a whisper.

His eyes are blue—very pale blue, like the sky at noon on a cloudless day. Blue like the water of the river we dragged ourselves from. Blue.

"That's impossible," I whisper, forgetting my discomfort at being so near to him and leaning in for a closer look.

This close, I can also more clearly see the speckles that cover his skin. They are irregular dots of very light brown over his pale complexion. My first thought is that they must be a symptom of some horrifying disease, but Pax does not look or act sick, and the spots are not unattractive.

He steps back to the trickle of water and dips his head forward into the stream. I wonder why he is getting himself wet again after we've just dried off, but his hair had never even been wet to begin with, protected beneath the helmet.

The water running off his head becomes dark brown. He's massaging his fingers over his scalp, and the color is draining away like paint from an easel. He does his face, too, rubbing at his eyebrows. I know my mouth is hanging open, but I can't close it.

It doesn't take long before all the color is gone. He removes his head from the stream and wipes his face on his sleeve. Then he shakes his head, spraying water droplets everywhere.

The pale eyelashes make sense now, and the pale complexion, for with hair his color—the color of light reddish gold—his features no longer look confused. There is unity in his coloring, and even in his slightly snaggled teeth.

His lips part, but I shake my head rapidly and step closer to him. I drop the gun on top of the nearest boulder with a clatter and clutch my hands together to stop the shaking. I'm breathing in shallow, hyperventilating breaths, because what I'm seeing, more than anything else that has happened this day, shakes the very foundations of my beliefs.

He is a study in recessive traits, traits I only ever learned about in the Agoge, traits that should no longer exist. This man, this *Pax*, whoever he is, is a fossil, a relic of a world long extinct. He shouldn't exist. And he most certainly cannot be a product of a Breeder. But the Controlled Repopulation Program has been in place since the end of the Great Incursion—no humans are born outside it, as all those not selected for the Program are sterilized at puberty. No Breeder in a hundred years has had recessive traits in her genes. Those were *weak* traits that made humanity *weaker*. Everyone who looked like Pax supposedly died out in the Great Devastations.

Yet here he stands. And if he isn't a product of the Program, then where has he come from?

"May . . . may I?" I ask in a halting voice, forgetting my aversion to touching him. I *have* to touch him to know it's real.

He nods, and I brush his cheekbones with my fingertips, hardly able to keep contact because I'm shaking so hard. I touch his eyebrows, his hair. The breath from his nostrils is warm on my hands as I trace his lips. He twitches and blinks when I touch his eyelashes, and I'm finally convinced the evidence I see matches the evidence I feel.

I stumble back a pace, on my guard again, and horrified that I've been touching him. I've been told of the evils and inferiorities of recessive traits my whole life, but looking at Pax, I see neither evil nor inferiority.

"You're . . . *beautiful*," I say. And then the shutters close in on my mind, and I sway sideways into the boulder. I'm dimly aware of Pax reaching out before the blackness takes me and I collapse.

Chapter 12

I awake to a stinging in my wrist. I twitch and try to pull my arm away even before opening my eyes, but Pax orders me in a steady voice to be still. Frowning, I peel my heavy eyelids apart and find I'm lying on my back before the cave, right where I'd fallen. I'm staring up at the tree canopy, and Pax has my wrist in a death grip. His head is bent over me, and he's holding an empty syringe between his teeth.

"What are you doing?" I ask in a raspy voice.

He removes the syringe from his mouth and says, "I have to remove your microchip. I should have done it right away, but hypothermia was the more pressing issue." He puts the syringe on the ground. It has a tiny needle on one end. "Local anesthetic" he says to my unasked question. "Keep your wrist still and don't sit up. It should be fully numb in another minute."

I look at where he's grasping me. There is a tiny pinprick of blood next to the blue vein on the inside of my right wrist. I sigh and ask, "What microchip are you talking about? I've never been microchipped."

"Yes, you have been. You just don't remember." He taps his finger on my wrist. "Can you feel that?"

"Just a little pressure."

"Good. Almost set." Keeping a hold of my wrist with one hand, he pulls a scalpel from a bag on the ground beside him. "Everybody is microchipped at birth, and then that microchip is replaced with a new one at age one, once tertiary viability is determined."

"Age *one*? Tertiary viability? I don't understand—"

"It's okay. There's no way you could know this stuff. Only med techs, science techs, and agents of the UWO are privy to it."

"So which are you?" I ask the question quickly, trying to catch him off his guard, but he doesn't even blink.

"None of the above. How about now?" He taps my wrist again.

"Nothing. Wait!" I shout when he's about to touch the scalpel to my skin.

He gives an impatient sigh and says, "Pria, if I don't remove this right away, Enforcers will track you and find you. They're probably already pulling up your location. Let me remove it and destroy it, and then we need to get away from here as fast as we can. I don't have time to answer all your questions right now."

He looks me straight in the eyes, and his voice is even and steady and urgent. He shows none of the telltale signs of deception. I believe him.

"Okay," I say, but only because the Program would have the Enforcers arrest me for treason if I am found in this situation. I have no choice but to follow through with my actions to whatever end they lead.

He touches the scalpel to the skin about a quarter inch from the blue vein and makes an incision an inch long. The scalpel is so sharp, my skin practically springs apart, and blood seeps out.

"Don't move a muscle," Pax says through tight lips.

I know enough of human anatomy to know why. It's delicate work, and if he cuts my vein, I could bleed to death. I don't have to ask where he got the scalpel or the syringe, or the rolls of white bandages peeking out of his bag. He roamed in and out of the Medical wing for weeks, as far I as know. He must have had plenty of time to steal supplies.

With the scalpel, he prods deep between my tendons. The deeper he goes, the more pressure I feel until a sharp sting makes me draw in my breath.

"Sorry," he says. "They plant them deep, and I couldn't get stronger anesthetic but I can see it now." He puts the scalpel between his lips and reaches into his bag before coming out with long tweezers.

I brace myself for another shock of pain when he sticks them into the wound, which is now running with blood, but I feel only pressure and a tug, and then he's pulling the tweezers out.

Held between the tongs and dripping blood is a tiny chip, shiny silver and white, about a quarter inch square. Other than two bent wires that look as though they must have secured it inside my arm, it's no thicker than a piece of paper. He nods and then extends the chip toward me.

I open my left hand and let him place it on my palm. After he puts down his tweezers and scalpel next to the empty syringe, he grabs a roll of bandages, mops up the blood on my arm, and puts pressure on the wound as he digs into his bag again. He pulls out a small canister with a spray top. It's a spray antiseptic—I recognize it immediately.

My arm is beginning to throb as the light anesthesia wears off, and I wince as Pax removes the bandage and sprays the incision with the antiseptic. Then he drops the canister and takes out another small container, this one with a lid that pops open to reveal a brush top. He squeezes it until a gooey liquid appears on the brush, and then he wipes the goo down the incision, holding my skin tightly together.

The glue takes only seconds to dry, and then he wraps a new bandage tight around my wrist several times over before he sits back with a sigh. "Let me see that," he says, gesturing for the microchip.

I hold it out and he takes it, his fingertips tickling my palm as he uses his fingernail to peel it up. It's sticky with blood and clings to his finger, but he scrapes it off flat on the boulder beside us. Then he takes up a rock and smashes it until it's in tiny fragments.

"There," he says, tossing the rock aside. "It's done. Let me help you up."

I want to protest, but my head is spinning and my arm is throbbing. I cradle my bandaged wrist to my chest as he lifts my shoulders. His hand only lingers long enough to make sure I'm steady, and then he's gathering his medical supplies and taking them to the trickle of water to rinse them off and scrub the blood from his hands.

"How soon do we need to leave?" I ask, remembering what he said about my being tracked.

"As soon as we can. There was ample time to pinpoint your location before I destroyed that thing, and the Enforcers will have taken note of its malfunction now. That will make it even more urgent to find you." He shakes his hands to get rid of the water and asks, "Can you stand? Will you be able to walk? Even if we can only move slowly, it will be something."

"Yes, I think so," I say. I touch the back of my head where there is a painful lump. "Did I fall on my head?"

Pax is shoving his rinsed medical supplies into his bag but looks up with a grimace. "Yes, sorry. I tried to break your fall, but you went down so quickly. I knew my appearance would be shocking, but I had no idea . . ." He creases his brow and seems to want to say more, but instead he shakes his head and finishes repacking his bag.

Wanting to be true to my word, I struggle to my feet, using the boulder for support.

"Here." Pax hands me the gun I'd put aside. "Tuck it into your waistband for now. I've turned the safety on, so you won't accidentally shoot yourself."

I take it, and then he shoulders the bag, followed by a second bag large enough to contain his Enforcer uniform and a number of other items.

"Let's go," he says, holding out a hand toward me. I look down my nose at it. With a wry smile, he lowers it and says, "Stay close on my heels and pay attention. There are more than mountain lions and coyotes out here."

Chapter 13

Pax's words send a thrill of fear through me. He must mean the Unfamiliars.

Although the Unified World Order made a pact of peace with them following the Great Incursion, everyone knows it's a tenuous peace at best and that reasoning with the creatures is far from reliable. It is said that to meet an Unfamiliar out in the wild without protection is to be killed by one. But these killings are infrequent, and people don't want to risk another war by reporting them to the UWO. Besides, nobody wanders the wilds anymore.

I snort, and Pax shoots me a look over his shoulder.

Well, nobody but us.

And the little girl . . . but I can't think about her, or I'll dissolve into tears again.

We're moving neither uphill nor downhill, but slantwise across the tilted landscape. The upward slope is to our left, which means the mountain range is to our left, so we're moving north. Somewhere far above us is Sanctuary, and I can't help but look up every few paces. I'm not sure if I'm longing for them to find me or dreading it. But they won't find me, not now that my microchip is removed. I can't believe I never knew it was there.

"Pax," I say, breaking a long silence. "When did you remove your microchip?"

"A long time ago," he says. He holds his hand up backward over his shoulder, and I'm walking close enough to see the faint scar on the inside of his wrist. He even has the speckled dots on his arm.

"What are those?" I ask. "All over you. The . . . dots. Are you sick?"

He glances back at me with a wry tilt to his lips. "Your kind would probably call me sick, but no, I'm not. They're called freckles." He looks forward again. "They're tiny deposits of concentrated melanin all over my skin. I know they must look strange to you."

"No . . . well, yes. But not like you're probably thinking."

"Right," he says. "I'm *beautiful*." He says it with a sarcastic emphasis, and I blush, glad he can't see me.

"Why are you mocking me?" I ask. "You're the one who told me I was different from the others. Is it so hard to believe I might view you differently than they would?"

Pax stops so suddenly I almost run into him, and he turns to face me. "Why, though? Why aren't you repulsed? You're the first person who's seen me and not threatened to turn me in. Usually I'm treated more like an Unfamiliar than a man. Why do you think I'm beautiful?"

I don't know why. Everything about my education taught me his kind were inferior, that they evolved out of the human genome long ago.

I shake my head and purse my lips. "I can't deny what I see with my own eyes. You saved my life, so you're not weak. You're clearly intelligent, so you're not inferior. You're not beastly like an Unfamiliar. You're a man. And how can I see a fellow human as anything but beautiful?"

He huffs. "You didn't learn that in the Agoge. There are rankings to humanity, remember? Survival of the fittest. It's only logical that some of us are inferior to others, that some of us don't *deserve* to live. You're a Breeder—you should believe that more than anyone."

I recoil. "Just because it's taught that way doesn't make it true."

Pax spreads his arms. "What is truth?"

I don't know. I'm running through the catalogue of my education in my mind and coming up empty. An ideology of breeding a better human race always seemed so logical to me, but what if the UWO conception of what makes for a better human race is tragically flawed? I take a deep, meditative breath and close my eyes. "I don't know what to believe right now, but I'll thank you not to snap at me when I'm trying to be kind."

Pax is quiet for a long moment, and I open my eyes to find him staring at me with a shrewd expression. He stands straight with his shoulders thrown back, despite the heavy bags he carries, and his lips are parted as though he was about to speak but stopped. Then he scratches the back of his neck and says, "You're right. I'm sorry. Let's just say it hasn't been easy growing up in this world looking like I do. I'm considered a criminal for something I can't control. It's meant that I'm always on the run or in hiding. I've never really trusted anyone before, and I'm not used to polite conversation. If I'm short with you, please forgive me."

I nod. He's standing so close, and his blue eyes mesmerize me. There are speckles of gold swimming around in them, like the gold dust that settles on the bottom of the mountain streams in Colorado Province—gold dust that, according to my history lessons in the Agoge, once drove men mad with greed and longing. Will the gold in Pax's eyes drive me mad? It's difficult to say. It is already a mad thing he's convinced me to do, and mad things he's convincing me to believe.

"So why do you trust me?" I ask.

He smiles and shifts his bags higher on his shoulders. "I told you. I may not understand why, but you're different."

There is a sudden crashing in the underbrush above, and we both look upward to see a herd of mule deer bearing down on us. Something has spooked them. They are flying in leaps and bounds around the trees and over the rocks. Pax yanks me to a thick-trunked pine and presses me to his chest with his back to the tree.

I try to pull away, indignant, but he tightens his grip and gives me a slight shake. "Not now," he says. "Let them pass. Do you want to be trampled?"

The deer pound past our tree, paying us no heed, and then we hear the hum of an approaching UWO hovercraft. It's a sound I haven't heard in years, not since before Sanctuary, but I still recall the broad, arrowhead-shaped crafts and how they could hover directly above or zip up into the stratosphere and fly off with a sonic boom.

"Damn it," Pax says. "They sent an X-1. It'll have heat sensors. Get down on the ground, curl into a ball, and don't move."

I hesitate, considering just letting them take me. Pax throws his bags to the ground and rummages around in the bigger of the two. Sensing I haven't moved, he looks up at me without speaking, as though giving me a chance to make my own decision.

"Terminate B-Seventeen. She's asking too many questions."

I don't want to die. And I want to know why I find Pax beautiful when the rest of my kind would see him as an ugly anomaly. I have already made my decision.

I squeeze my eyes shut and drop to the ground. Curling into a ball, I hug my knees to my chest and feel Pax tossing leaves and pine needles over the top of me. The thrum of the X-1 grows louder, but it's moving slowly, combing the mountainside. Then the sound diminishes as Pax throws something smelly and heavy over me—some sort of animal pelt, I think. He drops down beside me and curls up, dragging the pelt over himself, too.

He stills and then whispers to me, "The ground is warm from the sun, so their sensors shouldn't be able to differentiate us beneath this. And if they're looking out the window, they'll just see a pelt of lion's fur. They'll probably scan the whole area from above before sending ground troops to investigate."

"I left my clothing from Sanctuary in the cave," I whisper. "Won't they find them?"

"Probably. But that's good. They won't know what you're wearing now, so they won't know what to search for."

"But it will also tell them I'm still alive."

"Yes, but they might assume you've been kidnapped. The Protector saw me with you in the Med wing, and I'm the one who shot her. Pria, if you're ever caught—if *we're* ever caught—that's the story I want you to tell them. I kidnapped you. If they believe you had nothing to do with it, they might let you live."

"But they'll kill you for sure if I tell them that." I find, suddenly, that I don't want Pax to die.

"They've been trying to kill me since I was a baby," he says. "And they haven't managed to yet."

The thrum is very loud now, too loud for us to keep whispering, so we fall silent. It must be just above us, but Pax did his job well, for it doesn't linger but continues on toward the cave we left behind earlier in the day.

As soon as the thrum fades to silence, Pax throws off the pelt and springs to his feet. This time when he offers his hand, I take it and let him pull me up. He shoves the pelt into his bag and re-shoulders it. The air has grown cool, and the long beams of sunlight through the trees no longer reach down to us where we stand in the shadow of the slope.

"Let's put as much distance between us and that X-1 as we can before nightfall," Pax says. "Those heat sensors will be much more difficult to trick when it's cold after dark, but I know of another place we can hide. It's a bit east of here, but we can make it if we hurry."

He takes up his smaller satchel, too, and I hold out my hand.

"Let me carry it. I can help."

He gives me a quick, searching look, then nods and gives me the bag. "This way," he says, and we turn east down the mountainside.

Chapter 14

We move much quicker going downhill than across the slope of the mountain, but the shadows are gathering fast. We hear the thrum of another craft after about an hour, but it doesn't come close enough for us to see what type it is. Not that I could identify it anyway, but Pax seems well versed on the types of UWO aircrafts and what their capabilities are.

The trees change from pines to aspens, and the underbrush rises up in impassible thickets we have to skirt around. The rocks become less gray and more yellow and red. We finally break out of tree cover and overlook a bare slope filled with patches of low scrub and tall grasses. Down below us and to the east, the ground rises up in waves and folds of red rocks. Beyond that, miles away, I can see more trees through which the silver ribbon of a river is visible, and on the other side glow the lights of the Commune within the ruins of the city formerly known as Denver. The setting sun behind us casts the valley in shadow except for places where the rays find their way through breaks in the mountain range.

We pause for only a few moments at the edge of the trees, and Pax hands me a bottle of water. I drink deeply and hand it back to him, and he puts it to his mouth and does the same while I gawk. We never, ever, share eating or drinking vessels in Sanctuary. The unsanitary sharing of germs is more than a little frowned upon.

"What?" he says, finally noticing my unease.

"I . . . nothing."

He narrows his eyes, giving me a keen look, and then tucks the bottle away in his large bag. He points down the slope into the valley. "See that outcropping where the first fold rises up and meets the second?"

I nod. It looks closer than it is, as we're looking down from above. I judge it's probably a mile and a half away.

"There's a cave formed in the overlap. It's virtually invisible from above, and it will protect us from the heat sensors if they fly over looking for us in the night." He looks to the sky, and I know what he's thinking. An X-1 could be flying above us right now, so high we can't hear its engines, and although its sensors shouldn't work so high, it could drop down at any moment. We'll be terribly exposed on the slope until we reach the cave.

"Can you run the distance?" he asks quietly.

I bite back a sarcastic response. Of course I can. I may have been depressed for several weeks, but I'm every bit as physically fit as I've ever been in the past five years. I merely raise my eyebrows and nod.

We adjust our packs so they're taut against our bodies, and I feel a thrill of adrenaline I've never felt before a run on a treadmill. With a jerk of his head, Pax starts off.

I run close on his heels, and it feels good to really move—exhilarating, as though I've been wound tight all day and this is my relief. I *have* been, and it *is*. Pax is keeping an even pace, but it's slower than I can run, and we're losing light fast. I wonder if he's keeping it slow for my benefit, but he needs to know I'm no weakling.

I increase my gait until I'm abreast of him, my heels pounding heavily on the downward slope. I push the pace a little, and he increases to match me. We each zigzag around protruding rocks, and I almost twist my ankle once but keep going. We reach the bottom of the slope in no time, and the fold of rock rises up on the horizon across the valley, blocking our view of the second fold and everything beyond. I lengthen my stride even more until I'm running flat out, but Pax keeps easy pace. I'm fleeing my old life, and fleeing *for* my life, if Pax can be trusted. Every breath I draw, every footfall, takes me farther from Sanctuary, and the words *no going back* pound over and over in my mind. Tears sting in my eyes. I think it's sweat at first, but it's not.

A rock formation rises up out of the shadowy grass like a sentinel, and I careen around it toward a natural path cut into the rocks of the first fold, leading up toward the cave Pax indicated above. He grunts and falls back— he must have tripped—but I hear him continue a moment later, so I don't stop. I fly up the steplike path, my feet now on red rock instead of grass, my arms pumping. Near the top of the fold, it overlaps another and forms a triangular cave entrance. I duck inside and run straight to the shadowed back wall and catch myself against it with both palms.

My breathing is ragged, and I try to control my flood of emotions as my eyes adjust to the dark. Crying is for the weak. I will never cry again. I clutch my stomach and double over, squeezing my eyes closed.

Pax's feet echo as he enters the cave behind me. He slows to a stop but doesn't approach me. I hear him sling his pack to the ground, the sounds muffled in the enclosed space. He is quiet for a moment before he says, "Are you okay?"

"Yes!" I almost shout at him. "Just . . . leave me alone! Don't come near me!"

"Okay," he says, his voice level, calm.

I gasp and blink rapidly, determined to win this emotional battle. I pace to the far corner and brace a hand on the wall, my back to Pax. I've almost got a hold of myself.

There is a sound back here I can't place—a strange hissing rattle. I search the shadows at my feet a moment before a burst of green light illuminates the coiled shape that is about to strike. I shriek and leap back as its head explodes.

Pax has his gun drawn and a grim expression on his face. "Rattlesnake," he says. He walks over and picks it up by the tail. It drips blood onto my boots. "But at least we have meat for dinner."

Meat for dinner. I've never eaten meat in my life. Something about the decapitated snake unhinges my last measure of resolve, and I burst into tears and stumble backward until my back hits the wall of the cave. I shrink down and hug my knees to my chest, burying my face in my arms as I sob for the life I've given up. Even if it wasn't as perfect as I'd always thought, it was all I knew. And now it's over.

I will let myself cry this one last time. When I rise, there will be no more tears, and I will be a stronger person.

Chapter 15

Pax leaves the cave, and for a crazy moment I think he's abandoning me. But then he's back with a bundle of brush in hand, and he sets about building a fire in the center of the cave. I stay curled up in a ball against the far wall, ignoring him and mortified by my fit of tears, but he doesn't press me to speak to him.

By the time all my tears are spent, he has built a crackling fire that is filling the cave with smoke, due to the fact he has tacked up his lion pelt over the entrance. I drag myself close to the fire, as the cave was cool to begin with and getting cooler, and sit without meeting his eyes.

He busies himself yanking the skin off the dead rattlesnake. "Didn't figure you'd want raw snake for supper," he says, skewering the body on a stick and holding it over the flames.

"I don't know if I can eat that," I say, my voice raw and hoarse.

He raises an eyebrow. "First thing you have to learn out here is that it's a kill-or-be-killed, eat-or-be-eaten world. This snake would have killed you just now if I hadn't shot it, and there's no use in letting the meat go to waste."

That means he's saved my life—again—today. "Thank you," I say, but he just shrugs.

"I didn't say that so you would thank me. I would have had to kill the snake anyway. Animals are not the same as humans."

I open my mouth as an automatic protest springs to my lips, but he shakes his head.

"I know what you're going to say, but you're wrong. And you already believe me, deep down. If you didn't, the death of that little girl this morning wouldn't have bothered you like it did. Humans are mammals, but the core of what we are runs much deeper than it does in any animal. We rationalize, we imagine, we exercise choices based on motivations other than instinct or skill. We take dominion of our world. But most importantly, we have a spirit within us, a soul. And that, more than anything else, sets us apart. To kill an animal is just that—killing an animal. But to kill a human is murder." He rattles this off like it's a memorized speech—quickly, and with little inflection. He must have been using this as a prepared answer for some time. Or maybe he's just rationalized his own need to eat meat.

Still, the words he's just spoken are treasonous to the UWO. But I can't discredit them. "So that's really why you saved me? To keep me from being murdered?"

"That was the immediate cause, yes, but I've known you would be the one for some time now." He turns the rattlesnake so the other side is over the fire. I have to admit it smells good, although that could be because I missed my afternoon meals.

"How did you know my name?" I ask.

"You told it to me. You don't remember? Right after your procedure. I asked you what your name was, and you said it right before the drugs kicked in."

I frown and crease my forehead. I recall *thinking* my name, but I must have spoken it aloud, too. I don't know. The memory is so hazy. I rub my hand over my short hair and sigh. "You said you knew I would be 'the one.' The one for what? Who are you, and what do you want with me?"

What I really want to ask is, *Why did you ruin my perfect world?* But that's not a fair question. Pax may have planted some seeds of doubt, but my depression of the last several weeks was not his fault. My world has been crumbling for some time now.

He turns the snake again, and the firelight dancing along the bottom of his features casts his eyebrows and hair in shadow. Other than the reflection of the flames in his clear blue eyes, I can't even tell he's genetically recessive —I almost thought *inferior*, but I now know that's not true at all.

"I have . . . a couple of motivations," he says. "I've wanted to rescue one of you for some time, and not just so you can be of use to me."

I shiver and lean away. I'm not sure what he means, but it puts me on edge.

Pax sighs and rubs a hand over his face, staring into the fire. "I should

Breeder

probably start with telling you who I am. The rest won't make sense without it."

"Okay," I whisper.

"I am a product of the Controlled Repopulation Program, despite what you probably think."

I twist my mouth to the side and lower my brow, but he shakes his head.

"No, it's true. They've lied to you about so many things. Recessive traits show up all the time—there is no such thing as 'perfected genes.' Even you could be a carrier, but you'd never know it because they wouldn't let you know it. Most people like me are aborted before birth when the *defects*"— he spits the word—"are discovered through their testing methods. But a select few of us are born, whether by accident or for scientific purposes so they can study us. I was one of the latter." His grimace is almost terrifying in the flickering light, and he scratches the back of his neck before continuing. "I was born there, in Sanctuary, twenty-four years ago, and I lived the first year of my life with the rest of the—what do they make you call them? Contributions?—in the underground nursery set aside for determining tertiary viability. I think they were studying my behavior beside the so-called normal infants, but I've never known for sure. There are floors of secret labs and nurseries beneath Sanctuary. I only showed you the basement, where the . . . byproducts . . . are incinerated and discarded. But there's more, much more."

My mouth is hanging open, and I can't muster the will to pull it closed. What is he talking about, "tertiary viability"? And there are no nurseries in Sanctuary, let alone secret nursery labs. All our contributions are sent directly to the Commune nursery where they live until age seven when they are enrolled in the Agoge. I should know—I remember my own childhood!

But yet, here sits a man who shouldn't exist.

And how much can I really remember about my earliest years? I can't rule out he might be telling me the truth.

"What I do know is that the Breeder who bore me, my birth mother, found out I was still alive. She was so horrified that one of her own had been not only genetically flawed but also selected for genetic study, that she ordered my immediate termination."

This is simply too much to ask me to believe. I throw up my hands. "Wait. No. You've just proven to me you're lying. Contributions belong to the state. No Breeder ever finds out who their contributions are, so everything else you're saying must be false, and I'm horrified you would even insinuate what you're saying. You're trying to tell me the delivery med techs *kill* human infants . . . in Sanctuary. But that's . . . that's . . ." I can't find a word strong enough for my revulsion to the idea.

"Wicked?" Pax asks quietly, intently.

"Yes! And it's not rational. It doesn't make sense. We're trying to *re*populate Gaia Earth." I swallow, remembering how I said those very words to Mother earlier today and how she rebuffed them. But still, it's too radical what Pax is suggesting. "I just know . . . human beings don't do that to each other. Maybe long ago, but not now."

"Why not?" The fire dances in Pax's eyes, drawing me in. "If we're just animals, why wouldn't we kill our own young? You saw it earlier today, the refusal to save one of our own in the face of certain death. It's just the circle of life, isn't it?"

I feel a chill at the way he echoes Mother's words from earlier—almost as though he was privy to our conversation—and the way he's circling around and drawing me in to agreement with him. I know at this moment that Pax is every bit as intelligent as I am. Further proof he's not inferior at all.

"Nobody at Sanctuary killed that little girl," I whisper.

"Do not think for one minute they couldn't have prevented it." He leans forward. "Do you have any idea how many Protectors are stationed inside Sanctuary? How many Enforcers are stationed outside? I know—I've posed as one for long enough. That little girl couldn't have gotten through to the Looking Glass without being allowed through."

"Stop!" I cover my ears. "I don't want to hear any more."

He sits back and purses his lips, watching me.

I feel as though all the neurons in my brain are firing at once as his logic wears away at my long-held assumptions. "Animals kill each other all the time," I finally say, coming back to something we can agree on. "But it's different with people. We're not driven solely by instinct. When an animal kills, even when an animal kills a human, it's not murder."

Pax gives a slow nod.

"I don't believe we're just animals," I say, and then I slap my hands over my mouth, because it's true. I *don't* believe what I've been taught. "But . . . if we're not just animals, if we're above the way the animals act, then why would we kill each other?" I lower my hands and pierce him with a sharp look. "You haven't proven your story is true."

"If we have the ability to take a higher road, then we have the ability to take a lower road as well, and that sometimes means behaving like animals. Except, when a human behaves like an animal, he or she is without excuse. It *is* wickedness." He shakes his head and removes the cooked snake from the fire, setting it aside to cool. "I won't pretend to understand the human condition, but this I know—there is wickedness lodged in the very fabric of the Program. I can only know what I *am* and what was almost done to me. And my experience has taught me I'm not the only one. I escaped the fate intended for me, but thousands of others haven't. I can't sit by and watch it happen any longer."

He speaks with passion, but his expression is merely stern, and I'm left feeling flummoxed. If what he's saying is true, it means my entire life has been a lie. I haven't contributed to the repopulation of the earth at all; I've contributed to a scheme meant to keep humanity under control.

But I've always known that, haven't I? I'm a carrier of superior genes. What did I think they did with the inferior people?

I guess I always thought they were merely excluded from the Breeding program and assigned to other positions in society. It never crossed my mind that some of them were killed before even being given a chance at life.

But I don't know . . . I don't know . . . I wish I could unhear these things Pax is saying.

"They proved themselves capable of killing *you*, have you forgotten?" Pax asks in a whisper, but I close my eyes. "Look at me, Pria," he says, his voice firmer, and he waits until I do. He holds out his arms and rolls up his sleeves so I can see his freckles. "You yourself said I shouldn't exist. What further proof do you need?"

"Proof? What further *proof* do I need?" I jump up and wave my arms, overwrought. "You're asking me to believe the med techs, Mother, all of us, are privy to the murder of innocent human children. I've always been told every child born in the Program is a valued contribution to society—that we bear them because they are wanted and necessary to repopulate the earth with the very best of mankind! Yes, you're sitting here, and I can't explain that, but you were an infant when these so-called things happened to you in the so-called secret labs beneath Sanctuary. If, as you say, you're supposed to have been killed, then *why are you alive?*"

He stares at me with a sad, grim expression, his mouth pulled into a tight line and a crease between his eyebrows. Then he says, "Because a med tech took pity on me. She couldn't carry out my sentence. She saved me instead, and she left me with people who told me all about what happened once I was old enough to understand."

"And you believed them?"

There is a flash of anger in his eyes. "Why wouldn't I?"

"They could have been lying."

"Why should they?"

"To . . . to undermine the Program. If they're unhappy with their assignment in life, they might want to bring the whole system down. And there's something else about your story that doesn't make sense," I say.

He raises an eyebrow.

"What sort of Breeder would have the power to issue an order to kill a baby?"

I ask the question triumphantly, for I know the system well, and I know what authority Breeders have, which is almost none at all. Choice is not a part of our society. We can't even determine what we will eat for our meals, let alone who lives and dies.

Pax leans back and rests his forearms on his raised knees. "The Breeder who Carried and delivered me—my mother—is *Mother*."

Chapter 16

I let out a surprised breath and sit down hard. "What? How could you possibly know that?"

He rises and goes to his bag. From an inside pocket, he withdraws a yellowing slip of paper and presents it to me.

"I can't read, remember?" I say in a tight voice.

"And why do you think that is?" he asks, but then he quickly says, "Never mind. That's a discussion for another time. I suppose it will be harder to convince you without your being able to read this, but let me tell you what it says. I know you at least know your numbers."

I nod. That much was easy to work out on my own, since all of us in Sanctuary are designated according to them.

"Then you can see the number here," he says, holding the paper before my eyes and pointing. "Tell me what number it is."

An upright dash. A sideways squiggle beside it.

"Thirteen." I shift uncomfortably, because I know where he's going with this. It's not exactly a secret what Mother's Breeder designation was before her reassignment.

"That's right. Mother was Breeder Thirteen before her reassignment to Director Mother of Sanctuary. I was her final Carry when she was thirty-four years old. She was reassigned within the year. And it was as Director Mother that she discovered I was still alive. She is privy to all the information about everything that goes on in Sanctuary, after all. This paper"—he waggles it—"is a print-off of information from my first microchip. When the med tech who rescued me cut the chip out of my arm, she put it into a machine that could read the information on it and printed this off for me, so I would always have proof. It says I am the contribution of B-Thirteen and includes other medical data, like blood type, date of birth, etcetera. It is true, and I am who I say I am."

"But I can't read it, so how can *I* know it's real?"

"I suppose you'll have to trust me, if the evidence you've witnessed today isn't enough confirmation. Unless you want to go back to Sanctuary and take your chances there, that is."

"I can't exactly do that, now can I?" I fail to keep the bitterness out of my voice.

To his credit, he lowers his eyes.

"Even if that's real"—I raise my chin toward the slip of paper—"you could have gotten it anywhere."

"I didn't." He raises his eyes back to me, and his expression is defiant. "I got it where I said I got it."

Once again he displays none of the telltale signs of deception. If he's a liar, he's an exceptionally good liar.

"It was given to me by the people who raised me, and they got it from the med tech who rescued me."

"Then why aren't you still with them? Clearly they accept you for who you are. Why bother venturing out into a world that denies your viability?"

"Well, that's where you come in."

"Oh?"

"I was raised among a group of people who are outside the control of the UWO."

"There are no such people."

"There *are*, and I was among them."

I huff and cross my arms.

"How else do you think I could have survived as a baby in the world as it is?"

"So now you're saying not just that med techs kill human babies at Sanctuary and you were miraculously rescued from said fate by a rogue med tech, but also that there is a population of humans who exist outside of the control of the UWO? It's . . . a lot to process."

"Pria, according to your worldview, *I shouldn't exist*." He drags his hands through his hair. "I'm living proof you've been lied to by the UWO. You grew up in the Agoge—did you ever see anyone who looked remotely like me? You now know people like me exist because I'm sitting right in front of you, so where *else* do you think I could have been raised, if not by people outside of the established society?"

I bite my lips and consider his logic.

"Listen, you can believe I'm lying about everything if you want, but you can't deny who, and what, I am."

No. I can't. I take a deep breath and let it out slowly. "Okay, go on. I won't interrupt again, I promise."

"Thank you. Now, I don't remember what the group called themselves, because I was only with them until I was five or six. But there were a lot of people like me—different from the genetically accepted 'superhumans' of the UWO—and a lot of people who just didn't agree with how things are run. I can't remember when it happened, but the UWO found them and sent in bombers. My entire community was destroyed, and everyone was killed. I escaped only because I'd been out playing in the woods with a few other boys. Two of them ran back when the bombs started dropping and died, and one of them fled with me. He was older than me, and we helped each other survive. We tried to find another group, but groups are understandably elusive, and we didn't know whom we could trust. We always failed. My friend could get around better than I could in the Denver Commune, as he had dark hair and eyes. All he had to do was cover his mouth."

"Why did he have to cover his mouth?" I ask, so interested I ignore my promise not to interrupt.

"He had a deformity in his upper lip that made it hard for him to eat, and hard for him to talk, too." Pax touches his upper lip, whether purposefully or subconsciously, I can't tell. There is a faraway look in his eyes.

A deformity? I can't even picture what he's describing. Deformities, like recessive traits, disappeared long ago.

Pax lowers his hand. "But he managed to get us food and supplies when we needed them."

"He stole them," I say. "There's no other way he could have gotten them. Thievery in the Unified World Order is punishable by death.

"Only what we needed to survive," Pax says. "What would you have done?"

"So what happened to him, your friend? You're talking about him in the past tense, so I know he's no longer around."

Pax flicks a spot on his pants. "He got dragged away by some Enforcers."

"They caught him stealing?"

"No. He'd just been walking through the Commune. One of them ripped the scarf off his face. They must have grown suspicious of him for some reason. When they saw his deformity, they covered him up again, and I thought they were going to let him go, but I was young and naïve. They dragged him back behind a building and shot him through the head. I saw the whole thing from a hill above the Commune. I was only ten years old."

A tear, a real tear, slides down Pax's cheek. Do people cry over stories they've made up?

"I've been on my own ever since." He doesn't wipe away the tear, but his expression hardens, and no more of them fall.

"What was his name?" I whisper.

"Jacob. But his mother, when she was alive, called him little Yacov."

He had a mother who knew him and raised him? Who knew him well enough to give him a loving nickname?

"Little Yacov," I repeat. That tiny detail, so specific—too specific to have been planned out ahead of time—lets me know more than anything else that he's not lying. At least, not about anything he's experienced with his own eyes.

My chest feels tight, but I promised myself I wouldn't cry again, and I will stick to that promise. I don't want to accept this harsh new version of the world Pax presents, but he's convincing me, bit by painful bit. "So how can I help you find more of these people you're saying exist?"

"You just need to come with me," he says. "They want a Breeder."

Chapter 17

I lean back. "They *want* one? For what? Am I your prisoner, then?"

"No," Pax says quietly. "Never my prisoner. But these people are more than a little skittish. Every time I've gotten close to what I think is a Nest —"

"What's a—"

"It's what the UWO calls the communities of rebels. Every time I get close to what I think is one, I can't find my way in. They are very well hidden, and they don't reveal themselves for anyone they don't know, not even for someone who looks like me. Trust me, I know. I've tried. But it's easier to make connections with people outside the Nests who might know a thing or two, and I met a guy named Mack about five years ago who told me what I needed to know. Mack said he ran secret missions for the local Nest, and that they're locked down real tight but they have interest in getting a hold of a Breeder. It's for information—information about Sanctuary and how it's run. He said if I could bring them a Breeder, they just might let me in."

"And do you know where this local Nest might be?"

Pax shakes his head. "Mack said it was more than his life was worth to tell me that. But I've heard a rumor from other places that there might be a Nest northwest of the Commune and deep in the old mining ranges. Mack said if I could find them on my own, and bring a Breeder, all I would have to do is get close enough and they'd take care of the rest."

"You learned all this five *years* ago? What have you been doing all this time?"

"You think it's easy to impersonate an Enforcer? To not only fool the UWO but infiltrate Sanctuary as well? I may have been armed with the knowledge my savior left me about Sanctuary, but that was about all. Yes, it's taken me five years to establish myself in such a position as to be able to extract one of you but, all things considered, I think I've done fairly well."

I study his expression, searching for artifice and finding only determination. "And how are these people supposed to know I'm a Breeder?"

Pax snorts and looks me up and down. "It's written all over you. You're young, athletic, beautiful, and *bald*, I might add. Or close enough to bald."

I touch my head self-consciously.

"And you're painfully naïve. You spent half the trek today gawking at the trees and flowers and plants. Anybody paying any sort of attention will be able to see what you are from a mile away."

"You're basing all this off a lot of assumptions," I say. "And I'm not sure I appreciate your plan to use me as bait."

"They won't hurt you," he says. "Not if they're anything like the people I lived with. And not if you've actually given up your place in the UWO."

"And if they're not like the people you lived with?"

"Then I'll get you out of there. I promise." The small fire is burning low, but I can see his resolve in the flickering light that's left. "Just like I got you out of Sanctuary."

"So . . . you did that just to be able to use me?"

"No, Pria . . . no. Like I've said several times already. You're different. You're too good for the Program. You don't belong with them—your curiosity was proof enough of that. Do you know how many girls I visited in the Medical wing before you became the first one to tell me your name?"

He visited more of us? Nobody ever said anything or gave any hint. Of course, neither did I.

"The fact that you'd held on to that scrap of identity in the years since joining the Program told me more about you than you could possibly know. Most of the other Breeders are like robots going through their days. But not you. You're *alive*."

Alive. Alive and hurting. Alive and depressed. Does he know that, too?

"And you wanted to know more. You remembered meeting me, when all the others had the memory wiped away by the drugs. You clung to that, and you asked questions, you sought me out. Yes, I need a Breeder, but I chose you because I couldn't leave you there. I knew they would kill you when your curiosity came to Mother's attention. If she could give the order to kill her own son, what hesitation would she have over killing a Breeder she could no longer control?"

I think of the day I followed Pax through the door to the stairwell, and about the infant's cry I heard. A cry that cut off abruptly.

I twitch and close my eyes. What, *what*, had I been a part of in Sanctuary?

Pax is removing chunks of white meat from the stick, and he offers me a handful. "It's cold now. I'm sorry. I forgot about it while I was talking."

I take the snake meat with numb fingers and stare at it, my mouth dry, but my stomach rumbling.

"You must eat it," Pax says, but there is understanding in his voice. "If you don't, you'll weaken rapidly. You're off the drug and supplement regimen now. Without the supplements, you have to make up the nutrients somehow. And you should expect some emotional changes as well. Don't ever be embarrassed to cry in front of me, if you need to."

"I don't need to cry," I say sharply.

He nods.

I swallow hard and wonder what the meat tastes like and if I will like it. If I really don't believe animals are equal with humans, then I should be able to eat this meat to survive. I already feel myself weaker than I've ever been. And I'm so, so tired. I swallow again, and then I take a tentative bite.

It's bland, and squishy. The texture is harder to process than the taste, and I fight to swallow it.

"I have some bread, if that will help you get it down," Pax says. He's also pulled out the bottle of water we shared earlier. "It's a little stale, but it's edible." He breaks off a chunk and tosses it to me.

Together with the bread, I'm able to eat my handful of meat. The familiar grainy texture masks the unfamiliar one of the snake. When Pax goes to open the flap over the cave mouth and let out some of the smoke that's gathered, I discreetly wipe off the mouth of the water bottle before I take a drink. I'm full after only a small portion of food, as they fed us in six small meals a day at Sanctuary, but my stomach is churning and hopping.

It must be very late by now, and I am exhausted beyond words. I stretch out on my side and try to get comfortable, but I've always had a soft bed in which to sleep, and this rocky floor finds every one of my bones. I'm not sure I'll be able to sleep.

I'm too tired to continue asking questions, though, and I'm certain Pax also wants to sleep. He's given me so much to think about, I think I might be awake all night from the thoughts running through my head if not from the uncomfortable ground.

He comes back into the cave and says in a low voice, "I can see the lights of an X-1 out over the valley, south a bit. I'm going to kick out the fire just to be safe."

I nod and yawn, covering my mouth.

"It might get a little cold," he says. "I don't have any blankets. It would be wise for us to sleep close together for warmth—and in case anything comes looking for us in the night."

"Do not even think about touching me," I say. "I'd rather freeze to death."

He raises his arms. "Okay. But if you get too cold—"

"I'll never be that cold." I turn my back is to him and close my eyes, feigning sleep.

The last feeble light flickers out as he stomps on the embers, and then I hear him settle across the cave from me with a deep sigh. His breathing lengthens almost immediately, and I open my eyes and stare into the pitch black. My stomach won't stop churning, and I wonder if the snake meat has poisoned me.

I toss and turn as the minutes wear away. Can it really have been only this morning that I saw the little girl killed by the lion? That I had a conversation with Mother about survival of the fittest? Impossible. It must have been another life.

The churning in my stomach is turning to sharp pains, and it's all I can do to keep from groaning aloud. I curl into the fetal position and hold my abdomen like I've done so many times in the past weeks, but this time it's not because I feel there's something missing that used to be there, but because I know there's something there that wants to get out.

The realization that I'm going to be violently sick hits me with horrifying suddenness, and there's nothing I can do about it. I struggle to my feet and go to the wall so I can grope my way along it.

I'm holding my hand over my mouth by the time I find the lion-pelt flap, and I burst through it. Unable to cling to discretion any longer, I vomit all over the rocks outside the cave. It comes in body-racking waves until I'm heaving nothing but air, and I finally slump back against the rocks, spent and even wearier than I was before.

I rub shaking hands over my clammy face and steel myself to face Pax, who I'm certain must have heard me.

As I turn to reenter the tent, a fleshy, long-fingered hand comes out of the darkness and seizes me around the middle. I have time for only a surprised exhalation of breath before I'm lifted up and turned to face a harrowing visage with glowing red eyes and a gaping maw.

An Unfamiliar. I've only ever seen pictures, but there's no mistaking what it is.

It sniffs me and grunts, its red eyes piercing.

I scream.

Chapter 18

Its grunt is a metallic, grating sort of sound, and its fingers tighten around my middle, cutting off my breath and my scream.

Then green pulses of light zip through the air and strike it square in the chest, right where its heart would be, if it had a heart like normal, earthbound creatures. It flinches and takes a step back as I slip from its loosened grip.

I hit the ground hard, having dropped about six feet, and gasp as pain shoots through my heel.

Pax is standing outside the cave with his feet planted in a wide stance, both hands cradling the gun as he shoots repeatedly into the chest of the Unfamiliar. It gives a sort of roar, and then it bellows and falls backward, its long limbs flailing and red blood squirting and streaming from its wounds. Strange that they should bleed the same color we do.

Pax doesn't stop shooting until it lies perfectly still, and then he lowers the gun and says, "Good. It was about to overheat." He pushes a button on the side of the weapon and holsters it. He offers me his hand, and I take it without hesitation and let him pull me to my feet. He quickly releases me and turns to yank the pelt down from over the cave mouth.

"What are you doing?" I ask, hating the warble in my voice.

"We're leaving. We can't spend the night here. There could be more of them, and if there are, they will have heard that."

That. My scream. The shooting. The Unfamiliar's death throes.

I shiver and twist my hands together. I should help Pax pack up, but I'm

Breeder

too weary and distraught, and he seems to have it in hand.

He emerges from the cave after only a few moments with both packs cinched tight to his back. "Come on," he says. "We have to run again."

"Where will we go?" I ask.

"As far away from here as possible." He skirts the dead Unfamiliar, and I follow close at his heels, praying my adrenaline will carry me as far as it needs to.

We hit the ground of the valley, and the grasses rise up to meet me as I pound through them. Pax angles us northeast, toward the Commune. That can't possibly be a safe place for us to go, but I have no breath to question him. We do not see any more Unfamiliars, nor do any UWO crafts descend upon us. We run for at least an hour, but the time blurs together in a misery of shaking limbs and rattling breaths.

Finally, we splash into the middle of a slow-moving river. The water is fordable, not too high or strong, and I stumble over the rocky bottom, slowing to a walk alongside Pax.

"Drink," he says. "Now, while you can. You're probably terribly dehydrated after getting sick back there." He doesn't even sound winded.

I drop to my knees, letting the icy shock of water jolt me out of my tired malaise, and put my mouth right into the water.

When I'm finished, Pax hauls me to my feet and says, "Just a little bit farther. There's an old, abandoned building I know of, not far from here. I've stayed there before."

I nod. I don't have energy for talking.

We run on for at least another twenty minutes before Pax leads me up a sharp incline strewn with gravel. I slip and fall to my knees, and Pax doubles back to lend me a hand. Once we reach the top of the incline, he points to a building that rises above us and says, "That's it."

The building is actually one of many, although the others seem to be in ruins. The moon is high and bright, revealing metal steps along a breezeway through the structure. Pax goes before me, taking the steps with light feet, his gun in hand. When we get to the top, he finds a door and tests the knob. It's unlocked and swings open, revealing a space that's dark, but not pitch black, as the large windows along the wall let in the moonlight. Somehow, despite the ruins all around, the glass in this building is still intact.

"Wait here a minute," Pax whispers.

I hover in the doorway, shivering from exhaustion, cold, and fear, even though I'm burning up from exertion. Pax checks every inch of the space and then creeps down the dark and narrow hallway in front of us, his weapon held out in front of him. He opens two doors on the left and peers through them, and then does the same for a door at the end of the hall. I try not to cry out and go after him as he turns a corner and disappears from sight.

He returns a moment later, his gun lowered, and nods at me and gives me a grim smile. "All clear," he says, his voice still a whisper. He gestures me forward into the space and closes the door behind me. I hear a metallic toggling and look over my shoulder to see him turning a knob above the door handle. "Ah," he says. "Lock still works."

Despite being inside and behind a locked door, I feel exposed by the gaping windows. I wrap my arms around my chest and look around. The space is bare of furniture, but I get the impression it used to be a dwelling of some sort.

Pax follows my line of sight and gives me a nod. "Through here," he says.

I follow him down the hall to the first door on the left, and he opens it to reveal a dark empty space, about eight feet deep by four feet wide. It's windowless, probably an old storage closet of some sort. I go into the small room, and he follows me in and closes the door, engulfing us in blackness. I hear him sit, and then a soft *thump* I assume is him resting his back against the door. I stand in indecision for a moment before going to the far end of the room and lying down on the carpet. Even though it smells musty and feels chewed through in places by rats or mice, it's soft, and I'm so exhausted, I know I'll be able to sleep.

After a moment of hesitation, I shift so the bottom of my boot touches the bottom of his. I'm not ashamed to admit the events of the night have me terrified. Even in this confined space, I need the assurance of his presence.

He says nothing, and I'm thankful for that. He must understand.

I hear Pax fall asleep only moments before I follow. I sleep for a long time.

Chapter 19

I awake hungry, sore, and confused. It's still dark, although a hint of light comes in through the bottom of the door around Pax's dark form, which is still leaning against it. It takes me several moments to orient myself, and then I'm hit with a wave of remorse so strong, it's all I can do to keep my resolve of not crying.

I pull my foot back from where the sole of my boot was still touching his and roll to a sitting position, wincing and holding my ribs. I'm bruised in a circle around my middle, thanks to the Unfamiliar that attacked me last night.

How many times did Pax save my life yesterday? Did my life need saving in the first place?

Yes. Mother tried to kill me.

Even if I don't believe anything else Pax told me about Sanctuary, I must remember that, or I'll go crawling back.

My mouth is dry and my tongue parched. The packs are on the floor beside Pax—two darker lumps in the blackness of the closet. I reach for the bigger one, and Pax grabs my wrist.

I catch my breath and try to twist away, but his grip is like iron, his fingers fully encircling my wrist. The faint light glimmers off his eyes, which are now wide open, and he releases me.

"Sorry," he says. "Not used to being with someone I can trust."

I pull back my hand and rub my wrist. "It's okay. I was just trying to get a drink."

Pax digs into the bag and then tosses me the water bottle. "Here," he says.

It's full. He must have filled it at the river last night.

While I drink, he stands and stretches and then puts his ear to the door for several moments before cracking it open. Pale light pours into our space, illuminating dust particles floating in the air and several silky strands of spider webs in the seams of the walls and ceiling. There is a furry, brown spider crouching in a funnel-shaped web in the corner not a foot from my hand, and I yank myself away with a shudder and clamber to my feet.

There were no vermin or spiders inside Sanctuary, which was always pristine, but I learned about these sorts of creatures in the Agoge. Spiders had always frightened me more than any of the others, the way they wove their silken webs to ensnare unsuspecting prey, and the way they could descend on one unawares from any angle. I want to throw up, realizing I slept with my face inches from one of them.

I have to get out of here. I stumble across the room, wriggling past Pax and sloshing water onto his boots.

"Careful with that," he says, snagging the bottle out of my hand. "Fresh water isn't always easy to come by, you know?"

I don't answer. I'm busy brushing invisible silken strands from my arms and legs.

"Are you okay?" he asks.

"Spider," I say, gasping the word out.

Pax raises his eyebrows and leans back to take a look into the corner of the room in which we slept. I feel certain he's going to laugh at me, but he doesn't. He just says, "Right. Not used to those in Sanctuary, were you?"

I shake my head and give another involuntary shudder.

"I hate to break it to you," he says, pulling the bags out of the room and ushering me through, "but the world is full of monsters, Pria." He closes the door behind us.

"I'm getting that idea," I say. All my bravado yesterday about wanting to appear tough, and I'm undone by a spider. I huddle against the wall and look around, expecting to see more spiders crawling toward me, but the hallway stretching left to right is empty. The light filters in through the large windows in the main living area—windows I can't see around the corner in the hallway. But that's fine by me. If I can't see the windows, then nobody can see me through the windows either.

"There's a bathroom around the corner," Pax says, dropping the bags beside me and gesturing. "No running water, but it's an intact toilet, at least. I'll stay out here if you want to use it."

I blush and nod and leave him standing in the hall.

Around the corner at the end of the hall is a cracking sink with a mirror above it. There's a door on the left that must be where the toilet is, but I'm distracted by my reflection in the mirror. The surface is remarkably reflective, even though it must be over a hundred years since anyone lived here.

I touch my cheeks as I study myself through large, dark eyes. Other than seeing my reflection in Pax's Enforcer visor, it's the first time I've seen myself since being selected for the Program, and I'm amazed at the lack of recognition I feel. At Sanctuary, I always pictured myself as a copy of the sisters around me and assumed there was no individuality in my appearance. But now I see how wrong I was.

I am me. I am Pria. I am not a number.

I rub my inch-long hair and tilt my face side to side. Pax called me beautiful yesterday. He said it in a clinical, bitter way, implicitly criticizing a version of humanity of which he has no part. I've always known I'm genetically superior, but beauty was never emphasized in our education. I was always told my looks were for better adaptability to the demands of nature, but it makes sense that they would also be considered beautiful. I was bred as much for my looks as anything else, but they are not superior to Pax's at all.

How shallow I must appear to him. I let out a heavy sigh and turn away from the mirror.

When I rejoin Pax, it's to find him in the main living area. He's carrying a discolored plastic jug half-full of liquid, but he puts it down when I approach. In the light pouring through the windows, his eyelashes look gold, and I see he even has freckles on his eyelids.

"What's that?" I ask.

"Gasoline."

I laugh. I can't help it. "You're joking. Nothing uses gasoline anymore."

He draws his brows together and frowns. "Is that what they taught you in the Agoge? That everything only runs on clean fuels these days?"

I blink and frown at him in return.

He snorts and shakes his head. "That's what the UWO wants you to believe. Fossil fuels were outlawed before the Great Devastations but reintroduced during the Great Incursion when the army was trying to rapidly create new war machines to match those of the Unfamiliars. The UWO has used fossil fuels ever since, although they're still forbidden to the populace. I thought that was common knowledge."

"I guess you were wrong," I say, my voice tight. "So what do *you* need gasoline for?"

"I found something a couple of years back, and I've managed to get it running. It used to be called a motorcycle. It could draw attention to us, but we're going to have to risk it. We need to move fast, and walking just isn't going to do the trick."

A motorcycle. Whatever that is, it sounds ominous, especially if it runs on gasoline, which, if I remember correctly, is highly combustible.

"Where did you get the gasoline, then?"

"The basement of Sanctuary. I hid the container here a while back. I always intended to bring you here, if I ever got you to leave."

I sigh and shake my head. More bizarre claims for me to accept as truth.

"Give me your gun," Pax says.

"What? Why?"

"I'm just going to show you how to use it. Give it here." He holds out his hand, and I pass over the gun, feeling reluctant to part with it even though I have no idea how it works.

"This is called an Automatic Energy Rifle, fifth edition," he says. "But everybody calls it an Air-5 because the acronym—A E R—sounds like *air* when said quickly, and because it's so lightweight." He turns it over in his hand and shows me a switch, which he then toggles up. "That's the safety," he says. "If it's in the full down and right position, the weapon is locked." He toggles the switch down again, and then back up. "When it's in the middle position, like so, it's in individual shot mode. Squeeze the trigger once and hold it down all you want, but it will only shoot one energy bullet. Move the switch to the fully upright position"—he does so—"and it's in automatic mode. Squeeze and hold the trigger, and it can shoot as many as two hundred bursts a minute. But you have to be careful when you use it like that, because it can quickly overheat." He hands it back to me.

"Where does the energy for the bullets come from?" I ask, holding it limp in my hand.

"It's essentially converted light energy, but there's not an unlimited supply. Air-5s do have to be recharged."

"Do you have a way to recharge them?"

"No. But I'm hoping where we're going will." He moves to stand behind me, and I shy away, but he says, "I'm not going to hurt you, Pria. I just need to show you the proper stance." His voice is low and comforting like it was the first time he spoke to me in the Med wing.

I concede, but I'm tight as a rod as he puts both arms around me and lifts my arms out in front. He positions my hands on the Air-5 with my right index finger over the trigger and my left hand cradling my right.

"If the situation allows, always hold it in two hands like this for stability." His breath tickles my ear as he speaks, and it's all I can do not to turn around and push him away. "Your feet should be in a wide stance. You wouldn't guess it, but the Air-5 gives a hefty kickback, and if you're not prepared for it, you could fall over. Train down the top of the gun through these little ridges here." He taps them. "Those are your sights. Another good thing about the Air-5 is that it shoots straight. You line up those sights and squeeze the trigger, and the weapon'll do the work for you."

He steps back, finally, and I roll my shoulders. I start to lower the weapon, but he says, "No. Take a shot. But first . . ." He toggles the switch from automatic to single-shot. "Okay, now take a shot."

"What should I shoot?"

Pax narrows his eyes. "How about that spider?"

I shudder and feel a wash of cold over my body. But then I laugh. Me, with a gun, against a spider, and I'm still afraid. "Okay."

Pax gives me a lengthy, penetrating stare that wipes the smile off my face. I clear my throat and raise my eyebrows. He blinks and turns away.

"Are you ready?" he asks, his hand on the door handle.

"Yes."

He opens the closet door, and I train the gun toward the far corner and the small smudge of brown I can see in the web. But then I hesitate. All my life, I've been taught to harm no living thing. Mother would say this spider is worth as much as a deer, or a lion, or a human.

If they're killing human infants in Sanctuary, on the basis of genetic inferiority or otherwise, then what a gross hypocrisy that teaching is. I ate snake last night, and I *can* kill this spider.

I take aim and shoot. But I've already forgotten about the kickback Pax mentioned, and I stumble backward into him. He catches my shoulders and sets me upright fast enough for me to see I missed the spider but got close enough to spook it out of its hiding. It's scurrying across the floor toward me, a horror of spindly, jerking limbs. I shriek and shoot, but miss again. It dodges and keeps coming, and I practically crawl over Pax to get away.

Then Pax stomps his foot, and the spider is gone, pulverized beneath his boot.

I'm shaking violently, and I know it's irrational, but I can't control it.

"It's dead," Pax says. He takes my gun from my trembling grasp and fingers it to the safety position. "We'll practice again later." He hands it back, and I swear he almost smiles.

Chapter 20

After a breakfast of stale bread and dried fruit that does nothing to calm the ache in my stomach, Pax leads me out of our haven and down the steps into the breezeway. He goes to the entrance and spends several long, still moments studying the sky before coming back to where he left me at the bottom of the stairs. "I don't see a sign of anyone or anything. There's a heavy cloud cover today, which is good because it restricts aerial visibility."

I nod and shoulder the satchel. It's so silent here, the air of abandonment almost oppressive. I look over my shoulder repeatedly, but there's nothing to see but concrete and closed doors.

Pax walks through the breezeway to the last door on the right. It looks like another dwelling like the one we slept in last night, but when he opens it, I see a dust-covered black . . . I don't know what. He goes inside and rolls it out. It's got two wheels, a long seat, and a bar across the front that looks like it might be for holding on to. It's completely black, and some of the metal components are rusty, including the metal foot Pax folds out and rests against the ground.

Pax unscrews a cap on its front and pours in the gasoline from the canister he brought out with us. A pungent smell wafts toward me, and I cover my nose and squint. He empties all of it into the . . . motorcycle, I think he called it . . . and then he screws the cap back on the side of the vehicle.

"I'll be right back." He goes into the dwelling with the empty canister, leaving me alone with the motorcycle.

I touch it with light fingers. The seat is made of some spongy material that is also a little tacky. I can't identify it. And there are scratches all over the sides. The tires are smooth and look unreliable at best. No wonder mankind took to the skies as soon as hover technology was invented. Who wanted to trust their lives to air-filled rubber?

Apparently Pax does. He comes out of the door empty-handed and shuts it behind him. "Ready?"

"You really know how to work this thing?"

He nods.

"And . . ." I bite my lip and look the motorcycle up and down. "You really think it's safe for us to ride?"

"As safe as anything the UWO makes. And it's certainly safer than braving the walk through hostile Unfamiliar territory."

I touch my bruised ribs and nod. I don't ever want to meet one of those again.

Pax lashes down the large pack on the very end of the machine and asks, "Can you handle carrying the bag? Too many important things in there. If we have to ditch the bike for some reason, I don't want to lose it."

"I've got it," I say, and I tighten the straps over my shoulders.

Pax pulls a heavy, round object from the large pack before securing the last tie and hands it to me. "Wear that," he says. "If we crash, at least your head will be protected."

If we crash. Wonderful. I look down at the Enforcer helmet. My reflection in the bronze visor stares back at me.

"Here." Pax takes it back and fits it over my head before I can protest. It wiggles around a bit as I move, but it'll stay on. As soon as it's secure, a display of red lights appears in the periphery of my vision.

"What are the lights?" I ask, my voice coming out muffled and tinny.

"The helmet measures things like heart rate, temperature, breathing rate. It's meant to help Enforcers and Protectors be in control of themselves. If you focus intently on someone else, though, it provides a readout for that person. I guess the idea is to know your enemy."

I tilt my head and stare intently at Pax, focusing on his eyes. I know he can't see my expression, so it doesn't make me feel awkward. The red lights blink twice, then change and turn to green. "Huh," I say.

Pax swings his leg over the bike and straddles it, one foot on either side. "Come on," he says, holding out a hand to me. "Climb on behind me. You'll have to forget your fear of touching for a while."

"Why?" I ask, pulling back.

He gives me a grim smile. "If you don't want to go flying off the back of the bike, you'll have to hold on tight. Put your feet here"—he points below the seat—"and wrap your arms around me."

I blink and look at his middle, heat flooding my face. I'm both repulsed and attracted by the idea, but there's no way I'm going to admit that to him. I twist my mouth into a dissatisfied frown, thankful he can't see my face.

"Aren't you worried about someone hearing us?" I ask. "Or *seeing* us?"

"It's going to be loud, but it's also fast." Pax shrugs. "Nobody in the Commune has anything to rival this for speed. Except the Enforcers, of course, but they won't be looking for us."

"Why not?"

"Do you really think Mother wants to make it public that a Breeder has fled the Program with a rogue Enforcer?"

I see what he means. If control is the game of the Unified World Order, then they must keep up the illusion of total control. They wouldn't want anybody else to know about the cracks in the system.

"So you don't think anybody else is looking for us?" The thought is exhilarating, and I feel my shoulders straighten as an invisible weight is lifted off them.

"Other than the X-1s we've seen so far? No. We're going to follow this old highway here." He points out beyond the dilapidated grounds, opposite the direction we came in last night. "It will take us north to another abandoned roadway that loops for miles around the Commune. Beyond that, it's northwest into the mountains. The Program won't look for us that far north so soon. There's no way they could anticipate our having a means of speedy travel." He shakes his head. "They'll search in a walking radius around Sanctuary for days, and then hopefully they'll give us up for dead."

Pax seems good at basing decisions off assumptions, although I can't deny his logic. And what other choice do we have?

I swing myself over the seat and put my feet where Pax instructed me to. He hops up and down in a jerking motion, and the bike roars to life. It's so loud, even through the helmet, I don't see how we can possibly go undetected.

"What about Unfamiliars?" I shout in his ear.

He turns his head so I can read his lips. "Too slow!" he shouts back. "On foot, they'll never catch us!"

"What if they're not on foot?"

"They're not likely to attack!"

"Even if we're in their territory?"

Pax narrows his eyes and faces forward again. "Don't worry about it, Pria!" His shouted response carries back to me, and then the bike lurches forward.

Chapter 21

I grab for Pax's shoulders to stay upright.

"Waist!" he shouts, and I reluctantly slide my hands down and around his middle, holding him loosely as he navigates out onto a cracked concrete expanse. The foreign feel of the rubber tires bumping over the ground makes me bounce on the narrow seat. I've only ever traveled via hovercraft before now, and not since I was transported from the Agoge in the Commune to Sanctuary.

Pax zigzags around piles of rubble and tufts of tall grasses that look as though they might at one time have been decorative, and then he turns the motorcycle left onto a stretch of concrete that disappears over the horizon —one of the old highways. A coyote sits in the middle of the road about a hundred yards up, but beyond that, I see no living thing.

Pax shouts, "Hold on!" and then the bike roars and accelerates.

I'm almost thrown backward, just as he said, but I tighten my grip on his waist and lean closer to him. The landscape of broken buildings and rubble becomes a blur as the bike goes faster and faster. I'm assuming the coyote ran out of the way, but we're so quickly beyond the place where it was sitting, I can't tell.

Pax leans forward, tucking under the wind. I have no choice but to press myself to him and hold on with white-knuckled intensity.

He weaves the bike from side to side, avoiding gaping holes, and more than once I gasp and close my eyes, certain we're about to crash. But Pax manages to keep us upright somehow. His stomach is taut beneath my hands, his back hard and solid. It's both thrilling and comforting in a way I can't define.

I thought earlier that humans took to the skies as soon as hover technology was invented, but I remember now that isn't entirely true. Roads were maintained up until about fifty or sixty years ago, for transport vehicles. Then the old hover army transports were adapted for cargo purposes after the last truce was negotiated with the Unfamiliars, and that's when the roads were abandoned.

There's never been any need for pedestrian transport services, not since the Unified World Order took over. With the exception of people like the med techs, who get around via UWO hovercrafts, everybody lives for the rest of their lives where they are assigned after the Agoge. I would have been reassigned to a position within the Denver Commune at age thirty-five, or whenever I stopped producing viable offspring. It's a future that is now closed to me.

The motorcycle flies over a rise in the pavement and goes airborne for a few seconds. I catch my breath and grit my teeth, trying not to scream. We slam back onto the pavement, and the back of the bike fishtails. I stay on only by digging my fingers into Pax's ribcage.

We turn toward the mountains, and he accelerates again. I want to shout at him to slow down, but I have no breath left in my lungs. This roadway seems smoother than the one we left, and it curves around eventually to head north again. One long-limbed Unfamiliar lopes along the base of the red rock formations to the west, but it's too far away to pay us any real attention. After that, I squeeze my eyes shut and try to ignore the passage of time.

After maybe an hour or more, the motorcycle slows, and Pax turns it to the left. I crack my eyes open and sit up straighter. We're moving slowly enough now that I can do so without my head snapping back. My arms and back are sore, and I arch and look over my shoulder. We're high enough in elevation that I can see the blocky buildings of the Denver Commune on the horizon, probably twenty miles away. Hovering over it are several slow-moving black dots—UWO hovercrafts of some sort. I look south and see a couple more black dots, much closer than the ones over the Commune, moving back and forth over the valley at the foot of the mountains. I tap Pax's shoulder and point.

"Too far south to see us," he shouts. "They'll never think to look this far north, not this soon after our escape, and not where we're going."

"Where *are* we going?" I shout back.

"Up there!" He jerks his chin, and I follow the motion. I can just make out a narrow line that switchbacks up the mountainside, all the way up to the top. It must be seven or eight thousand feet of climb.

"Is that a road?"

Pax doesn't answer, just angles the bike onto a side road so broken apart it's more like rubble than concrete. My teeth jar in my mouth as we bounce along it.

"If the Nest is anywhere, it's up there," Pax says over his shoulder. "The tree cover is excellent in some of the passes, and they probably use old mine tunnels. Plus, the Unfamiliars don't like the elevation past a certain point. Ideal, if you ask me!"

This is crazy. It's crazy, and I'm going along with it. "What if we can't find them?"

"We don't need to find them—we need them to find us," he shouts back.

The gravelly rubble deepens at the seam beyond which the road starts climbing, and Pax slows to a crawl, maneuvering the motorcycle through it. I crane my neck and stare up at the expanse. The heights make me dizzy, and I close my eyes and look down again, focusing on the roadway as Pax frees the bike from the rubble in jerky bursts and starts up the steep incline.

There used to be a railing on this road. I can see the remnants of it—a post here, a twist of warped metal there—but the railing itself is long gone. It doesn't bother me until we pass a couple hundred feet and the wind picks up. Great swaths of strewn rock piles and boulders bisect the road at intervals. Pax is able to navigate through most of them, but at about two thousand feet there's a rockslide so thick we have to dismount to get over it.

The wind blows hard and cold this high, and the entire Denver Commune is laid out below us. More disconcerting yet, the hovercrafts over the Commune are lower in elevation than we are. They circle over and over, and I wonder what they're doing. I don't remember seeing so many during my time in the Agoge.

I shiver and wrap my arms around my chest. My whole body feels numb from the vibration of the bike, and I want to stretch and walk around, but the downward slope to my right is so steep and intimidating, I stick to the inside curve of the road.

Pax beckons me over to help with the motorcycle. It's heavy, and he asks me to heave the back end of it over the rubble pile while he lifts the front end.

I brace myself behind it and push as he strains to lift the front. When he gets the front wheel up on top of the rubble, the bike starts to tilt. I'm strong, but not strong enough to stop its slow fall to the side from where I am at the rear of the bike. With a shout, Pax leaps around to the outside edge of the road and pushes the bike back up while I push forward. The rear tire mounts the rock pile, and the bike tilts to the other side almost immediately.

Pax springs after it again, but the rocks on which he's bracing himself loosen and shift. With a clatter, they tumble over the edge of the road and careen down the mountainside. Pax gives another shout as his feet go out from under him and he falls to his chest, carried along by the rockslide that is now in slow motion, jarred loose by our struggling over it. The motorcycle rolls forward and crashes to the far side of the slide, its wheels spinning.

I dive toward Pax, but I can't reach him with the way the rocks are shifting and sliding between us.

"Pax!" I shout. The lights inside my visor are blinking rapidly, but I don't need a helmet to tell me I'm hyperventilating.

Pax is scrambling for purchase, his face twisted in grim determination. "Argh!" he shouts as his bottom half disappears over the edge, and then the rest of him is carried over.

"*Pax!*" I scream. I throw myself down on the roadway and inch forward on my chest to hang my head over the edge.

He's still there, about ten feet below the road on a steep portion of mountainside that looks as though it used to be part of the road itself. Just beyond his feet, the slope drops off in a cliff. He's managed to grab an old wooden post, probably a relic of the old guard railing, and his head is tucked into his chest as the rocks continue to fall, pelting him on their way down the mountain. The post he's clinging to lists toward the edge as though it wants to go over. There is no place for his feet to gain purchase. If he lets go, he'll slide another couple of feet and over the drop-off.

And I'll be alone.

But I care about more than that. I may not trust him completely, but I certainly don't want him to die.

Still, I can't do anything for him until the rocks stop moving. I remove my helmet and cast it aside. "Hold on!" I shout.

He doesn't acknowledge me. His fingers are whitening on the post.

I scramble back to my feet and look across the rocks to where the motorcycle lies on its side.

Rope. I need rope, and Pax secured the large pack to the back of the motorcycle with a length of it.

The movement of the rocks has almost stopped. I cast one more look over the edge to make sure Pax is still holding on, and then I tuck the helmet beneath my arm and take a flying leap over the rocks.

I land on the far edge, my heels twisting painfully in the jumble, and fall to my rear, unable to keep my balance. Ignoring the pain, I struggle upright and navigate the edge of the rockslide to get to the motorcycle. With shaking fingers, I work at the knots, but Pax tied them so tight I don't know how to undo them.

With a cry of frustration, I drop the rope and run back to the edge. Pax is straining at the post and digging his toes into the slope beneath him. He's not going to make it if I can't help him.

I look toward the pack tied onto the bike and picture what's inside it. The lion pelt. I dash over and dig into the pack through the spot I loosened trying to get the rope untied. With a yank, I extricate the pelt.

"Hang on!" I shout. "I'm coming!"

I sit down at the edge and brace my feet against an embedded boulder that sticks a couple of inches out of the ground. "Grab on," I say, wrapping one end of the pelt around my forearm and throwing the length of it over the edge.

I can't see Pax from this angle, but his voice carries up to me, strained and tight. "Too far away. Can you get it closer?"

I lean forward and look down. The end of the pelt hangs about four feet to his right, and two feet above him. I shift so it's my rear braced against the boulder and dig my heels into the steeply angled slope beneath me. The pelt flops a couple of feet closer to him.

"That's as close as I can get it," I say. "You'll have to throw yourself at it."

Pax looks up, his face dusty and streaked with blood. I see a flicker of fear in his eyes despite his efforts to hide it.

"Remember what I am," I say. "I'm strong. I won't let you fall."

Without further hesitation, Pax takes one hand off the post and, with a groan of effort, swings himself sideways, feet scrambling against the slope and sending several rocks rolling over the edge. He grabs the pelt with one hand and then the other as I lean back with all my might, my tailbone screaming against the rock and my arms feeling as though they're being pulled out of their sockets. The pelt feels like it's digging a new hole where it's wrapped around my wrist, and I want to scream from the pain.

I maintain my grip on the pelt as it sways from side to side. He's climbing. I can hear the scrabbling of his body against the slope and the trickle of dislodged stones.

A moment later, he grabs my ankle, and the pressure is dispersed between my leg and the pelt. I gasp and grit my teeth as my heel slips, but I'm lodged against the embedded boulder and leaning so far back I'm practically lying down. I don't budge.

Pax's grip on the lion pelt moves higher until he reaches my hands, and I release the pelt to grab his hand in both of mine. He pushes himself up with his other hand on my knee and, with a final heave, he flops over on top of me, pushing me back onto the road. Then he rolls to the side, releasing me from his crushing weight, and we both lie with our legs still hanging over the edge, staring up at the sky and breathing hard.

Pax throws an arm over his face and lies as if he's dead, neither moving nor speaking. My arms feel like jelly, and my wounded wrist is sending pulses of pain up and down my forearm and through my fingers. I can't even muster the strength to wipe the sweat from my brow.

I finally sit up and wince, stretching my back and prodding at my sore ribs. Pax watches me with a strange expression in his eyes—he seems somehow taken off his guard, surprised almost, but I can see the wheels turning in his head. He's trying to make sense of his brush with death.

"You saved my life. Thank you."

I give him a half smile and shrug, uncomfortable with his tone. He sounds different, like he's speaking to a stranger. I remind myself that we practically are.

"Now we're even," I say.

Something flickers in his eyes, and he blinks and comes back to himself. "Right," he says. He sits up and winces as I did. A trickle of blood is drying on his face from a cut above his eyebrow, and another from a cut in the center of a raised, purple bruise on the opposite cheekbone. He's covered in dust and rock particles, and he shakes his head and rubs his hands through his hair to dislodge them. The insides of his wrists are scraped and bloody.

He stands, testing his balance with his arms out for a moment, and then raises his shirt to look at a long, red welt and a pattern of scratches on his ribcage. I stare in mesmerized curiosity. His chest and stomach are pale and muscular and covered in freckles. I've never, not even once in the Agoge, seen a man's naked chest before.

I shouldn't be looking at him. It's indecent, and if he were to catch me staring, I think I might die of embarrassment.

I duck my head and study my hands, which are streaked with red stress marks. My hand above the spot where Pax cut out my microchip is now throbbing so bad I almost cannot stand to move it. I cradle it and look for the lion pelt, but it's gone. It must have slid over the edge and off the cliff.

I stand and brush my hands off on my pants, even though they're not really dirty. I sneak a glance at Pax, but he's still studying the injuries on his chest. I look away again and search for something to do until he's done.

I still have the bag attached to my back, and I swing it around to my front and dig out the water bottle and a roll of fresh bandages. The bottle is only about half-full, but I spare a little to wet a bandage. I walk over to Pax and hand it to him, my eyes still carefully averted.

"Thank you," he says, his voice clipped.

I look at him again a moment later to find he's finally lowered his shirt, and he's cleaning the blood off his face with the moist bandage I've given him. He meets my eyes and looks away. There is an awkward silence between us, but I don't know why there should be. It didn't feel this way after the times he saved *my* life.

He finishes mopping at his face and begins cleaning up his wrists. I give him the bottle so he can run some water over them and get out the gravel and dirt. After he hands it back, he holds the bandage against the worst of his wrists and looks around, his eyes scanning the ground.

"The pelt fell over the edge," I say. "Sorry. I couldn't keep a hold of it."

"Damn," he says. "Guess I'll have to kill another one."

"You . . . killed that lion?" I'm slightly revolted, even after seeing what a mountain lion is capable of.

He shoots me a sidelong look and says, "Yeah. I was fourteen and injured from a bad fall. It was stalking me, and I had to shoot it. It was kill or be killed."

I nod, trying to imagine a fourteen-year-old Pax alone in the wilderness. "You were only fourteen?"

"It was kill or be killed, Pria," he says again in a quiet voice. "What would you have done?"

"I'm not judging you," I say. "I think . . . I know you did what you had to do. You don't strike me as a cruel person."

He wrings out the bandage, now pink and patched with dark red, and looks away.

Chapter 22

We eat lunch before moving on, which gives both of us a chance to recover from the shock and exertion. Pax digs a couple of packets out of his bag and hands one to me. It is made of a thick papery material, and I examine it closely.

"It's a Commune ration." He tears his open and looks inside. "You've never seen one of these before?"

I shake my head.

"The paper is completely biodegradable. These packs are airtight until opened, but they'll disintegrate within twenty-four hours after that. We can leave them on the road. Not *everything* the UWO has created is bad," he says in a wry tone. "Now, the food inside is another matter." He pulls out a gray square. "I have no idea who this kind was made for, but it's all pretty bland." He bites off one corner, and some crumbs fall to the ground.

"What do you mean, who it was made for?" I ask, tearing open my own pack.

He chews and swallows before responding. "These are manufactured by the nutrition techs with the UWO, and they're specific to certain age groups and nutrition needs, and whatnot."

"So you stole these from someone," I say dryly.

He shifts and scowls. "It was a long time ago," he says. "I mostly eat off the land these days, but in situations like this"—he spreads his arms over the barren road—"it's nice to have something to fall back on, even if that something is a tasteless vitamin-packed Commune ration." He takes another bite.

I remove mine from the packet and sniff it. It smells like nothing and looks like dried paste, but I'm so hungry, I can't complain. I bite into it, and it's dry and coarse and bland. There is a slight saltiness, but otherwise it tastes like nothing I've ever had before. I swallow my first bite and ask, "How often do they eat these in the Commune?"

Pax raises an eyebrow. "Every meal of the day."

I choke on my next bite and cough to get the crumbs out of my throat. "What?"

Fresh food was always prepared for us Breeders in Sanctuary. They were small and simple meals, but tasty. In the Agoge, too.

"If you live in the Communes, it's all about utility," Pax says. "No frills, and no choice. You eat what the UWO prescribes so you can stay in what they determine to be optimum health so you don't become a drain on society. And when you reach a certain age, you . . ." He frowns and looks at his ration.

"You what?" I say. "What certain age?"

"Forget it," Pax says. "I've already told you more than you're ready to believe. Just forget I said that." He shoves the rest of his gray square into his mouth and balls up the paper. He tosses it onto the rockslide and stands, brushing off his fingers on his pants. Then he walks to the edge of the road and looks out, his hands on his hips, while I finish my food.

I try not to stare at him, but it's hard not to. How does he know everything he knows? And how has he gotten a hold of everything he has? He exists, and he's a real person, I acknowledge that. I can't get around acknowledging that. But I can't seem to stop staring at him either.

As a genetic anomaly, it must have been very difficult to navigate the world of the Unified World Order without getting caught. Even obtaining such things as the colored lenses he wore in his eyes and the color paste for his hair would be risky. And who provides those things, if not the very people he claims he's been unable to find all these years? Certainly the UWO wouldn't make a habit of engineering products that allow people to evade them. Everything about Pax seems either too good, or too terrible, to be true.

But I have no choice but to trust him. I can't survive in the wild on my own, and they would arrest me and execute me for treason were I to return to Sanctuary.

My mouth feels chalky after finishing the Commune ration, but Pax left the water bottle with me. I drink sparingly and then bring it back to Pax,

Breeder

who has returned to the motorcycle and is running his hands over it with a calculating look in his eyes. Probably checking for damage after its tumble over the rockslide.

"Pax," I say.

"Hmm?" He doesn't look up.

"What would they do with you if they found you? Would they kill you like they killed your friend Jacob?"

He does look up now, his eyes clear and piercing. "Yes. They would kill me. Enforcers are instructed to kill any genetic anomalies on the spot."

"But you're not a real Enforcer, are you? So how can you know that?"

Pax straightens and says, "I've spent enough time among them to pick up on their orders. With the uniform on, I'm virtually invisible to them. Just another worker bee." He's watching me with the same calculating expression he just used on the motorcycle. I think he senses I'm still not convinced of his full story.

So I opt for honesty. "I don't believe you." I cross my arms over my chest and straighten my shoulders. "The world isn't as cruel as you're making it out to be—it simply can't be. The UWO doesn't kill people just for being different."

"Then why would they teach people like you in the Agoge that people like me died out a long time ago? Why wouldn't they tell you the truth, if it's not that big of a deal?"

"I didn't say I don't think it's a big deal to them, because obviously it is. And they may be flawed in their rationale when it comes to what makes someone genetically inferior or superior." I look him up and down. "But I just can't believe it's as bad as you're making it out to be. I *see* you, and I acknowledge that either the UWO lied in my education or left out mention of recessive anomalies, but I don't believe they would kill you just for existing, and I certainly don't believe they're killing babies in Sanctuary! I think you've led a hard life because you're different, and you're angry about it, but I don't believe it's illegal to be genetically flawed."

I'm geared up for a fight, tense and ready for him to explode at me, but he doesn't. He just nods in a thoughtful sort of way and cinches the hole closed on the large pack.

"And what about my friend Jacob? Why did they kill him if not for his defect?"

"If they shot him, it was most likely because he was a thief. I'm sorry, but it's true."

Pax tightens his jaw.

"I'm not happy it happened, but he was a criminal—*you're* a criminal. And now I'm one, too, because I let myself trust you."

"And what about Mother's order to kill you?"

I lick my lips and feel my shoulders slump. "I'll give you that one. I . . . I can't deny she gave that order. And it's the only reason I came with you."

"The *only* reason?" Pax raises an eyebrow. "What about the death of the little girl? What about the baby's cry?"

"You know how I feel about the little girl," I say. "And I don't deny you've helped me realize I don't believe everything I've been taught about . . . about the order of things. But the baby's cry"—I look at the ground—"I don't know what that was," I whisper. "It could have been anything. It could have just sounded like a baby. It could have been the cry of a newborn being born."

Pax shifts closer to me, and I look up as I sense his nearness. But I won't give him the satisfaction of seeing me back down.

He says, "What if I told you that cry was of a two-month-old baby girl who had begun to show signs of developmental delay? What if I told you her cry cut off abruptly because they threw her, whole, into the fire of the incinerator?" He is so close he's practically breathing on me.

"Why must you make up such horrible stories?" I ask, my eyes stinging.

"Exactly," he says. "What would possess me to imagine something so horrible if it wasn't true?"

A blast of chill wind slams into me, and I put up my hands to prevent myself from falling into him. His reflexes are quick, and he grabs my wrists, holding me steady until the wind eddies away.

"Maybe you're making it up because you need a Breeder," I say. "You said so yourself. I've told you what I do believe, but I can't help wondering if you've made up some of these stories and mixed them with truths to get me to trust you."

Pax is quiet for a long moment, still holding my wrists. I can't read what's going on behind his hooded eyes.

Then he says, "I'm not lying to you. If you can't trust your instincts, trust what you've experienced already. I rescued you from certain death in Sanctuary, I removed your microchip, and now I'm taking you to the one place you can be safe in this society. And when we get there, you'll see that I've told the truth about the UWO. Maybe then you'll believe the rest about Sanctuary and the Controlled Repopulation Program."

"I guess, since you know I have doubts, we'll just have to trust each other," I say.

He gives me a solemn look. "That's true." He releases my wrists at last but then frowns and looks at his fingers, which are stained red. "You're bleeding," he says. He takes my right wrist again and turns it over. The bandage is soaked through with blood.

"I must have torn it open when I was helping you up the slope," I say.

"Give me the bag," he says. "I'll fix it up again before we go. We can't have you attracting predators."

It's almost as though the conversation didn't just happen.

I sit on a rock and watch him lay out his paltry medical supplies. My wrist is throbbing and feels warm and sticky. The throbbing has moved up into my head as well, and I close my eyes.

"If everything you're telling me is true," I say, my voice quiet, "then the world is full of all sorts of predators. If humans are capable of such monstrosities, then *I* could be a predator. Or you."

I open my eyes and stare at his thick, light, red-gold hair. He's bent over my wrist, unwrapping the soaked bandage with extreme care, and he doesn't hesitate.

He simply says, "Yes, I could be," and continues his work.

Chapter 23

The rest of the road is mercifully free of serious rockslides, but it's still slow going, and the sun is hanging low over the mountains when we come to a broken-down rock wall. Pax slows the motorcycle, and I hop off and remove my helmet when it comes to a halt. The air is thin and much colder up here, at about six thousand feet, probably. Patches of snow cling to the westward side of the rocks, the side that gets few hours of direct sunlight this time of year.

Pax and I drink the rest of the water in the bottle, and he goes to collect some snow. As he shoves the bottle full of it, I gaze out to the east. The Commune looks tiny from this height, and the hovercrafts like little bees. But I feel too exposed, like a sentinel standing above the world, now that most of the mountain is below us. I turn away from the edge and go to the broken-down wall.

It's about waist-high and circles almost all the way around an area free of vegetation. The view from this side of the road is spectacular—beyond spectacular. I bite my lip, enraptured. From the Looking Glass, we could see the mountains only as they appeared above the trees, but here I'm looking down, down, down into a canyon gorge where a silver ribbon of twisting river marks the bottom. The mountains rise up like sloped walls on either side and fold over each other all the way to the horizon.

"I never knew they went on for so long," I say. "The mountains, I mean."

"Didn't they teach you geography in the Agoge?" Pax asks, his tone a little mocking.

"They did, but somehow they never quite managed to convey this . . . this . . ."

Pax comes up beside me, shaking the bottle to agitate the snow into melting. "This what?"

"This . . ." I spread my arms wide. "Majesty, I guess." I don't know where I learned or heard that word, because I've definitely never had opportunity to use it before now, but it's the only word that fits what I'm seeing. "I always got the impression all of this was almost destroyed by humans even before the Great Devastations. But *look* at it."

"I am looking at it," Pax says, and there's a tone in his voice that makes me glance at him.

He's studying the landscape with a hunger in his expression, as though he's seeing his future out among the mountains. I can't deny that, even with the technology the UWO has to hunt us, it does seem as though we could disappear here.

"That Nest could be anywhere," I say quietly. "How long do you plan on looking?"

Pax's expression dims, and the look of hunger leaves his eyes. "As long as it takes."

Me and him. Alone in the mountains. For as long as it takes. I shiver and shake my head.

"Are you cold?" he asks.

"A bit."

"Why don't you put on the Enforcer jumpsuit over what you have on?"

I almost turn down the offer, but the air is biting through my tunic and pants, and I'm not used to physical discomfort. So I nod.

Pax digs it out of the bag and hands it to me, then pokes around among the scrub brush while I shimmy into it. It's baggy enough that I can easily tuck my tunic and pants down into it, and when I zip it up all the way to my chin, I'm immediately warmer.

Pax returns to my side with a handful of greens—some long stalks with tiny white flowers on the ends, others shorter and with purple flowers. He doesn't offer any explanation, just rolls them up and shoves them into the bag, which he then hands over to me.

"We're a little exposed here," he says. "Let's move on and find a campsite somewhere in the trees."

"Okay." I fit the helmet down over my head and climb onto the back of the bike.

The road continues upward, but the slope is less steep now, and it cuts

K.B. Hoyle

straight across the mountain rather than switchbacking up it. We enter pine cover, which further obstructs what sunlight is left coming in through the mountains to the west, and my vision through the Enforcer helmet's visor becomes increasingly tinted with green.

Pax steers the bike onto a side road and comes to a halt beside what looks like an ancient, semi-ruined structure. "Not enough light left," he says, "and I don't want to use the light on the bike. It's too risky that it will draw attention to us."

I look around, but the day still seems plenty bright to me. "I can see just fine," I say.

He taps the side of the helmet and says, "Night vision. I should have told you. Take it off and look around."

I do, and it's to find the world blanketed in shadow. The abandoned structure is nothing more than a heap of blackness before us.

Pax stretches and steps off the bike. "Plus, predators come out at night, and this looks like it could be a good, sheltered place to camp." He holds out his hand. "Here, let me see that."

I give him the helmet, and he puts it on. Then he unholsters his Air-5 and says, "Stay here while I check it out." And he leaves me alone in the darkness.

I try not to feel afraid as he melts away toward the black structure, but the world is big and vast and dark, and it's cold up here. I unholster my weapon and finger the switch so the safety is off. It's not that I want to shoot anything, but it gives me a sense of security knowing I'm not completely helpless. I turn in a slow circle, noting the glimmer of a few pairs of eyes up in the trees, but they're small—probably squirrels or birds.

A twig snaps beside me, and I spin around and instinctively fire my weapon.

"Hey!" Pax says. Then his hand is on my arm, forcing it down.

"Oh! I'm sorry. Did I hit you?" The thought makes me nauseous.

"Luckily you're a terrible shot, so no," Pax says, his tone dry. "Next time just look before you fire, okay?"

"Okay," I whisper. I quickly flip the safety back on, but Pax shakes his head.

"No. Keep it ready. You never know what could wander in up here." He looks over his shoulder. "The cabin, at least, is deserted. Better yet, it has a stone fireplace we can use to cook a hot meal."

"What's a cabin?"

"It's what they used to call these wooden structures," he says, jerking his head in the direction behind him. He wheels the motorcycle toward it, and I follow. "People used to live in them long ago, or use them for vacations."

"What's a vacation?"

"It's . . ." He parks the motorcycle and turns to me, pulling the helmet off. "Well, people used to have leisure time that they spent with family and friends."

I'd learned that people once lived in family units—it was part of what destroyed society and led to the Devastations—but I've never heard of this vacation concept before. "Leisure time scheduled by the government, right?" I ask.

"No." He gives a short laugh. "Free time. They could go whenever they wanted and do whatever they wanted." He walks up a couple of short steps and through the gaping hole of a doorway.

The very idea of what he's saying sends a shock through me. "Sounds dangerous," I say. "Getting to do whatever you want whenever you want . . . I guess that's why their society failed."

"Dangerous?" Pax turns toward me so I can see the gleam of his eyes in the darkness. "I suppose it was a little dangerous, but doesn't that sort of freedom tempt you at all?"

"No."

"Now I have to accuse *you* of lying," he says.

"What?" I sputter. "I'm not lying."

"Of course you are. You're here, aren't you?"

I close my mouth tight and purse my lips. "I didn't leave because I wanted freedom. I left because they were going to kill me and, well, you gave me a way out."

"Hasn't this been a little exhilarating, though?" Pax tilts his head.

"If by *exhilarating* you mean terrifying, hunger-inducing, and uncertain, then yes."

He gives me a thin smile and moves farther into the cabin. "You're enjoying yourself whether you admit it or not. You should have seen your face at the overlook an hour ago."

It was beautiful, but I won't say it out loud. Instead I say, "Pax, how do you know all this stuff? About cabins and vacations and how people used to live? You claim to not have gone through the Agoge, but you seem to know more facts than I do."

"I *didn't* go through the Agoge, but I learned a lot from the people I lived among as a child. And Jacob and I picked up a lot of information as we traveled. That's how I know what I do." He sets down his pack and grabs his Air-5. "Make yourself at home while I work out a fire."

The walls have gaping holes in them, but against the far wall is a stone box of sorts that must be the fireplace he mentioned. He kicks at a wooden frame that may have once been a chair, and it falls apart into fragments and shards. "Perfect," he says. He takes the pieces and arranges them in the fireplace. In no time, he's got a small fire going, and then he tells me he'll be right back.

I crouch alone by the fire, trying not to look around and find spiders and critters sharing our space. I toss a twig onto the flames and twist my mouth, unhappy that Pax seems to be chipping away at my reasoning. I've never really thought about freedom, but he must be right. I must have craved at least a little more freedom than I was offered at Sanctuary, or even Mother's threat of death would not have ousted me from that life. I desired, at least, to keep my own life, and that proves I never really believed the rhetoric about my life belonging to the Program. The thought is a little unsettling. In only two days, Pax has caused me to realize things I've believed for a long time without realizing I believed them. Yet Pax himself remains an enigma.

He returns shortly with a pot he's filled up with snow. I don't know if he found the pot in the cabin or if he had it in his pack all along, but he suspends it from a hook over the fire. Then he hands me some of the greenery with the purple flowers he picked at the overlook.

"When that boils, you'll see large bubbles appear," he says. "Tear up these flowers and throw them in. I'm going to hunt us a squirrel."

Meat. I frown. I don't want to get sick again.

"What are these called?" I ask, holding up the flowers.

"Bergamot," he says. "They're edible, and hopefully they'll help settle your stomach this time."

"Oh." Whatever Pax's real story is, I can't deny he's thoughtful. I shift and avoid his eyes, remembering how I've never detected a trace of the usual signs of artifice in him. I was so sure I didn't believe the horrible things he was saying earlier today, but it's hard to cling to that conviction when I weigh it against his actions.

When I look up, he's gone.

I tear the flowers and stems into tiny bits, waiting for the water to take on the large bubbles Pax talked about. Before he cooked the snake last night, I'd never seen food preparation. In the Agoge, and later in Sanctuary, food was always delivered to us already cooked.

I wonder who makes the chalky Commune rations we ate for lunch today.

There must be a factory in the Denver Commune. I wonder how I'd feel if that had been my assignment after my Agoge education instead of becoming a Breeder? Everything about the UWO was designed to maintain a classless, ordered society in which no one could consider him or herself better than anyone else. But isn't that exactly what Breeders have always been told? That we are better—genetically superior?

I toss the bits of flower into the water as it froths upward in bubbles and then wipe my fingers on my pants. Maybe it's human nature to fight for rankings and supremacy. Maybe I don't have any idea what's truth and what's lie.

Chapter 24

I stomach the meat better this time, but it still makes my insides twist and jump like they've come alive. I eat only a small amount of the squirrel Pax shot, mixed and boiled with the bergamot broth, which gives off a minty, herbal scent. I'm so very hungry, but I can't force myself to eat more than a small helping. Pax seems determined to make me adjust to three larger meals a day rather than six small ones. He says if we stop for six meals a day, we'll never get anywhere. Seeing as how he has no concrete idea of where we're going, I don't see how stopping for more meals would hinder our getting there.

"We should take turns at watch tonight," Pax says when he's finished eating. The fire is burning low, and the cold wind is blowing through the gaping holes in the cabin walls, making whistling and whooshing sounds. I'm thankful once again for the Enforcer uniform Pax is letting me wear. I tried to give it back before dinner, but he refused.

"What are you afraid of?" I ask.

"Anything," he says. "Everything. UWO vessels, Unfamiliars, bears, mountain lions, coyotes, snakes . . . you need more?"

I shake my head and twist my finger into the hair by my ear.

"I'll take the first watch," he says. "You go ahead and get some sleep. I'll wake you in about four hours."

I'm weary beyond words, and my wrist and ribs are aching, but the idea of him sitting awake watching me sleep makes me shiver. I open my mouth and close it. I know I'm being ridiculous. We've already spent one night together.

"I'm not going to hurt you, Pria," Pax says. "If I wanted to, I would have done so already. And I won't let anything else hurt you either."

"I suppose you can't, if you *need* me," I say.

Pax purses his lips and leans back, rubbing the back of his neck with both hands. "Just get some sleep, okay?"

With a sigh, I stretch out in front of the fire and rest my head on my arm. I can't decide if it will be worse to face him or to put my back to him, but eventually the floor decides for me, as the warped wood punishes my hips until I roll onto my back. Resting an arm over my face to shield myself from him, I close my eyes and let myself relax.

~

I'm having a vivid dream in which Mother inserts a long needle into my abdomen and tells me the implantation is going just as planned. Flora the cloned dog sits at my bedside, wagging her tail and licking my hand. When Pax shakes my shoulder, I start awake and clutch at my stomach as phantom pains assail me.

"Are you okay?" Pax's voice is low and concerned. "The squirrel   meat —"

"No . . . no. It's nothing. I'm fine."

Pax offers a hand to help me sit up, but I ignore it and push myself to my feet.

"My turn to watch already?" My voice is scratchy and rough, and my head feels stuffed with rocks. I can't remember the last time I got fewer than eight hours of sleep in a night.

"I'm sorry," Pax says, and he sounds genuine. "If I didn't have to drive the motorcycle, I'd take the whole watch."

I blink at him. "I believe you," I say. "But that's not necessary. I didn't mean to make you feel bad. I'm strong and capable—of course I can do my part."

"I know you're strong and capable, Pria," he says. "You don't have to convince me."

Silence, heavy and thick, falls between us. Awkwardness seems to creep up at unexpected times, and I wonder if it is always this way between women and men. I never felt awkward with any of my sisters, but whatever this is between Pax and me has a different feel to it.

"Anyway," he says. "I sat against the wall over there." He nods to an intact wall dividing the cabin into two spaces. "It's not the warmest spot, but it gives you a good view of the access points without making you visible from the outside. Take this." He hands me the Enforcer helmet.

"Okay." I pick my way around the broken-down furniture and dried leaves. "So I just . . . sit and watch?"

"Keep your weapon ready," he says. "If anything comes along, crawl over here and wake me up. But don't worry—dawn is only a few hours off. I never saw anything other than a band of mule deer."

I nod and settle against the wall, putting the helmet on so I can see. Pax lies down on his back right where I slept and falls almost immediately asleep. I watch his green-tinted chest rise and fall for several minutes before I remember I'm supposed to be watching the "access points," as Pax called them.

Jagged shards of glass poke out from around the edges of the windows. The doorway gapes at me, a dark yawning hole that looks ominous even in the green glow of the helmet visor. A set of glowing green eyes outlined by a furry form with pointed ears stops outside the cabin and looks at me. Another coyote. I train my Air-5 on it and hold my breath, but it loses interest and moves on, its nose to the ground. I let out my breath. Hopefully that will be all the wildlife I see tonight.

Pax was right, it isn't the warmest spot, but the cold air actually helps me to stay awake. Temperature, along with food and sleep, was highly regulated in Sanctuary so we never had to feel uncomfortable. As I think longingly about my warm bed in the dormitory, my head grows heavy and nods toward my chest. I jerk upright and stand to pace. I wonder how much time has passed.

Pax doesn't even stir once in his sleep, but his eyes move beneath his eyelids. He must be having vivid dreams, like me. I suppose if his life has been as tumultuous as he's painted it, he must have plenty to haunt his dreams.

How did I get here, pacing in the dark and cold in a structure well over a hundred years old with a weapon in my hand and meat in my stomach?

Just thinking about my stomach makes it growl, and I look around for the cook pot. It's sitting on the hearth next to the embers of the fire, and I hope it's still a little warm.

I pick my way over to it, stepping over Pax's legs to reach it. Then I squat and lift the pot to my lips, testing the heat of the metal against them before taking a drink. It's cool enough to touch, and I take several sips. The meaty flavor is still strange, but somehow satisfying.

Pax grabs my ankle, and I jump, spilling the broth.

"I'm . . . fifteen," he says. "Fifteen . . ."

His eyes are closed and roving around beneath his freckled lids, making his golden lashes dance. I think he's talking in his sleep.

"I know," I say. "You told me you're Enforcer Fifteen."

"Fifteen," he mumbles again. "Is . . . my . . . number." His grip relaxes and his hand falls to the floor.

I let out a careful breath and carry what remains of the broth back to my spot against the wall. I'm not sure what that was all about, but I'd rather be out of his reach for now.

Chapter 25

I'm asleep against the wall with the pot in my lap when Pax wakes me with a hand on my shoulder and a wry look. The sun is already high.

"I'm sorry!" I scramble to my feet, and the pot clangs to the floor. "I promise I watched most of the time. But when the sun started to come up, I guess I—"

"It's okay." He bends and picks up the now-empty pot and carries it to his pack. "How are you feeling this morning?"

I rub my arms and watch him cinch the pack up tight, two Commune rations under his arm. "How do you mean?" There are many ways I could answer his question, most of them in a negative way. I'm cold, stiff, tired, still hungry, weak, and homesick.

"Physically." He pats his chest. "This is day three of your being off the supplement regime. Are you holding up okay?"

That's probably why I feel so weak, but I don't want to admit that to him. "I'm doing fine," I say. "You don't need to worry about me."

Pax raises an eyebrow and shrugs. He tosses me one of the Commune rations, and I catch it. "Breakfast," he says, "since you finished off the soup."

I blush, unable to tell if he's mad that I ate the rest of it.

After tearing open the ration, I see this one is the same color as the one I ate yesterday. Pax is already consuming his in large bites—it looks as though he's hardly chewing. I suppose with how little flavor they have, that's not an illogical way to get the job done. I remove my helmet and we eat in silence before taking turns at using a dense thicket of bushes as a toilet.

When I finish and emerge from the thicket, Pax is already straddling the motorcycle with the far-off expression I noticed yesterday at the overlook. It jogs my memory of when he spoke in his sleep in the middle of the night, and I say, "Why fifteen?"

Pax's expression goes blank, and he looks at me. "I'm sorry?"

"When we talked in the stairwell at Sanctuary, you told me your Enforcer designation was fifteen. And again, in the middle of the night last night, you woke up and"—I swallow instead of telling him he grabbed my leg —"and told me you were fifteen. That it was *your number*. But you chose it, right? Because, if everything you've told me so far is true, you're not a real Enforcer."

Pax schools his expression so subtly I might not have noticed it if it weren't for how high I scored in perception in the Agoge. I'm a genius in many aspects but most particularly in the art of reading details and drawing deductions from them, especially when I'm paying close attention. He relaxes the muscles around his mouth and barely flares his nostrils, and his pupils dilate slightly. For the first time, I'm certain he's about to tell me a lie.

"The Enforcer I was impersonating when I stole that uniform was designation fifteen, but I only give it out as my designation if I'm directly asked. I stole the uniform off an Enforcer many miles south of here, closer to where I lived with the Nest that was destroyed."

"Why do you think you told me your designation in your sleep?"

"I don't know. Who can guess why people dream certain things?" He tosses me the helmet, signaling the end of the conversation. "Put that back on, but be ready to take it off if I say so. If we hit upon an area I think the rebels are likely to be, I want them to be able to see you."

"Mm-hmm," I say, sliding the helmet over my head. As the bike roars to life, I swing myself onto it and hold Pax's waist. I don't know what part of his explanation just now was a lie, but I know some part of it was.

Chapter 26

"Get down." Pax grabs the back of my neck and shoves my head into the underbrush, and the rest of my body follows suit.

"What is it?" I snap.

We've been puttering around the mountains for almost two weeks, back and forth over saddles of pine- and aspen-covered slopes, poking into abandoned mining tunnels, and eating off the land as best we can. We left the motorcycle several days ago, after concealing it by a memorable patch of boulders on an old mountain road, and then struck off over a ridge on foot. Pax figured the rebels might be spooked by the bike and the odd couple riding it. That and it was almost out of gas.

I don't have the energy to agree or disagree—my temper is wearing thin, and I just kind of want to go home. Which is impossible, of course.

In contrast to me, Pax has remained unerringly calm. He seems to have a bottomless pool of patience from which to draw, and he even makes our rambling search through the woods feel methodical. He's quiet more than he speaks. I've grown accustomed to it, so it's no longer awkward, but I can never read what's going through his mind. When I get upset, he remains steady. When I am impatient and ill-tempered, he doesn't react in kind. I don't know how he does it.

We've been descending all day into the valley on the far side of a ridge we just crossed, and Pax has been so even-keeled this whole time that I'm more shocked than annoyed that he's shoved me to the ground.

He puts a finger to his lips, which are now shadowed by red-gold hair he calls a "beard," and crawls forward to a rock. Lifting his head until just his eyes are above it, he stares down into the valley for a moment, and then he gestures me forward.

I crawl, too, the bag shifting back and forth between my shoulder blades, until I'm at his side.

"Unfamiliars," he mouths, pointing down.

I crease my brow as a cold chill goes through me. "I thought we were too high for them," I whisper.

He shakes his head and points again. "In the valley," he whispers back.

Cautiously, I roll sideways and look around the boulder. I can just make out the fleshy, lanky limbs of three Unfamiliars. They are about two hundred yards below us at the bottom of the valley, walking east with long strides. Their six-fingered hands hang at the ends of arms that dangle almost to their knees, and each one is well over twelve feet tall with the red-eyed, slack-jawed visage I'd been conditioned to fear as a child. Although naked, they appear sexless. We humans have never discovered how they reproduce.

They turn their heads from side to side as they walk, as though they're searching for something, and I hold my breath, hoping they can't detect us up here.

Pax squeezes my wrist where the wound from my microchip removal is almost healed, and I let him hold it. I can't tell if he's trying to comfort me or warn me to be still, but I don't care which it is. I'm thankful for the contact, as the sight of the Unfamiliars makes me shiver with fear.

One of the three turns its sallow face toward us, and even though we're far up the slope, it stops walking and stares. I feel its red eyes boring through me, and Pax's pressure on my wrist increases. But neither of us lowers our heads. I know, for my part, if I'm going to be attacked, I want to be able to see my attacker.

I hear a whisper of movement near our legs. With his other hand, Pax is unholstering his Air-5. He gives my wrist a firmer squeeze that I take as indication I should do likewise, and then he releases me. I fumble with my weapon and finger the safety to off. It's a good thing we haven't had reason to use our weapons for much more than hunting this week, because the charge on Pax's is already running low.

When I look up again, all three Unfamiliars are staring up the slope toward us. They then begin a slow ascent, and I swallow reflexively as my heart rate increases.

They might attack us . . . they probably will attack us.

Pax told me this week that the truce between our kind and theirs is mostly a sham. There won't be open warfare as long as we stay out of the territory they've claimed as their own, but they are far from desirous of being at peace with humanity. Pax and I have clearly violated that truce twice over already—when we camped in the cave south of the Denver Commune, and now as we are descending into this valley. The problem is, there's no way to know what territory they have or haven't claimed, and the boundaries are ever changing. The Unfamiliars don't build dwellings or settlements like humans do.

Pax and I are stuck. There's no place for us to go. If we move, we'll be exposed and they'll attack us for sure. But there are two of us and only three of them. We're armed and they're not. We should be able to take them down.

Pax toggles his switch to automatic. I do the same. The Unfamiliars are gaining on us, moving up the mountainside with spiderlike agility for creatures so big. I hear and see young saplings bend and snap as they are grasped in enormous hands and used as leverage for the giants to heave themselves up the slope.

All the birds have fallen silent in the forest except for an insistent robin that calls to its mate from across the valley. The call is answered by another bird somewhere behind us, and the two carry on a conversation, as if to warn each other of the impending danger.

Pax eases back so his feet are beneath him, ready to propel himself into a standing position, but I'm frozen in place, watching the Unfamiliars approach. The creamy tone of their skin is tinted a ghastly gray, and they are covered in wrinkles and folds that suggest their muscles hang suspended on bones that slide around within them. They have no hair anywhere on their bodies, and I want to know what makes their eyes glow like they do. But they are aliens, not yet well adapted to this planet, so they should look odd to me—unfamiliar, as they tactfully came to be called after the Great Incursion ended. Right about now, I'm thinking *unfamiliar* is not a strong enough descriptor.

My hands are shaking, and I bring my weapon up alongside my cheek, trying to steady it. If they give any indication of hostile intent, we will have no choice but to defend ourselves. Even the two robins have fallen silent now.

The Unfamiliars are so close I can see the cracks in the creases of their skin, and a sickly sweet, metallic scent precedes their arrival.

A dark shadow goes hurtling over my head and lands in front of me, firing green bursts of energy at the foremost of the Unfamiliars with a gun much larger than my Air-5. I expect it to be Pax, but it's not, although it *is* a man. I'm too shocked to scream or even move from my position as the Unfamiliars give throaty roars and swing out at the man. But he rolls to the side and comes back up on his feet, firing again within seconds.

A second figure joins him, running up from the bottom of the valley, the opposite direction the man had come from. Then three loud bangs sound behind me, jarring my teeth and making me drop my weapon. Blood sprays from the chest of the first Unfamiliar as it keels over with a groan. It lands with a loud crash.

I scoot down and turn over, putting my back to the boulder and the fight just beyond it. I scrabble for my Air-5 in the underbrush, but I can't find it.

And then I look up, and my attention becomes riveted on Pax. He is crouched with his hands raised and his expression sharp while a man stands beside him with a gun pressed to Pax's temple.

Chapter 27

"If you want to live, you will not move a muscle," says the man holding his gun to Pax's head.

"That goes for you, too," says another voice, and I wrench my gaze away from Pax to see a girl, probably about my age, training an Air-5 on me. I think it must be my own Air-5, because the underbrush around me is clear.

The shots, both the energy zips and the deafening bangs, continue to mingle with the roars and groans of the remaining Unfamiliars behind me, but I'm so confused by these people that those sounds fade to the background.

The man with Pax could pass for a regular citizen of the UWO. He's got dark hair and eyes and olive skin. But the girl—I can't take my eyes off her. Her skin is darker than any human's I've ever seen. She's brown, like the color of the bark on the pine trees, and her hair is black and sticks up in the middle, even though it's several inches long. She's shaved both sides of her head, leaving an extreme ridge of hair down the middle. Her eyes are light brown, lighter than her skin, and they are hard and humorless. She's smaller than I am, but muscles stick out on her bare arms, and her chest beneath the tight shirt she wears is almost as flat as a man's.

She catches me looking her up and down, and my shock must register on my face because she says, "What's the matter? Never seen a black person before?"

"No," I whisper. The sounds from the Unfamiliars have quieted, allowing my voice to be heard. "I was told your race died out long ago."

She snorts and draws the corner of her lip up in a sneer. "Listen to you, talking about my race, as though it's somehow different from yours. Think you're so superior because you grew up in the Commune? Because you're allowed to exist?" She spits at my feet, and I flinch, disgusted. But she presses forward. "There's only one race, and that's the human race. If you want us to let you live, you'd better get that through your head."

"Celine," says the man holding a gun to Pax's head. "Leave her alone. She doesn't know. Look at her—"

"I *am* looking at her, Elan. I know what she is. It's why we intervened at all."

I get the impression she's saying this for our benefit, Pax's and mine.

Celine crouches before me, and up close I can see she has a dark, swirling pattern marking her head on one side where her hair has been shaved.

"Well, are you or aren't you?" she asks in a low voice charged with hostility.

"Am I or am I not what?" I whisper back.

"One of the princesses," Celine says. "A Breeder."

I shoot a look at Pax, whose expression is now guarded and impassive. But I can see the tension just beneath the surface. *These* are the people he wanted us to find? They're coarse and mean and . . . animalistic. Can he possibly mean for us to join with them?

Pax gives me a barely perceptible nod. I don't see what choice I have anyway, given the circumstances.

"Yes. I am . . . I *was* a Breeder," I say. "I lived in Sanctuary until about two weeks ago."

"And why did you leave them?" Celine asks. "Didn't you have a perfect little life?" She presses the cold nozzle of the Air-5 up against my cheek.

A chill goes through me at her terminology, and at how many times I'd reminded myself of that very thing. "I left because I was unhappy."

That admission costs me something, a little bit of my inner self, and I see Pax blink and furrow his brow. But it's true—I had been unhappy, desperately unhappy for weeks and weeks, ever since my procedure. And it was only after I got away that I started to feel some of that freedom Pax talked about. I'm still not exactly happy, and I still wake up to phantom pains and terrible dreams, but I feel more at peace out here in the wild than I did the last several months in Sanctuary. I don't know that I've acknowledged it before now, but it's true.

"You were unhappy," Celine says, her voice dry. "*That's* why you left? Is that supposed to convince us you're not a spy?"

"No, there's more," I say. "They were going to kill me."

Celine's eyes narrow, but she doesn't remove the gun. "Why would they do that? You seem healthy enough to me."

"Because I . . . I was asking too many questions."

Celine looks at Pax, then at the man named Elan. "If that's true, she could end up being of some use to us. If it's not true"—she turns back to me—"you'd better make up your mind to tell the truth before we get you back to Asylum, or there will be hell to pay." She nudges me. "Stand up."

I do so. "You're taking us with you, then?"

"I said *you*. Haven't decided about *him* yet."

One of the men who was fighting the now-dead Unfamiliars appears and yanks Pax's weapon from his hands. "Come on. You, too. On your feet."

"But he's obviously one of you," I say, faltering a little. The man who took Pax's gun is as dark as Celine but dwarfs her in size.

"What do you mean, one of us?" the man asks. "You mean genetically inferior? You mean a freak?"

I don't know what the word *freak* means, but it doesn't sound positive. "I know you're not genetically inferior," I say, raising my hands in an effort to placate the aggression that seems to emanate in waves from these people. "Pax has taught me that much. But he's said a lot of things I'm unsure about. I'm really just looking for answers, and . . . and a refuge, I guess, because I can't . . . I can't . . ." I'm horrified to realize tears are threatening at the backs of my eyes, and I shut my lips tight and clear my throat, blinking them away.

"Oh . . . you going to cry?" Celine says in a mocking voice. "Forgive me if I don't empathize with your situation."

"So who are you?" the one named Elan says to Pax. "What are you doing wandering in our territory with a woman claiming to be a rogue Breeder, and how have you survived without a Nest? Or are you from another Nest?"

How has Pax survived without a Nest? I avert my eyes, not meeting his. That single statement seems to validate half of Pax's story right there. Or maybe *all* these people are paranoid and delusional.

Pax is on his feet now. He stands about as tall as Elan but several inches shorter than the big, dark man. I've gotten used to being around one man, but seeing several, and all of them bigger than me, reminds me of my first days with Pax and puts me even more on edge.

"My name is Pax," he says, "and I don't have a Nest. I've been on my own since my Nest was destroyed years ago."

Elan jerks his head toward me. "Tell me about her."

Pax says, "I met one of your people several years ago, a man named Mack. I'd been trying to find a new Nest for years, and he told me the only way you'd reveal yourself to me would be if I brought you a Breeder. I've been impersonating an Enforcer for some time, and I managed to infiltrate Sanctuary and get her out. She's right. They were going to kill her. And you can trust us, both of us."

"Oh, well if you say so," Celine says. "Although that does explain the uniform."

I frown and glance at Pax, wondering how she knows about the uniform since neither of us has worn it in days. It's been too warm.

"You ever heard of a Mack?" Elan asks the dark man.

"No." His hands tighten on his weapon, which is black and made of metal. I wonder if it's the one that made the loud noises when shot. "Oy, Henri," he shouts over my shoulder, drawing out the first syllable so it sounds like *Ahn-ree*. "You know a Mack?"

"Mack? Nope, no Mack." The voice that drifts back is so similar in sound to the man who just called out that I look over my shoulder in surprise.

The owner of the voice, Henri, is identical in every way to the dark man standing with Pax. Same skin, same facial features, same height and girth, same bald head. But I see as Henri picks his way forward that the physical similarities do not extend to expression. Henri has a curious light in his eyes, and his mouth is tipped in such a way as to suggest he finds the situation amusing rather than threatening. He comes up beside the other man, and I stare in gape-mouthed awe.

"What *are* you?" I ask. I can't help myself. I thought every human was unique.

Henri grins, but the other man scowls. "We're twins," Henri says. "You know—brothers who shared a womb. We may not be from the Breeding program, but we're all right, despite what it looks like at the moment."

"Henri!" Celine says.

"What? What's it going to hurt for her to know that we're twins? Let me guess, you don't want her to know you're our sister either?"

Celine snorts and mutters something under her breath.

Brothers. Twins. I had "sisters" in Sanctuary, but none of them were actually related to me. Knowing blood relations is strictly forbidden in the UWO because it is tempting to give highest allegiance to those incidentally related by mere chance of nature, rather than to the UWO and society as a whole. Family is dangerous and divisive to society. But clearly what I'm seeing here are products of an actual family, reproducing and living together outside of the rules and regulations of the UWO. The thought horrifies and intrigues me all at once, making me dizzy. I put a hand to my head.

Through my haze of confusion, I hear Elan say, "Well, we knew we'd have to take them to Luther if we intervened, so let's get on with it. I don't want to risk another fight today. Henri, get Brant. Etienne, check them."

Etienne is Henri's twin. The name sounds like *Eh-tee-en* and, like Henri and Celine, evokes feelings of something different. I can't quite put my finger on it.

Henri purses his lips and makes a call that sounds just like a robin. I do a double take and widen my eyes.

"That was you," I say. "Before the fight."

"Of course it was," Henri says, flashing me a bright smile. Something about his demeanor makes me feel warmer inside, despite our circumstances.

The feeling of warmth is erased a moment later as Etienne grabs my wrist in a painful grip and pulls it toward him so hard I stumble.

Pax says, "Don't hurt her. I've already removed it." His voice sounds tight.

"I'll be the judge of that." Etienne shoulders his big black gun and flips out a knife that catches glints of light from the sun.

I try to pull away, but it's like pulling against a rock. Etienne rips the bandage off my wrist, revealing the red, scarring wound. He raises an eyebrow and prods the wound with the flat side of the knife. I wince and suck in my breath through my teeth.

He bites down on the blade of his knife and pulls a small wand-like contraption from a pocket of the vest he wears. He pushes a button on it, and it begins to hum. He passes it slowly over my wrist, staring intently at a screen on the backside of the wand. After several seconds, it beeps, and the screen turns green.

"Clean," he says.

"Check the rest of her," Elan says. "If she's a plant, they'd remove the wrist chip, but she could have one somewhere else."

Etienne says to me, "Don't move." He takes his time sweeping the wand over and around all my limbs, not satisfied with any appendage until he gets the beep and the green light. Henri has another wand and is doing the same to Pax.

"Elan," Henri says. "Check this out." He holds up Pax's wrist. "He's got a scar."

Elan peers at it for a moment, then spears Pax with a calculating look. "How'd you get that? You were born in the Program?"

"Obviously," Pax says. It's the first time I've heard impatience in his voice in a long time.

"It's rare for someone like you to survive. How'd you manage it?"

"I was rescued by a med tech who couldn't stomach killing me. She removed my chip and brought me to a Nest."

"What was the name of this med tech?"

Pax shrugs. "I never found out. I was just a baby."

Elan stares into Pax's eyes for several long moments, almost as though daring him to blink first, and then he says, "Lucky you. Guess you had a guardian angel."

A small crease forms between Pax's eyes. I can tell he's as unfamiliar with the term as I am.

Etienne and Henri finish scanning us and finally declare both of us clean just as another olive-skinned, dark-haired man arrives. This must be Brant.

"Let's go," Elan says. "It's getting late."

"For the record," Etienne says, putting a hand on Pax's chest, "I don't believe you."

"Etienne, let's go," Elan repeats. "We'll let Luther decide what to do with them." He glances at Pax. "I guess you're getting your wish—you get to come with us to our Nest. But if you're a spy, you might as well just tell us now. I'll kill you quickly. I can't say the same for those back in camp."

"I'm not a spy, and neither is she," Pax says. He's still so calm. How can he be so calm?

"Luther will decide," Celine says. "Come on, princess." She jabs me between the shoulder blades with my Air-5. "Time to walk."

Asylum

Chapter 28

"My name is Pria," I say to Celine as she prods me forward. "Not Princess."

She's quiet for a moment, and then she says, "I didn't realize you have names. I thought they just numbered you—like cattle."

I don't know what that means.

"So . . . Pria, huh? Weird name. How'd you get it?"

"The other girls in my Agoge class. We named each other when we were old enough to realize we needed to call each other something. The teachers didn't forbid it." But then, because I feel like I should, I say, "You're right about Sanctuary, though. They don't allow names. I was Breeder Seventeen. I'd almost forgotten my name until Pax came along."

"Yeah. Pax." She comes up beside me so we're walking abreast of each other, but she keeps the Air-5 trained on me in the crook of her arm. "What's his story—his *real* story?"

I glance over at him. "To be truthful, I wasn't sure I believed his story until you all showed up. And there are aspects of it that I still . . ."

Celine pokes me on the arm. "Spit it out, princess."

"Pria."

She rolls her eyes. "Fine. *Pria.*"

We're hiking west along the slope, angling down all the time so the valley floor rises up to meet us. I'm distracted by our direction of travel, and I say, "Isn't the valley floor dangerous? Aren't you worried about running into more Unfamiliars?"

Celine cocks one eyebrow, and then she throws back her head and laughs. "Unfamiliars! Hey, Elan, when was the last time you heard someone use the term *Unfamiliars*?"

"Been a long time."

She snorts and shoots me a disgusted look.

"What is it?" I ask.

"Only UWO stooges call them Unfamiliars. The rest of us, those who are free, call them Golems."

"Golems? What does that mean?" I ask.

But one of Celine's brothers—it must be Etienne, because he carries the black gun—says, "Not another word, Celine. We don't know if we can trust her."

"I'll trust her over him." Celine jerks her chin toward Pax. He's not looking at us, but I can tell he's listening by the focused expression on his face and the way he tilts his head.

Etienne shakes his head. There is a glint of gold in his ear, and I squint at it, mesmerized. Celine has her head markings, and Etienne has metal through his ear. Genetics aside, these people are strange to me.

"You're such a sexist," Etienne says. "Just because she's a girl, you'd rather trust her. Look at her, she's one of them. At least he's screwed up like the rest of us."

"We're not screwed up!" Celine says, rounding on him. "If Mom could hear you saying things like that, she'd bash your head in."

"It's a good thing Mom's dead, then, so I can say whatever I want."

Celine stops in her tracks and strikes Etienne across the face. "*Salaud.*"

I frown, not recognizing the word.

Etienne rubs his cheek and glares, but the other brother, Henri, jumps forward and pushes them apart.

"Knock it off," Henri says. "Do you want our guests to think the stories are true and all of us rebels are savages?"

"I've never heard any stories about you until I met Pax," I say. "And he always said positive things."

"No stories at all?" Henri asks, his eyebrows raised.

I shake my head. "I thought the UWO was all there was left of human civilization in the world."

"Man. I thought we'd made a bigger impression than that. Luther will be so disappointed."

"My brother won't know what to make of it," says the man named Brant. His tone is grumpy. Like Elan, he, too, could pass for a citizen of the UWO.

"If he'd listen to me—"

"Stop. Talking," says Etienne, his voice like a growl.

Celine says, "*Quel est le problème? Si ce sont vraiment des espions, ils seront bientôt morts.*"

I gape at her. "What was that? I didn't understand it."

Celine just gives me a grim smile and falls back behind me. "No more friendly talk," she says. "Just walk."

Everyone falls silent, although I have a million questions buzzing around in my head. They keep Pax and me carefully separated, and I'm never once close enough even to talk to him, not that I know what I'd say. Now that we've been found by his "rebels," all my curiosity is directed toward them.

"How do you survive here, if it's Unfamiliar territory?" I ask once we've descended all the way to the valley floor, unable to contain myself.

"Golem territory," Celine says. "And it's not their territory, it's ours."

"Shut it, Celine," Etienne says.

She sighs.

"Blindfolds," Elan says.

They bring us to a halt, and Brant and Henri step up to us with strips of fabric in hand. I catch a glimpse of Brant tying one around Pax's eyes before Henri takes up my vision. He gives me a half smile and ties it loosely so I can still see the underbrush out the bottom when I look down.

"Sorry about this," he whispers in my ear when he's done. He pats me on the back, and then a hand takes mine to lead me forward. It must be Celine's, because it is much too small to belong to any of the men.

It's more than a little disorienting to walk along the valley floor without the use of my sight, and I stumble often. Celine is patient, though, and doesn't ridicule me or force me to go faster than I'm able. After what I judge to be a quarter of an hour, we begin to climb again. We pass through pockets of cooler air that I interpret as heavy tree cover and finally enter a space in which the air stays cool and our footsteps echo. There are whispers of other voices here, but they seem to come from far off. Through the bottom of my blindfold I see nothing but dark rock.

Caves. We're in a cave system, I think to myself, remembering how Pax had speculated they might take refuge in old mining tunnels.

I'm pushed forward so I almost fall on my hands and knees, and then a rolling, scraping sound comes from behind me, and all goes silent.

I freeze, unsure what to do. Have I been left alone? No, there's the scrape of a shoe against rock.

"Hello?" I say.

"Pria. Are you okay?"

"Yes. Do you think we can . . ."

Pax's hands touch my face, his fingers featherlight as he lifts the blindfold. "Better?" he asks.

Truthfully, it's not much. Wherever we are, it's pitch black, and I understand why Pax had to feel his way up my face to find the blindfold. It's cold in here, too, and I shiver and wrap my arms around my chest. "Cave?"

"Yes." He trails his hand down my arm and takes my hand. I don't object —it keeps me from feeling like I'm floating in a dark void. "They've locked us in."

"What do you think they intend to do with us?" I ask.

"They said they were taking us to see a man named Luther."

"And that he'll have us killed if he doesn't believe our story." I can't keep the accusatory tone out of my voice. Pax said these people would welcome us.

"He won't kill us," Pax says.

"How can you know that?"

"Because we *are* telling the truth." He tugs on my hand, leading me forward until he stops again. "There's the wall," he says. "Let's walk the perimeter."

The cave in which they've imprisoned us is small. I take only twenty steps to complete the circle. There's an indented section that must be where they rolled a rock across the entrance. There is no furniture of any sort.

We eventually sit with our backs against one of the uneven walls. It's uncomfortable, and the floor is damp, but my legs are tired, and I'm glad for the reprieve.

"Pax," I say.

"Hmm?"

"I believe you—about how the UWO treats people of genetic inferiority, at least."

His hand twitches in mine, but he doesn't say anything.

"I don't mean inferiority. I mean . . . difference." I lean my head back against the wall and stare blindly toward the unseen ceiling. "I don't think these people would be so secretive if they were accepted by society, or even if they were only persecuted. I believe you that they—you—would be killed if the Enforcers got a hold of you."

"Thank you," he says. "For believing me."

"I'm still working on believing some of the rest, you know."

"I know. It will come."

"What makes you so sure?"

"Because I'm telling you the truth."

In the dark, I imagine something Pax said to me on the first day we met. *"What is truth?"* Caustic. Sneering. Angry. That version of Pax clashes in my mind with this version of him, and I'm not sure which to believe. Whatever he pretends, though, Pax is not as secure as he wants me to believe he is.

The scraping, rolling sound comes again, and a crack of light appears. It's dim, but I cringe away from it, my eyes slow to adjust. When I'm able to look up, I see Celine and one of her brothers, I can't tell which, silhouetted in the entranceway, their features lit by a glowing lantern her brother holds aloft.

Celine looks at our hands, which are still twined together, and she narrows her eyes. I pull my hand out of Pax's and stand.

"Luther is ready to see you now," she says. "Both of you."

Her brother lifts his lip in a sneer, and the light catches on a glint of gold in his ear. Etienne.

K.B. Hoyle

Chapter 29

They don't blindfold us again, but Celine keeps an Air-5—probably mine—trained on us from behind as Etienne leads us through twisted tunnels. They wouldn't have needed to blindfold us before, either, because I'm hopelessly lost within a few minutes.

There are cords strung up along the ceilings and attached to old wooden beams that frame the tunnels through which we're walking. Every hundred feet or so, there's a lantern like the one Etienne holds hung up near the ceiling. The light given off is pale blue, almost white, and without warmth.

A murmur of voices grows louder the farther we walk, and we emerge into a cavernous area with a suddenness that takes my breath away. Here there are enough lanterns hung that it's positively bright, and people are gathered in clumps around a strange mix of furniture and artifacts. Some of it is wooden and ancient-looking, and some of it looks like it could have been taken directly from the halls of Sanctuary.

I don't have much time for observation as we're marched straight across, people parting before Etienne as though used to his surly attitude. As we pass, silence falls among everyone but the children, who are running and playing everywhere. I gape and turn a circle, watching as a small girl with flowing blond hair shrieks with laughter and chases a skinny boy practically over my toes.

"Oy, watch it, you!" Celine shouts after them, but she doesn't sound angry.

"Children," I say. "There are *children* here! Where . . . where do you get them?"

Celine snorts. "We *make* them."

"What do you mean?" I trip over a protrusion of rock on the floor, and Celine rights me by my elbow. "You have implantation facilities here?"

Celine blinks and raises an eyebrow. "You know, for someone whose job it is to reproduce for humanity, you're shockingly naïve."

And then we're across the cavern and ducking through another corridor that ends in a wooden door, fitted to the shape of the tunnel and shut tight across it.

Etienne knocks twice. "Luther. We have them," he says in a loud voice.

The door is opened from within, and we're chivied inside. The space is well lit by the lanterns along the walls and several candles that drip wax into artful puddles at the bases of their bronze holders. All the furniture is old-fashioned, the sort of which I've only seen pictures of in the Agoge. Wooden shelves filled with colorful, thin, rectangular things stand around the walls, and there is a broad wooden table in the center of the space surrounded by several mismatched chairs. A curtain with a pattern of blue, white, and black stripes hanging on one side of the room might cover a second exit, but I can't tell for sure.

Sitting at the table with papers spread out before him is one of three of the men who were in the room already before we entered. I cannot gauge his age, but his olive-skinned face is lined and craggy, and he has gray hair sprinkled throughout his otherwise dark brown curls, with one prominent patch of white hair about an inch square above his right ear. His eyes, though, are green and deep set and sharp—the eyes of a young man. His forearms are well muscled. Although I'm more accustomed to seeing youth than seeing age, this man looks to me like a young man who has aged prematurely. His features spark a hint of familiarity, too, and I glance at Brant, who is standing beside the door. Brant had called Luther his brother, and the resemblance between the two is undeniable. The man at the table is Luther.

It was Brant who opened the door, and he scowls at us now as he closes it tight. At the table standing beside Luther is a stoop-shouldered man with light hair and pale blue eyes. He has hair covering his chin and jaw, and he wears a wire-and-glass contraption over his eyes. He straightens when we draw near, and he's actually quite tall when he isn't stooping over.

Pax's bags—our bags—are lying against the far wall. They are closed and look intact, but I'm sure they've been searched.

"Don't worry," Luther says, waving a hand toward the packs. "It's all there. We don't have the same qualms about private property as the UWO does. You can have them back if we decide you're telling us the truth." He looks at the stoop-shouldered man with the light hair. "Thank you, Bishop. You can go."

The man called Bishop nods and gathers a bundle of papers from the tabletop into a haphazard armful. He walks around toward us, and I can't help staring at him as baldly as he's staring at me. He's thin and a little twitchy, but his expression is kind and curious. He adjusts the wire and glass contraption farther up his nose, and then he ducks out of the room. I watch him until the door closes in his wake.

Luther rises from his chair. He comes around the table and stands with his arms akimbo, looking us up and down. His shirt is loose with the sleeves rolled up to his elbows, and a wrap of some sort is looped around his neck. He wears heavy boots like Pax and pants with many pockets. Now that he's closer, I can see that his muscular forearms are laced with scars, and he wears a gold band around one of his middle fingers.

After several long moments, he lifts my wrist and runs his thumb over my microchip scar. Then he adjusts his hand so his fingers press lightly to the spot where my pulse beats. He steps close enough that I can see the lines in his green irises. I flush red and look down, but he says, "No. Look at me. This is a test. I'm not going to hurt you."

I steel myself and meet his gaze. I try to be unflinching, but I've never even stared Pax in the eyes like this, and certainly not from so close.

"Good. Just like that," Luther says. "Now, Elan tells me you're a Breeder and a deserter. Is that true?"

"Yes."

"Why?"

I look over my shoulder at Celine and her brother. "I already told th—"

"Look at me," Luther says, and I do. "I know you've already told them, and they've already told me, but I want to hear it from you."

I lick my lips. "I was growing unhappy there, and I didn't know why. I still don't know why, but I . . ." I look at Pax, then back at Luther before he can chide me. "Pax came to me and told me I was different. So, when Mother tried to kill me, I guess I was already prepared to trust Pax. He said he could get me out, and he did."

"Why was Mother going to kill you?"

"In her order, she said it was because I was asking too many questions."

"And what have you learned about the world since you left Sanctuary?"

I blink. How can I possibly answer that question? Does he know what my life was like in Sanctuary before I fled with Pax? I answer the only way I can. "A lot of things."

"Do you believe all of them?"

"Some." I lift my chin. "But not all."

Luther nods slowly then releases my wrist and steps back. "Sit." He points to a chair at the table.

"Well?" Celine says.

"That's it?" Etienne says. "Aren't you going to ask her anything else?"

Luther walks to Pax and says, without looking at either of them, "She's telling the truth about Sanctuary and why she left. That's all I need to know from her for now. The rest will come later."

"Doesn't mean she'll help us," Celine says.

"No. No it doesn't. But it's a start."

To my surprise, Celine sits down beside me, giving me a sharp but not unkind look. "What do you think?" she whispers as Luther positions himself with Pax like he did with me—fingers to wrist, faces close.

"About what?" I ask.

"Luther." She jerks her head toward him. "His little trick." She lowers her light-brown gaze on me and waits, her eyes bright.

I narrow my eyes and watch as Luther asks Pax a few introductory questions. He's studying his eyes, no, his pupils, and watching his breathing.

"He's able to detect when people are lying," I whisper, turning back to Celine. "And he's good at it."

"The best," she says. "That's one reason why we elected him our leader."

"Elected?"

"Yeah, you know, democratically. We took a vote, and he was chosen. Of course, that was years ago—I was only a kid—but he's been reelected every couple of years since. He's a good leader. Too bad about his wife, though."

"His wife?" I'm doing an awful lot of repeating what Celine says, but she keeps saying things that make no sense to me.

"Yeah . . . oh, that's right, you wouldn't know anything about marriage, what with it being against the law and all. Sorry, I was born and raised out here, so your ways are almost as foreign to me as mine must be to you." She scratches the side of her nose. "Um, yeah, but his wife died giving birth to his son."

"She died giving *birth*?"

"Okay, you've got to stop repeating me like that, princess."

I'm too shocked to insist she use my name. "How could she die giving birth?"

Celine's expression turns sour, and she leans away from me. "We don't always have the best medical supplies available to us, seeing as how we're criminals and all." Her tone is icy, and she suddenly looks at me as though I've been wheedling information out of her. She pushes away from the table, and I stare after her, my mouth open.

Celine retreats to the door and leans against it, studying her nails, so I turn my attention to Pax and the others, who have been listening to Luther's interrogation. He's taking much longer with Pax than he did with me, and I'm struck with uncertainty. What if Pax has been lying to me this whole time? I thought I was good at reading signs of truthfulness, but I've never applied the tactics Luther is applying now. If Pax is a liar, am I brave enough to remain here alone, without him? Would I want to?

Pax has finished telling Luther everything he's ever told me—about how he was born, how he was saved by the mysterious med tech, about the attack on his Nest and the death of his friend several years later, and about how he's been on his own since then. Finally he gets to the story of when he met Mack, and Luther leans in, watching him even more closely.

"He told me I'd never find you on my own—that I would have to let you find me. And for you to reveal yourselves to me, I'd have to bring a Breeder."

"How many years ago did you say this was?"

I don't for one second believe Luther forgot that piece of information. I think he's testing Pax to see if his story changes.

But Pax says, "Five years ago," appearing unconcerned but harboring that energy beneath the surface I'm used to seeing by now.

"I've never heard of Mack before," Etienne says. "None of us have. He's got to be lying."

Luther drops Pax's wrist and gestures for him to take a seat at the table beside me. I'm sitting on a frayed cushion, but the seat Pax takes is rigid and wooden. He sits with his spine straight against the back of the chair.

"I can detect no lie in his story," Luther says as he sits across from us. "Although . . ." He taps his fingers against his lips. "Mack." He leans back and studies the wall behind us, his hand over his mouth. "*Mack.*"

"What are you thinking, Luther?" Brant asks.

"I wonder if he's talking about Mackenzie. I never heard him go by Mack, but it could be possible."

"But Mackenzie—"

Breeder

Luther holds up a hand, and Brant falls silent.

"Describe him, this Mack."

Pax says, "Tall, over six feet at least. He had dark brown hair when I saw him, but it could have been dyed since he was in the Commune. Brown eyes."

"That could be practically anyone," Etienne says.

"He had a birthmark on his right cheek about the size of an acorn. He covered it, but I could see the outline beneath the makeup."

Luther raises his eyebrows at the others in the room. "The man's name was Mackenzie," he says. "I don't know why he gave you a shortened version. Perhaps he didn't trust you fully, but it was him."

"Was?"

"Mackenzie is, as far as we know, dead."

Pax frowns and leans forward. "When?"

"Around the time you're describing. We'd sent him to the Denver Commune to do a job. He was one of our best topsiders—someone who can pass for a citizen of the UWO—except for that birthmark, of course. But he was able to keep it covered pretty well. I'm surprised you noticed it." Luther leans forward and rests his elbows on the table so he and Pax look like they're facing off. "Mackenzie disappeared off the map. It wasn't the first time it happened to one of ours, and it won't be the last. You know how easy it is to get caught."

"Yes."

"Which makes your story that much more remarkable. I've heard of people living on the fringes of UWO control out in the middle of nowhere, but I've never met anyone like you, who's spent so much time in and around the Communes without getting caught. I've never met anyone who's infiltrated Sanctuary."

"I'm careful," Pax says.

"No one's that careful."

Pax steeples his fingers and matches Luther's stance. "I'm lucky."

Luther narrows his eyes, and Etienne and Celine make simultaneous sounds of disbelief.

"Was I lying?" Pax asks. "You tell me."

Luther gives his head a slow shake. "No. You weren't lying, and you aren't now."

Pax leans back.

"One could almost say you're *too* transparent."

"Well, what else would you expect?" Pax spreads his arms. "I've been trying to find you for five years. I'm rather eager to stay."

"See, that's part of the problem," Luther says. "I'm afraid your information is a little out of date. For some years now—between when you met Mackenzie and now—we've been actively trying to extract people from the Communes. It's . . . funny . . . that we should never hear of you, or vice versa. The people of Denver have gotten restless, and we've been feeding the flames. Have you never noticed?"

I watch Pax's expression carefully. Other than a flutter of his eyelashes, he doesn't seem surprised.

"I don't have much opportunity to talk with people," he says. "It's always been too dangerous. After I stole the Enforcer uniform, I had to lay low for a long time so I wouldn't be caught. I've been focusing on extracting a Breeder, after all."

Extracting a Breeder. The way he says it makes me sound like a means to an end, which is what I've always been to Pax, if I'm honest with myself.

Luther holds out his hand, and Pax lays his wrist in Luther's palm. Luther presses his fingertips to Pax's pulse again.

"How did you get in and out of Sanctuary all this time?"

"I didn't," Pax says. "I lived there."

I gasp, and then I laugh out loud. "No. No way."

Etienne snorts, and Celine lets out a chuckle.

Luther raises an eyebrow and looks at me, then back at Pax.

"There are no men allowed in Sanctuary," I say. "There's no way he could have lived there undetected."

"Explain," Luther says to Pax, who hasn't looked at me, despite my outburst.

"I only had to get in once," Pax says. "I did that about a year ago. Enforcers *do* enter Sanctuary, but only through the basement, where the labs are located."

I'm about to laugh again, but Luther looks so grave I swallow it.

"But how did you remain undetected for so long?" Luther says.

"There are places beneath Sanctuary where few people ever go. It wasn't that difficult to find a place to hide, and I was careful about covering my tracks. The medical staff turns over every two weeks, so even if I was spotted by one of them, they had no reason to think I wasn't one of the sanctioned Enforcers who work from time to time in the labs. By the time they could have grown suspicious, they were moving on. From the basement of Sanctuary, I learned the passcodes, hacked the system, and gathered information on all the Breeders I could."

"All to get here."

"All to get here."

"Simple," Luther says.

Pax narrows his eyes. "Hardly."

"And what do you plan on doing now that you're here?" Luther asks with a tilt of his head.

Pax leans in. "I plan on helping you execute your revolution."

Chapter 30

Luther releases Pax's wrist and sits back. He looks at his brother, Brant, who has made a noise of protest.

"There is no revolution," Brant says. "Not yet. And if it can be avoided —"

"Brant, not right now."

"I still don't trust them," Etienne says. "I don't care what Luther says."

"Don't be an ass," Celine says.

Luther sighs. "They are telling the truth. You know what we're doing here. Would you have me refuse them asylum?"

"We have to put it to the vote," Brant says.

"Yes, of course." Luther looks at Celine. "Will you call the assembly?"

"Sure thing." Celine pushes herself off the wall and yanks open the door.

"You'll have to stay here until the voters are assembled, I'm afraid," Luther says. He twists the gold band on his finger.

Pax nods, but I look around, unsettled. Etienne glares at me, and Brant chews his thumbnail and watches his brother. I cross my legs, then uncross them and tap my fingers together.

"I'm sorry," I finally say, "but you didn't seem surprised when Pax mentioned the labs in the basement of Sanctuary. I'm not even sure I believe they exist, but . . ."

Luther just watches me as I glance at Pax, then I close my eyes. "I can't believe some of the things you've told me, Pax. I just can't." I press my fingers to the crease between my eyes. My hands are shaking.

"We've suspected for some time now that labs exist in Sanctuary," Luther says. "But what that information means to us will remain private until the assembly has voted on whether or not to let you stay."

"This is my life," I say. "I want to know."

"Listen to the little Breeder talking about *her life*," Etienne says. "Didn't think any of you soulless cogs in the CRP ever had an original thought."

"Etienne," Luther says sharply. "There are just as many victims in the Controlled Repopulation Program as anyplace else. You will keep your thoughts to yourself, or you will leave."

Pax stands suddenly. "Bathroom?" he asks.

Luther gestures toward the curtain to my right. "Through there. Etienne, go with him."

Etienne purses his lips and comes forward with his weapon trained on Pax. Together, they go through the curtain, leaving me alone with Luther and Brant.

After several moments of silence, during which Luther arranges the remaining papers on his table and Brant stares at me, I twist my finger into the hair at my right ear. Realizing this makes me look nervous, I drop my hand and let out a careful sigh. Pax and Etienne seem to be taking too much time getting back.

Luther must have the same thought, because he looks toward the curtain and frowns. "Brant, go check on what's taking them so long."

Brant goes without challenge, and then it's just Luther and me.

He looks at me and says, "You should know, not everyone will trust you. It will be easier for most to trust your friend—"

"Because of how he looks," I say. "And because of what I am."

Luther nods. "Prejudice was not introduced by the UWO, although sometimes we like to pretend that was the case. It lives in the heart of every human being, and for those here who have been oppressed by the UWO, it can be especially difficult to accept defectors into our midst. But I won't let any harm come to you if it's in my power to prevent it, and neither, I suspect, will Pax."

"I don't see why Pax should care what happens to me now," I say. "I've gotten him what he wants."

Luther opens his mouth to respond, but there's a scuffling sound beyond the curtain, and he rises. A moment later, Brant and Etienne come through, dragging Pax between them.

I jump to my feet, my mouth open. Pax's eye is swollen shut and purple, and a trickle of blood runs down his face from a crack beside his eyebrow.

Etienne, likewise, has a dark spot on his jaw, and his nose is bleeding.

"What happened?" Luther asks as they deposit Pax into a chair.

Pax straightens and glares at Etienne through his good eye. I instinctively reach for him but then pull my hand back. I don't know how he would interpret comfort from me. Are we friends? We're comrades, at least, allies in a common cause. But now that we're here, I'm not sure.

Etienne locks his jaw and wipes at the blood flowing from his nose. I notice he doesn't have his gun anymore—Brant is carrying it.

Brant rolls his eyes and takes Luther's arm. He draws him to the far side of the room and whispers in his ear. Luther looks at me, then Pax, and then Etienne. He takes the weapon from Brant and carries it back to Etienne. I think he's about to hand it back, but instead he punches Etienne across the face with his other hand.

Etienne reels back with a grunt.

With an expression of disgust, Luther shoves the gun at Etienne's hands, but before he releases it, he says, "Say anything like that ever again, and I'll expel you from Asylum."

Etienne gives Luther a poisonous glare. "Not without a vote. You really think the people will choose them over me?"

"If you maintain your position, they deserve to be chosen over you. But it doesn't have to be that way. Go clear your head and think about what's important. You're not welcome at the assembly."

Without another word, Etienne brushes past Luther and out the door. He makes to slam it behind him, but Celine is on her way in and catches it with her hand, looking after her brother in bewilderment. She raises her eyebrows and comes into the room. "I would ask what his problem is, but I think I know."

"I should have had Henri go with Pax instead," Luther mutters.

Brant snorts, and Luther hands Pax a piece of cloth, which Pax presses to his bleeding head.

"It's unwise to solve problems that way with Etienne," Luther says. "There's a reason he's one of our best soldiers. You're not likely to come out on the winning end."

"I wasn't trying to win," Pax says. "I was trying to make a point."

"I would like to say you succeeded, but it's more likely you just made him angrier. Next time, come straight to me."

Pax lowers the rag and turns it to the clean side. "I thought you said you would expel him if there's a next time."

Luther looks at me and says carefully, "There could be more than just

Etienne."

I'm so confused, I don't even know how to begin formulating my questions. I cross my arms and blink, my mouth hanging open.

Luther turns to Celine. "Is everyone gathered?"

"Yep. Assembled and waiting on you."

Luther nods and gestures for Pax to rise. As he makes to lead the way out of the room, he pauses next to me and says in a low voice, "Stay close to Celine. You can trust her."

I can trust her to what, protect me? Is that what Pax was doing? Looks more like he was protecting himself, unless he threw the first punch.

But I can't ask these questions, because Celine is taking my elbow and leading me through the doorway into the corridor beyond.

Chapter 31

The cavernous space, which had seemed so chaotic when they brought us through it earlier, is now organized. A large crowd of people stands before a raised platform. It's difficult to judge the size of the crowd because I've never seen this many people gathered in one place before. There were about forty Breeders at Sanctuary, and this crowd looks to be at least four or five times that size. Children and teenagers stand in a clump off to one side, and in front of the crowd of adults, a much smaller group of elderly people sits in a row of chairs.

"Making almost all the voters stand keeps the debates from going on for too long," Celine whispers in my ear.

I don't really understand what she means by *voters* and *debates*, but I nod as though I do.

"Intimidated?" she asks.

"Yes."

She grins. "Good. That's the point."

We mount the stage. It's not high, but it makes for an awkward step up, and I have to put my hand down on the wooden planks to give myself a push. The crowd, which was mumbling in low tones, falls silent, and I feel every eye on me. I blush and look down. Never in all my life have I experienced this much personal attention.

On opposite corners of the stage are two large, empty jars, and I can't figure out what they might be for.

Henri hops up on stage beside Luther and Brant and gives me a smile and a wink. I cringe at first, thinking he's Etienne, but then I realize almost at once that Etienne would not be that friendly to me.

At Henri's heels is a black, white, and brown dog with a droopy face and lolling tongue. I'm reminded of our dog at Sanctuary, Flora, and I wonder if this dog is a clone, too. The dog barks once, then sits and wags its tail.

"That's Arrow," Celine says. "He's Henri's."

Pax shifts so he's standing closer to me, and I lean toward him without meaning to. I don't want to look uncertain, but I feel uncertain, and Pax is the most familiar presence I can claim here among these strange people who look at me with a mixture of curiosity and hostility.

And the colors of their skin . . . it's enough to make me dizzy with the implications. A couple of people are as dark as Celine and her brothers, but many more people have lighter skin and a variety of hair colors. There's even a woman with hair the color of the setting sun and skin as pale as milk. Even though she stands in the middle of the crowd, I can see she's as freckled as Pax is, and her eyes are brilliant green.

"What happened to him?" shouts a man from the crowd before Luther can begin.

"There was a disagreement," Luther says. "But it's been sorted out now. I want to make it clear these people are among us because they seek asylum, and that means they're under our protection."

"But this is different," another man says. "These aren't ones we brought in from the Commune. Celine says that one's a Breeder and that they found us. How can we trust them?"

"I've tested them," Luther says, "and found them to be telling the truth. That should be enough for everyone here. We're not determining their viability. We're determining whether or not they may join us. I cast my vote already." He pulls a stone from his pocket and tosses it into one of the jars where it makes a hollow *clink* and rattles before it settles. "I wanted you to see them before the debate. Their names are Pax and Pria."

"She doesn't look so perfect to me," a woman yells.

"What makes her better than the rest of us?" another asks.

Luther raises his hands, palms out. "We all know the system is flawed! That's not what we're here to discuss today, and comments like that can be saved until after they've left the assembly."

"What, concerned about their feelings?" asks a man standing just behind the line of elders.

"Yes, I am," Luther says simply. "We operate here under the premise that all humans are created equal, and that holds true regardless of nationality, gender, constitution, age, or"—he glances at me—"background. I ask you all to remember yourselves and what you believe if you want to be a part of this assembly and, more importantly, if you want to remain in Asylum."

Most of the people in the crowd nod at Luther's short speech, but the man who spoke up a moment before asks, "Are you threatening us?"

"No. I'm stating a reality. If you don't hold to these beliefs, then you belong better with the UWO."

The man juts out his chin and clamps his mouth shut, but judging by the dark look he shoots me, he's far from converted to Luther's way of thinking. There are some others in the crowd giving me similar looks, but the majority seem friendly enough. Luther's statements about equality ring through my head, awakening feelings I can't quite categorize, and I find I want to stick around and hear more of what he has to say.

But Luther gestures, and Celine nudges me toward the edge.

"That's all?" I whisper.

"That's it. Open discussion can't really be had while you're standing here," she says.

"Where are we going?"

"To a safe place until the debate is over. It's not real comfortable to listen to people discussing your fate," she says. "Oh, hang on." Celine takes a stone from her own pocket and lobs it into the same jar into which Luther tossed his. It's a long throw, and she hits it with precision. "Now we can go."

Pax steps down and offers a hand to me, which I ignore as I hop off the stage. A buzz of conversation starts up again behind us, and I hear a third stone hit the jar. Then Henri appears at my elbow.

"I've made my decision already, too," he says. "Come on. We can go to my shop."

"Are you sure that's the best place?" Celine says.

"What place better?" He grins. "Might as well make them useful while they're here, for however long that ends up being."

"Yeah, sure," Celine says. "Just keep your dog from slobbering all over me."

The dog, Arrow, sniffs at me and Pax and then leads the way with his long tail held high.

Chapter 32

Henri's shop is a large cave, well lit by the usual hanging lanterns and also by a roaring fire in a manmade stone structure. There are a variety of implements scattered throughout and heaps of larger items lying in what looks like no discernible order. There are a couple of exits off the cave, several chairs, and an old fraying couch on which Arrow immediately stretches out.

"Sorry about the heat," Henri says. "I was working on forging some new bullets. Etienne's orders."

"Wouldn't want to disappoint Etienne," Celine says. She perches on the arm of the couch and picks at her nails. Arrow waves his tail and lifts his head to lick at her, but she shoves his head away.

I stand in uncertainty, my gaze traveling around the space until Henri says, "Take a seat. It could be a while."

I take the closest chair, but Pax says, "I'll stand," and begins a circuit of the cave.

Henri puts out the fire, but instead of using the large basin of water beside it, he lowers a hood over it until the light diminishes to the unnatural whiteness from the lanterns.

"That's better," Henri says. He mops his forehead with a rag he wears around his neck.

"How did you get this?" Pax asks, his voice sharp, and I look over, as do Henri and Celine.

Pax pulls back a cloth from what can only be our motorcycle, and I frown and lean forward.

Henri just smiles and says, "Well, we were watching you for days, obviously. When you ditched the bike, it was too good to pass up."

"It's mine," Pax says. "You stole it."

"Nah, I didn't steal it. I just brought it here to make some improvements on it. Usually this sort of thing is Celine's department, but she's busy with the larger vehicles, and I wanted to tinker with it a bit. Here, look." Henri goes to Pax and flings the cloth the rest of the way off. Shiny, flat, black panels have been attached to the back and sides. "I outfitted it with solar panels. It needed something, because it was almost out of gas. This way, both systems can work together, and you'll get a lot more life out of it."

Pax runs his hand over the panels, his expression unreadable, especially from where I'm sitting, because I can only see his swollen eye.

"You can have the bike back, whatever they decide," Henri says.

"I thought you said they'd kill us if they decide we're lying," Pax says.

"We already know you're not lying. Luther'd have figured it out if you were, and despite a few people—"

"And Etienne," Celine says.

Henri nods once. "Despite what people like my brother might think, everyone else trusts Luther when it comes to his lie detector test. They're just trying to decide, based on your story, whether or not to let you stay."

"They'll let you stay." Celine looks up from her nails. "The vote always goes with Luther."

"Not always."

"Okay, what I mean is the vote always goes with Luther when it comes to refugees. We're all big softies at heart. Besides"—she squints at me—"we need her, remember?"

"Need me for what?"

Celine purses her lips, and Henri shifts from one foot to the other.

"Whatever it is," Pax says, "it had better be something she's given a choice on. I won't see her used."

"You're one to talk," Celine mutters.

But Henri says, "Of course! We're all about personal liberties here. It's just probably better if we don't say anything about it until the vote is cast."

"If you hurt her—"

"Come on, man, do we strike you that way?"

"Some of you do, yes."

Henri's gaze travels to Pax's black eye. "Don't judge us all by one man," he says. "Etienne is angrier than most, but he won't hurt her."

Pax draws his mouth into a thin line and turns back to his motorcycle.

"Hmm," Celine says, so quietly I almost don't catch it.

I turn questioning eyes on her.

"Nothing," she says.

"Is it finished?" Pax asks, returning to the topic of the bike.

"Almost. Give me another week or so with it, and I'll have it purring like a kitten."

Pax nods, and Henri drops the cloth over the bike.

"Why didn't you approach us sooner, if you'd been watching us for days?" I ask.

"We had to figure you out first," Celine says. "You've been in our territory almost since you entered the mountains. We don't have surveillance as good as the UWO's, obviously, but we have our ways of knowing when people are snooping around who shouldn't be. If you'd been dressed as an Enforcer out here by yourself," she says, nodding at me, "we would have had to kill you on the spot. A lot of people's lives rely on our remaining in secret. But you have this guy with you." She gestures at Pax. "He clearly wasn't a citizen of the UWO, and neither was he your prisoner. Some of us came and went—like Henri brought your bike here and started working on it before coming back to meet the rest of us—but we never lost sight of you. When you blundered onto the Golems, we had no choice but to intervene."

"Ah, we needed to take those three out anyhow." Henri kicks back on the couch, and Arrow leaps off. The dog shakes himself, his long ears and jowls flopping, and then comes over to me.

I look into his doleful eyes as he lays his chin on my knee and drools all over it. "Is he a clone?" I ask.

"What, Arrow? Nah, he's natural born."

"We do have some clone livestock, though," Celine says. "We skim them off the UWO flocks."

"Isn't that dangerous?" Pax asks.

I turn to look at him. "Because it's stealing?"

"No, because all cloned animals are embedded with a computer uplink to the UWO main databases."

"To communicate with their brains, yeah. But why would that be dangerous for them?" I wave a hand toward Celine and Henri.

"The uplink doesn't just communicate with their brains—it transmits their location, not unlike the microchips they put in us." He touches his wrist.

"We have a guy who can detach the uplink part from the main computer. So they're still given necessary brainwave instructions via the computer that remains in their head, but the UWO can't track them anymore," Henri says. Then he winces. "Eh . . . I probably shouldn't have told you that."

I'm too intrigued to care about what he should or should not be saying. I lean forward over Arrow's head. "Why bother with the risk, though? They can't reproduce, so their flocks aren't sustainable. Wouldn't it make more sense to just cultivate some natural-born flocks?"

Henri frowns and twists his mouth to the side. He rubs the top of his bald head and glances at Celine.

"You might as well just tell them," Celine says. "You've already spilled that we steal cloned animals and know how to disengage their uplink."

Henri sighs. "Yeah, all right. Okay, well . . . we're keeping tabs on the UWO's progress, with cloning, you know?"

"Why?" Pax asks.

"Isn't it obvious?" Celine asks. "It's only a matter of time until they perfect it on the animals, and when that happens, humans will be next."

I laugh. "No. No way. Why bother? They have the Controlled Repopulation Program. What purpose could there be for cloning humans?"

Celine's mouth stretches into a smile as she raises her eyebrows. Then she doubles over with laughter. "So . . . naïve . . ." she says through her fit.

Henri flicks her. "Knock it off."

"I'm sorry, it's just that . . ." Celine closes her eyes and leans back, resting one arm over her forehead. "I just can't believe you can really be so naïve."

I feel a flicker of anger, the first I've really felt since these people have captured us. "If I'm naïve," I say, "it's only because I haven't had the opportunity to learn. So teach me."

Celine sobers and narrows her eyes at me, lowering her arm. "Well, you're supposed to be a genius, right? Otherwise you wouldn't be a Breeder. So *you* figure it out. Impress me." She folds her arms over her chest.

Henri says, "Celine—"

"No. I want to see if she can do it. I want to see if there's any validity at all to the Program."

I suppress my natural skepticism toward everything I've learned in the last several days. I can't work through this based on my preconceptions, anyhow. I have to just take the facts as presented. To distract myself from Celine's open stare, I stroke Arrow's head and listen to the *thump thump*

thump of his wagging tail hitting the floor.

Human cloning. If these rebels' version of the world is the true version, how would human cloning fit into the UWO's objectives? I think back to the last dispatch from the Oligarch I listened to. All dispatches say basically the same thing in different ways. I close my eyes and think.

"The Controlled Repopulation Program exists to ensure the propagation of a more perfect humanity. Controlled human breeding will result in a human population that never exceeds 300,000 people, the greatest number we can ensure will not be a burden on the environment. Controlled human breeding will result in a human population free from disease and malady, and therefore free from poverty, famine, and war. We strive to perfect humanity's genes so that one day we will exist in a utopia where every human knows his or her place with no painful divisions among us. Through the noble work of the Program, the disease of self-determination will be expunged from our midst, and the only higher powers necessary will be those whose jobs are to oil the machinery of the Program's inner workings. On their shoulders lie the greatest burdens, and you in the Program can rest in the knowledge that your task is laid out before you, planned down to the very last detail to ensure the greatest probability of producing viable contributions to society."

Viable contributions. I wrinkle my forehead. That word, *viable*, reminds me of something Pax told me about in our first hours together. *"Everybody is microchipped at birth, and then that microchip is replaced with a new one at age one, once tertiary viability is determined."* I hadn't had a chance to ask him what that meant, and I really don't want to think too deeply on it, but Celine has challenged me to figure out why the UWO would clone humans, and the answer might lie there.

"What's she doing?"

Celine's whisper cuts through my inner dialogue.

"She's thinking," Henri says.

"No," Pax says. "She's remembering."

I open my eyes. "Both," I say.

Pax is standing next to my chair with his arms crossed, looking down at me.

"I'm trying to synthesize what I know with what I've been told with what I've experienced to come up with the answer to your challenge."

Henri smiles broadly and puts his hands behind his head. "This is fun."

Celine raises an eyebrow. "So?"

I straighten and let my hand drop from Arrow's head. "Pax told me there are levels of human viability that are determined at different ages." I watch her expression carefully, because the implications of the stages of viability are so horrifying that I'm still not sure I believe Pax, but Celine just nods.

"If that's the case," I whisper. Then I clear my throat and continue in a stronger voice. "If that's the case, then the Controlled Repopulation Program is not as close to perfecting human genetics as they'd like us to believe."

Celine taps the side of her nose twice and points at me. I frown, not understanding the gesture.

"But I believe the UWO hasn't lied about their goals, which means that a lot of time and resources are poured into an imperfect program. But if they could meet their goals for humanity another way, by circumventing the Program entirely, and come up with better results, then that might be justification for human cloning."

Celine raises another eyebrow, waiting.

"In their eyes, at least," I add.

"Not bad," she says. "That's what we think, too, more or less."

"It makes sense, really," Henri says, his hands still behind his head and his long legs stretched out before him. "They plan on releasing the animal clones into the environment, reproductive blocks removed, of course, once they've perfected that process. It follows that they would do the same with human clones but in a more controlled manner. No more levels of viability to deal with, because you could create in a test tube exactly the sort of human you want."

"I'm sorry, but . . . wouldn't that be a good thing?" I ask. I look at Pax. He told me viability determined whether or not a child was allowed to live. "It would mean no more killing of Contributions, right?" I shudder. I can't help it. "That is the implication of determining viability. The Program kills the Contri—the babies—if they don't measure up?" It sounds so ludicrous, I almost can't say it, and I don't meet his eyes.

But it's Henri who answers. "Whatever we suspect goes on in Sanctuary, replacing the human population with human clones is not the answer. It would mean no more babies born at *all.* Why bother with Breeding when you can just create?"

"It would spell death for all of us," Celine says. "We'd be in even more danger than we are already. Once they figure out how to do that, they'll kill all those born in the Program first, and then they'll hunt the rest of us down."

I don't protest, though every molecule in me wants to. These people believe such horrible things, but every time I disagree, I'm proven wrong. Instead I say, "But they can't replace *everyone* with clones."

"Oh, of course not," Celine says. "Just the worker bees. The ones in charge, the bigwigs in the UWO and whatnot, they'll get to stay natural born, just like they are now."

"Wait . . . *what*?"

She gives a humorless laugh. "Something else you didn't know, huh? Yeah, they get to have their own children and marriage and families and the whole lot. Every now and then they adopt a genetically superior kid from the Program to infuse their lines with new, *better*, blood, but aside from that, they're the only ones who lead remotely normal lives."

I press my hands to the sides of my head to steady myself. "But you really think they would kill everyone else?"

"Of course. We've managed to stay hidden for years, and there are probably thousands of Nests all over the world—people who hid themselves away during the Devastations and never resurfaced—but if they're able to produce waves of cloned soldiers to hunt us down, they will. Eventually."

"Not to mention the soul issue," Henri says. "Would clones have souls? Would they have that spark that sets humanity apart from animals? And should humans really be engineering other humans? There's something intrinsically wrong about all of it."

I shove my fists into my stomach and jump to my feet, feeling sick. I pace to the far side of the room and place my hand on the covered motorcycle, my back to the others.

"It's a lot to process," I whisper. "You say they're trying to clone humans, but it just seems . . . impossible." I turn to Pax. "And *you* say they're killing humans—infants—who don't measure up to their standards."

"Why should the age of the person matter?" Celine asks. "They'd kill us if they had a chance. If they'd kill an adult for being genetically different, why not a baby?"

"Because it's just . . . just . . . barbaric! And I can't think about the possibility that I was part of something like that!"

Henri leans forward. "Hey, you didn't know."

"But I believed their ideology."

"And you don't now?" Celine's question sounds like a challenge.

"How can I?" I gesture toward Pax, then toward her and her brother. "You people aren't inferior—you're amazing. And even if you were inferior, it's not like I'd want you dead."

Celine and Henri exchange a look, then Celine smiles at Pax. "Nice choice," she says. She doesn't sound sarcastic. "There aren't many in her position who would feel that way."

Pax nods.

"But what do you people want me to do about all this?" I ask.

"There'll be time to discuss that at a later date," Luther says as he enters the cave. "Good news—they voted almost unanimously to let you stay." He's carrying our bags, which he tosses toward Pax. They land on the floor at his feet with a *thwump*. "Good news for you two, too," he says to Celine and Henri, "since apparently you decided to divulge some of our secrets."

Celine studies her nails while Henri coughs and sits forward, dropping his arms.

"For now," Luther says, turning back to Pax and me, "let's just worry about getting you settled in."

Chapter 33

"We'll get you sorted out in separate living quarters, unless"—Luther raises an eyebrow at us—"you prefer to be together."

It's on the tip of my tongue to say being together would be fine, as I've grown used to sleeping with Pax nearby, when Pax says, "It's not like that, but I would like to stay close, for obvious reasons." He touches his swollen eye. "One living space, two beds, if that's possible."

I frown. What does Pax mean, "it's not like that"?

Luther looks at me, and I shrug and say, "Sure." There's too much going through my mind right now to care about sleeping arrangements, even though I'm bone tired.

"That can be arranged," Luther says. "Celine, why don't you come along?"

"Sure," Celine says and hops down from the arm of the couch.

Henri makes to rise and come as well, but Luther says, "No. I need you to focus on that netting. I'll send Elan along to help you out, but the south quadrant is getting pretty ratty after the last storm. Do you think you can get it repaired by nightfall?"

"Shouldn't be a problem," Henri says, shrugging his broad shoulders. "Send Elan, and Etienne, too. He could use the heavy labor."

Luther raises an eyebrow. "True words."

"Tell Elan he still owes me a rematch," Celine says over her shoulder as we exit through one of the curtains. "I'm holding him to it."

I cast a look back at Henri as he waves in dismissal. His warm brown eyes rest on me for a moment longer than everyone else, and then the door closes between us and we're in a narrow, poorly lit, winding tunnel.

"You'll need to learn your way around," Luther says from the front of the line. "It can be something of a maze here. But that's worked to our advantage, security-wise. Unlike many of the other Nests, we haven't had to move around much. We've been in this location about eight years."

"Yep," Celine says. "I was eleven when we came here. It was the year my mom died."

We come out of the tunnel into a wider area with many branchings. Luther chooses one on the left, and we follow. We pass many closed doorways, some covered only with curtains, but others with custom wooden doors fitted to odd-shaped entrances. There are boxes with numbers outside many of them, and shoes laid out neatly before others. I hear the sounds of laughter and soft conversation, and finally we come all the way to the end of the hall.

"We opened up these tunnels to be living quarters. These couple at the end are empty." He pats the wooden door beside which he's standing and nods at the one opposite. "There used to be a family that lived down here, but . . . they're gone now."

I shoot a questioning glance at Celine, but she's digging the toe of her boot into the ground.

"If you want to be together, you can take this one here." He removes a key from his pocket and opens the door to reveal a black, cave-like space. He gropes around the inside of the wall next to the door, and then lights flicker on. Luther steps inside and puts his hands on his hips. "They were a married couple, so there's a double bed"—he points to a surprisingly normal-looking mattress and frame on the far wall—"but behind the partition there is where their daughter slept. That bed might be a little tight for Pax, but you should fit just fine, Pria. There are even clothes left in the bureau. They were pretty well liked around here, so nobody wanted to go through their stuff after . . ." He winces and looks at Celine.

"After they died," I say. I'm guessing, but it's the obvious guess.

"Yeah."

"What about the room across the hall?" Pax asks.

"I thought Celine could move over there to keep you guys company."

Celine looks up and frowns at Luther. "Why?"

"It would be wise, given the unique circumstances, for them to have someone around they can trust."

"But I already have a living space."

"I know. Let's make it a temporary move, until things settle down a bit."

Celine raises her chin, her nostrils flaring. "Fine." She stomps out of the room and disappears down the hall.

Luther turns back to us. "I'll let you two get settled in. Oh, there's, uh, no bathroom facilities in the separate living quarters. It just wasn't feasible. But if you head back the way we came, through the fifth curtain on the left are the bathrooms. Laundry facilities are there, too. Food is served in the mess hall morning, noon, and night, if you decide not to eat in your apartment. And here. This will get you started until we can line up jobs for you." He digs into his pocket and pulls out a handful of gold coins that he dumps on a rickety wooden table near the door.

I pick one up and turn it over. "Is this real gold?"

"Yeah," he says with a grin. "That's one thing we've got plenty of." He looks around and raises his arms. "I think that's about it for now. Generators turn off at ten to conserve power. Come and see me in the morning about job assignments."

"Thank you," Pax says.

Luther smiles at us one more time and sets the key on the table by the door with the coins. "If you take that to Henri tomorrow, he'll make a copy of it so you can both have one." Then he backs out of the room and pulls the door closed after him.

The silence that falls between us is heavy with uncertainty. I'm shaking from exhaustion and hunger and the shock of everything that has happened today.

Pax goes to the table and fingers the gold coins. Then he walks around to the other furniture. There's a single chest of drawers, another larger table with three chairs around it, and a mirror hanging above a shelving unit that holds a few pots and pans and a box with metal coils and a dangling cord. The large bed stands on the far wall and is covered with two pillows and colorful blankets. The space is divided by a wood-framed partition that doesn't quite reach the ceiling, which is about eight feet tall. Between the wooden frame is stretched a piece of thin yellow fabric with a pattern of pink flowers on it.

While Pax explores the rest of the room, I go around the partition to look at the smaller bed. Luther said the couple's daughter slept here. The bed is narrow and short, probably just long enough for me but definitely too short for Pax. It is covered with a faded blue blanket with yellow stripes. There is a small table beside the bed on which sits a mirror and a tiny latched box. I sit on the bed and sink in further than I would have thought. The mattress is soft and a little prickly—stuffed with something I can't identify—and it rests on a simple wooden frame.

I pick up the mirror and hold it up to my face. The light is poor, as there's only one lantern humming far up near the ceiling, so my reflection is shadowy, but I can still see myself. My hair is a dark wavy cap on my head. My dark eyes are large and vulnerable-looking, framed with dark lashes, and my complexion is pale with strain. I don't think I look very beautiful, and certainly not genetically perfect—not after all the beautiful diversity I've seen today.

I catch a shadow out of the corner of my eye and jerk around, startled, my cheeks coloring. I put the mirror down on the table with a snap.

Pax stands in the gap between the end of the partition and the cave wall, holding a neat stack of fabric. He looks at the mirror I just put down and then back to me. "I found these in the drawers," he says, handing me the stack. "I think they might fit you."

"Thank you." I take the clothes and hold them in my lap. I'm about to move them aside and stand when Pax sits beside me on the bed. The cushion depresses even more, and I have to lean away from him so I don't slide down to meet him.

"What do you think?" he asks in a low voice. "Do you want to stay here?"

"Here in this room, or here in Asylum?"

"Here in Asylum."

"You're giving me an option now?"

"You've always had an option."

He's watching me, and I stare back, alternately looking into his uninjured pale eye and studying his face. We're close enough that, even in the dim light, I can see the paler freckles that mark his eyelids and his lip line. I wonder how long his left eye will be swollen shut. He still fascinates me after all this time, and the pull I feel to look at him is confusing, but at times compelling, like now.

"The whole point of searching the wilderness was to find these people," I say. "Where else would we go?"

"But do you think you'll be happy here?"

"I don't know what it is to be happy, Pax."

He reaches over and takes my hand. I twitch, my first instinct as usual being to pull away, but his warm grasp is actually comforting, so I let my fingers rest in his.

"I barely remember what it is to be happy either," he says, "but I know I was happy once long ago. I think we have a chance of making a real life here."

"We." I twist my lips to the side. "You know, you don't have to feel obligated to do what I do, to go where I go, now that we're here."

"I don't feel obligated." He lowers his gaze so all I can see of his good eye is golden lashes feathered over his cheekbone. "We're friends, aren't we?"

Friends. I blink. "Yes, I suppose we are."

Pax smiles then, the most real, non-grim smile I've ever seen him give. It's a little lopsided, and it shows his snaggletooth, but it's genuine. The effect makes his swollen eye pucker, but it also sends out lines around his good eye and turns him from intimidating to amiable. I smile back.

He releases my hand and looks around, scratching the back of his neck. "I'm sorry you have to take the smaller bed. If you want to sleep in the bigger one, I'll—"

"Don't be ridiculous. This bed fits me. And the privacy back here might be nice."

"Oh, right."

A knock sounds on our door. "Let me get it," Pax says.

He rises, and I stand behind him, wondering who could be coming to visit.

Pax tenses and then opens the door, but it's only Celine.

"I thought you might be hungry," she says, shoving a couple of loaves of bread and two metal canisters at us. "And there's this." She pulls the Air-5 from the satchel she wears and hands it to me. "Now that you're one of us, it didn't seem right for me to keep it."

I take it back. "Thank you."

"It's almost out of charge, but if you plug this into the power strip over there, you can charge it here in your room." She hands me a contraption that has metal tines on one side and an oblong rod on the other. "I took it from the armory."

"Thanks . . . again."

We all three stare at each other, and then Celine scratches her nose and clears her throat. "I'm sorry about stomping off earlier." She gives a short laugh. "It's just that I don't like change."

"It's okay," I say. "I can understand that."

"Yeah, I suppose you can. Listen, in the morning, come get me before you head back to see Luther. I can introduce you around as we go."

"Sure."

"Okay, well, good night, then."

"Good night."

Pax closes the door and locks it. "I'll plug that in for you," he says, taking my Air-5. I follow him so I can watch how he plugs the tines into the power strip on the floor and then slides the rod into the base of the handle of the weapon. "If it lights up green, like so, you know it's charging," he says.

I nod. "Here." I hand him one of the loaves and metal canisters.

He opens the canister and takes a sniff. "Just water."

I take a tentative sip and find the water to have a metallic taste, but I'm so thirsty I can't afford to be picky. The water may not taste great, but the bread is warm and fragrant and makes my mouth water. I sink into one of the chairs at the table with a sigh and eat, ignoring Pax as he putters around the shelves, munching and sipping sporadically as he goes.

When I'm finished, I stare at the wall, feeling my body digest and relishing the sensation of having a full belly and solid furniture beneath me. Around this time, in Sanctuary, I would be doing evening meditation, and I let myself slip into the familiar relaxed state, my eyes half-closing.

Pax pulls me out of it when he says, "I'm going to change my clothes and go to bed. You might want to go behind the partition if you don't want to see."

"Oh, yes of course." I rise, feeling as though my body weighs twenty pounds more than usual. I wave a hand in dismissal, too tired to do anything else, and walk around to the far side of the room.

Behind the partition, I can see just the faintest outline of Pax's shadow as he shrugs out of his clothes and pulls on what are presumably a new shirt and pants he found in the dresser. He sighs, and I hear the bed creak as he collapses on top of the mattress.

I rouse myself enough to look through the clothing Pax found for me. There is a long-sleeved nightgown that, when I put it on, comes down only to my knees and is a little short in the wrists, but it's baggy otherwise and soft, so I leave it on. I wonder how old the girl was who'd owned these clothes. I toss my dirty clothes in a pile on the floor, feeling a thrill of rebellion. That never would have been allowed at Sanctuary. I turn down the blankets on the bed and am about to lie down when I realize the lights are still blazing in the room.

Tiptoeing around the partition, I reach for the light switch and glance toward Pax. He's already asleep, lying half on his stomach with one shoulder drawn up higher than the other and one leg bent. His face is hidden beneath his arm, and I creep forward and look down at him, drawn by some magnetic force that also twists a knot in my stomach. His clothes are way too big on him—the shirt is practically draped like a blanket over his shoulders with a wide neckline revealing the ridge of his collarbone, and he's cinched the pants so tight they bunch at his waist. He's barefoot, and it's the first time I've seen his feet outside of boots. It strikes me as funny for some reason, and a smile tugs at my lips.

I shiver. It's chilly in this underground room, and Pax has fallen asleep on top of his blankets. I hesitate, biting my lip, and then go back into my part of the room. Three blankets are layered on my bed, and I peel off the top one with care.

Back at Pax's side, I lay the blanket over him as slowly as I can, holding my breath and hoping he doesn't wake up. He snorts once and mumbles something, then rolls so he's completely on his stomach, and I jump back, dropping the blanket. I dart back to the light switch and switch it off with trembling fingers.

Absolute darkness falls, tempered only by a sliver of light that filters in through the bottom of the door. I creep back to my bed by feeling my way along the wall. When I lie down, I fall asleep almost immediately.

Chapter 34

I wake from a dreamless sleep to a warm hand on my face. Blinking and frowning, I try to focus on the form sitting on the side of my bed.

"Sorry," Pax says, removing his hand. "You were hard to wake up. You must have been exhausted."

"Hmm," I say, my voice gravelly. "First time in a bed since we left Sanctuary."

"I'm sorry to have to wake you, but it's getting late, and you were shivering." He touches my face again. "Why did you give me one of your blankets?"

I pull myself into a sitting position, which is difficult with Pax pinning down one side of the blankets. I lean against the wall and am immediately regretful, as the rock proves to be ice cold and bumpy. I lean forward instead, hunching over my knees. "You would have been cold," I say. "You fell asleep on top of your blankets."

He raises an eyebrow. "You were watching me sleep?"

"No!" Blood rushes to my face. "I just noticed when I went to turn the lights off."

There's a loud knock, and Celine shouts through the door, "You guys up yet?"

Pax stands, leaving my third blanket folded at my feet. He goes to open the door, and I pull the blanket up, unfolding it and tucking it under my chin. I really am freezing. But I also feel content this morning. I didn't have any nightmares or phantom pains.

"Sheesh, we need to find you some other clothes," Celine says, traipsing into the room and looking Pax up and down. "Although it's not a bad look, up here." She taps his exposed collarbone and winks at him.

I frown, and the knot returns to my stomach.

"Anyhow, I told Luther I'd check on your progress. He was expecting you hours ago."

"We had a long day yesterday," Pax says.

"Mm-hmm, and slept about twelve hours after it." She looks around the partition at me. "Hey, princess, want me to show you the bathrooms?"

"It's Pria," I say through gritted teeth.

"Yeah, yeah." Celine waves her hand dismissively. "So you want me to or what?"

"Um . . . yeah, okay."

"Come on, then. We don't have all morning." She looks at Pax. "You'd better just put on the clothes you arrived in, if you don't want to draw too much attention to yourself. Then meet us at the end of the hall, and I'll show you where to get some food."

Pax nods, and I grab a pair of pants and shirt at random from the pile Pax gave me the night before and follow Celine out into the corridor.

Five doorways down on the right, Celine draws back a curtain to let me look inside a room that is surprisingly spacious. The ceiling soars up twenty feet, and I can hear rushing and splashing water. The floor is constructed of wooden slats, and in the gaps between the slats, the sound of water hitting rock echoes up out of the darkness. I can't tell how far down the natural cave floor is.

"When they were opening up these tunnels, they happened upon this cavern, and it became our main bathroom facility."

A wooden wall with five doors stretches across the space in front of us, and large basins line the walls.

Celine pulls the first door open, and the splashing sound gets louder. "This is the shower, but I warn you, it's cold."

A small waterfall pours out over a lip above and splashes onto the slatted wooden floor.

"The water falls naturally from there," Celine shouts over the noise. "You wash in it, and it drains through these slats to the underground stream below. The other four doors open to toilet stalls, so the waste drops into the stream and is carried away. Not into our water supply, obviously. Brilliant, huh?"

I'm hugging my chest, trying to stop my shivering from the cold, wet air.

It's a little disconcerting to see running water beneath my feet, and I wonder how they suspended the floor over the underground stream, but I nod. There's a bench by the door inside the shower room, and I set my new clothes on it.

Celine reaches beside the door and pulls up a wooden tab until it sticks. "When you come in to shower, pull this tab here. It lets everyone know the shower is occupied and locks the door. But we all have to share in this wing, so . . . quick showers, yeah?"

I can't imagine wanting to linger in the coldness anyway. "Yeah."

"Soap's in that bucket there." She points. "All right, I'll leave you to it. I'll be right outside the door."

Celine closes the door, and I turn a circle. As quickly as I can, I strip naked and approach the water. I test it with my hand, and it's every bit as frigid as the mist promised it would be. I take a deep breath and plunge in, crying out despite myself and tensing all my muscles. I'm shivering so violently I can barely get the soap out of the bucket and scrub myself down, but somehow I manage it. And then I'm dancing free and drying myself on my nightshirt because I don't have a towel. In minutes, I'm dressed in the new clothes, which fit in the waist but are short in the arms and legs again. After a quick visit to the toilet, I join Celine outside the bathroom.

She grins. "Cold, isn't it? You look positively purple. I'd like to say you get used to it, but you don't really. You forgot your boots," she says, shoving them at me. "Pax brought them by."

I don't have any socks, so I push my damp feet into the boots bare. "What do I do with this?" I hold up my wet nightshirt.

"Hang it here." Celine takes it and hangs it over one of several hooks by the door. "It's too damp in the bathroom and too closed up in many of the rooms for clothes to dry properly, so a lot of people use these hooks. Don't worry, we don't usually have to worry about people stealing stuff."

A door opens and closes down the hall, and a girl with long, light brown hair comes toward us. She stares at me the whole way before ducking into the bathroom.

Celine snorts. "It's not you—well, it is. I mean, most of us have never seen a Breeder before. But it always takes people a while to warm up to new recruits."

"Uh-huh." I twist my fingers and look down the hall. I'm eager to rejoin Pax, if for no other reason than the sense of normalcy he offers. Funny that he should have become my new normal.

Celine catches the direction of my gaze and jerks her head down the hall.

"You two are pretty tight, huh?"

"Tight? I don't know what that—"

"Close, like, you've been through a lot together. I mean, why else would you let him share your living quarters?"

I start walking down the hall as I think about how to answer Celine. Her tone suggests that she's digging for more information than just a basic answer to her question, but I can't imagine what it is she's looking for. "I haven't known him for very long," I say. "But he's the closest thing I've had to a real friend since, well, ever." I shoot her a furtive glance. "I don't make friends easily. And he did rescue me from Sanctuary when they were going to kill me, and he's helped me survive in the wilderness. I don't know. I guess you could say we're 'tight.' "

"But you don't really know any different, do you?" Celine says. "I've heard they don't allow any men in those Breeding facilities. At least, not where you lot can make contact with them. Had you really never seen a man before you met him?"

I shake my head. "Not since the Agoge, where some of my instructors were men. But that was five years ago, and I was just a kid. Being around men now is . . . different, somehow."

Celine laughs, showing straight white teeth. "You don't say."

We come out into the main branching, and Pax is leaning against a wall with his arms crossed over his chest and his expression watchful. He straightens and looks me up and down.

"Don't worry, she's in one piece," Celine says. I don't know why.

Pax's black eye doesn't look any better today. If anything, it looks worse, and the spot where the skin broke open is scabbed over and angry-looking. I feel a twinge looking at it and wonder again why he and Etienne fought and what it had to do with me.

"This way," Celine says, standing back to allow a few people to brush by us. They shoot us curious glances, but no more. She leads us down a broad tunnel back to the main cavern in which the assembly gathered last night. I smell food, and she directs us toward another cave off the main one where the smell gets stronger.

There is a collection of tables in this space—the same eclectic mix as I noticed in the cavern the day before—everything from stainless steel to plastic to warped wood.

"Where do you get all this furniture?" I ask, brushing my hand along the top of a table that could have come straight out of the dining room at Sanctuary.

"We don't steal it, if that's what you mean. Some of it we make, others are cast-offs we find in the trash heaps or in dilapidated old settlements."

A long counter at the end of the cave stands before a partitioned-off space behind which steam and smoke rises. Celine hops up and slides over the counter. "Hang on. I'll be right back." She goes behind the partition, and I hear her talking with someone.

I raise my eyebrows at Pax, but he just shrugs.

Celine emerges a few minutes later with two bowls filled with a beige substance and drizzled with golden honey. "The cook was packing up the breakfast stuff, but I managed to scrape some oatmeal out of the bottom of the pot for you. It won't be the greatest meal you've ever had, but it's something to fill your stomachs, at least. Oh, and food is free here for everyone, as long as you come at meal times. We don't like to see people go hungry. If you want extras, at odd times of the day or because you want a luxury item, you need to pay for it at the store. I'll show you where that is later. You can buy clothes there, too. All sorts of stuff."

Pax and I each take a bowl and sit to eat as Celine disappears again. The oatmeal has a slightly burnt taste to it and sticks to the roof of my mouth, but the honey helps. Celine comes back and plops two handled cups down in front of us. The liquid within is dark, almost black, and steaming. It gives off a strong nutty scent.

"What is this?" I peer at it and lean my face into the steam.

"Coffee," Celine says. For some reason, she's smiling.

I take a sip and cough and sputter as my mouth is filled with bitterness that only remotely resembles the intriguing smell. "That's disgusting." I wipe my mouth and push the cup away.

Celine throws back her head and laughs. "It's an acquired taste. I figured they'd never given it to you in Sanctuary, but it's the lifeblood of most of us here. Henri drinks it by the bucketful."

Pax takes a drink and makes a face. "It's . . . interesting."

"What, you've never had it before? That surprises me. It's not like you've lived in Sanctuary your whole life."

Pax takes another drink and then pushes his cup away. "Yeah, I'll pass on that."

Elan enters the dining cave and walks toward us.

Celine looks up and straightens in her seat. "Hey."

"Hey. Luther's wondering what's taking so long."

"I'm introducing them to coffee."

"Ah yes. The nectar of life. And how do you find it?"

I wrinkle my nose, and Elan laughs.

"Okay, well, hurry up and finish. Luther's got other business to get to today, but he wants to be sure to get you your work assignments first." He turns to leave.

"What are you up to today?" Celine asks, drawing him back. She sounds brighter, friendlier, and I squint at her. There is high color in her cheeks, barely visible under the dark tone of her skin.

"Helping your brother with the netting over the south quadrant. He couldn't get it finished before dark last night."

"How about a rematch tonight, after work?"

Elan smiles. "Sure. My place?"

"Got it."

"Bring our new friends." Elan nods at us and then leaves.

Chapter 35

A little boy with dark hair is playing on the floor beneath the table, and his sputtering imitations of vehicular sounds distract me from Luther, who's trying to explain the job system here in Asylum.

"Everybody who's able contributes here, but you'll be paid for your work. A small allowance is taken out of your wages to pay the cooks and the people who hunt and cultivate the crops, because everyone partakes of the food. Other than that, your wages are your own. So what's it going to be? What would you like to do?" Luther leans forward, his hands on the table, and stares us down.

What would I *like* to do? I have no idea. Like and dislike never played a part in determining usefulness to society in the UWO.

Pax says, "You know what I want to do."

"Yes, and there will be time to talk about that. I'm interested in the information you have, obviously, but before I let you into my inner circle, I need to know you're trustworthy and a hard worker. It's not easy being a Free Patriot in this world. People die. Are you prepared to be one of them?"

Pax folds his arms. "If it means fighting for the freedom to exist and determine my own fate, then yes. I am prepared to die for that."

"What about me?" I ask. "You want me to do something for you, don't you?"

A small hand touches my ankle, and I jump. I look down to see the little boy smiling up at me. He must be Luther's son, the child his wife died bearing. He's a little copy of Luther.

"Yes," Luther says. "But I won't ask it of you now. You need time to adjust to this new life, and the people here need time to adjust to you. Then, when you're ready, we'll discuss how you can help us and whether or not you'll be willing."

There's a part of me that wants to scream, *Just get it over with!* but the greater part of me appreciates Luther's sensitivity.

"So, in the meantime, what would you two like to do?"

Pax doesn't answer, but I blurt out, "I want to learn how to read. Is there something I can do that will teach me that?"

Luther comes around the table and wrinkles his brow. "You don't know how to read?"

"It wasn't considered necessary for a Breeder."

He nods and strokes his chin. "Bishop's been complaining about his workload lately. I bet I could convince him to take on a paid apprentice, and he'd be happy to teach you how to read. He loves showing off what he knows."

I nod, picturing Bishop—the bent man with the blond hair and the contraption on his face who was in Luther's office yesterday.

"You want to put her alone with a man?" Pax asks, his tone guarded.

"Bishop is not one we need to worry about," Luther says. "He's married to his work. I doubt he's ever thought about anyone in a"—he looks sidelong at me—"romantic way."

Romantic. Another word I don't know. "If I can learn from him, then I'll be happy to work with him."

"Good."

"He can take on two apprentices, then," Pax says.

"No, I'm afraid that would be a bit much for him. He's used to solitude. But I can put you close by. Henri's shop is just around the corner from Bishop's archives, and he can always use a hand. What do you say? You'll get to learn some practical skills, and you might even have some knowledge to offer him."

"He does have my motorcycle." Pax looks at me. "All right. I'll work with Henri, and Pria will work with Bishop. When do we start?"

"Right away. Celine will show you the way."

Chapter 36

"You didn't bring your Air-5, did you?" Celine asks me over her shoulder as she leads us back to Henri's shop. I'm busy counting turns and not paying attention.

"Huh?"

"Your Air-5. It's still in the room, right?"

"Oh, yes. I didn't think about it."

"I did," says Pax, and he grabs my wrist from behind and presses the cool weapon into my palm. "Always carry it, Pria. Promise me that."

I freeze, and Pax collides with me. I round on him. "You said we were supposed to be safe here, and that if we weren't, you'd get me out."

Celine stops and looks back at us, her expression impatient.

"Then last night you ask me if you think I'll be happy here. But now you want me to carry a weapon with me everywhere I go, and I *know* this has something to do with all of this, too." I point at his swollen eye. "So which is it—are we safe here, or not? Is this someplace I can be happy? I don't know, but I'm tired of people talking circles around me!"

It's Celine who answers, in a low and patient voice. "It *is* safe here, Pria. As safe as the world gets these days, at least. But because of what you are, there will always be some people who resent you, and there's a possibility some of them might try to hurt you to prove a point."

"Is that what happened between you and Etienne?" I ask Pax. "Did he hurt you to prove a point?"

"No. He threatened to hurt *you* to prove a point. I let him know what I

Breeder

would do to him if he did."

I blink, surprised by the depth of conviction in his voice.

"You wanna leave?" Celine asks. "Fine. But the world out there is a lot uglier than the world in here. If the Enforcers catch you, they'll torture you for information about us, and then they'll kill you. At least here you know you can be yourself, and you have friends."

"Do I have friends?"

"Of course. Stick with me, stick with Pax, and Henri and Elan and some others I'll introduce you to. Whatever you do, don't wind up alone in a room with Etienne or any of his friends. There are things they could do to you that would, in their words, make you useless to the Breeding program."

I don't know exactly what sorts of things she's talking about, but her tone makes me shiver.

"What's going on out here?" says a familiar voice from down the hall. I jump, thinking it's Etienne, but it's clear that it's Henri when he appears a moment later, wiping his hands on a rag and grinning in a bemused sort of way.

"I've just been telling her not to wind up alone with Etienne."

"Oh . . . yeah." Henri's grin fades. "Don't worry, I'll get him sorted out. There's nothing like a big brother to knock some sense into someone's head."

Celine snorts. "Big brother by two minutes."

Henri spreads his arms. "And proud of it. Are you guys coming to see me?"

"Yeah, I have a helper for you." Celine nudges Pax forward. "He wants to work with his hands, so Luther assigned him to you."

I notice she didn't say anything about his wanting to stay close to me.

"Uh, sure. I guess that's fine." Henri looks over his shoulder. "I've just been working on your bike, actually."

We all start walking again, down the corridor toward Henri's shop.

"What's Pria's job assignment?"

"She's going to apprentice with Bishop."

Henri laughs. "Really? Oh man, I'd die of boredom. Have fun with that."

"She wants to learn how to read," Celine says.

"You don't know how to read?" Henri stops and looks at me. "For real?"

I sigh. "As I keep telling people, there wasn't any reason for me to know how."

Henri gives an incredulous laugh and continues walking. "Man, the UWO really knows how to keep people under their thumb." He holds open the curtain at his shop, and we go through. "So how did you learn anything in the Agoge?"

"It was all done orally," I say. "And there were some pictures and videos."

Henri shakes his head. "You really must be a genius. I could never learn that way."

"Pria, let's get on to Bishop. Pax," Celine says, turning to him, "Bishop's archives are around the corner at the end of the hall. There's a big wooden door with a knocker on it."

"Got it," Pax says.

I give a short wave and exit with Celine.

"Have fun," Henri calls after me.

"What am I supposed to do with this thing?" I ask, holding up my Air-5. "I don't have my holster."

"Once you're in Bishop's archives, you can put it down. Just don't forget it's there." Celine lifts the heavy knocker on the door and lets it fall with a loud *clang*.

"Who is it?" Bishop calls from deep within the chamber.

"Celine!" she calls back. "I have a new recruit for you—the Breeder."

I frown. "Why not just give him my name?"

"Because he has a natural curiosity. He might not remember your name yet, but he'll have been itching to talk with you about the Program," she whispers.

The door flies open. The wire and glass contraption is shoved up on Bishop's head, and he squints at me a moment before pulling it down to rest on the bridge of his nose. "Hello," he says, peering through it.

"Hello," I say.

"Come in, please."

"Thank you." I follow him into a space that opens up above me to staggering heights. My mouth drops open as I turn a circle and then bump into a table because I'm staring up instead of watching where I'm going. The ceiling tapers to a crease probably a hundred feet above me, and colorful rock formations hang and jut out from spots along the walls. Wooden shelving units and ladders stuffed full with stacks of papers, colorful rectangles, and bits of things I can't even begin to identify dot the curving walls, and wires are draped all along them with multiple lanterns lighting the space. The sight of it all, without even knowing what it is, floods me with longing and possibility. "This . . . this . . ."

"Pretty amazing, isn't it? It's all natural formations," Bishop says, gesturing at the ceiling. "We broke through to this cavern in the construction, and I claimed it as my own. I do, after all, need a lot of storage space. Even better, it's dry." He holds up his hand. "Feel the breeze?"

"There's ventilation in here?"

"Somewhere far above. It's not enough to let in light, but it keeps my manuscripts dry."

"I didn't realize we were so deep inside the mountain," I say, looking all the way up again.

"It rises above us at this point."

Celine shifts and clears her throat. "Right, well, listen. Luther's assigning Pria to you as your apprentice—your *paid* apprentice. Can you handle that?"

"Oh!" Bishop squints at me. "Are you interested in my work?"

"Truthfully, I don't have any idea what you do. But I said I wanted to learn how to read, so they brought me to you."

"Excellent. They brought you to the right place."

I smile, feeling my shoulders relax, gratified he didn't act shocked or look at me like I'm stupid.

"Since you've hit it off, I'm going to go." Celine backs toward the door. "Don't leave until Henri or I come to get you, yeah?"

"What about lunch?"

"I have food here," Bishop says.

I shrug. "Okay then."

"Where should we start?" Bishop asks as soon as Celine closes the door. He throws a lock on it and turns to me, his expression open, friendly, and eager. "You can put that down, by the way."

I place my Air-5 on the table and then spread my arms. "What *is* all this? What do you do here?"

Bishop straightens his curved back and beams. "This is all the written history I've managed to collect predating the Great Devastations, and a few artifacts as well, of course."

"Predating? I thought everything was destroyed during the devastations."

"Ah." Bishop's expression saddens, and he clasps his hands together. "That's what you've been taught, isn't it." He paces to the closest shelf and puts his hand on a stack of colorful rectangles. "Everybody believes there were only three Great Devastations, but I maintain there was a fourth—a Great Destruction of information—although I cannot prove it. There was, of course, the Famine, the Pandemic, and the Incursion. But somewhere in there, I believe the Unified World Order decided information was dangerous. All literature, all histories, all religious texts, all art and music, everything that could be considered culturally divisive, suddenly *poof*"—he makes a starburst with his hand—"disappeared."

"You believe the UWO did that?" I wrinkle my nose. "They said everything was destroyed during the fighting and chaos. It makes sense, doesn't it?"

"But, my dear girl, it happened so fast. What they won't have taught you is that one day the electronic and net databases were full of information, and the next day they were wiped clean. That does not happen via war."

"What about the physical copies of things?"

"Destroyed, systematically. I don't have proof, as I've said, but everything I've ever found intact has been hidden away in a cache of some sort, or half-burned in an otherwise untouched building. The marks are everywhere that it was all hunted down, sought after, targeted." Bishop shakes his head. "Not everyone believes me, but I've no doubt."

"Was nothing kept?"

"Some things were, yes, and who knows what exactly the UWO elite have preserved on their databases or in their estates. I do know they kept that which they deemed of value to unify and preserve their vision for humanity. Although those bits have often been rewritten to promote their own agenda. But all the access to that information is highly restricted."

"Is it such a bad thing to want to unify humanity?" I ask, almost in a whisper. "It does make for peace, doesn't it?"

"Unity and peace that come at the cost of freedom, of conscience, of liberty, of individual identity . . ." Bishop's voice has risen to almost a shout. He slams his fist down on a table, and I jump back. "That is not true unity or true peace at all. It is slavery. Do you know what slavery is?"

"No."

"I will teach you."

I put my trembling fingers to my forehead. "But if it happened the way you think it did, it's not an official Devastation, your Great Destruction. And if—*if*—the UWO carried it out, who's to say it wasn't done with good intentions? The world was falling apart! Something had to be done. Can we fault them for trying?"

Bishop stands back and purses his lips. "This might be a bit too much for you to start with, considering where you've come from. Let's leave off with it for now. But sometime, sometime soon, I'll ask Luther to take you to see the Golems. Then you can tell me what you think about the UWO's good intentions. Now, if you're to be of any use to me as an apprentice, you must learn to read, and learn to read fast. Here." Bishop brings a large piece of paper to the table and lays it out in front of me. "This is the English alphabet, upper and lowercase letters matched up. You do at least recognize the letters, do you not?"

"Yes, I recognize them, although I don't know the sounds they make."

"You must be adept at oral learning, yes?"

I draw my shoulders back. "Very."

"Good. Pay attention as I give you the various sounds, and then work them through over and over while I finish the archiving I'm working on."

In about a half hour's time, Bishop has taught me the most common sounds of each letter in the alphabet and left me to finish his work. It's another hour or more before he comes back to check on me. "Now, tell me what sound each letter makes."

I go through each one flawlessly, and Bishop steps back a pace and gives me a frank stare. "Amazing," he says. "I've heard your kind are geniuses, but I've never seen it at work before. It would have taken a child a week to learn that by heart, and most adults several weeks. Your memory must be astounding."

I blush and look down. "I was bred this way. I can't really take credit for it."

"Yes you can. Of course you can!" He adjusts the contraption on his face up his nose.

"What is that?" I ask, my curiosity finally overwhelming me. "On your face."

"This?" Bishop taps the contraption, and I nod. "Glasses," he says. "Or spectacles, whichever you'd like to call them. They correct my vision, which is regrettably poor."

"Oh, I remember learning about people like you, but I was taught—" I snap my mouth shut and sigh. "I really need to stop being surprised by you, by all of you, here. I've already seen so many different types of people I was taught no longer existed. It's just . . . a lot to wrap my mind around."

"I imagine you're having an easier time adjusting than you think."

"Why do you say that?"

"How long since you left Sanctuary again?" he asks.

"Almost two and half weeks."

"So for two and a half weeks you've been without their drugs. Your mind should be clearer now than it's ever been, better able to take in new experiences and process them, better able to process emotions. More likely to believe radical claims—that is, more likely to believe the truth. Have you not felt that way since you left?"

"I . . ." My knees feel weak, and I pull myself onto a high bench at the table. "My mind has been sharper, yes, but not just since I left Sanctuary." I close my eyes and think back. Most things that happened before my procedure are a blur in my mind, but ever since I woke up from that procedure to find that my Carry had failed, my memories are crystal clear. "It's been several months," I say.

Bishop tilts his head and scrutinizes me. "You must have begun fighting the drugs. It happens for some people. Some of those who've joined us grew discontent that way."

I lean forward over my knees. "But the Program only drugged us when we were Carrying to help the process go as smoothly as possible. I wasn't drugged when I wasn't Carrying."

Bishop chuckles. "That's what you think, but you're wrong. Everyone who lives in the UWO is drugged." He brings down a couple of covered bowls and canisters of water. He shakes a canister so I can hear the water sloshing around inside and then sets it before me. "I don't know how they conveyed the drugs to you in Sanctuary, but in the Commune it's in the water supply. It's something of a mild sedative—it keeps people pliable, controls mood, basically makes people into perfect worker bees. Most people have no idea what life is like without it."

"Why do they do that to everyone?" I'm barely able to keep my mouth from hanging agape.

"Because humans are naturally independent." He makes a fist. "We're fighters, Pria. We fight for what we believe to be right, and we *know* we are meant to be free. That's why some people can't be fully harnessed by the drug. But the UWO can't brook any individual liberty, any threat to their authority. You know this, for I'm sure it's what you've been taught. Serve the UWO because the state supersedes all else, yes?"

"Yes," I whisper.

"I'm telling you now that's wrong. The state does not supersede any person's right to life, liberty, and pursuit of happiness." He gives me a wry smile and leans back in his chair. "I read that in one of my manuscripts. It's a nice turn of phrase, isn't it?"

"Sure."

"But it's true, Pria. Can you not feel the truth in it?"

I can. And it fills me with warmth.

Chapter 37

By the end of the day, Bishop has taught me to combine several of the letter sounds into words. He's also taught me to write my name and given me the piece of paper on which I practiced to take back to my living space. In return, I helped him organize the colorful rectangles—which he calls books —on one of the shelves into double stacks to make room for new information he says he needs to archive.

It's Henri who comes to collect me at the end of the day, with Pax on his heels. I clutch the piece of paper to my chest and follow the two men out of Bishop's archives.

"What's that?" Henri asks, looking down at my hands. He tugs on the exposed corner of the paper, and I let him take it.

"I wrote my name," I say with a swell of pride. I'm beaming.

"Eh . . . so you did! Nice job. Very pretty." He gives me a broad smile as he hands it back. "Your friend made something today, too, so it's new experiences all around."

"Yeah?" I look over my shoulder at Pax, who's following just behind me. He's been quiet since they picked me up, and even now he takes a moment to answer. He's turning something over and over in his hand.

"I made a copy of our key," he says, his voice low. Then he takes my hand and presses it to my palm. "I actually made it. Henri showed me how to use the machine, and I . . . I . . ."

Henri clears his throat, and Pax releases my hand, leaving the small metal key in my grasp.

"You two are something else," Henri says with a laugh. He turns down an unfamiliar corridor, and we follow it into what is clearly another living space wing. This corridor winds and twists up and down, and there's a lot more noise. "I live down here with Etienne, and Celine—well, not right now, obviously, but usually she lives this way, too. A lot of us single folk share this space because none of the families want to put up with us."

Single folk. I've no idea what he means by that. Don't they pride themselves on being members of families here?

We squeeze past a couple entwined together, and I stop and stare. The two have their arms around each other and are pressed very close, and their mouths are touching. And moving.

"Come on." Henri tugs my arm. "It's not polite to stare."

"Don't they know anything about *germs*?" I hiss. "Why would they . . . what possible reason do they have to . . ."

Henri's looking at me with an expression of barely concealed mirth. "You really don't know?" He stops before a wooden door and knocks twice.

I frown and think back. *"We make them,"* Celine said yesterday when I asked about the children. They taught us in the Agoge that long ago people had reproduced just like the animals, but that the act was barbaric, unsanitary, unpredictable, and savage. They never told us *how* it had been done, but I know it had to have something to do with human biology.

The door pops open, and Celine says, "You made it! Finally. Come in!"

Henri's shoulders are shaking as he watches me mentally work things through, and he nudges me forward. "Come on, Einstein. Go on in."

"What did you call me?"

"Einstein. He was a genius, like you. It's a compliment." Henri steps back so Pax can come in, too, and says, "You can't be as . . . uninformed . . . as she is, can you?"

"I don't know what you're talking about," Pax says, sounding stiff.

Henri laughs out loud. "Okay, well, I take it you two aren't together, then. I've been wondering."

"What do you mean, 'together'?" I ask.

"He means romantically involved," Celine says. "You're living together, so everyone's going to assume you are."

"I don't know what *romantically involved* means." I look to Pax for help, but his expression is stony and unreadable.

"It means . . . oh brother, how do I explain this?"

Henri shakes his head and goes to plop down on a ratty couch. "Don't look at me."

There's a short table in front of the couch on which Elan is setting up wooden pieces on a board. "You ready to start?" Elan asks.

Celine waves her hands. "In a minute. I need to try an experiment first." She walks to Pax, and her posture resembles that of the prowling lion I saw through the Looking Glass at Sanctuary. She stops in front of him and tilts her head up, staring into his frown. Then she wraps her arms around his neck and presses her lips to his.

A coiling sensation, like I swallowed something alive, churns in my stomach, and I clench my fists so tightly I'm ruining the paper I wrote my name on. My pulse is racing, and when Celine pulls away from Pax, I feel an irrational desire to smack her across the face.

She steps back and, for some reason, glances at Elan, who is frozen in a half-bent posture over the table. Then she looks me up and down, and a slow smile creeps over her face. "Mm-hmm," she says. "*That* is called a kiss. It's a rather integral part of romantic attachment."

Pax is wide-eyed and still as a statue.

"That didn't really teach me anything," I say, trying to slow my heart rate. "Other than you people have a shocking disregard for sanitation." Whatever it is I'm feeling, it's uncomfortable, and I've never felt anything like it before.

"Oh, but it taught me a *lot*," Celine says. She grins and slaps Pax on the shoulder. "Relax. I was just messing with you." She goes over to the table and sits beside Henri, who gives her a disgusted look and shakes his head. "Now I'm ready," she says. "Let's play!"

Chapter 38

Pax and I stand right where we are as Celine and Elan settle in. One look at Pax tells me he's as much at a loss as I am. He's standing with his head slightly forward and his brow creased as though trying to make sense of Celine's behavior.

"Come on, you two," she says, waving us over. "You're going to have to get used to normal human behavior if you're going to live among us." She shakes her head and squints at Pax. "I mean, *her* I get, but I thought you said you grew up in one of these Nests."

"Only for a few years," Pax says. "I've been on my own most of my life."

"Yeah, but you've at least observed human behavior, haven't you? And you're not made of stone. You've got to be, what, twenty-five years old? Are you trying to say a good-looking guy like you has never—"

Henri clears his throat. "Boundaries, Celine."

She rolls her eyes. "Whatever. Well, come and sit and watch me dominate Elan."

We make our way forward, moving carefully as though the ground might give way. The living space is warm, and there are alternating red and yellow shades covering the hanging lanterns that add to the warmth. There's a neatly made bed on one wall, a rack of clothes, and a kitchen like Pax and I have. Then there are the chairs and couch and the table on which the game is set. I sit on the couch beside Celine, and Pax sits in the other free chair beside Elan, who is leaning over the board with a look of concentration on his face.

"What is this game called?" I ask. We had plenty of games at Sanctuary

—it was something to do to pass the time—but I've never seen this one before.

"It's an old game called chess," Elan says. He moves a white piece forward and sits back. "It's a game of strategy, so naturally the UWO made it illegal to play. It's on the list of banned games."

"There's a list of banned games?" I ask in a weak voice.

"Oh yeah. Wouldn't want people thinking too hard. Might put ideas in their heads."

Henri gives a short laugh and stretches his arms behind his head. "I don't know why I bother to watch you two play. You always take forever."

"You hush," Celine says, staring hard at the board. She still hasn't moved a piece. "You're just jealous because you suck at this game."

"It's a stupid game."

"It is not a stupid game just because you're bad at it." She moves a piece toward the center of the board and rests her chin on her hands.

Henri snorts.

"If it's illegal, then how did you get a copy of it?" I ask. "Did you get it from Bishop's archives? He told me today his theory about the UWO destroying everything like this." I wave my hand at the board.

"Yeah, we're a suspicious group here by nature, but Bishop's one of the most conspiratorial," Henri says.

"Bishop found an old box with the rules intact somewhere, but no pieces or board. Elan read the rules, figured it out, and then carved all these pieces," Celine says. "Beautiful, aren't they?" There's a note of admiration in her voice.

"So you don't believe Bishop that the UWO destroyed everything?" I look across Celine's back at Henri.

Henri shrugs and tilts his head. "Ah . . . I don't know. The evidence does suggest it, but we've never found anything that outright says that's what they did. It could be true, but it could also be that everything really was destroyed as collateral damage in the Devastations. Does it really matter? It's gone either way, and we know the UWO regulates what people have access to now. I'm not convinced they didn't just take advantage of the situation as they found it."

"If you're going to rebuild the world," Celine says, watching Elan leap a piece over another line of pieces, "why not do it according to your own blueprint?"

Henri yawns.

"If you're going to act that bored, why don't you make yourself useful and go get us some dinner," Celine says, kicking him. "Elan, you don't have any food here, do you?"

"Not really," Elan says.

"Typical. Henri, go. Get us some sandwiches or something." Celine prods him until he gets up off the couch.

"All right, all right. I'll be back." Henri leaves, grumbling under his breath.

"You guys can turn some music on if you want. The player is over there."

But I don't want to listen to music. I'm too intrigued by the patterns I see forming on the game board. "How do you play?"

"Basically the whole thing is about capturing the other person's king," Elan says. "We each have one, and we get one move per turn to use all the other pieces to capture as many of the opponent's players as we can, but all with the ultimate goal of working our way toward the king. Hang on." He considers the board and then makes his next move, taking one of Celine's pieces off the board. "See? Like that. She left her rook wide open."

"Only so I could draw out your bishop. Sucker," Celine says, moving another piece. "And the goal may be to capture the king, but everyone knows the queen is the most important piece." She taps a tall, narrow figure on the board and gives me a look that seems loaded with more than just information about the game.

Elan says, "Yeah, well. A good player has to know how to use them all." Then he tells me the names of all the various pieces and how they move across the board.

"Careful," Celine says. "She's a genius, you know. She'll probably turn into an expert, and then you'll never win again."

"Pax is a genius, too," I say, rather absently because I'm studying the game so hard.

Celine laughs. "You're joking. What are the odds of that?"

Pax just clears his throat and says, "I don't think so, Pria."

I look up at him. "Of course you are."

"Why do you say that?"

"How can you not know?" I wrinkle my brow. "I've seen you work through things, figure stuff out. You think just as quickly as I do, and you analyze people and situations down to the last detail. Did you think that was normal?"

Pax scratches the back of his neck. He seems disconcerted by my assertion, but I can't imagine why.

"Well, you two are quite a pairing, whatever the case," Celine says. "I didn't get a chance to introduce you around too much today, but I'll make sure you meet some new people tomorrow."

Henri returns with an armful of sandwiches and Etienne at his heels. "Look who wanted to come and watch the showdown," he says in a careful voice when they enter.

Pax clenches his fists and stands, sending his chair skittering backward.

"Easy," Henri says. "He comes in peace."

Pax is silent, staring Etienne down with his good eye.

"Why did you really come?" Celine asks, her hand poised over the chessboard.

"I thought someone should be around who hasn't been completely taken in by these two," Etienne says.

"That's what I thought." Celine sighs and makes her move. "Why can't you just ease up, Etienne? They passed Luther's test, and they passed the vote. They're with us now. And you know she could be valuable."

I glance at Celine. These people keep making offhand remarks about something I can do for them. I wish they would just tell me what it is.

"Or she could be a massive liability," Etienne says. He raises his chin at Pax. "Sit down."

"I think I'll stand," Pax says.

"Suit yourself." Etienne walks toward Pax until they're almost nose to nose, and then he ducks behind him and takes Pax's seat with a haughty smirk.

Pax looks at me. "I think it's time we go."

I stand, every nerve in my body tingling from the poisonous look Etienne is giving me.

"You don't have to go just because of him," Celine says, jumping to her feet.

"It's fine," Pax says. "We're new here, and it's been a long day."

Henri clears his throat. "Ah, okay then. I'll show you the way back to your wing."

"I know the way," Pax says. "There's no need."

"Still." Henri sets down all but two of the sandwiches. "You shouldn't wander alone just yet. Let me walk you."

I don't know what the protocol is for leaving someone's residence, so I don't say anything. I just follow Henri out the door, and Pax brings up the rear.

"I'm . . . ah . . . really sorry for bringing him back with me," Henri says. "He asked if he could come, and I thought maybe if he got to know you a little bit, he'd come around."

"It's okay. I understand," I say, and Pax walks silently beside me.

"I didn't mean to make you uncomfortable," Henri says, looking at me with an earnest expression.

I shrug. We turn down our corridor.

"Well, what did you think of chess? At least, as much of it as you saw." Henri seems to be trying to make polite conversation.

"Seemed easy enough to play," I say.

Henri raises his eyebrows. "You know, normal people wouldn't say so. Did you have a lot of strategy games at Sanctuary?"

"No, nothing that made us think too deeply. Mostly cards and dice games."

We stop at the end of the hall before our door, and Pax goes to unlock it.

"Why is Celine playing poorly, though?" I ask Henri.

"What do you mean?"

"I was watching her moves, and the movement of her eyes around the board. She always saw the best move to make, but then chose something else—some other move that wasn't as good. I thought the point of the game was to win."

Henri laughs. "You mean to tell me she's throwing the game? That's perfect. I should have guessed."

"Why? What do you mean?"

Pax is standing inside our room, waiting for me.

"Celine likes Elan, has for a long time. But he's . . . oblivious, I guess you could say. She's probably creating excuses to get together with him, and if she loses, she can claim a rematch."

"He's not oblivious," Pax says. Henri and I turn to him, and I raise an eyebrow in a knowing way. "He knows full well how she feels toward him, and he reciprocates the feelings."

Henri spreads his arms. "What is this? Do you have Luther's gift of reading people?"

"I just observed," Pax says. "When she kissed me, Elan was noticeably aggravated. His posture changed, his breathing changed, and he wouldn't look at me for the rest of the night."

"Huh." Henri reaches around our doorframe and tosses the two sandwiches onto the small side table. "Well, maybe he's putting her off because of the age difference. He's ten years older than she is. At any rate, I hope you enjoy the sandwiches. See you in the morning, yeah?"

Pax nods, and I smile at Henri. He's so different from his brother that it's hard to imagine they once shared a womb.

"Night, then." Henri raps his knuckles on the doorframe and leaves.

I close the door and lock it, and then I turn to see Pax staring at me. "What is it?" I ask.

"Nothing," he says.

I unwrap a sandwich and hand it to him before taking up the other one for myself. Pax holds and stares at it. "Maybe we should leave here," he finally says in a low voice.

I shake my head and slump back against the wall. "Now you want to leave?"

"Etienne will hurt you if he gets the chance."

"I know. I've already been told. But Henri seems to think he'll come around."

Pax purses his lips, turns his back, and goes to the larger table by the shelves and puts his sandwich down. "I didn't think it would be this way," he says. It doesn't even sound as though he's talking to me, standing with his face toward the wall.

I don't know what to say in response, so I take a bite of my sandwich.

Pax turns back to me. "Where is your Air-5?"

I swallow. "Oh . . . I forgot it in Bishop's place." I grimace. "Sorry. I didn't mean to."

"I'll go get it," Pax says. "You shouldn't be without it."

"Wait, Henri said we shouldn't wander alone yet."

"Pria, I don't want you to be without it, not even for one night. I can take care of myself." He goes to the door.

"Clearly." I touch his shoulder, and he flinches for some reason. I nod at his black eye. "That looks awful enough. Don't get into any more fights."

He stares at me for a long moment, and then he says, "I'll be right back. Lock the door after me. I have my key."

I nod, and Pax slips out. I throw the lock and press my ear to the door, my heart thudding almost too loudly to hear anything down the hall anyway, but I'm desperate to make sure he gets to the end of the corridor without being accosted. I hear a burst of muffled laughter and a child's playful shriek, but other than that, nothing. With a deep sigh, I turn away from the door and go to sit at our table to wait.

I've just taken another bite of my sandwich when a key scrapes in the lock and the knob turns. I frown and look around. It's too soon for Pax to have gotten to Bishop's and back already.

The knob finishes turning and the door swings open. Etienne steps inside.

Chapter 39

Not taking his eyes off me, Etienne closes the door with a snap and locks it. I gasp and skitter back, trying to put the table between us, but there's really no place for me to go, no way for me to defend myself.

I'm considering screaming, but the thought has barely entered my mind when Etienne is standing before me with his hand on my throat. He pushes me until my back is against the wall and then lifts beneath my jaw so I'm on tiptoe and can barely breathe.

"I could kill you right now by crushing your esophagus, and if you make a sound, I will, do you understand?"

I blink and try to nod, but he has my head in too tight a hold.

"Now listen closely. I don't know how you fooled Luther, but nobody gets into or out of Sanctuary who isn't working for the UWO, *nobody*." His lips are mere inches away from my face, but he moves closer, tickling the side of my cheek. "I know you and your boyfriend are spies, and I'll be watching you. If either of you do anything to endanger these people here, I'll kill you."

He raises his other hand up before my wide eyes so I can see a glint of bronze. "My fool of a brother made several practice keys before he let your boyfriend make the key to this place. I found them in Henri's discard bin, and I took them and gave them to my friends. We're going to keep them just so you know we can get to you any time, any place. My friends would like to do a lot worse to you than I'm doing. Do *not* think you are safe here. If you tell Pax about this"—he jabs me with the key—"about any of this, we will kill him, even if we have to sneak in here in the middle of the night to do so. If you tell Luther or Celine or Henri or anybody else, Pax is dead. If you try to change the lock on this door, Pax is dead. There are many of us who can get to you, and you'll never know who we all are. Luther will never be able to have us all arrested before one of us can kill your boyfriend and make it look like an accident. Are we clear?"

I try to make my assent clear through my eyes, and I must succeed, because Etienne says, "Good," and releases the pressure on my neck until my feet can fully touch the ground and I can breathe again.

I gasp and massage my neck as Etienne steps away.

"We're not spies," I say in a wheezy voice. "We're not lying."

Etienne snorts. "With everything the UWO is capable of doing, you could be spies and not even realize it." He takes a step toward me again, and I flinch away. "My friends think they can break you. Let's hope it doesn't come to that." He pockets his key to our living space, walks to the door, and just like that, he's gone. I hear the scrape again and see the knob turn back into locked position.

I slide down the wall until I'm crouched in an upright fetal position next to the pieces of my sandwich that I dropped when he pushed me up against the wall. I will not cry, I will not cry. If I cry, Pax will know something happened, and his life will be in even more danger than it is already.

With shaking fingers, I gather the bits of my sandwich and dump them into a basket that looks as though it's for waste. Then I straighten my clothes and try to be calm, but I'm still shaking, and I know Pax will notice. I go around the partition to my side of the room, determining that if I can't act normal, I must hide from sight.

When the lock scrapes again, I look toward the door, my heart slamming up in my throat. But it is Pax this time, and he's carrying my Air-5. I retreat to sit on my bed and busy myself taking off my boots.

"Pria?" Pax says.

"I'm here."

"Can I come over there?"

"Not right now, please. I'm changing." And then, because that's what I said I was doing, I change slowly from my clothes into the nightgown.

"You didn't eat your sandwich," Pax says.

"I ate some of it," I say. "But I . . . wasn't feeling well, so I threw the rest away."

Silence. I wonder if Pax is considering the tremor in my voice.

Then he says, "Are you ready?"

I clench my hands and take a deep breath. "Yes."

Pax appears a moment later with my weapon. "Here, it's still charged. Keep it beneath your pillow or just under the bed. Someplace you can reach it quickly if needed."

I reach for it, but when I take hold, he doesn't let go. "What's wrong?" he asks. "You're shaking."

"I told you I'm not feeling well." I don't meet his gaze. He doesn't release the weapon.

"Do you need a medical technician?"

"No. I'd just like to go to sleep."

"You're lying," he says. "You're not sick. Something is wrong. Something happened while I was away."

Etienne's cold voice enters my mind. *"I will kill him."*

"Nothing happened," I say in as firm a voice as I can. "I said I'm not feeling well, and that's the truth." I force myself to hold his gaze. But he's shaking his head and squinting his good eye at me. I yank the weapon out of his grasp. "You've only known me for a few weeks, Pax. Stop acting like you know everything about me."

"I may not know everything about you," Pax says, unfazed, "but I know you well enough to know when you're not acting like yourself. What happened?"

"Nothing happened!" I shout. "Leave it alone, would you?"

Pax blinks and steps back. "Fine." He sets his jaw and walks away.

I'm trembling even more now, and I sit down hard on the bed. I shove the Air-5 under the frame, pushing against a box of something that's already under it, and then I drop my head into my hands, miserable. I hurt Pax's feelings, and I made him feel like I don't trust him. But if I saved his life by doing so, it was worth it.

Chapter 40

It's more than a week before Celine and Henri say they feel comfortable letting us wander the caves without them.

"Does that mean you're moving back to your old living space?" I ask Celine.

"No. I think I'll hang out with you guys a little longer." She smiles.

I smile back, still a little shy at the notion I might actually have made my first real friend—other than Pax, of course. And that relationship is too complicated to call a true friendship at the moment. He's sullen and watchful, rarely talks, and never lets me out of his sight except for when we're working or when Celine and I go to the bathroom together. His eye has healed enough that he can see out of it again, but it's still ringed with yellowish skin.

I don't resent his watchfulness, or Celine's constant presence, but I hate that it causes other people to view me as weak. But I *am* weak, at least, weaker than I ever imagined. I can do nothing about the way Etienne seems to follow me sometimes, and I can do nothing about how his eyes trail me every time we're out someplace public, like the dining hall, where we are now.

"I'll admit," Celine goes on, picking at her salad, "I was a little put off when Luther made me move down to your wing, but this week and a half has been really . . . fun. I never expected someone like you to be so likeable."

I frown. "Someone like me?"

"Yeah, you know, a UWO cog."

Cog, I've come to learn, is the unfriendly term applied to people who are a part of the UWO system. We're just "pieces of the machine," as Celine told me.

"Individuality is so discouraged in the UWO, I half-expected it to have been bred out of humanity by now."

"You can't breed out individualism," Henri says, sitting down with a bowl of stew. "It's a part of what makes us human." He grins at me. "Hey, Pria. Pax." He gives Pax a short nod.

"Maybe individualism is part of what they're trying to get rid of in the cloning research," Celine says. "I mean, human clones wouldn't be *real* people, so why would they have real human personality traits?"

"It's all theoretical, Celine," Henri says. "All theoretical."

Pax pushes his empty plate away. "When do you think Luther will want to talk to us? Now that we've been here over a week—"

"Simmer down. He'll get to you when he gets to you," Celine says. "How's your reading coming, Pria?"

I shrug and nod at the same time. "It's going well, I guess."

"What, not reading full-length novels yet?" Henri asks. Then he grimaces and scowls at his bowl. "This is disgusting. What did he put in this today?"

"It's leftovers from yesterday—a bunch of stuff mixed together," Celine says. "I wasn't stupid enough to go near it."

Henri brushes his bowl to the side. "I'll just buy something at the store later."

"You'd better not let Orson see you waste that. You know how he feels about wasting food around here."

Henri looks around and whistles sharply. A moment later, Arrow runs toward us, his long ears flapping and his tail wagging.

"Here you go, boy." Henri plops the bowl on the floor. "There. Not wasted."

"You know Orson hates animals in here almost as much as he hates waste."

Henri waves a dismissive hand.

"I'm sorry, but what's a novel?" I ask.

Henri looks up. "It's a long story that's been written down. You know what a story is, right?"

"Sure, I guess."

"Well, a long time ago, people used to write stories down and distribute them for people to read."

"Why? What purpose did that serve in society?"

"Pleasure, entertainment . . . because they could." He looks at Celine and shrugs.

"To communicate messages, too," she says. "They weren't just for fun. Messages can be tucked away inside stories without readers even knowing it."

"I bet that's why the UWO decided they were too dangerous to remain in existence," I say. "Messages they couldn't control. I wonder if some of Bishop's books are novels."

"Oh, I wouldn't put it past him to have a few tucked away," Henri says.

Pax drums his fingers on the table. He's staring at a spot on the wall as though he's not really seeing it. "Back to work, then?" he says to Henri.

"Ah . . ." Henri gives me a sidelong glance. "Yeah. Let me just swing by the store to pick up something edible."

I almost ask if I can come along—I have a small pile of coins to call my own from my short time at work with Bishop, and Pax and I visited the store several days ago to pick up some clothing that fit better than what we were given. It was a bright, colorful place, full of almost as many items as Bishop's archive. I could spend an entire day there exploring.

But Bishop is expecting me. Celine and I stand, and we all leave the dining hall together. A few people smile at me as I walk by, but most of them give Pax searching looks. He hasn't exactly made himself approachable since we got here.

We part ways in the tunnel system, and Celine walks me to Bishop's archive.

"Has he always been like that?" she asks me.

"Who—Pax?"

"Yeah. I've never met anybody so tightly wound, and I grew up with Etienne." She gives me a knowing look.

"I haven't really known him that long, you know," I say. "But yes, he's always been a bit tense." And full of hidden energy, which I've seen beneath the surface since that day in the stairwell at Sanctuary. "But he's also . . . steady, reliable. You know what I mean?"

"Uh-huh." We stop before Bishop's door, and Celine lays a hand on my arm to stop me from knocking. "He likes you, you know."

"Of course he likes me. I don't think he would have stuck around if he didn't."

"No, sweetheart, you don't understand. Pax *likes* you. He's such a robot I'm not sure he even realizes it yet, but he definitely does. He stares at you constantly when you're not paying attention."

I shrug. "He's keeping an eye on me. You know he's designated himself my protector."

"It's more than overprotectiveness, trust me."

"Okay, so he likes me a lot. So what?" I look up. "Wait . . . is this part of that romance stuff you've been trying to teach me about?"

Celine huffs. "You're impossible. All right. Get to work. I'll be back to get you later." She lets Bishop's knocker fall, and he opens the door a moment later.

"Hold up!" Luther calls from down the hall, and Celine, Bishop, and I turn to look. "I'd like Pria to come with me this afternoon instead. Bishop, you'll have to do without her."

I raise my eyebrows. I haven't seen Luther except in passing since our first days here.

"Yes, sir," Bishop says.

"Pria." Luther nods my direction. "Let's go for a walk."

"Do you want me to come, too?" Celine asks.

"No. The six-wheeler needs your attention. I'll get her back to her place safely tonight."

"Shouldn't we get Pax, too?" I ask.

He shakes his head. "This is just for you. And I'd rather you didn't say anything to him about it just yet. Got your Air-5? Good. We're going outside."

"Outside?" I feel a shiver down my spine.

Luther gives me a grim smile. "It's time you see what the Unfamiliars really are."

Chapter 41

When we step out into open air, it's surprisingly dark, although the fresh wind on my face takes my breath away. I close my eyes for a moment and soak it in, realizing now how much I've missed it while living holed away in the tunnels. Of course, years of living in Sanctuary had conditioned me to living inside, but the sense of freedom and openness out here is delicious.

I open my eyes when I feel Luther pressing a wad of cloth into my hands.

"Camouflage," he says. "Put it on. Once we're outside the netting, you'll need it."

It's a simple tunic, and it's mottled dark green, brown, and gray. Celine, her brothers, Elan, and Brant were wearing something similar when they first apprehended us. I slip it on and let it settle on my shoulders.

"The netting?" I ask, raising an eyebrow at the fibers crisscrossed between the tops of the trees far above.

Luther folds his arms and looks up. "One of our greatest inventions, and something the UWO still hasn't figured out, even though it's so simple. It's densely woven, but not so dense the trees can't get enough light, and camouflaged so it looks like trees if you're flying over it. The fibers have cooling elements running through them, so it fools the heat sensors of the UWO flying crafts. They would have to find us on foot, and this isn't good terrain to land in." He grins. "It was Wallace's idea, years ago. Have you met Wallace yet?"

"No, I don't think so."

K.B. Hoyle

"You'd remember if you had. Anyhow, having this netting over our entrances means we can keep the animals penned up outside, and people can get some fresh air without having to worry too much about discovery. We also have the whole perimeter watched for miles around. That's how Brant and the others found you."

"They weren't hunting those Unfamiliars?"

"Is that what they told you? No. We'd been tracking you. They just happened to also discover the Golems in the area."

Luther starts off, away from the cave entrance, and the guards who stand there watch silently. I hurry to catch up.

Once we're out of earshot of the guards, I ask, "Why didn't you want Pax to come with us?"

Luther casts me a sidelong glance. "How close are the two of you?"

"We haven't known each other very long," I say. "But in that time, we've been through a lot together. I know he cares about me." I frown, thinking about Celine's assertions, and then trip over a tumble of rocks.

Luther pauses to help me up. "You okay?"

I nod and wipe my hands on my tunic.

"I ask because he's something of an enigma," Luther says.

I squint up at him. We've moved outside the netting now, and the surroundings get brighter as afternoon sunlight cuts through the trees in sparkling shafts, catching on the liberal sprinkles of gray in Luther's hair. "You don't trust him."

"Not fully, no. Does that bother you?"

"I . . . I understand you have to keep your people safe, so no, not really. But why don't you trust him? You let us stay."

Luther shrugs and shoulders his gun to help me over a sharp rise. "He passed my test, so I had no reason not to let him stay. But there was something in his demeanor as he answered my questions that was . . . odd. Usually I have to wade through natural nervous reactions to determine when someone is telling me truth or falsehood, but Pax was so assured of himself that there was no nervous reaction at all. Truthfully, I found it suspicious, but what was I to accuse him of? Being too confident of the truth of his story?" He gives me a wry expression. "And he certainly fits the mold of those we take in here. Quite frankly, I can't believe he's survived all this time on his own."

"But you do trust me?"

"You were—are—an open book. I can read every emotion on your face. I've no doubt you're telling the truth about your experiences, and that's why you just might be the one person who can help us."

We're descending now into a valley, and Luther tightens his hold on his gun.

"Pax wants to talk to you, you know," I say. "He's eager to help."

"I know, and I will talk with him soon. I'll talk with *both* of you soon, as you both have inside information about Sanctuary that could be invaluable to us. But I wanted to let you adjust to life with us first, and let you determine if *you* trust *us*."

I purse my lips.

"So?"

Do I trust them? I think of Etienne and his threats, and I almost blurt out the whole story to Luther. It would be the perfect time. We're alone, and Luther could have Etienne arrested before he ever knew I told on him.

But Etienne has friends, and I don't know how many. I can't risk it.

"Pria?" Luther asks. "Is everything okay?"

He can read every emotion on my face, he said. I school my features and say, "I'm just figuring out how to answer you. Obviously I trust *you*, or I wouldn't be out here alone with you. And . . ." I think of Celine, Elan, and Henri and their friendships. I think of Bishop and his enthusiasm for learning and history, and all the children of all different colors racing around the tunnels. I think of their grandiose claims about how the world is. "I trust most of you, and some of what you say. But you have to understand that this life is, in many ways, much harder than life at Sanctuary, and it goes against everything I've ever been taught. I think I want to help you. And I definitely don't want to hurt you."

"That's good enough for me," Luther says. "We're almost there."

We proceed in silence the rest of the way, and Luther keeps his eyes sharp and his gun ready. He whistles a birdcall once, and it is answered from a hundred feet away by a person I can't see. And then the smell reaches me. I cough and cover my nose with my forearm.

"They're pretty ripe," Luther says. He pulls a cloth from his pocket and hands it to me. "Tie it around your face. It'll help." He does the same with a second cloth. "Recognize where we are?"

I look around, the smell somewhat dampened by the cloth over my nose and mouth. We're in the bottom of a rift valley between sharp slopes, but there's nothing remarkable about it.

"It's where Brant and the others picked you up. Come on. This way." He leads me up the slope to our right, and the smell gets stronger. "I thought they would have decayed enough by now."

I breathe through my mouth and nod, even though his back is to me, and I don't really know what I'm nodding about.

When we get about halfway up the slope, the smell is almost unbearable. I can even taste it in my mouth, and I swallow hard, trying not to gag.

"Here we are," Luther says. He gestures for me to come forward, and I see the three dead Unfamiliars lying in the underbrush. They look enormous and somehow more alien in death, with their garishly long arms and legs and elongated faces. Their skin, usually grayish, is now white and mottled purple in places, and their open eyes are black in death. Great chunks of flesh have fallen away, either through decay or through scavenging animals, revealing lumpy muscle mass and flesh, thick tubular veins lined with black coagulated blood, and white bones.

I shake my head and press the cloth against my nose. Why did he want to show me this?

"What do they look like to you?" he asks.

"Dead aliens," I say.

Luther, for some reason, grins. "There's no such thing as aliens."

Chapter 42

Luther points his gun at the closest Unfamiliar and fires. It's larger than my Air-5, and brown instead of green, but it's the same sort of energy weapon. It makes the same *zipping* sound I'm used to, but I flinch back anyway, surprised he is shooting at a dead body.

I give him an alarmed look as he fires a few more times and then shoulders his weapon. In the decayed hole where he's fired, bone is visible, and now there are char marks on the bone. He stoops to one knee and pulls another rag from his pocket, which he then uses to wipe at the charred spot.

I shake my head and back away, uncertain.

"There we go," he says. "Usually takes several shots to get through the enamel. It's virtually impossible to do through the skin and flesh. What do you see now?" He sits back on his heel and looks up at me.

I stare at the spot he's wiped clean. Then I squint and look closer. I can't believe it. There is metal—shiny, silver *metal*—showing through beneath white enamel that has been chipped off by his shots. "What is that, an implant of some sort?"

Luther shakes his head. "All its bones look like that beneath the enamel."

All its bones. Forgetting the stench, I drop down beside him. "They're . . . they're *machines*?"

"That's right."

"But this is real flesh and blood! They're decaying!"

"*Real* is a relative term here," Luther says.

"Is this just . . . just the form of their bodies, then—some sort of mix of living and mechanical?"

"They are technically not living at all. They're manufactured." He points to a vein sticking out of the decaying flesh. "Plastic," he says. "Porous and filled with blood, yes, but artificial blood. This flesh is real flesh and decays as such, but it's all been grown in a lab. We don't know how it works exactly, but there is a system that circulates the blood through the body and regenerates the flesh to give it the appearance of life. The frame is mechanical, and the eyes are just infrared heat sensors." He waves his hand. "Wallace can explain it better than I can."

"But—but they must be alive in some sense, or why else would they have invaded the earth?"

Luther shakes his head. "They did not invade the earth. They were created here. They came out of the warehouses of the UWO."

I sit back and squint at him. "You know this for a fact?"

"We've dissected them completely, and we have one whole frame back at Asylum. They have no nervous system, no reproductive or digestive systems, and the marks of human engineering are all over them. It's the same technology we find in the UWO aircraft and vehicles we salvage. In place of a brain, each has a computer chip at the base of its neck that is connected to the UWO mainframe. It's the same sort of chip we find in the cloned animals."

"But these things aren't clones."

"No, not at all. That's why we call them Golems—because they're not alive, they're just animated. They are machines cloaked in flesh to give the appearance of life, but they are not clones, human or otherwise. It is unsettling to wonder how far they've come in their experiments if they were able to create these things over a hundred years ago, don't you think?"

I raise my eyebrows. "So you're saying the UWO created them and set them loose on humanity under the guise of a third Great Devastation? You're saying they engineered the Great Incursion—that they made it all up?"

He nods.

"Why would they do that? The Incursion killed hundreds of millions of people!"

"Exactly."

I shudder and close my eyes. "No . . . no. We're supposed to be rebuilding humanity. It's the sole purpose of the Breeding Program!"

"Breeders are to rebuild humanity along the lines of what the UWO says is acceptable, and never to give any thought to how the world was purged of the unacceptable humans in the first place."

"Of course I gave it thought." I open my eyes and glare at him. "But their version made—makes—sense. There were three Great Devastations that decimated the human race, and our job was to restore it. That makes sense! What *doesn't* make sense is destroying humanity just to rebuild it." I jump to my feet and pace away.

Luther rises as well and watches me. "Then why else would they create these things? Give me another explanation that makes sense, and I'll listen."

I search my brain for several minutes, but I can't think of any logical reason why the UWO would invent a race of aliens, stage an invasion, and lie about it. "I don't know," I finally say. "I just don't know."

Luther takes my elbow to steer me down the slope of the rise back into the valley. "I know it's not easy to learn these things," he says in a low voice. "But it's better to live in truth than to walk in lies, yes?"

"What is truth?" Pax once said. In Sanctuary, I thought I could trust my existence. I thought I could trust what I saw with my eyes and heard with my ears. I now know that existence was not consistent with reality. *Reality* is a group of societal misfits living together and resisting the power of the UWO. *Reality* is a downed machine in the forest masquerading as a living creature.

"Show me," I say. "Show me the dissected Unfam—Golem. I want to see it with my own eyes."

Chapter 43

"I can do that," Luther says, helping me over a fallen tree.

"What are the other implications of the Golems being manufactured by the UWO?" I ask. My voice sounds dead to me. I lower the rag so I'm wearing it loosely around my neck. "What else do you know?"

"Well, I'm hoping that's where you can help us out."

I wrinkle my forehead. But I'm ignorant—I know absolutely nothing. If this excursion outside Sanctuary and into the heart of the wild has taught me anything, it's exactly how little I know about reality. So I don't ask him what he means. I figure he'll get around to it when he's ready.

Luther leads me back to Asylum along a different path than the one we took to get to the Golems, up and over the opposing ridge and then into another valley. Before long, we come into a natural clearing that abuts the side of the mountain rising above us. Luther takes me around a bend in the terrain, and then we're facing a wall of the netting they use to cover the trees. It's woven much more thickly here, and Luther lifts one corner and gestures me forward.

I duck beneath the netting, and it takes a few moments for my eyes to adjust to the dim light inside the cave, so I can't immediately see where I am or what's around me.

"You're back already."

I turn to find Celine emerging from beneath a black vehicle with six wheels. She's wiping her hands on a rag and grinning at me. I look around and see several more vehicles of various sorts, including what looks like an

X-1.

"So what'd you think?" she asks, coming up to me. There is a smudge of grease on her cheekbone.

"I . . ."

"I know, right? When Luther showed me, all I could think for a long time was, *bastards*. But there's no use being mad. Better to channel that energy into doing something useful to take them down."

I look back at Luther and raise an eyebrow. "Is it here?"

"No, it's in Wallace's lab."

"Wallace's . . . you going to show her the skeleton?" Celine asks.

"She wants to see it."

"Good."

"Come along with us, Celine," Luther says.

"Sure thing." She tosses her dirty rag back toward the vehicle she'd been working on and falls in beside me as I follow Luther through the garage. It's a vast underground space supported periodically with beams and filled with vehicles that materialize out of the gloom like ghosts, and I realize there's much more to Asylum than Pax or I have discovered . . . or been shown.

Off the main space, there's a wooden door with a metal box set into the wall beside it. Luther presses a button on the box and says, "Wallace? Come and open the door, will you?"

"Just a minute," a man says through the speaker, and a hiss of static follows.

Luther releases the button, and the static cuts off.

"It will be *exactly* a minute—watch," Celine says. She holds up her wrist, and there's a device on it I'm not familiar with, but she seems intent. After a moment, she softly counts down from ten, and when she gets to one, the lock on the door in front of us squeaks open, followed by the door itself.

"Right on time," Celine says, grinning. "Every time."

The man called Wallace is, for some reason, not what I'm expecting. So many people here are different that I've come to expect surprises around every turn, but Wallace could be right out of the male gene pool of the Breeding Program. He's tall, broad-shouldered, olive-skinned, and dark-eyed, with strong features and thick hair that is almost black.

"It's the Breeder!" he says. "Hello. I've been waiting for Luther to bring you to see me." He speaks very fast, and in the second since he's opened the door, I can tell by the flitting about of his eyes that he has observed everything in his line of sight.

"Pria, meet Wallace," Luther says. "He was an engineering tech for the UWO before he fought off the effects of the drugs and defected to us. How long ago was that?"

Wallace blinks once. "Ten years, three months, twelve days, two hours, and twenty-nine minutes ago."

Luther smiles. "He's a little . . . exceptional, not unlike you."

"Exceptional?" Wallace snorts. "I'm a freakin' genius, but never mind that. It's nice to meet someone who was on the other side of the Program." He shakes my hand and nods.

It seems I wasn't far off in my assessment. "You were in the Breeding Program, too?"

"I was one of the donors, yes, if you can call it *donation* when you don't have a choice in the matter. After that short phase of my life—it's much less time consuming for the men than for the women, you know—they noted my massive intellect and assigned me to engineering."

Without warning, he turns and walks back the way he came, through a narrow passage in the rock. We follow, and Luther shuts and locks the door behind us.

"It's a little disconcerting, though," Wallace says, coming up against another door that he opens with a key, "thinking of all the kids out there that could be mine. Maybe even one of yours." He raises an eyebrow.

"I doubt it," I say. "I only delivered one contribution. My second failed."

"Failed, or was terminated?"

I blink. "I . . . don't know."

"Flawed either way, I suppose. Definitely not one of mine, then."

I pale, and Luther clears his throat.

Wallace looks from Luther to me. "Sorry. That was inappropriate," he says. "I'll admit, I'm a genius in every area except humor."

"It's okay," I say. I look around. His shop is much larger than Henri's, but the items it contains are no less mysterious to my untrained eyes. He has what looks to be pieces of some of the vehicles out in the garage, as well as many things that hum and buzz and blink with lights. And, for some reason, at the far end of his shop, he has a small pen with two sheep and a goat.

"The benefit of coming out of engineering is that I took a lot of knowledge of their tech with me," Wallace says. "They're improving every day, though, and it's hard for me to keep up. They have *me* several times over, if you take my meaning, where Asylum only has the one." He says this without conceit, and he idly spins a tool between his fingers. "My specialty was mechanical engineering, not human or animal engineering, although I have made some progress in tracking their cloning procedures."

"You're the guy, then, who can disconnect the cloning computer from the UWO uplink without killing the animals," I say.

"That's me, although the procedure is far from perfect. All I have to do is convince the computer to continue communicating instructions to the brain without pulling the instructions from the uplink. The animals live, yes, but not as long as natural animals do. I'm still working on it." He gestures toward the penned animals. "But I doubt you're here to talk about my clones. No . . ." He squints at me and steps closer. "Pale, locked jaw, sweaty palms . . . Luther showed you the Golems, didn't he? Bet that was a shock. So you must be here to see Pat."

"Pat?" I wipe my palms on my camouflage tunic.

Wallace walks toward a tall partition that reaches almost all the way to the ceiling. "An androgynous name for an androgynous creature." He pulls the partition aside and steps back so I can see. "Pat!" he shouts with a grin.

Chapter 44

Hanging from hooks in the ceiling is a gleaming metal skeleton. It's unmistakably that of a Golem, for its size and for the six fingers on its hands and six toes on its feet, but I never would have believed it if Luther hadn't shown me the metal bones of the decaying ones first.

I walk forward until I'm standing just beneath it, dwarfed by its size. The toes of the dangling feet hang just inches above the floor, and I can see that white enamel still clings to the bones in places. An elaborate system of plastic tubing is attached to the bones in places, all leading back to the chest cavity where there is some sort of machine.

Wallace drags a stepladder over to the skeleton and mounts it so he's level with the Golem's chest. "This hydraulic chamber here pumps the blood through the body, keeping the flesh, well, alive, for lack of a better term."

"So it is real flesh?" I ask in a whisper. "It's organic?"

"Oh yeah," Wallace says. "They figured out a way to grow it and sustain it on these titanium skeletons—as long as the system is working, that is." He taps the machine in the chest. "The same hydraulic system animates the limbs. These things don't move using the artificial muscles they've grown. Everything is powered by the skeleton, the hydraulic system within the skeleton, and the implant in the head that's linked to the heat-sensor eyes. That's why, when you see one of these suckers in action, their flesh seems to sag on them."

Celine shivers beside me. "I used to have nightmares of these things as a kid."

Breeder

"It makes sense that you would have," Wallace says. "I believe they first created them to resemble creatures the human psyche would naturally find fearful. In a way, they're just bogeymen."

Bogeymen. I don't know that word. "Did you find, in their makeup, any other reason for their existence other than . . ." I purse my lips, not sure how to phrase it.

"Other than killing humans? No. These things are human-killing machines—literally. They were designed to kill with their bare hands. The hydraulic system makes their grip powerful enough to rip off limbs or crush a skull. And their sole target is humans. We captured this one alive, and before I took it apart, we tested it with animals. Put a sheep or a goat in front of it, no reaction. Put a human in front of it, it goes berserk. Make no mistake, they were created with a singular purpose."

"But they had to make them appear organic, too," Luther says, "and that means they couldn't make them invincible, or people would have caught on eventually."

"Yeah," Wallace says. "Open up enough veins, and they will 'bleed out,' rendering the hydraulics ineffective. But the eyes keep transmitting to the computer in their heads until they go black. The eyes go black, and you know it's done."

I shake my head. Such an elaborate deception, and for what? "How many people know about this?" I ask. "How many people have you told?"

Luther sighs. "Well, all the leadership here knows, but not all the people. A lot of people have lost loved ones, and if they were to know that the UWO organized the Third Devastation, I don't think I would be able to contain the outpouring of rage. They're already angry enough knowing how they're oppressed by the UWO. It wouldn't achieve anything to riot, except all of our deaths. We have to be organized first on a large scale before we can act."

"And that's what you're trying to do," I say. "Organize so you can act."

"We're working in that direction, yes."

I spread my arms. "But what about the first two Devastations? If the UWO created the third one, who's to say they didn't engineer the first two as well?" The thought makes me immediately sick, and I sway. There is a stack of crates to my left, and I walk over to them and sit so I don't fall over.

"I like her," Wallace says, getting down from his ladder. "She's quick."

Luther's expression is grave. "Those of us who know the most about how the UWO does things believe they did engineer all three of the

Devastations. Wallace, me, Bishop, Elan—"

"Me and my brothers," Celine says.

"Among some others you have yet to meet."

"But other than a manmade Golem," Luther says, pointing at the skeleton, "we don't have any proof, and until we do, there is slim chance of getting all of the Nests to unite."

"Why? I thought you all wanted to overthrow the UWO?"

Celine mutters something under her breath that I can't understand, and Luther says, "It would be very, very risky. Many people would lose their lives, and our chance of success would be minimal. Most of our kind don't want to fight, they just want to lay low and survive. They believe that if we ignore the UWO, the UWO will ignore us."

"Stupid," Celine says with a scowl. "How many of us does the UWO have to kill before people realize they won't stop until they have their pure human race? Until every human on the planet is subject to them? They will never stop hunting us. Those creatures are proof enough of that."

"Is that what the Golems do?" I ask. "They hunt and kill you?"

"Yes. They leave the Communes alone, except to show themselves from time to time just to remind people they are out there," Luther says. "The so-called truce was only instated to keep humans and Golems from mingling, but it's something of a joke. Why bother making a law that they can't mix when people can't leave the Communes without permission anyway?"

"Ah, they just wanted to cover their butts," Wallace says. He's moved on to another part of the cave and is tinkering with an object with blinking lights. I get the impression he needs to always keep himself busy with something.

I drop my head into my hands and massage my temples, trying to stay focused despite Wallace's distracting frenetic energy. "So you need proof that the UWO engineered the Great Devastations." Facts about the first two, the Great Famine and the Great Pandemic, swim through my head. All that hurt, and all those lost people . . . could the Unified World Order really be behind all that? And how could they have gained the power to do so in the first place?

"Proof, yes," Luther says. "But information on more than just that. We need to verify what the Controlled Repopulation Program is doing. There are so many rumors and very few facts."

"Pax says there are secret labs and nurseries beneath Sanctuary," I say and then close my eyes. I don't want to think about it.

"We know there are infant nurseries—there must be, because children do not appear in the Commune nurseries until age three, and they don't enter the Agoge system until age seven. The youngest children must be kept somewhere, and if they are, then for what purpose?"

"Viability," I whisper. "That's what Pax told me. They go through stages of determining viability. But he can tell you more about that." I open my eyes. "I know even less than you all do. I'm completely ignorant, and I'm still not even sure what I believe about everything. You should be confiding in Pax, who is trustworthy, despite what you might think. What on earth do you want me for?"

Luther and Celine exchange a look.

"Isn't it obvious?" Wallace asks from across the room.

Luther shoots him an annoyed look. "We want you, Pria, because you can get back in."

Chapter 45

The shock of Luther's statement stays with me all the way to his office. Just outside his door, he stops me and Celine and says, "Please don't tell Pax about the Golems. When I'm certain I can trust him completely, I'll tell him myself."

I nod, numb and not caring about Luther's scruples. How could they want me to go *back*? He whisked me away before I could respond, almost as though he knew I would need peace away from Wallace's energy to let it to sink in.

We enter his office to find Pax, Henri, and Bishop already there with a silver-haired woman Henri introduces as Mari. Celine brightens when Elan slips in behind us a moment later.

"Sit, please, everyone," Luther says.

We do so, silently.

"Don't you want Brant and Wallace here?" Henri asks. I notice he doesn't ask about Etienne.

"You know how Brant feels about this," Luther says. "And we just came from Wallace's. He's busy. I'll catch him up later."

"Is that all the leadership, then?" I ask, going through the names in my head.

"No, not all," Luther says, but he doesn't elaborate.

"We sometimes have differing opinions on what needs to be done," Celine says. She's twirling a metal bit from one of the vehicles on the table.

"I thought you voted on things," Pax says.

"On things that affect the community at large, yes. On covert operations, no," Luther says. "It wouldn't be wise or safe for everyone to know everything."

Celine twitches, and the metal bit falls to the floor. She doesn't pick it up.

"Pax, you've been here for over a week now," Luther says. "I trust you've settled in?"

Pax nods, his gaze steady and his lips pursed.

"Then it's time for me to tell you there are aspects of your story that puzzle me." Luther leans forward and clasps his hands together. "I believe you told me the truth about infiltrating Sanctuary, living there, and eventually liberating Pria and yourself, but I'm troubled. How did you manage to do such a thing, when we've been trying for years without success?"

"How am I supposed to know how and why you failed?" Pax asks, his tone matter-of-fact rather than hostile. "I only know how I succeeded."

"Sanctuary is a veritable bunker," Luther says. "Only the medical technicians come and go, and our attempts to infiltrate their ranks always fail. But now you're telling us that Enforcers come and go as well?"

"Enforcers and some Protectors," Pax says. "Although the presence of the Enforcers is one of the most highly guarded secrets of Sanctuary."

"Then how did you find out about it?"

"Time. And I paid attention."

"You make it sound so simple."

"It took me five years."

Luther unfolds his hands and leans back, but I can tell he's still not satisfied with Pax's story. "Fine. So tell me about what you witnessed while you were living beneath Sanctuary."

Pax shoots me a sidelong look. "There are some things I'd rather not say in front of Pria. They will be upsetting, given her previous station there."

"I'm afraid Pria must hear what you have to say if she's to make an informed decision," Luther says.

"An informed decision about what?"

"About whether or not she will return to Sanctuary to gather information for us."

Pax jumps to his feet, his chair skittering back onto two legs and then falling over. "You can't be serious." He puts both his hands palm-down on the table and leans toward Luther. "You *can't* send her back."

"It's her decision to make, not yours," Luther says, calm in the face of Pax's outburst. "And you owe it to her to tell us what you know."

Pax shakes his head, more agitated than I've ever seen him. "If you send her back, they will kill her—or—or they'll experiment on her, and *then* kill her. She's useless to them now, corrupted, a traitor. They have no reason to let her live."

"Unless—and forgive me, Pria, I know we haven't told you this part yet —but the plan is to have Pria go back and claim to have been kidnapped by you. If she convinces them she was taken against her will, they may allow her to reenter Sanctuary. Especially if she claims to have information about us."

Pax drops his head and breathes deep. "In this grand plan of yours, what is she supposed to do once she's there, and how will she get back out?"

"We're hoping she can gather intel for us. Access to the UWO mainframe is limited depending on the department. The sort of information we need, top-secret information about the Program, will be accessible only via direct access. It's impossible for us to hack into the uplink and mainframe remotely, even with Wallace's genius.

"But there is a hack we can give Pria that she can hook up to the main computer in Sanctuary. The virus on the hack can download files directly to our computers here and then self-destruct when all the files have been transferred. *That* will be the simple task. The other one . . ."

Luther looks at me, and his expression is grave. "The other one will be more difficult. I'd like her to investigate the floors beneath Sanctuary. Unless I'm wrong, due to the nature of what we expect goes on down there, none of that information will be on a computer, at least not one uplinked to the mainframe. She will have to observe with her eyes and ears and take note in her mind. Once these things are complete, she can escape in a manner we will have prearranged and report back to us."

To my surprise, Pax laughs. It begins as a sarcastic chuckle and progresses into a manic belly laugh, but at no time does he truly sound amused. "You—you make it sound like—like it's actually possible," he finally manages to say. His laughter drops off, and his voice steadies. "You have no idea what you are asking of her. If you think for one minute this plan of yours will work, you are sorely deluded."

Luther considers Pax for a long moment and then turns to me. "What do you think, Pria?"

I lick my lips. "If I can convince them I was kidnapped against my will, and that I have information for them about all of you, I stand a chance of getting back in." I hear Pax snap his teeth together. "You said it yourself, Pax, when we first escaped. If I was ever recaptured, I had to claim to have been kidnapped by you. The rest of it . . . I don't know."

"You don't need her to investigate the labs beneath Sanctuary," Pax says. "I can tell you everything you need to know."

"And I expect you to. But your account must be verified. If we based all our judgments here on the witness of one person only, we'd be fools."

"Then kidnap an Enforcer or a medical technician as they're leaving Sanctuary and torture the information out of them!" Pax shouts. "I can show you when, where, and how they come and go without detection."

"I expect you to tell us when, where, and how the Enforcers leave Sanctuary, because that will likely be Pria's only way out. However, if there is any other way, we do not obtain information through coercion and torture," Luther says. "We must keep our tactics above that."

"But you'll sacrifice an innocent woman to obtain an uplink to information on their computer mainframe?" Pax slams his fist on the table. "They were about to kill her when I got her out! There must be another place you can infiltrate to get the information you want."

"True. There are other places we could infiltrate, but none that would contain the files we need on the Breeding Program. And we need firsthand accounts—plural—of those labs. Pria can feed them information about us—doctored, of course—in small enough doses to prevent them from killing her until her task is complete. She will be too valuable for them to kill her right away."

Pax pushes away from the table and paces, raking his hands through his fair hair. I wonder if I should feel as aggravated as he does. It is, after all, my life that will be put on the line for this, but I just can't muster the feelings. Instead I feel a sense of destiny. Maybe this is what I'm meant to do.

"Did you never wonder why Mackenzie told you we needed a Breeder?" Luther asks Pax in a quiet voice. "We have tried, and failed, to send in imposters in the form of medical technicians, Protectors, and even Breeders, but they were always flagged and killed on the spot. The only person who can get back in, and who can gain access to the places we need her to, is a legitimate Breeder. Pria is our only hope."

Pax paces to the far wall and leans his hands against it, his back to us. "You are right about one thing," he says.

"What's that?" Luther says.

Pax turns and drops his arms. "Only a Breeder can get to the files you want. The only computer in Sanctuary that contains the uplink to the Program mainframe is Mother's personal computer in her office. It is the most secure place in Sanctuary, and she never invites technicians, Protectors, or Enforcers up there. But Breeders . . . sometimes she does call Breeders there for a chat."

"Then it's settled," I say. "I have to go."

Pax shakes his head. "You don't. Don't let these people make you think you *have* to do anything."

I stand, my eyes blazing. "Then I choose to go."

We face off for a moment before Pax turns to Luther.

"If she goes, then I go with her."

Chapter 46

"I'm afraid that's out of the question. It would destroy her story. For what reason would her kidnapper return to the scene of his crime?"

"Then forget it. I'm not telling you what I know." Pax folds his arms and stares around the room.

"I can still go," I say.

Luther taps his fingers on his table. "No. You can't. We need to know details of the layout beneath Sanctuary and the secret ways in and out before I'd be willing to send you in. Pax is the only one who can provide that information."

"Unless he's being obstinate because his story is false," says the silver-haired woman named Mari. "Perhaps he does not have any information to give."

"He's not lying," I say, irritated because I'm angry with Pax and because, despite that, I still feel the need to defend him.

"She's right. I'm not," Pax says. "But that's all I will say until you give up this mad plan."

"You know, I didn't have to tell you what we're planning," Luther says. "I could have asked you for this information a week ago and gotten it, but I chose to be forthright, to treat you as an equal. I'll ask you to remember that."

Pax's gaze falters for a moment, but he sets his jaw.

Luther sighs and stands. "I can see you won't be persuaded by more argument. I can give you time. If you want to be of use to this movement, as you claim, you will give us the information we need."

"Not if it leads to your sending Pria in there by herself."

"She needs the information you can give her."

"Send me instead," Pax says. "I can get back in."

"But you can't access the computer mainframe. You said so yourself." Luther clasps his hands behind his back. "If it comes to it, I would be willing to send you in through the secret ways you've alluded to for the purpose of helping her escape, but that's all. And not without your sharing the information with me first."

Pax purses his lips and looks away.

"You may have some time to think it over. For now, we have other plans to discuss—plans that don't involve you." Luther gestures toward the door, and Pax stalks over to it. "Pria, you may go as well," Luther says.

I wrinkle my nose and follow Pax. I don't want to be alone with him right now, but I've been dismissed.

"Do you want me to walk with you?" Celine asks in a low voice.

"No. I'll be fine."

"Really, I can go with you and come right back."

"Celine." I put up my hand. "I'll be fine."

I follow in Pax's wake down the corridor, out through the great hall, and on into our residence wing. He doesn't speak to me until we get back to our room, at which point he locks our door, tosses his key on the table, and yanks his large pack out from under his bed.

"What are you doing?" I fold my arms and watch him shove some of the clothes he bought this week into the pack.

"We're leaving," he says. "Get your stuff."

"Excuse me?" I lower my arms, my mouth agape.

"I said we're leaving. I can't keep you safe here."

"Oh really? And where would you suggest we go?"

"We can find another Nest."

"Where? How? We don't even know if there *is* another Nest within a hundred miles."

"Then we'll travel a hundred miles!" Pax shouts. "Now get your stuff."

"You don't . . . you don't *own* me, Pax!" I throw my arms in the air and march over to him. "I'm not going anywhere!"

Quick as a flash, he grabs my wrist and pulls me closer to him. "Do you even understand what it is they're asking you to do?" he says, so close I can count his eyelashes. "It's a suicide mission, and none of them are brave enough to do it themselves."

"They've tried, weren't you listening? Everyone who's tried has been killed for it. I'm the only one who can do this."

"And die in the process?"

"Not if you tell me—tell them—what you know about the layout of the floors beneath Sanctuary and how the Enforcers come and go," I say. "If I need to, I can just escape the same way you and I got out, but I'd rather walk out a door." I tug on my wrist, but he holds it tight. "Why won't you cooperate? I don't get it."

"You don't—" Pax huffs, his breath warm on my face, and studies me from forehead to chin.

His proximity is making me nervous. My stomach is knotting, and I feel almost sick. "Let go of me," I say.

"You're really stupid, you know that?" He releases my wrist with a jerk and steps away. "I promised I would keep you safe," he says.

I glare at him, rubbing my wrist and smarting at his insult. "As you keep saying. But if that's really what you want to do, then you're going to have to stay right here, because I'm not leaving unless it's to go back to Sanctuary to get the information they need." With my back straight, I walk away to my side of the room and sit on my bed. I can hear Pax muttering on the other side of the partition, and something heavy—probably the pack—hits the floor. But then his bed frame creaks and I know he's sat down, too.

I kick my feet, angry and confused about my feelings. I want to hit him in the face, but the thought of hurting him makes the knot in my stomach tighten even more. I wish I could know why he feels such a heavy burden to take care of me, because just helping me escape Sanctuary doesn't seem reason enough.

My heel strikes against the box beneath my bed, and I reach down and under to pull it out. I'd forgotten about this box. It's heavy, and I strain to pull it onto my lap. The outside of it is decorated with tiny, connecting flowers, and I run my fingertip along the patterns, forgetting some of my anger and wondering if the girl whose room this was drew the flowers. Nobody has told us the names of the people who lived here or how they died.

I open the box and cough at the cloud of dust that arises. Inside are stacks of yellowing paper with drawings and lines of handwriting on them. I take out several sheets and page through them. My reading has progressed to the point that I can recognize words here and there, and I can read few simple sentences, but I can't piece together the entirety of what the girl wrote. I flip through several sketches of people, including one of a boy that repeats over and over. She must have liked drawing him.

I sift through the pages for at least fifteen minutes, and Pax doesn't try to talk to me from the other side of the partition. A knock sounds on the door, and I hear the creak of his bed as he rises to answer it. I carefully place the pages back in order and put them in the box before shoving it back under the bed.

"Hey," says Henri, his voice bright when Pax opens the door. "They released me early from the meeting, so I came to see if you two wanted to go have dinner."

"No," says Pax. "I'm not hungry."

"Well, I am." I come around the partition and smile at Henri, whose broad frame fills the doorway. "I'll come with you."

"Great." Henri raises his eyebrows at Pax, offering a silent second invitation.

Pax's gaze flickers between me and Henri. He shakes his head and goes back to his bed.

"Your loss," Henri says. "The hunters brought back fresh game. There won't be any reheated mush tonight."

Pax lays back on his bed and stares at the ceiling.

I watch him a moment longer, guilt twisting in my stomach even through my anger. "Would you like me to bring you something?" I ask.

"No. Thank you," Pax says, his expression unreadable.

I nod and close the door.

"Having a bit of a fight over this, huh?" Henri says, walking beside me down the hall.

"A bit, yeah."

"You know, I get the impression he just doesn't want you to get hurt."

"He's not exactly subtle about it," I say, pulling my mouth to the side and raising an eyebrow.

Henri smiles. "True. And you're not . . . I mean, you're *sure* you two aren't . . ."

I frown at him. "Aren't what?"

"Never mind."

I swing my arms, feeling freer now that I'm out of Pax's stifling protectiveness and condescension. "You know, I'm not actually that hungry right now. I just kind of wanted to get away."

"Do you want to go to my shop for a bit? I promise Arrow will be happy to see you."

"Sure."

He redirects us, and I say, "I don't mean to sound unkind toward Pax. It's just that he seems to think he can make my decisions for me."

Henri nods in a knowing sort of way.

"What do *you* think I should do, Henri?"

He stops and faces me, his expression serious. "I think nothing and nobody should tell you what to do—not Luther, not Pax, nobody. You should do whatever you want to do."

I chew on the corner of my lip. "But it would help, wouldn't it? If I decide to go back."

"Well"—Henri shrugs—"yeah. Of course it would. If you succeed, it could make the difference between—between life and death for the rest of humanity, for all of us the UWO would see killed." He starts walking again, shoving his hands in his pockets. "But it's still your decision, Pria."

"My decision." I laugh.

"What's funny?"

"I never had the opportunity to make my own decisions before leaving Sanctuary, and now I have the weight of the world resting on a decision I have to make. A month ago, the very idea would have seemed . . . wrong. And the person who's responsible for giving me the opportunity to make my own decisions now wants to start making decisions for me. It's confusing. I should feel grateful to Pax. I *am* grateful. But I'm angry, too."

"I don't blame you," says Henri. "*C'est la vie.*"

I wiggle my finger at him as he stops to unlock the door to his shop.

"What is that?" I ask. "Those words you and Celine say sometimes that don't make any sense."

Henri chuckles and steps back so I can walk past him into his shop. Arrow bounds up from the couch and runs toward me.

"They do make sense, just not to you or, to be fair, to almost anyone these days." He flips his lights on. "I'm speaking another language. It's French, and *c'est la vie* means 'That's life.' Although once upon a time, that phrase was well enough known you wouldn't have needed to know French to understand it."

"French," I say, trying out the word on my tongue. It doesn't seem to fit the beautiful, melodic words Henri spoke.

"A long time ago, there were thousands and thousands of different languages spoken on the earth."

"Well, I do know that," I say, scratching Arrow's ears. "They teach that in the Agoge. It's part of what divided the peoples of the world into warring factions."

Henri snorts. "Yeah, they *would* teach it like that. Diversity bad, conformity good."

I twist my mouth to the side. "So how do you know French?"

"Ah." Henri goes to his workbench and sits. "Our mother taught us, and her mother taught her, and on down the line. We come from a long line of people who believed that holding on to our heritage was important. That it would keep us from devolving into savages like those who run the UWO."

I plop down on the couch, and Arrow hops up beside me, eager for more ear scratching. "So it's a part of your heritage. What does that mean?"

"Our ancestors were what was known as French African, long before the Devastations. They spoke French as their primary language. When the Devastations struck, a group of French Africans banded together and escaped here, to North America, where things were rumored to be better. But as everyone knows, the Devastations eventually purged the entire earth. My people built their own sort of Commune in these mountains, but over the years they diminished until there were hardly any of us left." He picks at a knot in the wood and doesn't look at me. "Eventually we joined up with the people here at Asylum when Etienne and I were just babies. Celine and Guy were born a part of this Nest."

"Guy?"

"Our youngest brother. He's dead now."

"Oh. I'm sorry."

Henri sighs and continues to pick at the knot on the worktable. "Etienne believes we should preserve our race by only having kids with other black people—that we need to stay racially set apart. But I view that as just a perverted version of what the UWO is doing." He looks up at me. "I believe preserving our heritage has much less to do with the color of my skin than with passing on our language, our history, and our customs. I couldn't care less what color my wife will be, as long as she holds dear the same sorts of things I do." He ducks his head again. "What are skin color differences, after all, but a slight genetic variation?"

I squint at him. I've never heard someone talk about such things. Celine is always going on about romance, but Henri's talk of preserving his heritage and choosing a wife runs deeper than all that. I lean forward. "Will you say something else for me in French? It's so beautiful. I'd like to hear more."

Henri holds my gaze and smiles. Then he says, "*Vous êtes si belle et si gentille, j'aimerais pouvoir vous dire à quel point vous avez déjà touché mon coeur.*"

I smile, letting the sound of the words wash over me. "What does that mean?"

"Ah . . . no. I think you'll have to just learn French yourself and figure it out." He winks.

"*Tu es un idiot.*" Celine comes through the curtained entrance and rolls her eyes at her brother. "That means, 'You're an idiot.' Henri. Not you, Pria."

"Why is Henri an—"

"Never mind." Celine puts her hands on her hips. "Henri, Etienne's on the warpath. He wants to know why he wasn't invited to the meeting today."

"He knows damn well why he wasn't," Henri says, rising.

"Yeah, well, you'd better head him off before he finds her here." Celine jerks her head toward me.

"All right, all right. Sorry about this, Pria."

"No, it's okay," I say quickly. I don't want Etienne to find me here either.

Henri whistles, and Arrow trots after him as he hurries out the door.

"Jeez," Celine says. "Everybody's upset today about something." She perches on the arm of the couch beside me. "Getting to know Henri better, are we?"

"I kind of had to get away from Pax for a bit."

"I don't blame you," she says. "Just, you should know . . ." She shakes her head.

"I should know what?"

"Never mind."

Chapter 47

We sit in silence for a few moments, and then I say, "Henri mentioned you had a younger brother."

Celine flinches. "Guy. You know, a good deal about why Etienne is so bitter is because of Guy." She fingers a thread on the couch.

"What happened to him?" I whisper.

Celine sighs. "It was ten years ago, before we were set to move here, to Asylum." She looks around. "We had picked up a couple of people from the Denver Commune who told us they were fleeing from the UWO. We put them in captivity, not unlike what we did with you and Pax, until we could get Luther to check their story. But the problem was, Luther was away. He was here, actually, scouting out this location, and we didn't know when he would be back. After a week, those in charge decided to trust the defectors and let them out. Guy was just a kid, seven years old."

She smiles sadly, her gaze distant. "It was always a hundred questions with Guy. He followed the defectors everywhere, asking them anything and everything he could think of, and pretty soon they began to have trouble answering his questions. All lies break down eventually, you know, and Guy was reporting to our mom, in his childlike way, their inability to answer him. Well, Mom grew suspicious and brought Guy with her to confront them. As soon as she started to express her doubt, one of the defectors exploded some sort of device he'd carried in with him. We think they had bombs sewn into their skin, because we'd searched them thoroughly. But we'll never know for sure. We didn't have the detection equipment then that we have now. Anyway, Guy died in the blast, as well as several people who were nearby. Mom was badly injured, but she recovered. Physically, at least."

I gasp. "That's horrible!"

"Mom never got over it, and she blamed herself for bringing Guy with her. Eventually the guilt overwhelmed her. Right before we moved here, she shot herself in the head."

I gape at her. I don't know what to say.

"So . . . yeah. Try not to judge Etienne too harshly. He acts like a complete and total ass half the time only because he's never let himself get over their deaths. In his opinion, we ought to kill them all, as if that will somehow magically bring Mom and Guy back." Celine picks at a thread on the couch.

"What happened to your father?" I ask.

"Don't know," Celine says. "He left on a mission thirteen years ago and never came back. But we never received word that he'd been captured or killed either."

"A mission to do what?"

"Something top secret. Nobody's ever told me what. Henri likes to think he's still alive out there, somewhere, but I don't want to cling to false hope. If he *is* alive, I hate to think what they've done to him." She peers at me. "This is a dangerous life, you know. There are other, safer Nests you and Pax could have taken up with. And they probably wouldn't ask you to do what we're asking you to do."

I purse my lips to the side. "Yes, Pax's thoughts exactly."

"He want you to leave?"

"He tried to *make* me leave. I said no." I square my shoulders. "I want to carry out this mission for you."

"Why?"

I'm silent for a moment, thinking over her simple question. Why *do* I want to? I barely know these people. I'm not deeply invested in their lives.

"I guess I want to know the truth," I say. "From the moment Pax started telling me my life in Sanctuary was a lie, I started to question everything. Well actually, I guess it goes back even before that," I say, thinking about my long months of depression—depression that has all but disappeared since I've been in Asylum.

"But the point is, if you and Pax and the rest are telling the truth about the Program and the UWO, then I must help you because it is the right thing to do. If you all are lying or mistaken, then I deserve to be caught and tried for treason against the UWO. And the only way either of these things is going to happen is if I go back to Sanctuary and find out for myself. Does that make sense?"

Celine nods, and then she says, "You're very brave, Pria. I'm sorry I was so mean to you when we first picked you up."

"It's okay," I say.

"Are you going to go through with the mission even if Pax doesn't come around?"

"Yes."

"But how will you get out of Sanctuary?"

I grin. "Haven't you heard? I'm a genius. I'll figure out a way."

Chapter 48

Despite Pax's contention that he wasn't hungry, I bring him some food anyway when Celine and I finally meander back to our wing. Orson, the cook, made a delicious red stew with fresh venison and bread. I can't believe how normal eating meat has become, but now I can hardly imagine a meal without it.

I say good night to Celine and go into our apartment. Pax is sitting at the table with his head in his hands, and I feel a pang of remorse.

I place the bowl and wrapped bread down beside him and sit in the other chair.

He stares blankly at it for a moment and then reaches out and takes my hand. "Thank you," he says, his voice hoarse.

I freeze, looking at his hand, feeling its weight over my fingers. That simple gesture awakes feelings in me that make my stomach twist and clench and blood rush to my face. I pull my hand away.

"It's good," I say. "And fresh. I didn't want you to miss out."

He nods but makes no move to eat.

We sit in silence for several minutes until I finally say, "Have you changed your mind?"

Pax shakes his head. "I can't. I'm sorry."

I frown. "What do you mean, you can't? You're always going on about personal freedom and liberty. Of course you can help if you decide you want to."

But he says again, "No, Pria. I can't." He swallows and laces his fingers behind his head, massaging as though he has a headache. "I am sorry, though, that I tried to force you to leave here. It wasn't my place to do that. Now, though, there's a large part of me that wishes I had never brought you here at all."

If he knew about Etienne and his threats, he'd feel that way even more. I shift and lower my eyes, afraid he'll see the fear in them. Etienne and his mysterious "friends" are only a handful of bad people in this place full of people who have otherwise accepted me and Pax.

"But I can't change that now," he says. "And if this is really what you want to do, I suppose I can't stop you. But I strongly urge you to reconsider. Your death would achieve nothing."

"But you won't help."

"No."

I sigh and push away from the table. "Good night," I say before going over to my side of the room.

Sometime later that night, I'm awoken by Pax thrashing about and muttering. I throw off my covers and stumble around to his bedside in the darkness, but Pax is still sleeping. As my eyes adjust to the dark, I see he's twisted up in his blankets and his eyes are moving beneath his eyelids.

"I'm . . . fifteen," Pax mumbles. "Fifteen is my number."

I place my hand on his arm. It's sweaty and tense.

"They . . . killed . . ." He throws his head to the side and arches his back.

"Pax," I say. "Wake up."

"I'm number fifteen!" he shouts, sitting bolt upright.

"I know," I say. "Pax!"

He turns empty eyes on me, and for a long moment I'm sure he's still asleep. But then his focus sharpens and he blinks. "Pria," he says in a croaky voice. "What are you doing here?"

"You were crying out in your sleep. I thought somebody was attacking you."

He rubs his face with both hands. "I'm sorry for waking you." He kicks his covers away and swings his legs over the side of the bed.

Despite having bought clothes that fit him, he still sleeps in the too-large shirt and pants that belonged to the previous owner of our apartment. They hang askew on him, revealing the pale skin of his shoulder, and his hair sticks up on one side. He scratches the back of his neck as he rises and goes to pour himself a cup of water from a pitcher we keep on a shelf. He takes it down in one long draught while I watch.

"Who did they kill?" I ask. "Your friend Jacob?"

Page 224

He lowers the cup slowly, his expression confused.

"You were saying, in your sleep, 'they killed.' Were you dreaming about your friend?"

"Oh . . . yes. I was dreaming about Jacob," he says. "I'm sorry. The dream slipped away from me as soon as I woke up, but now I remember." He slumps his shoulders and puts the pitcher and cup back on the shelf, averting his eyes.

I'm certain he's lying to me, and I step up to him. "You're hiding something," I say. "You weren't dreaming about Jacob. You were dreaming about something else you witnessed—something that has to do with why you chose the number fifteen when you made yourself an Enforcer. You didn't forget your dream—you just don't want me to know about it."

Pax raises his head and looks at me, his mouth a thin line.

"You don't have to tell me what it is, but please don't lie to me."

He purses his lips tighter, and his whole body goes rigid.

Tentatively, I touch his clenched fist. I don't know anything about the romance Celine talks about, but I do know my heart hurts to see Pax in pain. And I know I want to comfort him if I can. "Will you be okay to go back to sleep?" I ask.

Pax relaxes his fist and our hands slide together. I don't pull away, even though the action makes me feel like my skin is on fire. He raises my hand until it's beside his face and then presses my palm flat against his cheek. He closes his eyes and breathes deep, and then he releases me.

"I'll be fine," he says in a low voice.

He steps away and returns to his bed, leaving me with my breath caught up in my throat.

Chapter 49

"Have you made up your mind to do it, then?" Bishop asks me the next day.

I straighten the pile of books I've been working on moving for him and turn around. "Yes. I will do it."

"It's very brave of you," he says, adjusting his glasses.

I look away, uncomfortable with his praise. "It just feels as though I should, you know?"

"It's still brave." Bishop hands me another couple of books and then scratches his chin, as though his beard is itching him. "Put these with the stack labeled *B*, please."

I do so, noting that the pages are frayed and burned. "When you found out about the Golems being machines of the UWO," I say, "is that when you started to theorize that the UWO might also have ordered the destruction of all of this stuff?" I sweep my arms around.

"Oh, I suspected it long before that. The UWO has never tolerated anything *different*. Speaking of which, look at this!" He holds up a wooden doll, naked and featureless except for round joints.

"What is it?" I ask.

"I have no idea," he says, posing it in a posture of thinking, with its hand touching where its chin would be. "But it sure fills me with whimsy." He plays with it for another couple of minutes, posing and reposing it. I think of the lifeless Golem hanging in Wallace's cave, and I shiver.

"I'm going to wait a few days before I give Luther my final answer, though," I say. "Pax is against my going, as you know, and I want to give him time to come around."

"He must come around, mustn't he?" Bishop says with a frown. "If you're going to be able to escape, you need the information he has."

"Not necessarily." I shrug. "I could always get back out the way Pax and I got out in the first place." Assuming everything goes as smoothly as planned.

Bishop gives me a look that says he's not convinced, but he doesn't say anything more on the subject. "Here. Sit down for a bit and practice reading this." He hands me a thin, colorful book. "It's a children's book."

I take it and sit at his table. "The . . . Red . . . Hen," I sound out. I raise my eyebrow at Bishop.

"I told you—it's a children's book. It's going to be a while before you can tackle anything harder, even at the rate you learn. That book is at your current reading level."

I sigh and start in, and he's right, it does still take me a good while to sound my way through the words. He helps and corrects me when I make errors, all the while puttering around his archives.

At the end of the day, Celine comes to collect me. We go to dinner together, but Pax and Henri do not show up. Celine says she thinks they are out working on the netting again and will probably be late. We go back to our wing, and I stare in hesitation at my door, knowing Pax is not inside and I will have to be alone for a while.

It's on the tip of my tongue to ask Celine if I can stay with her for a bit, when she squeezes my arm and says in an excited whisper, "I think I may have a date with Elan tonight!"

"A . . . a date?"

"It's like a romantic get-together," she says, waving off my confusion. "He asked me to come by his place after dinner. I would ask you what you think, but I know you're totally clueless," she adds with a wry smile.

"Oh, okay. So are you going, then?"

"Are you out of your mind? Of course I'm going! I'm just letting you know I won't be around for a bit. Are you going to be okay down here on your own?"

I shrug, even as my stomach drops. "Sure."

"Great! Just keep your door locked, yeah?"

"Yeah," I say.

Celine is already looking past me down the hall as though she's eager to be off. I can't ruin her night by asking her to stay, and I get the idea I'm not invited on this "date" thing.

"Okay, see ya." Celine winks and walks off.

I unlock my door with shaking fingers, wondering when Pax will be back and hating how insecure I feel. I'm strong and capable, I should be able to take care of myself. But here I am, racked with fear all because I'm alone.

Once inside, I lock the door, knowing it will be pointless if Etienne decides to pay me a visit, and go over to my side of the room. It's chilly in here, and I shrug into a second shirt and leave my boots on. Then, because I don't know what else to do, I sit on my bed, cradling my Air-5 and tapping my fingers on my knee in a rapid pattern. Could I use it against Etienne if he comes? Probably not. I don't want to kill anybody, and if I injure him, he'll retaliate by sending someone after Pax.

If Etienne comes, I'm stuck. But there's no reason to think he'll come, is there? Does he know Celine and Pax are both away?

Yes. He probably does. He's always watching.

Why do I want to help these people, whispers a voice in the back of my mind.

Because it's not about people like Etienne. It's about people like Celine, and Pax, and Bishop, and . . . my list could go on and on.

And it's also about the truth.

The lock turns with a grating sound. I stand, letting my Air-5 drop to my bed, and face the door with my heart beating in my throat. *Please let it be Pax, please let it be Pax, please let it be Pax.*

It's not. It's Etienne, and he's brought some friends.

Chapter 50

Etienne enters the room like a prowling lion. He gestures his friends forward with a tilt of his head—three men whose names I don't know and a hard-faced woman with tightly curled hair and a shiny scar across her cheek whose name is Rayna. She spots me first where I'm standing, half-hidden by the partition, and her lip lifts in a snarl.

"There she is," Rayna says. "Hiding behind the screen, the little coward."

Etienne waves for one of the men to stay in the hall as the other two stride toward me. Etienne shuts the door and secures the lock. I stand with my back straight and try not cringe away when his friends wrap their hands around my arms and drag me into the main living space.

My breaths are coming in giant heaves. I have to think of something to say to convince him I'm not a spy.

"Celine told me about Guy," I blurt out before I have time to consider whether it's wise or not. "I'm so sorry, Etienne. I understand how that must have made you—"

Etienne lands me a glancing backhand across the face, and I'm thrown back, blinking stars and tasting blood. I stay upright only because of the two men holding my arms.

"Don't you ever speak his name," Etienne says. "*Ever*, do you hear me? I'll kill you the next time you speak his name." His expression is contorted in pain and anger.

I nod, my eyes wide. The side of my face feels like it's on fire, and I'm pretty sure there's blood dripping from my mouth to the floor.

"The nerve," Rayna mutters.

Etienne rubs his hand over his bald head and turns away. "Against the wall," he says.

They force me backward until I'm jammed up against the wall beside Pax's bed. The stone is cold and uneven, and I shiver through my double layer of shirts.

"What did they tell you in the meeting?" Etienne asks, coming close.

My head hurts, and I'm still reeling from his blow. Etienne was not invited to the meeting yesterday—does that mean Luther doesn't want him to know what they've asked me to do?

Etienne nods to Rayna, and she grabs my outer shirt and rips it from collar to hem. The two men release my arms, and she yanks it from my shoulders and casts it away.

"What did they tell you?" Etienne asks again.

I'm confused and cold. I wrap my arms around my chest and say, "I . . . they told me what they want me to do for them."

"What information did you weasel out of them?" Etienne asks, getting down in my face.

"I didn't weasel anything out of them! They told me everything voluntarily." I cringe against the wall as Etienne leans closer.

"You've been manipulating them," he says.

"I haven't! I swear I haven't."

Etienne nods again, and Rayna slams my head against the wall so I drop my arms. Then she yanks my shirt up and over my head. I gasp and cover my chest, blinking tears. All I have left on is my undergarment.

"Is that what perfection is supposed to look like?" Rayna says with a sneer. "What makes you any better than me, huh?"

"I'm . . . I'm not," I say. "I don't claim to be any better than you."

Etienne is studying his hands, but the other two men look me up and down in a way that makes me feel nauseous.

"What do they want you to do?" Etienne asks in a low voice.

I swallow hard against the tears that keep threatening and try to ignore the two menacing men. I don't know why they're removing my clothes, but I'm certain they will hurt me if I can't figure out how to satisfy Etienne.

"They want me to return to Sanctuary," I say through chattering teeth. "I'm supposed to plant a virus that will download information from the mainframe computer at Sanctuary to your computers here. And I'm supposed to explore the secret labs beneath the compound. That's what they want me to do. I promise, that's all!"

Etienne sucks in a breath through his teeth and peers at me. "So you convinced them to send you *back* to Sanctuary with all the information you've gathered about us?"

"I didn't convince them—*they* asked *me!*"

Etienne leans close again. "You know our location, you know who our leaders are, you know the layout of Asylum. Do you expect me to believe you're not going to spill all that to the UWO the moment you get the chance?"

"I'm only going to give them the information Luther tells me to give them—the information I'll need to give them to stay alive!"

"Liar," Rayna says.

"I'm not lying!"

Rayna punches me in the stomach, and I double over with a grunt.

"Get the truth out of her," Etienne says, turning away. "Luther won't be convinced she's a spy unless we can get a confession out of her. Do whatever you need to do."

The two men move forward with leering expressions. One of them grabs my wrists and forces my hands above my head, while the other puts his rough, sweaty hands on my stomach. I whimper and twist, but I'm trapped. He presses close so I can smell his sour breath and rakes his hands up to my shoulders. "I always wanted to know—"

A pounding sounds on the door, and the man touching me freezes and looks over his shoulder.

Henri's angry, muffled voice comes from the corridor outside. "What are you doing here, Graham? Did my brother put you up to this?" There's a thump, then Henri says, "Pax, you'd better get in there."

The lock turns on the door, and Etienne jerks his head at the men holding me. The one holding my hands releases me, but the one with his sweaty hands on my shoulders hesitates a moment too long. Pax bursts into the room and takes in the scene with one quick look.

In a few strides, he passes Etienne and Rayna and grabs the man with his hands on me. Pax punches him across the face and then grabs his neck and lifts him up against the wall. "You think you can touch her and get away with it?" He slams the man's head back into the stone.

The other man grabs Pax's shoulders to wrestle him away, but Pax twists and kicks him in the groin. The man goes down with a groan, and Pax turns his attention back to the man he has pinned against the wall. In the background, Henri and Etienne are shouting at each other, and Rayna has disappeared without a trace. Shaking, I grab the pieces of my torn clothing and clutch them to my chest.

Pax's hand tightens around the other man's throat, and the man's face is turning purple. "How dare you?" Pax says.

"She's . . . jus . . ." the man says, his voice strangled as he clutches at Pax's hand, "a cog . . . b . . . ch."

Pax's expression hardens, and he slams the man into the cave wall again. All the remaining breath goes out of him in a huff, and his eyes cross and then slide closed. Pax releases him, and he crumples in slow motion, leaving a smear of blood on the wall behind him.

Chapter 51

Pax yanks a blanket off his bed and throws it around my shoulders. Then, without even asking me if I'm all right, he holds my chin and tilts my head from side to side, inspecting the damage from Etienne's blow. His nostrils flare and his jaw tightens, and he turns toward Etienne and Henri with clenched fists.

"You did this," he says, cutting through their argument. "You did it. You threatened to on the first day we arrived, and I told you I would make you sorry if you ever touched her." He advances on Etienne, who draws himself up with a defiant look.

"Dude, Hunter is dead," says the other man, the man Pax downed with a kick to the groin. "Etienne, are you hearing me? He's dead!"

"Well, it wasn't a *date* after all." Celine's disgruntled voice carries ahead of her as she comes around the corner into our room. She's scowling, but her face goes blank when she takes in the scene. "What the *hell*?"

"Celine," Henri says. "Go get Sing and her guys. And Luther."

Celine stands with her mouth agape and doesn't move.

"Now!" Henri shouts.

Celine jumps and runs off.

"He's dead. The bastard killed him." The other man begins to moan.

Henri steps between Pax and Etienne. "Stop," he says. "It's over. The authorities will be here soon."

"Let me go check Hunter," Etienne says. "See if what Ben is saying is true."

Pax is seething, held back by Henri, who nods at his brother. "Don't try anything stupid," Henri says.

Etienne hurries to Hunter's side and feels for his pulse. After a few moments, he shakes his head and turns Hunter over so he can see the back of his skull. It's indented and matted with blood. "*Je n'y crois pas.*" He turns wide eyes on Pax and then launches himself forward.

He almost lands a punch, but Pax catches his fist and twists. Etienne cries out in pain as Pax keeps twisting until there is a loud snap.

"Enough!" Henri shouts as he wrestles the two of them apart.

"See?" Etienne shouts, then groans and pulls his broken arm to his chest. "Can't you see? He's a spy! He's been trained to kill us all!"

"Are you out of your mind?" Henri gestures with both hands. "What do you think you were doing here?"

"I had to make her talk," Etienne says. "Somehow. You were going to trust her. You were going to send her back to them with information about us."

"Etienne, she's *not a spy!*"

"You can't know that!"

The man called Ben is inching toward the door. I shrink away from him with a glare.

"Don't even think about it," Henri says, pointing at him.

Ben freezes and gives Pax a wide-eyed look. "Don't let him kill me," he says.

"*Quel fouillis.*" Henri wipes his hands over his face and shoots Pax a disgruntled look. Pax is clenching his fists and breathing fast, barely containing his wrath. "Don't touch anybody else, yeah? You're only making things worse."

Pax gives a short nod.

Henri comes over to me, touches my cheek, and grimaces. "Are you okay?" he asks.

I nod. I don't trust myself to speak.

"I'm so sorry," Henri says. "I don't know what to say—"

"What is going on here?" Luther strides into the room, followed by a compact woman with jet-black hair and a round face and several men wearing matching charcoal-gray armbands and carrying guns. Security officers—I've seen them around Asylum.

Celine scoots in behind them and hurries to my side. She gives me a quick, searching look before turning to glare at Etienne.

"He killed Hunter!" Ben shouts, pointing at Pax. "He's a murderer!"

Pax crosses his arms over his chest and says nothing in his defense. Luther gestures to one of the security officers, who goes to the fallen man and holds his fingers at Hunter's throat.

"Dead, sir," the security officer says after several tense moments.

Luther turns to Pax. "Why did you do this?"

"I returned from work to find these men in my apartment with Pria." Pax's shoulders have relaxed and his fists are no longer clenched, but I can tell by the gleam in his eyes that he could erupt again at any moment. "They had her cornered, they'd ripped her clothes off, and that one, Hunter, was . . . *touching* her." Pax's voice is steady, and he hesitates only on the last couple of words. "I responded the way I promised Etienne I would should he or any of his friends carry out the threats he voiced to me on our first day here."

Celine puts her arm round me and says something in French.

Luther looks at me. "Pria?"

I nod, unsure how to vocalize my feelings of violation, and even less sure I want to.

Luther blinks, and he looks me up and down, taking in the blanket wrapped around me and Celine's protective stance at my side. He gives resigned sigh. "Is he telling the truth?" Luther asks Henri and Etienne.

"Yes," Henri says.

Etienne tightens his jaw and looks down. There are beads of sweat on his forehead despite the coolness of the cave, and he's still clutching his broken arm to his chest.

"What were you going to do, Etienne?" Luther asks, his voice dangerous. "*Rape* her to get some sort of confession out of her?"

"If that's what it took," Etienne says.

Luther steps back as though stunned and shakes his head. "Arrest them," he says to the black-haired lady named Sing. "Etienne and Ben. And Pax."

I make a noise of protest and start forward, but Luther holds up his hand. "He killed someone, Pria. I can't let that go unpunished. He'll have to stand trial."

"Luther," Celine says. "He was just—"

"No. I have to follow protocol."

I look at Pax to find him staring at me. I raise my eyebrows, but he just gives a curt shake of his head and allows two security officers to take his arms.

"There was a woman here, too," Henri says. "Rayna. She fled when we arrived. And Graham was keeping watch outside the door."

"We'll find them. Sing?"

The black-haired lady nods and leaves.

"How did you get in here," Luther asks, turning back to Etienne. "Did you force your way in?"

Etienne grits his teeth and flinches as a security officer grabs his good arm. He shoots me a warning look, and I know that, even now, I must say nothing about his previous visit. He could have more friends out there, friends who might be able to get to Pax, even in jail. I look at the floor.

"Pria?" Luther asks.

I shake my head.

Luther nods. "I see how it is. I'll get it out of him one way or another. Take them away." He sounds tired.

The security officers escort Pax, Etienne, and Ben out of our apartment.

"Henri, please see to it this mess gets cleaned up," Luther says, gesturing at the dead body. "He deserves a proper burial, no matter what his crimes were."

He comes to me and reaches for my shoulder but seems to think better of it when I flinch. "I'm deeply sorry this happened," he says. "Are you feeling all right?"

"I . . ." I feel dirty, but how can I explain that to Luther? "I'm fine," I say instead, trying to put on a confident expression.

He narrows his eyes. "Go with Celine. Stay the night with her, and don't open the door to anyone. I'll have your locks replaced." He turns away but then hesitates and turns back. "I know this must color your perception of us, but I assure you I will see they are punished according to the full extent of our law. I hope you don't let it dictate your decision."

Right. My decision to help these people. To put my life on the line for them. I feel Hunter's sweaty hands on my skin, and I shiver.

But Hunter, Etienne, Ben, Rayna—they are not like the others in this place.

I shake my head. Then I ask, "What's going to happen to Pax?"

"The court will have to decide," Luther says.

"Please don't hurt him," I whisper.

"If it's in my power, he'll receive the lowest sentence possible," Luther says. "I promise you, Pria. I'm not blind to what Etienne and his friends are capable of."

"He was just defending me. Doesn't that count for anything?"

"It does." Luther shoulders his weapon. "But he didn't have to kill him."

I shoot a look at Henri. His shoulders are hunched and his hands are in his pockets.

"Come on, Pria." Celine tugs on my elbow. "Sleepover at my place tonight."

Chapter 52

There are clothes lying in piles all over Celine's floor, and her bed is a mess of twisted blankets. She grabs a few blankets and tosses them onto the ratty couch against the wall. "I'll sleep on the couch," she says. "You can have my bed."

I nod, my teeth chattering. The only thing I brought with me from my apartment is my Air-5, which I clutch protectively to my chest.

Celine blinks and grimaces sympathetically. "Hey," she says, coming close and touching my arms. "How are you doing?"

I squeeze my eyes shut and look down.

"Pria . . . you can cry if you want. I won't judge you."

I shake my head vigorously.

She sighs. "Don't worry about Pax," she says. "Henri saw what happened. He'll testify that he was just defending you."

"What . . . what does *rape* mean?" I ask, remembering the word Luther used.

Celine stills and her eyes go cold. "Uh . . . I'd rather not explain that. Let's just say"—she pats my Air-5—"if anybody ever touches you like that again, you shoot him, got it?"

"But Pax—"

"If it's you defending yourself, you won't get put away for it," she says. "And even if you did, better that than the alternative."

I nod.

Celine goes to a pile of clothes and collects a baggy shirt and pants. "Come on. I think you'll feel better after a shower."

Breeder

She follows me into the bathroom and waits outside the shower door as I let the frigid cold water push into my head and shoulders. I quickly go numb, but I welcome it, as it erases the sensations that cling to me. Hunter's hands on my stomach. Etienne's knuckles across the side of my face. The sting of my cut lip. Rayna's ripping my clothes off with an expression of scorn.

"So this is what perfection looks like."

I rub my hands over my stomach and down over my thighs. *I am perfection. Physical perfection.* The thought makes me want to vomit.

"Are you okay?" Celine's voice comes muffled through the boards and the water in my ears. "You're going to catch hypothermia if you stay in there much longer."

I watch the water course down between the slats beneath my feet. Even my toes are perfectly formed, my nails strong and healthy. For what? So I can perpetuate a lie? So I can pass on perfect toes to another generation of approved humanity? For the first time, I wonder what became of my child, the one who survived. He—or she, I don't even know—would be three years old now.

"Pria, you're making me nervous!"

I shake myself and step out of the stream of water. Not bothering to towel off, I slip into the clothes Celine gave me and then step out into the main bathroom. Water drips from my short hair down my face, and the clothes cling to me in damp patches.

"Jeez, girl, you're blue." Celine takes my hands and rub them between her own. "Why didn't you dry off?"

I shake my head, my teeth chattering.

She rolls her eyes and keeps rubbing my hands.

"Celine," I say, and she looks up. "Do you resent me because of how I look?"

Her rubbing slows, and she looks me up and down. Then she says, "Don't be ridiculous."

But her hesitation has told me everything I needed to know.

"I'm going to do it, you know," I say. "I'm going to go back to Sanctuary and find out the truth. Because life can't go on like this—they can't be allowed to continue to manufacture their idea of perfect humanity while the rest of you struggle to survive. I *will* uncover what's going on. I owe that much to you, to Henri, to—to Guy."

Celine's eyes fill with tears, and she throws her arms around me. "Thank you," she says.

Chapter 53

"Remember what I said about how I think Pax feels about you."

My heart rate increases, and I nod. "It's . . . such a strange thought."

"I know you're not convinced, but trust me. I've never seen a man treat a woman the way he treats you without being madly in love. *Trust me*, he wouldn't care half as much about you going to risk your life if he didn't at least have an inkling of romantic feelings for you."

"But you care about me going, and you don't feel that way about me," I say.

"Yeah, and I'm willing to let you go and do it, aren't I?" Celine gives me a wry smile. "Friendship is one thing, romantic love is another thing entirely. Remember, don't let on that you know how he feels, just hint that you *might* know, but be firm about the fact that you *are* going. More than anything, he doesn't want to see you hurt. He'll give in and tell you what he knows."

I don't waste any time the next day in going to Luther. After a somber breakfast of potatoes and eggs, and a conversation with Celine about flirting that's both enlightening and disturbing, Celine escorts me to Luther's office. He opens the door almost immediately after the first knock, as though he's been waiting there for me, and ushers us in with a haggard wave. His son plays with blocks beneath his broad table.

Luther gestures for me to sit, but I decline, feeling too nervous to be still.

"Rayna and Graham were caught last night trying to leave Asylum," Luther says in a gravelly voice. There are deep circles beneath his eyes, and

I wonder if he slept at all. "They're locked up now. Was there anybody else involved with the attack that you know of, Pria?"

"No."

He nods and sits in his usual place, his shoulders sagging wearily. "I am, again, very sorry this happened to you. We don't tolerate that sort of behavior here, but I should have anticipated the level of animosity some people here would have toward you. But I assure you the majority of us—"

"Luther." I put my hand up. "I've already decided to do it. You don't have to convince me of everybody else's good intentions."

He blinks. For a moment, the only sound is the clacking of blocks beneath the table.

"But you'd better send me soon," I say, touching my bruised face. "I want these bruises to be fresh. It will help convince them I was kidnapped."

Luther swallows, the lump on his neck bobbing up and down. "Are you certain?" he asks. "It will be dangerous."

"I have to know the truth," I say.

Luther exchanges a quick look with Celine and then stands and approaches me. He rests his hands on my arms and looks down at me with a grave expression. "You could save us all," he says. "If you succeed, and if our theories are proven, you have no idea what this will mean for us, for the Free Patriots, for the coming revolution."

His son crawls out from under the table and blinks up at me with wide eyes.

"I think I have some idea," I say. "Just let me talk with Pax one more time before I go. I think I can convince him to tell me how to get out." I look at Celine, and she smiles. "And whatever you do, don't hurt him. Whether I come back or not, just don't hurt him."

Luther nods. "Rayna and Graham confessed to the crime. If only Pax hadn't killed Hunter, he wouldn't even be in jail right now, but—"

"I know. I understand," I say. "So what's next?"

Luther steps back and crosses his arms. "Wallace has the hack ready to go, and it shouldn't take too long for him to explain to you how it works. We can probably have everything set up for our departure this evening."

I raise my eyebrows. "*Our* departure?"

"A few of us will be keeping an eye on you for as long as we can. You won't be able to carry a gun, you know. Too suspicious if you're caught with it. You have to be able to convince them you fled from your captors with nothing but the clothes on your back."

My heart starts to hammer in my chest as fear over the plan grips me for the first time. "It will take me a long time to get back to Sanctuary, though, won't it?"

"We'll drop you under cover of night as close as we dare. We won't make you wander the wilderness alone for longer than you have to. And we'll point you in the right direction."

"I'm going to need to be dehydrated," I say. "And hungry and weatherworn. They must know there's not a Nest within fifty miles of Sanctuary. If they let me back in, they'll send me straight to medical for an evaluation." I grimace. "I shouldn't have eaten breakfast today. They're going to know."

Luther frowns. "We should wait until tomorrow night, then."

"No. I need to look as though I've been in the wild. We'll go tonight, but don't drop me too close. Give me a couple of days' walk."

"Pria, that's insane," Celine says. "You could die before you get there!"

"Do you want this plan to succeed or not? You don't understand the level of medical technology they have there. They may not have a human lie detector"—I nod at Luther—"but they'll be able to tell by reading my vitals whether or not I'm actually dehydrated, and whether or not I've actually been out in the elements for a few days."

Luther nods, and Celine sighs and wraps her arms around her chest.

"Take her to see Pax," Luther says. "I'll go let Wallace know she's coming."

Celine is quiet as she leads me through unfamiliar tunnels, away from the hustle and bustle of the main caves. Every time I glance sideways at her, she's chewing the corner of her lip.

"What are you thinking?" I finally ask.

She looks at me, her dark eyes sad. "I'm thinking I don't want you to get hurt or killed. I don't know if you've picked up on it, but I don't have a lot of friends." She gives a hollow laugh. "Here you are, going to risk your life, and I'm still thinking of myself."

"I've never had a lot of friends either," I say. "I don't think I had any real friends among my sisters in Sanctuary. Friendship, attachment to anything other than the UWO, wasn't encouraged. And for what it's worth, I don't want to die either."

"Glad to hear it."

We're coming up on some guards in an otherwise deserted corridor, and Celine stops and draws close to me.

"Remember what we talked about at breakfast," she says in a low voice. She twists her lips to the side and narrows her eyes. "Really, this shouldn't be too difficult for you, given the circumstances."

"What do you mean?"

She rolls her eyes. "*Vous êtes un tel imbécile.* Part of your appeal is your dewy-eyed innocence, you know that?"

I frown.

She pokes me in the chest. "I can see your hands shaking. How's your heart rate treating you?"

"Well, I'm—I'm nervous," I say. "Obviously. If I can't get him to tell me how to get out, I'll be stuck trying to escape the same way Pax and I escaped a few weeks ago, if that's even possible."

"Okay, you're just going to have to figure out your feelings on your own," Celine says. "But trust me, he'll tell you." She tugs me forward, and we pass the first set of guards and proceed on to the next set, who stand before a thick wooden door in the rock. "She's allowed to see him," Celine says to the guards. "Luther's orders."

The guards nod and one of them unlocks the door. When they swing it open, I see Pax inside, sitting on a low cot with his hands clasped in front of him. The space is lit by a single lantern. He stands as I enter, and the guard closes the door behind me.

Chapter 54

We stare at each other for several moments. My hands are sweating, and I rub them on my pants as I try to read him. He looks tired—exhausted, actually. The shadows under his eyes are offset by the golden stubble on his chin and jaw that catches the light from the lantern. Absent is his usual barely contained energy. His blue eyes are dull and vacant, and he stands with rounded shoulders.

"Cozy up to him a bit. Give him some hope."

I take a step forward but then stop. I don't want to be artificial with Pax. Two feelings war within me—an actual, real desire to reach out to him, and a fear that I'll come across as manipulative if I do.

"I'm so sorry you're in here."

"You don't have to apologize," he says. "You didn't do anything wrong." He clears his throat and searches my face.

My hands are shaking, and I clasp them in front of me. Pax catches the movement and takes a step toward me as though to comfort me. I swallow and look at the floor.

"Pria."

I look up, and he moves another step closer. There're only a couple of feet between us now.

He takes a breath then steps even closer.

I can't breathe and my thoughts feel muddy. Why am I here, again?

He touches my cheek so lightly I almost can't feel it. I close my eyes. What's happening to me?

"Don't go," he says. "Please don't go."

Oh yes. That's why I'm here.

I open my eyes. He's so close, but I want to draw him closer. I can't believe I actually want to feel his arms around me.

But I have to tell him the truth, and it will make him angry. "I'm going," I say. "Tonight. I'm sorry."

Pax drops his hand and steps away, shaking his head. "They'll kill you."

"They won't." I touch the bruise on my cheek, my split and scabbed lip. "They'll believe I was kidnapped, and they'll want the information I have. They'll know I couldn't have injured myself like this. In a way, Etienne did me a favor."

Pax's eyes flash, and I know I've said the wrong thing. "Don't say that," he says. "Don't ever say it's a good thing for someone to have hit you."

I feel a rush of warmth and know my face has gone red. "Regardless, I am going. I came to give you one more chance to tell me what I need to know."

"Is that the only reason?"

I blink and waver. "And . . . and to see you one last time, just in case."

Pax's mouth tightens, and something shifts in his eyes. He hesitates a moment more and then covers the distance between us in two long strides. I stiffen and almost step back out of habit but force myself to remain still as he wraps his arms around me. He lowers his head, and for a terrifying second I think he's going to press his lips to mine, like Celine did to him over a week ago, but instead he tilts his head so his cheek brushes mine, his scruff scratchy and his breath tickling my ear and neck.

I forget to breathe. He's warm and solid, and being embraced by him feels like . . . feels like . . . I close my eyes. I can't express what it feels like, but I like it. As if they have a mind of their own, my arms come up around his back, and I cling to his shirt.

Pax breathes deep, reminding me to breathe as well.

"Pax, I—"

"No, listen to me," he says, his voice urgent and low in my ear. His arms tighten around me. "Pay close attention. There's a tunnel, a long tunnel, from Sanctuary to the Commune, but it's guarded. Once you've planted the virus and discovered what you need to in the basements, return to the first floor beneath the Med wing.

"You'll need to have stolen a Protector's uniform, because you'll need the access codes that will show up inside the helmet. You can find Protectors' uniforms in the lockers in the hall behind the kitchen. That door will be locked, but the nutrition techs prop it open when they're serving meals. Slip in and steal a uniform from one of the farthest lockers. From that moment on, do not be seen without it.

"In the first basement, you'll find an unmarked door across from Nursery Six—the nursery where they study the deformed ones. There's an access panel by the door, and the code will show up on the inside of your visor when you look at the panel. The door opens straight to the tunnel.

"There are guards along the way, but they won't question you as long as you are in uniform and nobody's been alerted that a Protector's uniform has gone missing. The tunnel drops you out in the Enforcement Center in the Denver Commune. That's where it will be trickiest, because you won't have transfer orders. You're going to have to convince them there was a glitch in the system and the orders never came through to them. Be confident and assertive, and if they give you too much trouble, tell them you'll report them to Colonel Haymond. Everybody's afraid of him, so that should shut them up.

"Once you get outside, get out of the Commune as quickly as you can and disappear back into the forest. If you get caught at any time, shoot to kill. If you leave an Enforcer alive behind you, the distress signal from their suit will alert the entire system. Can you remember all that?"

I nod. I don't trust my voice.

Pax pulls back so he's looking down into my eyes. My breath is coming in quick hitches, and I can't look away. Without breaking eye contact, he leans closer until our lips are almost touching and waits. Just waits. I don't know what to do. I don't want him to pull away, but I'm terrified of what it might mean if he comes an inch closer.

A heavy fist pounds on the door, and a guard shouts through it, "You two just about done in there?"

I jump, my nose brushing Pax's as I leap away.

"Leave them alone, you idiot!" Celine shouts, outraged.

"Yes!" I call back, my voice too high. "We're finished."

Pax blinks, and a wrinkle appears between his eyebrows. He laces his hands behind his neck and paces away, breathing hard. Without turning back to me, he says, "I guess you got what you came for."

I press my hands to my cheeks, trying to cool them. I'm shaking. "Thank you," I say.

The door opens with a grate and a squeak of rusty hinges, letting in a blast of cool air.

"Pria," Pax says as I turn to leave.

I look back at him, searching his expression for some hint of what is going through his mind, but his stoic mask is back in place.

"Just don't die," he says.

I nod, and the door closes between us.

K.B. Hoyle

Chapter 55

I walk down the hall without waiting for Celine, and she has to hurry to catch up with me. "Sorry about that," she says. "The guards seemed to be under the impression they needed to rush you. I hope it didn't interrupt."

I shake my head.

"Oh. Good." She peers sideways at me. "Did you get it?"

"Yes. He told me how to get out of Sanctuary."

Celine lets out a long breath. "*Good*. Does it sound . . . doable?"

I shrug. "Maybe. I don't know." I'm walking aimlessly, and Celine tugs on my arm to direct me away from a turn I'm about to take.

"What else happened in there?" She takes my hand. I can't hide the trembling. "Did he kiss you?"

I shake my head.

"Did you kiss him?"

I shake my head again.

"Henri will be happy," she mutters. "Was I at least right about how he feels about you, though?"

"Maybe. Probably? I . . . I don't know, Celine!"

"Hey, calm down. It's okay."

I stop and face her. "I don't understand all these cues and signals and touches and looks and . . . and *affection*, can't you see that? I wasn't ever taught anything like this!"

"Well, tell me what he did, and I'll tell you what it means."

"He . . ." I put my fingers on my forehead and close my eyes. "He put his arms around me and brought his face down like he was going to kiss me, but then he just stood there. He didn't do it, but he didn't pull away. It was like he was having an argument with himself."

"Something must have been holding him back," she says. "Maybe he thought you didn't want him to do it."

"Well, I wasn't exactly pulling away!"

Celine brightens and pokes me. "So you *did* want him to do it."

"Kind of—maybe—yes. But I . . . I don't even know why."

"Well, what else happened? Did he say anything, other than how to get out?"

"He told me not to die."

Celine snorts. "That's romantic."

I blink. I don't even know how to respond to her sarcasm. "Can we just not talk about this?" I say, moving off down the corridor again. "I have enough to worry about as it is."

"Sure, sure. Whatever you want," Celine says, her tone amused.

We walk in silence for several minutes, Celine directing us toward the garage caves and Wallace's workshop. I'm vaguely able to identify the path, but I'm much too distracted by what happened with Pax.

Just outside Wallace's door, I ask, "Does it mean I have romantic feelings toward Pax if I *did* want him to kiss me?"

"I thought you said you don't want to talk about it," Celine says, pressing the buzzer on Wallace's entrance.

"I don't."

Celine laughs. "Well, yeah. It could mean that. Of course, it could also mean that you're just attracted to him."

"I also feel a little sick when I'm around him . . . a lot of the time."

"Sick how?"

I sigh and roll my eyes. "In my stomach."

"Uh, yeah. That could be romantic feelings. Didn't they ever teach you about internalizing emotions in the Agoge?"

"Not really, no."

Celine hits Wallace's buzzer again. "Listen, as you said, you have enough to worry about right now as it is. Let's just focus on getting you through this mission alive, and then when you get back, I'll tell you all about what love feels like."

"Ah, excellent!" Wallace says when he sees us outside his door. "I'm glad you decided to cooperate with our little scheme, Pria. We'll all owe you a great debt if you succeed."

I try to ignore the specter of the Golem skeleton hanging from his ceiling and focus on his words.

"Luther said you'd have the virus chip ready for her," Celine says.

"Yes, I do." He comes forward with something tiny held between his thumb and forefinger. "All you have to do is place it within a few feet of a computer attached to the UWO mainframe, and it should self-activate. You don't have to hook anything up or flip any switches. It's set to hack into the closest computer within range."

He holds up his finger, and at first I don't see anything. Then I notice a flesh-colored circle about half the size of a fingernail on the tip of his finger.

"It's sticky," he says. "Quite sticky. I painted it to match your flesh so it will hopefully escape notice."

"What is it?" I ask. "How did you make it?"

He jerks his head toward the hanging Golem. "I took this one from Pat there, but I've practiced on ones I've taken from the cloned animals we steal. The Golems have the same computer implant as the cloned animals, remember. I disconnect this little part of the implant, and it disrupts the uplink to the UWO computer. Of course, with the animals, I have to train what's left of the computer in their brains to continue communicating vital, life-sustaining information to them, but I didn't have to worry about that with the Golem." He waggles his finger. "I got to thinking, if this little thing can uplink to the UWO mainframe over a great distance, then surely I could reprogram it to hack into a close-range computer and transmit the information to me."

"Oh, surely," Celine says, her tone dry.

But I say, "But it does work? Have you tested it?"

"Have I—of course I've tested it! On Commune computers, but the principles are the same. But it has to be *close*, Pria, within a few feet, do you understand? It doesn't know which system to hack if it's trying to read all sorts of signals flying about."

I lick my lips. "So I just place it and leave it? How much time does it need?"

"It should connect instantaneously, and the file download should take no more than a couple of minutes."

"So . . . I don't even have to put it down by the computer. All I have to do is place myself close to the computer, and it will pick it up?"

He blinks. "Yes, that's right. If you can get yourself beside the necessary computer, the hack will take care of the rest."

"Will there be any way for me to know whether or not it's worked?"

"No. But you get it close enough, and it will work."

"Won't there be all sorts of security on the mainframe computer, though?" Celine asks. "How can you possibly have written a program into that little thing that will allow it to effortlessly hack into the system? Won't it set off alarms?"

"I've designed it to disguise itself as a—you know what?" Wallace waves his arm. "We don't have time for this. Just trust me. I've been working with these uplinks for years, and I know computers better than anyone. This will work, and it will work without alerting them to the fact that we're stealing their data. Are you ready?"

I look at Celine, who still seems unconvinced, and then nod at him.

"Okay. I'm going to place it inside your ear, like so." He folds the inner cartilage of my ear forward and presses his finger to the inside of it, leading to the ear canal. He removes his finger and steps back. "Go ahead and touch it."

I do. It's barely noticeable, just a slightly raised bump inside my ear, and it's smooth, so it must be that only one side of it is sticky.

"If you're going to place it, you'll have to use your fingernail to peel it off. Otherwise, as you said, just stand close to the computer for a couple of minutes, if you can."

I nod.

"Okay," he says. "Let me see your wrist."

I hold out my hand, and he examines the fresh scar from where Pax cut the tracking chip from the inside of my wrist.

"That shouldn't raise any suspicion," he says, rubbing his thumb over it. "It will match when you fled, and they'll believe your 'kidnapper' would have removed it as soon as possible." He gives me a grim smile. "Any questions I might be able to answer?"

I cast another look at the hanging Golem skeleton. "If I come across one of those out there, what do I do?"

"Run," Wallace says.

"But we'll be keeping an eye on you, too, as long as we're able," Celine says. "Don't worry, we'll keep you safe." But her smile doesn't reach her eyes.

Chapter 56

I pack nothing to take with me, and I drink only sips of water for the rest of the day. By the time Luther comes to Celine's room to collect us, I'm lightheaded and second-guessing my decision to go, but all their hopes are resting on me. That and I really do want to know the truth.

Luther and Celine walk me to the garage caves where Henri and Elan are waiting. They're all wearing camouflage gear and are heavily armed, and Henri tosses Celine a jumper when we walk in.

"You all right?" Henri asks, looking me up and down. "You sure about this—about going with nothing but the clothes on your back, I mean?"

"It has to be this way," I say, my voice already a little hoarse from lack of water.

"We'll drop you close to a stream," Luther says. "Don't be afraid to drink deeply. They'll assume you'll have found *some* water on your way, and there's no need to put yourself in any more danger than you have to."

Celine zips up the front of her camouflage jumper and waves her hand. "This way. We're taking the boat."

I frown and follow the others around the vehicles in the large cavern. The "boat" turns out to be a small hovercraft—the smallest the UWO makes, according to Celine—that is shaped like a rectangle with the ends turned slightly up. The enclosure over the base looks barely large enough to fit the five of us who are gathered. Aside from the camouflage paint that covers the entire thing, it does look like a boat.

"It's going to be something of a squeeze," Celine says, "but it's the most effective vehicle we have for this sort of thing, especially to avoid notice. And it's fast. If anything happens to you, we should be able to get to you pretty quick."

"We'll drop you three days out and follow you for two," Luther says. "On the third day, we'll have to ditch the boat and follow you on foot. After everything is finished, when you get through the tunnel Pax told you about and flee the Commune, we'll be waiting for you in the trees, as close as we can come, do you understand?"

I nod. "Yes. Yes, I've got it." I'm tingly and bouncing on the balls of my feet. My stomach is rumbling with hunger, and I'm almost eager to get out into the woods so I can start to forage for some of the things Pax taught me to find when it was just the two of us.

"All right, everyone. Let's go," Luther says.

Celine squeezes my hand and then climbs into the driver's seat of the boat. I follow the men through the small opening into the main body of the craft. There are four seats, two on each wall, with five-point harnesses. We can't stand upright because the ceiling is so low, and when I sit, I'm still slightly hunched forward along the curvature of the wall.

"Sorry about the discomfort," Celine says, calling back from the cockpit as Elan squeezes in and takes the seat beside her. "The UWO didn't build these suckers to transport people, just supplies. I added the seats."

"If it's just a transport vehicle, then why is it so fast?" I ask, buckling my harness.

Celine grins at me over her shoulder. "I made a few modifications." She flips a couple of switches and the boat starts to hum. She eases back on a stick between her seat and Elan's, and we rise a few feet off the ground, swaying back and forth. A rushing sound fills my ears, and I clutch at my seat. I've only ridden in a hovercraft once before, and that was a very short journey from the Agoge to Sanctuary when I was thirteen.

Luther reaches around me and pulls the door closed, and the rushing sound quiets. Celine points the nose of the vehicle toward the mesh-covered opening of the cave, and a guard pulls the mesh back to reveal the dark, mottled landscape of the forest beyond. She eases us forward, out of the cave and under the net that covers the surrounding area. The trees are nothing but black shadows rising like sentinels out of the darkness.

"Okay, everyone. Hold on tight," Celine says after we've cleared the net. She punches the throttle, and we shoot up and over the trees.

My stomach lurches back into my spine, and I close my eyes, fighting back queasiness.

"We can't get much height in this thing, especially not weighed down as we are," Celine shouts over the increased rumble of the engine, "but it's still fast!" She sounds downright exhilarated. I nod, keeping my eyes shut.

If I tune out everything except the hum and rush of the engines, I can almost pretend I'm in a meditation chamber in Sanctuary with white noise lulling me to relaxation. After several minutes, and finally feeling as though I have my queasiness under control, I open my eyes and stare ahead. Henri sits across from me, and when he sees me emerge from my reverie, he gives me an encouraging smile.

"First time flying, huh?" He's holding a bar above his head with one hand, probably bracing himself forward against the awkward curvature at his back.

I nod. Second time, actually, but I think it's best to keep my mouth closed.

"Well, you're doing great," he says.

I want to say thank you, but all I can manage is a tight smile.

"Listen," he says, "if anything happens to you in there, I want you to know . . ." He shoots a look at Luther and falls silent. I don't press him to continue.

It's hard to judge how long we're airborne, especially because looking out the front window—green-tinged for night vision—renews my nausea, so I spend the time studying either Henri's knees or the floor at his feet.

Elan seems to be trying to carry on a hushed conversation with Celine, but seeing as how she responds in curt, one-word answers, I'm guessing she's still sore over whatever he'd wanted of her instead of the date she'd expected the other night. Luther remains alert, but Henri dozes off several times, jerking awake whenever Celine banks suddenly.

I wish I could get some sleep as well, but I'm too consumed with thoughts of what's to come, and what I've left behind in Asylum. I wonder if Pax is sleeping or lying awake, thinking of me.

"Luther," I say after a long period of silence. I can talk now without feeling sick, and the small victory makes me proud.

"Hmm?" He looks sideways at me.

"If I do manage to do everything you've asked me to, and I can escape and get back out to the woods, what do I do if I can't find you? How do I find my way back to Asylum?"

"We'll be waiting for you," he says. "I promise."

"But what if you're not?"

He sighs. "Fair enough. If none of us finds you within a day, you can assume we are dead, and the safest thing for you to do would be to return to the Commune."

"What?"

He nods. "In the dead of night, return to the Commune and go to the public records house. The woman who runs it is one of ours. Her name is Helene. Knock three times, wait five seconds, then knock six times. That's our signal, and she can get word to Asylum that you made it."

"Why not just go to her in the first place?"

"Too risky. She's already in a great deal of danger being situated as she is. I won't risk drawing attention to her if we don't have to."

The boat loses altitude in a swoop that leaves me breathless and nauseated again, and I close my eyes. Celine seems to be swerving between tree trunks now, as we're rocking back and forth with enough force to throw us against our harnesses over and over again.

Henri wakes up with a jolt and says, "Oy, Celine! Stop showing off. You're making us sick back here!"

I'm glad I'm not the only one.

"Almost there," Celine says.

The boat comes to a shuddering stop in midair, bringing with it sweet relief, and then it descends until a bump tells me we've touched the ground. She keeps the engines revving but undoes her harness and leans back over her seat to look at me. "This is it, Pria. Are you absolutely sure?"

No. "Yes," I say, swallowing my fear.

Celine nods.

Henri unbuckles, as does Luther, indicating I should do likewise, and then Henri squeezes around me to open the door. He exits first into darkness, and I follow with Luther close on my heels.

The night is cool but not cold, and I'm immediately grateful. The clothes I chose to wear—a simple tunic, pants, and boots—will not keep me warm.

Luther must have chosen the drop spot, because he seems to know exactly where we are, even though the night is dark as pitch. He points into the trees beyond the nose of the boat. "That way is south," he says. "If you head due south, you'll eventually run into Sanctuary. It will be easy to find —just keep the ascent on your right and the descent on your left and head as straight as you can.

"In two days, you should come out in a bare stretch that will give you a view of the plains beyond the mountains. You'll see Denver Commune on your left and the woods that hide Sanctuary on the horizon ahead. That's where we'll have to ditch the boat and follow on foot, but if a UWO craft appears before then, we'll also have to make ourselves scarce."

"Could be good for you, though," Henri says. "If they pick you up, you won't have to walk all the way to Sanctuary."

I swallow and nod.

"In the meantime, we'll be doing a wide circle and keeping eyes on you as much as possible. Celine outfitted the boat with a sensor for anything mechanical, which means Golems will show up on it as well. We'll let you know if you're in danger."

"Here," Henri says and hands me something that gleams, catching the faint beams of moonlight making their way through the trees. It's a six-inch knife.

"I can't take anything like that," I say, backing away. "Too suspicious."

"Actually, I think it will be suspicious if you don't have anything on you. They'll expect you to have escaped somehow, yeah? You can tell them you stole it from your guard." He holds it out farther. "Come on, Pria. Take it. You have to have some way of defending yourself out here, and if you need help and we're not around, you can signal us by catching the light with it."

I look at Luther, and he shrugs and nods. "Henri's right. A knife shouldn't raise suspicion."

I take it, the hilt solid and assuring in my hand.

"Any other questions?" Luther asks.

I touch the virus hack I have stuck inside my ear and squeeze the knife hilt until my knuckles turn white. "I don't think so," I whisper, trying, and failing, to sound confident.

Luther claps me on the shoulder. "Thank you," he says. "Be safe, and good luck. We'll see you soon."

No *hopefully*, no *should*. Is he really so sure I will succeed?

Henri steps forward and envelops me in a hug before I know what's happening. It's the second time in a day I've been embraced by a man. Treason, treason, and treason again. How many reasons does the UWO have to kill me now? But they never have to know about these secret embraces, and besides, I'm going to convince them I was kidnapped. I have to. It's my only hope of survival.

Henri is taller than Pax, and I feel dwarfed by his size. His smell reminds me of Etienne, and I stiffen against my will.

He must sense my discomfort, because he pulls away and gives me a quick, searching look. "You'll be all right," he says. "You're tougher than you realize."

Am I? I seem to spend a lot of time unsuccessfully trying to convince myself of that.

He takes my chin in his hand and tilts my face up so I'm looking him in the eyes. "See you soon," he says with the same sort of conviction Luther used. Except Henri's words are warmer, and suddenly I'm blushing.

"Let's go," Luther says.

Henri releases my chin and steps away. He stares at me until he's back inside the boat and Luther closes the door. Celine presses her hand against the windshield and gives me a sad smile, and then she eases the boat up until they're far above my head and my short hair is buffeted by the downdraft from the hover propellers.

And then they're gone. I'm all alone in the forest, and the dark and stillness closes in on me like a living creature.

Criminal

Chapter 57

After taking several deep breaths to calm myself, I reorient so I'm sure I'm facing the direction Luther pointed me. South, toward Sanctuary and my old life. Toward the answers to everything or a whole pack of lies. Maybe both.

The darkness doesn't seem so oppressive anymore now that I'm past my first panicky moments, and I hear a gurgle of water not far ahead of me. My mouth salivates with longing, and I hurry forward, thankful Luther was true to his word to drop me by a stream. I have nowhere to tuck the knife Henri gave me, as I'm not wearing a belt, so I keep it clutched in my right hand and hold it out in front of me as I walk.

I find the stream without difficulty, stumbling among the rocks at its edge until I splash into the shallows. It's shockingly cold, but I plunge my face in and drink deeply, trying not to wet the entire front of my clothes.

Once my thirst is satiated, I crawl back a few paces until I'm out of the water and lean against a rock. Three days in the wilderness on my own. Unless I'm picked up, as Henri said. And if that happens before the three days are up, I should do everything I can to make it look as though I've been journeying for days, not mere hours.

The mud beside the stream is rough with gravel, not great for concealing, but good for weathering my clothes. I take up handfuls of it and rub it into the bottom of my pants, already wet from the stream. Then I rub some at random all over my body. Next, I find a sharp stone and dig at my pants and sleeves until I've opened up a few tears. I hope that and what I will put my body through in the next couple of days will be convincing enough.

"Okay, Pria. Time to go," I say to myself. The hour and my tiredness are catching up to me, and I want to find a dry patch of ground and curl up and sleep, but I should move instead. I have a lot of miles to cover, and I should look as exhausted and harried as I can when I get there.

I splash across the stream, able to see in the moonlight that it's narrow, and I head south. Bushes and tree limbs reach out of the darkness and grab at me, and I make little effort to avoid them. Scratches and scrapes are good. Scratches and scrapes are what one would expect to find on a desperate, fleeing woman. It's only after a couple of hours that I worry the scent of my blood will attract predators, but it's too late now. At least I have a knife.

The sun comes up so gradually I don't realize how light the forest has gotten until colors start to show. I stop, breathing hard, and appreciate the beauty of the light green of the spring trees and the wildflowers dotting the ground in the wider spaces between them. I never would have seen this in Sanctuary—at least, not more than we could see from the Looking Glass. I'm amazed at how much the landscape has transformed even since Pax and I entered Asylum.

I continue walking after a brief respite, but I'm trending east, down the slope. I stop and correct myself several times before I realize it's no good. I'm too tired, and my body wants to take the easier course. It's time for a rest.

I hear a hum and a rush overhead and instinctively duck, but it's just the boat, making a pass. Celine dips the nose of the craft, and I raise my hand, and then they're gone. With a sigh, I look around for a place to sleep. Between two large rocks is a spot cleared of leaves as though an animal once burrowed there. It's wide enough for me to curl up in, and I like the idea of sleeping with a rock at my back and my front.

I go and settle down on the cleared earth, and then I check myself over. There is a long scratch on my arm that stings and is bleeding freely. I tear off my sleeve at my elbow and tie the strip awkwardly around it to staunch the flow. Other than that, I seem to be free of serious injury.

My stomach growls. I didn't forage for any food during the night. With the darkness and the adrenaline fueling me forward, I didn't even stop to think about it once I was on the ground. But I'm too tired now to do anything about it. Sleep commands all my attention. With a deep sigh, I curl up, tucking my knees to my chest and one arm under my ear, and hold the knife in front of my chest. I'm asleep almost as soon as I close my eyes.

Chapter 58

I wake to a snuffling and a coarse wetness on my leg. It takes me a moment to orient myself, and then I realize there is an animal licking my ankle. With a shout, I shoot upward, brandishing my knife, and the creature disappears. My heart is beating in my throat, and I look around wildly until I find it—a coyote, sitting about ten feet away, studying me with yellow eyes.

I scream and fling my knife at it, not sure what I'm hoping to accomplish. It spins through the air, and the coyote dodges away and runs off into the trees.

With a groan, I heft myself up from my little hollow, all my muscles screaming at me, and scramble after my knife. Once it's back in my hand, I feel marginally safer, but my head feels stuffed with rocks, and there's a pounding pain between my temples. My tongue is dry, and my stomach feels so hollow it makes me ill.

Get moving. Head south. Find water. The basic instructions drum through my head with each pulse of my headache.

I stumble forward, heading down the slope, and then stop. No. That's not right. I have to head across the slope. How far did I walk last night? I have no idea. What time is it? The light slants through the trees from slightly west of straight above. It's afternoon, but early afternoon. I'm surprised I slept so long.

Finally heading the right way, I trudge along, one foot in front of the other. I'm amazed how lack of food has drained me. And the lack of water. Water. My every waking moment is consumed with desiring water.

I have enough presence of mind to recognize an edible plant after about an hour of walking. I can't remember what Pax called it. I just know it won't poison me. I tear off a handful of leaves and chew on them as I go, but without water, it's almost torturous to swallow. The leaves turn gummy in my mouth, and I know I must find water soon, or I'm in serious trouble.

I come to a broad tumble of rocks that looks like it was part of some long-ago landslide. I stop to put my hands on my hips and consider my path across. If I were healthy and hydrated, this would hardly give me pause, but right now it looks like a near-insurmountable barrier. The sky above the slide is open, and the sun shines bright upon the gray rocks. Will Celine and the others make another pass soon? I haven't seen them since I fell asleep.

I can't avoid navigating the rocks any longer, and going around either side is out of the question, so I finally begin to pick my way over it. The sun is surprisingly hot, and soon I'm sweating and cursing the fact that I'm sweating. I can't afford to lose any more water.

I'm almost to the other side when the rock I'm standing on tilts, pitching me down and pinning my leg. With a gasp, I drop my knife and catch myself as sharp pain shoots through my ankle. The pain doesn't relent, and when I try to pull myself free, it turns white-hot and I actually black out for a moment. I can't get free.

I groan and close my eyes. What am I going to do?

Signal them. That's what Henri told me to do if I got into trouble. Use the knife to signal them in the boat. But I dropped the knife. I look around for it as much as I'm able, gritting my teeth at every fresh stab of pain, but I can't see it anywhere. It most likely disappeared into one of the many crevices between the rocks.

I am totally helpless. But they'll be around soon for another pass, won't they? They have to be. And I'm in the open, so they'll see me. I close my eyes and rest my head on my arms. Surely they'll see me.

An hour passes. Two. I can't feel my ankle anymore unless I move, which brings renewed waves of pain. What an utter failure I am. I am not the fittest, and according to Mother's worldview—to the worldview I was taught in the Agoge—I don't deserve to survive.

I pass into a state of semiconsciousness, and when the sky darkens above me, at first I think it's night falling. But then the rush of hovercraft engines buffets me in the face, and I crack my eyes open to see the shadow of a craft just above my head.

"Celine," I whisper.

There is a sting in my neck, and the world goes black.

Chapter 59

"Seventeen."

Beep. Beep. Beep.

"Seventeen."

My eyes feel as though they've been taped shut, but I manage to peel them open, only to squeeze them shut again. The light is too bright, and the darkness behind my lids too cool and comfortable.

Beep. Beep. Beep.

"Seventeen." Mother's voice.

With a gasp, I shoot upward, gripping the edges of the bed on which I'm lying. A tube trails from my arm to a hanging drip, and a silver and white medical cuff is attached to my wrist.

Mother sits beside me, smiling warmly. "There you are," she says. "Welcome back."

I slap my hands to my chest as though I can contain the racing of my heart. I'm clean and whole and hydrated and in a room in the Medical wing of Sanctuary. It is just me and Mother.

She looks exactly the same as she did when I left.

Suddenly my story swims through my head. I thought I would have to use it to get myself readmitted to Sanctuary, yet here I am. But I still must cover my tail if I'm to succeed in my mission.

"I was kidnapped," I say. "How did I get here?"

Mother gives a slight shake of her head, and her expression takes on a pitying grimace.

I'm not sure how to read her reaction, so I keep talking. "There was an Enforcer, he—he broke me out. I didn't want to leave—"

"Shhh," Mother says, putting her hand on my arm. "Don't worry. You're almost better now. You can rejoin your sisters in just a few days."

"I . . . don't understand." I frown.

"How are you feeling?"

"Fine, good, but—"

"Good. That's what I wanted to hear." Mother smiles again. "Some disorientation is to be expected, but that will fade quickly. I expect, now that we've got you healthy again, you'll be ready for your next Carry within the month."

My mouth drops open. "I don't understand what's going on," I say.

Mother steeples her fingers beneath her chin and leans forward. "Let me see if I can explain it in a way that will cause you the least confusion. Every now and then, a Breeder responds adversely to a lost Carry. Depression can foster all sorts of side effects, including delusions, and I saw you spiraling out of control.

"When you did not respond to the usual drugs, I had no choice but to take these measures or lose you—one of our most valuable Breeders. When I sent you to solitary meditation, I had the Protectors render you unconscious. We brought you here instead and kept you in an induced coma for a week to medicate you and get you healthy again. We studied your brain activity, too, which was quite active while you were unconscious, so I had no doubt you would wake up having gone on a fantastic adventure—all in your mind, of course."

"What?" I can barely get the word out. "No . . . no, that's not right. A *week*? I've been gone for at least a month! I've been gone! I was kidnapped by a rogue Enforcer!"

Mother shakes her head. "You have been in this bed for a week. There are no Enforcers in Sanctuary, and there never have been."

My mind is reeling, and I lay back down so I'm staring at the blue ceiling. "This can't be. I swear to you, I was *gone*."

Mother is quiet for a moment until I turn to look at her. "Tell me something about your story," she says. "Something that happened to you. Something that would have left a mark, for example."

Something that would have left a mark. "Right after I . . . I was taken," I say in a halting voice, "my kidnapper, he . . . he dug my microchip from my wrist."

"Your microchip?" Mother's mouth quirks to the side and her eyebrows shoot up. "What an imagination you have, Seventeen. So this left a scar?"

"Yes," I say, and I raise my arm.

"Where?" Mother asks.

I touch the inside of my wrist, and we both look to where I'm pointing.

But there's nothing. My skin is as smooth and whole as it was before Pax removed my chip. There's not even a trace of a scar.

"I . . ." The cuff on my other wrist beeps as my heart rate increases. "It can't be," I whisper.

"Easy now," Mother says. "Take a couple of deep breaths."

I do so, but I can't calm down. There's no way it was all a dream. My heart twists in a painful knot, and I fight against tears.

"It's okay to be emotional," Mother says in a soothing voice. "It's common when waking up from a coma."

I gasp and swallow, fighting back the tears. "I was injured," I say. "My ankle."

"This ankle?" Mother rotates my right foot, but I feel nothing. "Or this one?" She rotates the other to the same effect.

I bite my lip and shake my head, my buzzed hair scratching against my pillow. I'm losing my fight against the tears, and one slips out of the corner of my eye and down into my ear.

"And . . . my face . . ." I reach up to where Etienne struck me and press my fingers into my flesh. There's no bruise. No cracked lip. I am smooth and unblemished. An inarticulate sound escapes my lips. I can't stop shaking, and my cuff won't stop beeping. I cover my face.

"Shhh, shhh," Mother says, stroking my arm. "It will fade. It will feel less real as the days go on. I promise. But I know it can be disorienting at first. That's why I wanted to be here when you woke up. Is there anything I can do to help you feel better before I go?"

I uncover my face. "Yes," I say, almost gasping the word. "Yes, please. Show me . . . show me what's through the door at the end of the hall."

Mother frowns. "The storage closet? Why?"

"Because it's where—I thought—he took me. There was a staircase through that door to basements beneath Sanctuary. Will you show me, please?"

Mother sighs. "You really shouldn't be out of bed just yet, but if it will help, of course I will."

She pushes a button on the side of my bed, and moments later a medical technician enters pushing a wheeled chair. She looks vaguely familiar to me, but I don't know that I can trust any of my memories right now.

Mother and the technician help me into the chair, and then the technician wheels me behind Mother as she leads us out of the room and to the main corridor. The door at the end beckons me, and I'm sure that what I'll find behind it will answer all my questions.

Mother gives me a kind smile before tapping in the security code on the panel beside the door.

She pulls it open and steps aside. Within are shelves and shelves of glass-vialed medical supplies. The shelves span from wall to wall and all the way up to the ceiling, where they're bolted in.

There is no staircase. There are no basements beneath Sanctuary.

With a shuddering sob, I cover my face and give in to the tears.

Chapter 60

Of all the things that turned out to be a figment of my imagination, the most difficult one to wrap my brain around is Pax. He consumes my thoughts as I slip in and out of sleep. How could I have invented a man—an impossible, genetically extinct man—and then come to care about him? How was my brain even capable of that? And why, now, does my heart hurt so much?

I shouldn't grieve over something I never had, but I can't seem to help it.

I think Mother is keeping me sedated for longer than she had planned. She seemed genuinely shocked at my emotional breakdown outside the closet and ordered the med tech to take me straight back to my room. I fell immediately into a dreamless slumber, and I've been sleeping most of the time ever since.

But the dreams are coming back now, for I keep waking up with gasping breaths and Pax's name on my lips. I have no idea how long it's been, but the memories from my dream are not fading as Mother said they would. If anything, they're haunting me more and more.

The med tech keeps close tabs on me, and one day when I'm awake, she says, "You can leave here tomorrow and rejoin your sisters." She puts a cool hand on my forehead. "Does that make you happy?"

"I guess so." I blink and look at her, sure as I was on the first day I awoke that I've seen her before. She smiles, and a tiny whorl appears above her lip. It hits me. "I've met you before," I say. "Haven't I?"

She pulls back, a crease appearing between her eyebrows. "Yes, actually.

Months ago." Then she seems to think she's said something wrong, for her eyes widen slightly and she turns away to straighten some things on the counter.

"How is that, though?" I ask. "I don't know that I've ever seen the same med tech twice."

"Oh, you have. I'm sure you just don't remember. We're on a rotation, you know, so we always come back around here eventually."

"Oh." I struggle to recall when it was I'd been treated by her in the weeks leading up to my delusion, but everything blurs together and I can't, although I feel like I've had this very same conversation with her before. "But you've treated me ever since I've been in my coma, right?"

She turns back to me. "Mother thought it would be good for you to have something constant to help ground you to reality when you woke up." She gathers up some linens from the end of my bed and goes to the door. "If you need anything, just ring," she says with a smile, and then she leaves.

After she's gone, I wriggle my feet and stroke the inside of my wrist, obsessively looking for the physical signs I know are not there. The med tech is right—I should feel happy that I get to rejoin my sisters tomorrow. Back to normalcy. Back to the life I was bred and trained for. At least knowing none of it was real assures me none of the nightmarish things Pax told me are true either. I don't have to feel guilty about my role in the UWO. We're working for the betterment of mankind.

But then how did I invent all those nightmares? The thought carries me to sleep.

I wake shivering. The vent above my bed is blasting cold air directly on me. Why is it doing that? The air conditioning in the building must be malfunctioning.

I roll out of the path of the vent and come to a sitting position on the edge of the bed. I'm about to ring for my med tech when I notice my IV has been removed. So has my cuff. I'm wearing nothing more than a medical tunic, which is loose and short-sleeved and comes only to my knees. When I stand, a tie dangles from the flap that swings open, and I quickly yank it back over myself to cover my nakedness. I wrap the tie twice around my waist and knot it.

The tile floors are like ice, but it feels good to stand. I stretch, testing my muscles. I seem to be in excellent condition, just as Mother said I was. That must be why they disconnected me.

I think it's the middle of the night, because the lights in the corridor outside my room are dim.

My door is cracked open.

I tilt my head and frown. That's odd. Did my med tech neglect to close it all the way the last time she left?

I open the door and peer out into the hall. All is dark and silent. Deserted. Where are the night med techs doing their rounds? Overcome with curiosity, I tiptoe down the hall and poke my head around the corner into the main corridor. There's no one in sight.

I shake my head and am about to turn back to my room when I see the door at the end of the hall, the door to the storage closet, is standing several inches open.

Chapter 61

My vision hones in on the open door. Am I hallucinating again? Did Mother put me back under because I was regressing? I grab at my wrist, but there's nothing there. If this were my hallucination, wouldn't I have my scar? My sprained ankle? The injuries on my face? But I'm just as whole as I was when I woke up a few days ago. I could be implanting new material into my old fantasy, I suppose, but something tells me that's unlikely. Or maybe I want it to be unlikely. Or maybe everything Mother told me after I woke up was a lie. Either way, I have issues.

"Someone forgot to close it," I whisper to myself, walking down the hall. "That's all. Someone forgot to close it." When I reach the door, I take a deep breath and pull it the rest of the way open.

The shelves are gone, vanished as though they'd never been there. I reel against the doorframe and blink rapidly, trying to clear my vision. The staircase Pax took me to, the one down which we escaped, is yawning before me like the mouth of a beast, and to go down these stairs will change everything, I know. But I'm drawn to it. Of course I am. What else can I do?

I descend to the landing beside the first door, my bare feet making almost no sound on the concrete. But there I stop and stare. How will I get in? Pax told me I'd need a Protector's uniform to get the access codes, and here I am standing practically naked, like a crazy woman, and totally unprepared.

But because I have to try, because it would be stupid *not* to try, I take the handle and turn. The door clicks and swings open. Shaking my head and holding my breath, I creep past it and close it behind me.

I'm standing in a long hallway that stretches into shadows. On each side are doors, some with glass panes in them, others solid metal. There are faint whimpers and cries, and all at once I'm seized with a paralyzing fear of what I'm about to see. If this is real—if I'm awake and this is *real*—then I'm about to witness some of the horrors Pax alluded to.

If this is real, then so is Pax.

I close my eyes and count to ten before I continue. I need all my wits about me.

There are numbers on the doors on the right but not on the doors on the left. When I reach the first door with a glass windowpane, I stop and look in, steeling myself. But there is nothing to be afraid of here.

There are about ten cribs lined up in a tidy row, all but one containing a tiny infant swaddled in a white cloth and hooked up to what looks like a feeding mechanism. Most of the infants are sleeping soundly, but two are squirming, and as one opens its mouth to squawk, the machine attached to its crib lowers a rubber nipple into its mouth.

I move on. It's strange to think my child, the one who survived, was housed down here and fed like that. I wonder how mothers in Asylum feed their babies.

The next four rooms contain cribs of increasing size to hold children of increasing age. There are no attendants, but small cameras dot the corners of the rooms. Who is watching the cameras, and from where? Can they see me creeping along in the hall outside the doors? If they can, they're ignoring me.

The sixth door is the first one without a windowpane, and there are cries and whimpers coming from within. Holding my breath, I try the door and once again find it unlocked.

This time I know I'm caught on camera as I enter the room, but I barely think of it. The cribs in here are more like cages, and the mattresses inside them are bare. The children, ranging from infants to toddlers, sleep fitfully, clad only in diapers with wires and tubes taped to their limbs and trailing across the floor to machines. One wakes when I enter and cries out, holding out skinny arms to me. I press my hand to my mouth to keep from echoing the child's cry, for he has a gaping hole from his nose through his lip that is oozing saliva. How can he eat like that? Why hasn't somebody helped him?

Because this is the Program, and these children are unfit to survive. *"Nursery Six, where they study the deformed ones,"* Pax told me. Most they abort, but some they choose to study. Is this where Pax lived until he was rescued?

The child with the split in his palette is crying louder. He's woken up a small girl with a moon-round face and unnaturally small ears and eyes. She lolls her head against the bars of her crib and stares at me. Just stares. The other children are stirring. I can't help them. To unhook them from the machines could kill them. I have to get out of here.

Tears sting my eyes as I back out and slam the door, and the sound echoes down the empty hall. I stumble, half-blind, farther along, not trying any of the handles on the doors I pass—the ones without windowpanes.

At the end of the hall, I come to a long bank of windows that look in on another nursery. Inside are cages, not cribs—not even cribs that look like cages as in the nursery with the deformed children—but legitimate cages, and the children inside them are naked, and most of them frail.

A cage near the back holds a boy who looks about a year old, and he stands gripping the bars and screaming, purple in the face. He's healthy, but judging by the state of the rest of the children in the room, he won't be for long. Distended bellies, stick-thin arms, sunken eyes, and deathly pallor greet me everywhere I look.

It's obvious what this room is for. This is where they starve unworthy children to death. A few of the children, I'm sure, are already dead.

I press my hands to the glass as tears stream unchecked down my face and a new feeling, anger, rushes through me in a dizzying wave. The Breeding Program is full of monsters. *We* are monsters.

"What are you doing here?"

The med tech's voice—*my* med tech's voice—echoes down the hall, preceding the sound of her slapping feet as she runs toward me. She's not wearing her head wrap, and her long dark hair floats around her shoulders. She's younger than I thought.

"You're not supposed to be here!" She skids to a halt beside me and puts her hand on my shoulder. "They'll kill you!"

"Like they kill these babies?" I ask. "You . . . *all* of you . . . know about this, don't you?"

She purses her lips and grabs my arm. "Come on," she says. "I don't know how you got down here, but you have to leave *now*."

"No!" I shout, wrenching my arm free. "This can't go on! We have to do something about this! We have to save him!" I point at the screaming boy. "*Save him!* Don't you care?"

"Of course I care!" she shouts. "But what am I supposed to do? I can't get in there—only Mother has the key!"

I step back, stunned. "She's the one behind all of this?"

The med tech waves her arms in the air. "Her. The other *Mothers* in charge of the other breeding houses. The Director of the Program. The Oligarch. All of the above. And all of *us* are implicit"—she jabs herself in the chest—"because we don't have a choice."

The door across from Nursery Six bursts open, and an Enforcer rushes into the hall. I freeze, my eyes widening.

I've failed. I found the evidence the rebels in Asylum need, but there's no way for me to fight off an Enforcer. I never stole a Protector's uniform. He'll recognize me immediately for what I am.

The Enforcer looks left and right, then does a double take and runs toward us. The med tech spins around, gaping, and I raise myself as straight as I can go. The med tech lunges as though to flee around the oncoming Enforcer, but he levels his Air-5 on her and shoots. Either it was a warning shot or he's a terrible marksman, because it misses her shoulder by an inch and burns a hole in the wall.

"Don't move," he says, and she freezes. Then he looks my way. "It's me," he says. "Pria, it's me." Pax takes off his helmet with one hand and casts it away.

I clutch at my chest and sag against the wall, so surprised and relieved I'm unable to even call a greeting.

"What is this?" the med tech asks, her eyes wide as she takes in Pax's appearance. "Who are you?"

Pax levels the barrel of his Air-5 against her forehead. "Someone who's here to get *her* out, and if you try to stop me, I will kill you."

"Do it," she says, staring down the barrel of his gun. "I'm begging you. Do it and put me out of my misery." She closes her eyes.

Pax waits a long moment then mutters a curse. "Don't get in our way," he says and lowers the gun.

He steps around her and comes to me. "You're alive," he says, and his voice breaks. He grabs my arm and hauls me to him, then takes my chin and studies me, turning my face side to side. "They didn't hurt you?"

"No," I say. "Why—why did you think I was dead?"

"Why did I think . . . don't you know?" He blinks at me. "You've been here for three months! All your injuries are healed—didn't that make you wonder?"

"What? But Mother told me . . ." I look at the med tech, and she sighs and nods. I reel against the wall and press my fingers to my forehead. I knew it. Or I should have known it. "Then . . . then how did you know to come and get me *now*? And aren't you supposed to be in jail?"

"Wallace equipped the hack to be sensitive to movement. When it went silent three months ago, after you were taken, we assumed you'd been killed. Then earlier this week, suddenly he got a signal and told Luther that either you were alive or they picked it off your long-dead body and were moving around with it, which seemed unlikely. Luther had no choice but to trust me with the information and send me back in here to rescue you."

"The . . . hack . . ." Of course. I reach up with trembling fingers and touch the slight raise inside my ear. Nobody found it.

He tugs on my arm. "Come on, we need to go."

"No." I dig in my heels. "*No*. Pax. I'm not leaving without that little boy!" I point at the screaming baby, his cries muffled behind the thick glass.

Pax looks through the glass, and his expression contorts. "I can't get you both out," he says. "I'm sorry. There are hundreds of babies who die here every year. It's a fact of life."

"But that one we can save!"

"I *can't*, Pria!" he shouts.

"Someone saved you. Have pity and do the same!"

Pax blinks and steps back as though I've struck him.

"Take me with you," the med tech says. She squares her shoulders and looks between the two of us. "Take me with you, and I'll take care of the baby. Please. I can't live like this anymore, and there's no way out for people like me."

Pax rubs his hand through his hair. "He's probably going to get us all killed." He releases a long breath. "Fine. Open the door."

"I don't have the key," the med tech says.

Pax points his Air-5 at the handle and shoots until it bursts open. The boy's screams come much louder as the three of us hurry into the room.

The smell is horrific, and I gag and double over, but Pax and the med tech head straight past me for the boy's cage. I catch my breath and hover over a tiny infant, her breathing coming in short, shallow bursts, her tummy enormous. I reach my hand through the bars and touch her fingers as Pax fires his weapon again. The baby girl doesn't respond to my touch.

"She's too far gone," the med tech shouts, lifting the naked boy out of the cage and clutching him to her chest. He's fallen silent but is breathing in shuddering gasps. "She'll be dead before the day is up."

I pull my hand out and clench my fist. I want to scream, but there's nothing I can do.

"We're going now." Pax pushes me ahead of him, out of the room of death.

We run down the hall, and when we reach the unmarked door through which Pax came, I stop and yank it open.

"Not that way," Pax says. "More Enforcers are coming. I had to kill one on the way." He leads us into the stairwell, and we slam through the door. Pax stops on the landing and looks around.

"What are you waiting for?" the med tech asks.

"I have to think about our little friend," Pax says, jerking his head toward the baby in her arms. "We can't exit the way Pria and I did before. He'll drown. But I have a few things . . ." He pats his pants where the many pockets are stuffed full. "Hopefully it's enough. Upstairs."

We run up the stairs and out into the dark corridor. Even though it's the middle of the night, I'm surprised all our commotion hasn't raised the alarm.

"Freeze!" a female voice calls out.

I've thought too soon. Three Protectors jump out from hiding around the corners of the branching hallways.

Pax doesn't hesitate. He shoots and hits the first two before they can react, but the third gets off a shot that grazes his arm. Unflinching, he runs forward, drops and rolls. Then he jumps to his feet and shoots down the hall. A grunt and the sound of a body hitting the floor tell me he hit his mark.

"There will be more," he says. "Don't hesitate."

We hurry out the door of the Med wing. The boy hasn't cried since the med tech picked him up, perhaps out of shock, perhaps out of an understanding that he needs to be quiet.

Pax is leading us to the Looking Glass room. I don't know how he expects us to get out through there. He shoots another Protector in the hallway, then two more that appear around the corner.

We descend the three stairs into the room, which is bathed in moonlight that makes the Tree of Life glow, and Pax heads straight for the glass. He removes something that looks like gray clay from a pocket and sticks it to the edge of the glass.

"What is that?" I ask, and then I gasp and fall as a beam from an Air-5 pierces my thigh.

Pax whirls around and shoots the Protector who just shot me. "Pria!" He rushes to my side. "Where are you hit?"

I'm in too much pain to answer, my leg on fire, but the med tech says, "It didn't hit an artery. She'll be fine as long as we can get it bandaged soon."

"Yes. We wouldn't want *Pria* to be permanently damaged, now would we?"

Through the haze of my pain, I look up and see Mother standing by the Tree of Life.

Chapter 62

Pax levels his Air-5 on Mother, supporting me with his other arm. I cling to him, trying desperately to get to my feet. The baby boy starts to cry.

"Holly, I'm surprised at you," Mother says. "Abandoning your post and stealing UWO property." She shakes her head. "Such behavior does not become a medical technician."

Mother takes a step forward, and Pax says, "Stop right there. Don't come any closer."

"Or what? You'll shoot me?" She spreads her arms. "I'm an unarmed woman."

"How archaic of you," Pax says through gritted teeth. He slips his arm around my waist and boosts me up so I have my feet under me, even though I can barely stand to put any weight on my right leg. "Don't think I won't do it." He moves me forward, around the first heavy settee, and then the next, inching us away from the Looking Glass. I bite my lip to keep from screaming.

"Oh . . . I don't think you will," Mother says.

Pax keeps walking, dragging me with him, and Holly follows close on our heels. He's circling around Mother, putting her between us and the Looking Glass.

"Where do you hope to go?" Mother asks in a quiet voice, turning in place to follow our movement. "Hundreds of Enforcers will be here at any minute. You can't possibly get away."

As discreetly as I can, while her gaze is fixed on Pax, I reach up into my ear and peel off the virus hack. Even after three months, it's still sticky. We're close to Mother now. I may only have one chance at this.

"You lied to me," I say. My voice is weak. "You lied to me about everything."

Mother's smile is predatory. "Try to put yourself in my position."

"Never in a million years."

Mother sighs. "It was all in the name of science, Seventeen. In the name of advancement. In the name of humanity."

"My name is Pria."

Behind us, the baby boy wails louder, and Mother's countenance falters. "Can't you shut that monster up?"

Adrenaline shoots through me, and I lunge. Pax shouts and reaches after me, but I've done what I needed—I've made contact with Mother.

She shrieks as I tackle her to the ground, and I hit her across the face with one hand while I grab her sleeve with the other. The hack isn't on my finger anymore, and I can only hope it's stuck to her sleeve where I intended it to go.

"You're the monster," I say, and I hit her again.

She grabs my thigh and shoves her fingers into my wound. I scream and black out for a moment as searing pain shoots through my leg and warm blood gushes out. Pax yanks me off her, and I cry out again and collapse at his feet. He's pointing the Air-5 at Mother, and judging by his breathing, he's barely maintaining control of himself. She stares up at him with a poisonous glare, blood trickling from the corner of her mouth.

"Kill her," Holly says. "Do you know how many deaths she's responsible for?"

But Pax just grits his teeth, and I remember something he told me a long time ago. *The Breeder who Carried and delivered me—my mother—is Mother.*

He can't do it, no matter what he threatens. He can't kill his own mother.

"Holly," Pax says. "Get down by Pria."

Holly does so without hesitation.

Pax narrows his eyes on Mother. "You're not worth the waste of energy." He raises the gun and fires toward the Looking Glass. Then he throws himself over me and Holly, sheltering the baby against his shoulder.

The explosion rocks all of Sanctuary. Whatever the gray clay stuff was, it punched a hole right through the wall, shattering the Looking Glass and sending shards of glass rocketing through the room. The first settee is pulverized, and the second one, behind which we're crouching, skids sideways.

"Let's go!" Pax shouts as debris rains down around us. His voice comes across tinny and faint as the effects of the blast ring in my ears.

Holly leaps to her feet and runs for the gaping hole where the Looking Glass used to be. I try to follow, but I've lost so much blood that I can't even get to my feet with Pax's help, and there's no way I can run. He swings me up into his arms, keeping his Air-5 trained forward beneath my back, and surges for the hole.

I clutch at his shoulders as I bounce along in his arms, each footfall sending jabs of pain through my leg. I almost wish I could lose consciousness, but then I'd be really worthless, dead weight. I can't do that to Pax.

We plunge into the trees and overtake Holly, who's waiting for us in the darkness behind a patch of bushes.

"This way," Pax says. "Don't stop until I say so."

We run uphill, and I don't know how Pax maintains his speed while carrying me and in the semidarkness. My hearing clears as we go, but my vision clouds with dots and a haze that refuses to lift. At first I think it's just the dim, predawn light, but before long I understand it's a physiological response to my injuries.

Sometime later, Pax grinds to a halt and drops to his knees, jostling me to the ground. I think he's finally lost his stamina, but he says, "It's now or never. We have a small window of time to remove the microchips. All of you, even the baby." He flips a knife out of his pocket. "I'm sorry, this is going to hurt. I didn't grab any anesthetic."

"My . . . microchip?" I blink up at him in confusion.

"They will have implanted a new one on your return." His mouth tightens into a straight line as he places the tip of his knife to my wrist.

"Wait!" Holly says, putting her hand on his arm. "Let me. I'm trained in surgery, at least. You wrap up her leg before she bleeds out, and then bandage your arm." She lays the baby down in the undergrowth. Her arms are bare as she wears an undershirt only—her medical tunic is wrapped around the child instead.

Pax hesitates a moment, then hands over his knife. From a pocket of his pants, he pulls a roll of gauze and sets it beside her. Then he unzips the top of his Enforcer uniform and pulls his arms out so he can remove his undershirt. I hear him tearing it into strips, but my attention is drawn back to Holly as she positions the knife. She's sweating, and a couple of drops fall onto my arm.

She mutters something about needing more light, then she says, "Sorry," and slices me open with a deft stroke.

I arch my back and groan, trying not to scream. It's agony, fire, worse than my leg. I pass out and come around a moment later to Holly wrapping my wrist in tight gauze. Her lips are pursed, but her hands are steady. There is a tugging on my leg, and I look down to see Pax tying strips of his shirt tight around my wound. My whole body is in paroxysms of pain.

"Okay," Holly says, wiping off the blade on the hem of her shirt. "I suppose I can't sterilize this." She moves to the baby and uncovers his arm. "You, Pax," she says. "Help me a moment. If he flails, I could kill him."

Pax ties off the last strip on my leg and joins her.

The screams of the child are torturous to hear, and I'm crying again. But it has to be done, or they'll track us and we'll all be killed. At least Holly works efficiently, and it's over within a minute.

I drag myself into a sitting position and watch as she bandages his wrist. He seems to have lost the energy to scream and is lying still, shuddering and whimpering, with his eyes half-closed. Blue eyes. Is that why they were going to starve him to death?

Without another word, Holly grits her teeth and gets to work on her own arm. Only then does her hand shake, but she gets her microchip out and crushes it between her fingers. Then she sits back, breathing hard, while Pax bandages her wrist.

"Your arm," she says in a thin voice when he's done. "You still haven't bandaged your arm."

Pax presses his hand to the bloody streak on his bicep and it comes away sticky, but it's not bleeding freely anymore. "It's fine," he says. "We've taken too much time here already."

"How are you going to keep carrying her with an injured arm?" Holly nods my direction.

"I got her this far, didn't I?"

Pax picks me up again as though I weigh nothing. The pain in my leg is down to a throbbing ache now that it's wrapped, and I think I could hobble along with help. But we need to run, and I can't do that.

Pax nods toward the hill. "The rendezvous point is at the top of the ridge. My people will be there in one hour. Let's go."

I can hardly hold on any longer from loss of blood, and I rest my head against Pax's shoulder with my eyes closed as he climbs. Bushes and tree limbs reach out and snag my bare toes and legs, catching and leaving scratches. I'm dimly aware of Holly following with the baby. A distant siren sounds.

After a while, Pax grunts and shifts me to free his firing arm. "Can you hold on to my neck for a bit?" he asks, his voice low in my ear.

I tighten my grip, fighting to stay lucid, and feel him holster his Air-5. Then he uses his other hand to grab at tree trunks to hoist us up. It's getting steeper. I wish I could help.

"Why hasn't a UWO craft caught up with us yet?" Holly asks, her voice labored.

"They'll have expected us to go east, down the slope. It's much easier, especially with two of us being wounded," Pax says. "It's why we chose the ridge as our rendezvous point."

Finally Pax lowers my feet to the ground and says, "I have to put you down. I'm sorry. Can you stand? Brace yourself here." He places my hands on two boulders that rise above my head on either side.

I keep my injured leg elevated and push hard against the boulders, managing to stay upright. I nod.

"Good." Pax turns to Holly. "Give me the baby." He takes him and, unzipping his uniform down to his waist, hugs the boy to his chest. Then he zips the uniform back up over both of them, keeping the child secure.

Pax looks up and shields his eyes against the early-morning sun. "We have to climb," he says. "I'll go up first, and you can help hand Pria up to me. Do you think you can follow?"

"Yes," Holly says.

Pax scales the crack, bracing his arms and legs against the opposing stones until he reaches the top, a few feet above my head. He kneels and holds down his arms. "Pria, your turn," he says.

Holly makes a stirrup with her hands, and I manage to hop my good foot into it. She hefts me upward, and I catch Pax's forearm. His fingers wrap around my bandaged wrist, and I cry out once before sealing my lips shut. He hauls me backward, and I tumble over onto the top of the boulders, panting. Then he leans back over to lend a hand to Holly, but she's already almost to the top.

Craning my neck upward, I see a tumble of gray rocks and boulders stretching up into the sun.

"We're almost there," Pax says. "As far as you can see—that's the top. It doesn't go beyond that. And it's not all this steep."

Holly lends me her shoulder now, as Pax is carrying the baby and picking our trail for us. I'm shaking and in terrible pain, but I push on, able to hop and scramble over most of the rocks except for a few places where we have to repeat the operation that got us to the top of the first set of boulders.

By the time we reach the flat top of the ridge, I'm at the end of my stamina. I collapse to the sun-warmed rock, losing my grip on Holly, and lie facedown, breathing in the scent of earth and stone. The sun is hot and I'm drenched in sweat, but I feel cold and clammy. I shiver and close my eyes.

"She's going into shock," Holly says. "Where are these friends of yours?"

"They'll be here," Pax says.

The baby cries.

A rushing sound bursts around us with wind that buffets my thin medical shift and makes Holly cry out in alarm.

"It's an X-1!" she shouts. "They found us!"

"No," Pax shouts back. "Holly, wait! Don't run! It's my friends. It's *their* X-1."

I roll over onto my side and squint up at the black, arrowhead-shaped craft overhead. It lands beside us with a roaring hum, and the door opens and lets down a ramp.

Celine runs down it, her eyes wide, her mouth forming my name.

Chapter 63

"Come on, we've got to go, go, go!" That's Henri shouting nearby.

Arms heave me up off the rock, and the world spins as I'm carried into the cool interior of the X-1.

"What's wrong with Pria?" Celine's anxious voice sounds in my ear.

"She's been shot," Holly says.

"Who are you? Who's the baby? I didn't realize we were taking on refugees," Celine says.

"Holly helped us escape, and Pria wouldn't leave the baby," Pax says.

"Another Breeder?" Henri asks.

"Medical technician," Holly says.

"Oh, right. Of course . . . hair."

"Come *on*. Get that door closed!" Elan shouts. "We're on radar. We need to disappear *now*."

The door shuts with a mechanical grinding of gears.

"I've got to get that oiled," Celine mutters, squatting down beside me.

When was I placed on the floor?

"Do you have a medical kit on board?" Holly asks.

"Here." Henri must toss it, because I hear something heavy land in Holly's arms.

"Are you sure you know what you're doing?" Celine asks.

"If you want her to keep that leg, you'll get out of my way and let me work," Holly says, her tone cold.

I feel a sharp sting of pain near my hip, and then numbing coldness sweeps through my body. I let out a gasp of relief and open my eyes.

Celine kneels by my head, her hand on my shoulder. Henri stands behind Holly, staring at me with an anxious expression, but he breaks into a broad grin when he notices me looking at him.

"Hey, Pria," he says. "Good to see you."

"Celine, I need you up here!" Elan shouts from the cockpit.

"All right," Celine says. "Don't die. I've got to go help fly the craft."

She's replaced by Pax, who crouches next to Holly and asks, "Do you need help?"

Holly shakes her head. "The good thing about energy gun shots," she says as she unwraps layer after layer of bloody bandages, "is there's nothing to dig out. Just tissue damage . . . hopefully." She tosses the last strips of Pax's undershirt aside and grunts as a pool of blood suddenly expands across the floor. "Put your hands here and press hard," she says, waving Pax over. "You"—she snaps her fingers at Henri—"get me a string or a tie of some sort."

Henri ducks away to do as she asks, and Holly holds up a needle and thread she's readied as Pax presses on my leg with both hands. He no longer has the baby, and I wonder who he handed him off to.

"It's a little too deep for the sealant glue," Holly says.

Henri returns, holding a long piece of string.

"Good," Holly says. "Tie my hair back."

He hesitates.

"*Now*," she says. "I have to be able to see, and I can't do it because my hands are covered in blood."

Henri does as she asks, his large hands clumsy at the task.

"Now go get some blankets for her, as many as you can find."

Henri hurries away again.

"Okay, ready?" Holly raises her eyes to Pax. "I'm going to do this fast. She's already lost way too much blood. When I say, I need you to release pressure but pinch the hole together, do you understand?"

Pax nods.

"Now," she says.

I watch the first stitch, and then, because I'm going to be sick if I watch any more, I look away and stare at the swaying supplies suspended in mesh nets from the ceiling.

After a couple of minutes, Holly says, "Good. We can wrap it up."

I'm still numb, so I can't feel any more than a vague tugging, and then a pile of blankets is spread over me and tucked in around my arms and legs.

Pax leans over me with a rolled blanket and lifts my head to place it like a pillow beneath me. He hesitates, then holds his hand to my forehead. He's splattered with my blood, and the front of his uniform is smeared with it as though he wiped his hands down his front.

"Rest," he says. "You're going to be okay."

I extricate my hand from the tight tuck of blankets and hold it out to him. He takes it and folds it between his own.

"Pax!" Celine shouts. "Luther's on the radio. He wants to hear the report from you!"

Pax nods and turns to go, but I squeeze his hand and hold him back. He raises an eyebrow.

"Tell him," I whisper, "tell Luther I placed the hack on Mother. If she goes to her office today, we'll have the files."

Pax gives me a slow smile. Then he brings my fingers up and presses them to his lips. I close my eyes, and when I open them, he's gone.

I either fall asleep or fall unconscious, I'm not sure which, but when I wake, I have the sensation of having slept for several hours. Pax dozes beside me, his arms propped on his raised knees and his head in his hands. Henri leans against the wall to my right, fiddling with his firearm, and Holly is curled up asleep beside him with the baby boy tucked inside the circle of her arms.

My pain has returned, and when I try to sit up to look at my elevated leg, I groan.

Pax starts awake and drops his hand to my shoulder. "Don't try to move," he says. "Just stay still."

Henri looks up. "How are you feeling? In pain?"

I nod. "But it's not too bad. Don't wake Holly," I say. I lick my lips and look at Pax. "What did Luther say? Did we get them? Did Wallace get the files?"

"We got them," Pax says.

I look between the two of them as Henri breaks into a smile. "You did it, Pria."

"They're encrypted," Pax says, his expression more cautious than Henri's. "It will take some time to break through and read them."

"Ah, you need to lighten up." Henri leans forward and touches my shoulder. "You did great," he says. "And don't worry about the encryption—Wallace will break it."

I cover my face and sigh. After all that, at least I got the job done.

"Pax says you witnessed some of what goes on in the basements, too. If you want to talk about it——"

"No," I breathe. "I'm sorry, I can't just yet."

"I understand. Sorry, I shouldn't have asked. Really, I'm just happy you got out safe in the end. We were sure you'd been killed."

I nod behind my hand.

"And now you're really one of us," Henri says. "There's definitely no going back after all that."

One of them. I lower my hand and stare up at the swinging supplies. After what I witnessed in Sanctuary, there's no group to whom I'd rather belong.

"How much is left of our flight?" I ask.

"We've been flying in circles a bit to make sure we don't have any tails before we head back, but we should be there soon," Henri says.

"We're almost home," Pax says.

I catch his eye. "Thank you for coming after me."

Pax nods, but he doesn't smile. Lacing his hands behind his neck, he hangs his head and stares at the floor.

Chapter 64

I was an approved Breeder for the Controlled Repopulation Program. I believed what they told me. I believed I was superior. I believed the Great Devastations that led to the depopulation of the earth happened as a natural result of overpopulation. I believed the Unified World Order saved humanity, and that I was a privileged part of that noble effort.

But I was wrong. Humanity is not better, or stronger, or smarter, or more versatile because of people like me. My genes may be nearly perfected, but I am no better, no more worthy of life, than anyone else.

I now live in a world of manufactured monsters, both human and alien, and I see Sanctuary for what it is—a slaughterhouse, not a breeding house. I was once a Carrier for them, but I never will be again.

I am on the run, and I will do everything in my power to see this world turned upside down.

I choose life among people who should not be alive, and because of that, I am extremely dangerous.

I am a criminal.

Pria's story continues in *Criminal*, book 2 of
The Breeder Cycle

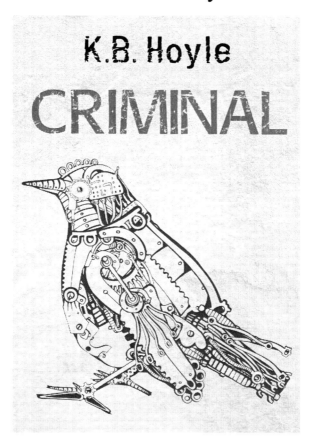

K.B. Hoyle

CRIMINAL

Pria thought leaving Sanctuary would be the greatest
treason she would ever commit. She was wrong.

Coming 2015

Acknowledgement

As usual, producing a novel is a team effort, and I'm so thankful for all the people who walk alongside me and make sure my books are the best they can be! Thanks so much to my editing team, Hayley German Fisher, Michele Milburn, Andrea McKay, and Lea Dimovski. Thanks also to Jenn McGuire, who made my dream for the cover into a reality, and Amanda Hayward for making the publication of this book possible at all. Cindy Bidwell and Catherine Edwards, thank you for your tireless work behind the scenes, and thanks to my writers group for giving me the earliest feedback on the manuscript. Thanks also to my beta readers, Elise Montgomery, Maggie Rapier, Griffin Gulledge, Megan Riley, and Melissa Bell. And for the French translations in the text, thanks so much to Rémy Vaneuil and Audrey Pagès. Lastly, my highest thanks goes always to my husband and three sons for your patience through my hectic writing schedule, and to my God for giving me the strength to endure.

About the Author

K. B. Hoyle is a bestselling author, a public speaker, a creative writing instructor, and a classical history teacher who uses her knowledge of the ancient and medieval worlds to pen speculative and fantasy tales for people of all ages. She has been married since the age of twenty to the love of her life, with whom she has four wonderful children. Find out more about her at **www.kbhoyle.com.**

CPSIA information can be obtained at www.ICGtesting.com
Printed in the USA
BVOW02s0339310815

415839BV00008BA/76/P